THE THIRD Q

A NOVEL

THE THIRD Q

ARNOLD FRANCIS | ROBERT LUXENBERG

GREENLEAF
BOOK GROUP PRESS

Published by Greenleaf Book Group Press
Austin, Texas
www.gbgpress.com

Distributed by Greenleaf Book Group LLC

For ordering information or special discounts for bulk purchases, please contact Greenleaf Book Group LLC at PO Box 91869, Austin, TX 78709, 512.891.6100.

Design and composition by Greenleaf Book Group LLC and Alex Head
Cover design by Greenleaf Book Group LLC

Publisher's Cataloging-In-Publication Data
(Prepared by The Donohue Group, Inc.)
Francis, Arnold.
    The third Q : a novel / Arnold Francis [and] Robert Luxenberg. — 1st ed.
    p. ; cm.
    ISBN: 978-1-60832-187-2
    1. Chauffeurs--New York (State)—New York--Fiction. 2. Philosophers—Fiction. 3. Self-realization—Fiction. 4. Conspiracy—Fiction. 5. New York (N. Y.)—Fiction. 6. Billionaires—New York (State)—New York—Fiction. 7. Suspense fiction. I. Luxenberg, Robert. II. Title.
PS3606.R26 T57 2011
813/.6   2011931383

Printed in the United States of America on acid-free paper

11 12 13 14 15   10 9 8 7 6 5 4 3 2 1

First Edition

ACKNOWLEDGMENTS

First and foremost we would like to thank the amazing team at Greenleaf Book Group who believed in our vision and our books from the very start.

Thank you to Kris Pauls and her team of editors for their insights and counsel; to Thom Lemmons and Aaron Hierholzer for their editing magic; and a special thank you to our editor Bill Crawford for his patience and understanding, his commitment to our vision, and his amazing talent.

To Chris McRay, Hobbs Allison, Jr., and Tanya Hall, thanks for your commitment and hospitality.

To Sheila Parr and the design team, thanks for making the book look so amazing.

To Katelynn Knutson, thank you for making us a priority. It's nice to feel wanted.

To the sales and PR teams, thank you for your support and that little extra nudge to get us onto the shelves.

To the many others at Greenleaf and elsewhere, thank you so much.

Among the legions of supporters that stood by us to make these books a reality, we'd like to single out Chris and Margaret Riddell of Deliverabilities.com. Our special thanks and heartfelt appreciation go out to you, dear friends, not only for your boundless energy and expertise in putting us on the map, but also for making the responsibility for these books your very own.

And of course special thanks goes out to our families, not just for putting up with us, but because without them this journey would not have been filled with as much joy and purpose.

We would also like to thank each other for the friendship and brotherly love and understanding that carried us through the ups and downs and allowed us to share this journey with you.

And finally, to you the reader, we send our heartfelt gratitude for having the courage to learn and move fearlessly toward a new and amazing life.

Thanks to the trainers, teachers, and authors who have been an integral part of our journey of growth and understanding, many of whom we mention in the acknowledgments section of our companion book to *The Third Q, Unlocking the Secrets: A Third Q Book.*

NOTES OF APPRECIATION

To Bob, for your endless insight, energy, and friendship.
I am forever grateful.

To Arnold, for your brilliance, wisdom, and friendship.
You are my brother. Thanks for sharing this wonderful journey.

THE THIRD Q

PROLOGUE

Blood flowed through the streets of Jerusalem as the Romans positioned their battering rams at the base of Herod's Temple. With the last of the Temple Guard now slain, the unprotected Kohanim, the Aaronic priests, retreated to the holy inner chamber and turned their faces to the heavens. They knew they had the power to withstand any challenge. Even as the temple shook and cracked around them, they held faith in the mystical power they controlled.

They could not be defeated. The chosen one, the High Priest; he possessed the power of the Name. Compared to that, the military might of Rome was nothing.

And then, as the temple trembled beneath a blow from the Roman siege engines, a stone block fell from the ceiling, crushing the High Priest.

Shocked, the other Kohanim stared at the High Priest's body. Had they been wrong to entrust the sacred mystery to a single Kohan? Were they as individuals strong enough to stand against the Romans? Had their pride blinded them to the true power of the sacred word? As the temple blazed and fell to pieces around them, the true name of God vanished in the dust of destruction.

*   *   *

1959, New York City, Dusk

In a bed as large as a railroad car, the old man gasped for air. His chest collapsed into itself, as the weight of uncertainty pressed heavily on him. A young man approached, choking back tears.

"Is that you, Max?" the old man panted.

"Yes."

"Come closer."

With a shaking hand, the old man pointed to a small wooden crate, barely visible in the flickering candlelight.

"You must keep searching," the old man said, his voice strained and barely audible.

"I promise," the young man replied.

"Don't tell anyone what we found."

"Why not?"

"Because it's our secret! At least until you find the rest . . . You'll need them all."

The old man's eyes widened at the sound of fists pounding against the door. Panic stricken, he looked toward the crate.

"Keep it from my son . . . promise me."

"I promise," the young man replied.

"Go, quickly . . ." He tried to say more, but his voice faded away like dust on the wind.

With a sharp crack, the door began to splinter and give way. The young man slipped silently down a hidden staircase, clutching the wooden crate under his arm, hiding it beneath a tattered cloth.

CHAPTER 1

Present Day, Wednesday, The Bronx

Zoro ducked as the chipped dinner plate flew past his head, bounced off the trunk of the limo, and shattered on the pavement behind him.

"Don't ever come back here," Gina yelled down at him from the second-floor window, her long, dark hair swirling around her face as the wind rushed down the street past the shabby tenements. "I'm through with a loser husband like you," she said.

"I'm not the loser, Gina. You are." For a moment, she stared down at him with her mouth set, her gaze hardened. Then she ducked back inside, slamming the window shut.

"Great," Zoro grunted under his breath as he stared at the place where the plate had hit the trunk. "My wife kicks me out, and then she scuffs the damn limo. Nice way to start a new job."

He gripped his lapels, pulling his collar tight against the cold wind. Under his hands he could feel his heart beating—a rhythm of regret, a rhythm of yearning for things to be the way they were when Joey was here.

Zoro slid behind the wheel of the short stretch Bentley limo, rubbing the morning from his eyes and already feeling beaten. He resigned himself to a world of uncertainty, where nothing was sure except pain.

Zoro couldn't say for sure who he was, but he knew exactly who he wasn't: He wasn't a man who moved his life. Instead, it moved him and sent him stumbling. And today would probably be just another aimless stumble. So he had a new job, chauffeuring for some rich geezer—so what? Something would go wrong. For Zoro, something always did.

Looking around, he could hardly recognize the old neighborhood. Once the pride of the Bronx, Little Italy had lost its luster—it looked worn out. Mike's Deli and Pete's Meat Market, Umberto's Clam House and Tommy's Tavern . . . all of them were faded, shabby, sad echoes of a time that was long gone. Like an aging supermodel who has lost her sex appeal, the old neighborhood couldn't hold Zoro's interest any longer.

Zoro had been out of work for nine weeks before finally landing this driving gig. He'd had his fingers mentally crossed the whole nine weeks, but this was the longest he'd been unemployed so far. It seemed like each time he was out of work, it took longer to find a job. Carmela, his mother, had set him up with the job. Zoro imagined she'd charmed an old acquaintance of his father's, lightly sweeping her hair over her shoulders as if she'd forgotten she was sick. Carmela still acted as if she was the attractive brunette of her youth. Zoro resented it, but he never spoke up; Carmela could smack him down without breaking a sweat. A couple of words, a tone of voice, and she'd make him wish he'd kept his mouth shut. As bad as he needed this job, Zoro already half hated whomever it was that cared enough about Carmela to toss her son a bone.

He turned the key in the ignition and the engine purred to life. Zoro rubbed the supple leather upholstery. *At least the car is classy*, he thought, shifting the transmission lever into drive and pulling out into the street.

CHAPTER 2

As Zoro drove, he tried to figure out how he felt about his new boss. If the guy really was some high roller, how did he know Carmela? And even more important, if he knew her, why would he listen to her? Something about the whole deal was bugging him, but he couldn't quite put his finger on it.

Judging from the car, Zoro's new boss was the type of person who was steeped in violence. The windows were tinted and bulletproof; the custom-built, steel-reinforced doors and puncture-proof, foam-filled tires would enable the limo to withstand some pretty heavy firepower and still keep going. From what Zoro could tell, the car was also equipped with its own air filtration and recirculation system. It was like being behind the wheel of an armored car. Who the hell would need a rig like this?

Zoro fished around in his pockets as he navigated the light morning traffic. He pulled out handfuls of partly used matchbooks, half-crumpled business cards, creased photos, and other pieces of paper. They all had names and phone numbers scribbled on them. It was his filing system. This was what he'd managed to save from his stuff that Gina had tossed out the second-story window. He piled everything in a loose stack on the seat beside him and shaped it into a wad he could grab with one hand. Then he crammed it under the visor above his head. He perched his plastic coffee mug on the middle of the dash. The steam from his coffee made a small circle of mist on the windshield.

Turning onto East 189th Street and getting swept into the swelling flow of traffic, Zoro began thinking about the damned mess he'd already been through this morning. He couldn't really figure out why Gina had decided to throw him out. "You can't keep a job," she'd said, but what was so different now from the past few years? "We live in this shit hole," she'd screamed, but this was where they'd been for the past seven years. Why was she picking this particular moment to shove him into the deep end?

Zoro thought about it for a couple of blocks, then gave a mental shrug, thinking, *Who the hell knows?* In his life, this morning was just par for a generally crappy course.

A few blocks later he spotted a familiar shapely feminine backside. He knew Holly's walk anywhere, even under layers of fall clothing.

Zoro had started giving Holly rides about a year ago. Holly was streetwise, but she was also damn good looking—and she had better listening skills than any bartender Zoro had ever met. Zoro needed somebody to listen to him this morning, so he glided over to the curb beside Holly and tapped the horn while rolling down the passenger-side window. Holly peered in and then flashed him a fifty-megawatt smile and reached for the door handle.

Holly slid onto the seat beside Zoro, and then he eased the car back into traffic.

"Nice ride, Zoro . . . so what's up?"

Zoro rolled his eyes and shook his head.

"Fight with Gina again?"

Zoro nodded toward the pile of his clothes in the backseat of the limo.

"So I still have a chance?" Holly said, smiling.

"If not for Gina, you'd be the one, Holly."

"Guess my chance isn't as good as I thought," she said. "She throws you out, and you still got an 'if' in front of my name?"

Zoro sighed. "She hates my guts right now, but she's still my wife."

"Yeah, too bad for me. And maybe for you."

Zoro shrugged, "I'm gonna stop by Johnny's later, see if he'll put me up for a while."

"Johnny's? You sure?"

Zoro nodded. Even though he wasn't exactly sure about Johnny, what other choice did he have?

"You're crazy, you know," Holly said. "You always get into trouble around Johnny."

"Ah, Johnny's easy, once you get to know him like I do."

"It isn't about being easy, it's about being safe."

"You got any aspirin, Holly? I just can't shake this headache."

"Nope, sorry."

Zoro wished he hadn't made it sound like he was coming on to Holly. It wasn't fair to either of them, and he tried to think of something he could say to make it a little better . . . or take it back. When they reached the parking lot of the place where Holly picked up her hot dog cart, he put a hand on her arm before she got out.

"About before, Holly . . . I owe you an explanation. I didn't mean—"

She held her hand up. "You owe me nothing, Zoro. It's okay."

"So we're good?"

She smiled. She got out and walked away, giving him a little wave over her shoulder. Zoro watched her go, trying to decide if he was feeling relief . . . or regret.

He shook his head, then checked his rearview mirrors. He nudged the Bentley back into traffic.

Just drive, Zoro, he thought. *It's the only thing you're good at, so don't think; just drive.*

CHAPTER 3

Zoro ploughed through sloughs of traffic, working the steering wheel skillfully, with precision. Zoro felt safe inside the limo, inside his own small world. He felt solid, with no misgivings. He chuckled as a preoccupied businessman stepped off the curb in front of a cab; the angry cabbie laid on the horn, and the Armani-suited pedestrian nearly dropped his smartphone as he beat a hasty retreat to the safety of the sidewalk.

But on the corner of Third Avenue, something sudden and inexplicable happened to Zoro: he wavered. For one of the very few times in his long driving career, Zoro lost focus on the traffic around him and stared at a woman standing on the corner.

Her deep eyes mesmerized him; her skin flowed in smooth perfection across every angle of her face. He was dizzied by her youthful beauty. She raised an arm, possibly to flag a cab, but her outstretched arm seemed to beckon to Zoro. Though he never stopped moving, the moment seemed frozen in time. Then, suddenly, the sun burst through the gap between two skyscrapers and blinded him.

The moment was shattered and Zoro's attention snapped back to the road, just in time for him to see a small blue figure standing dead center in the road ahead of him.

His heart jumped into his throat as he slammed his foot on the brake pedal. He had fucked up again, and Joey's face leaped into his mind. The limo's tires screeched in agony, laying down a strip of hot rubber on the road. The momentum threw him forward, and the pieces of his motley filing system spilled from the visor, scattering across the dashboard and the front seat. His coffee mug upended, flinging coffee everywhere.

I must be seeing things, he thought fleetingly. *There can't be anyone in the street.* And then, he felt and heard a thump.

Oh, my God! Not now, not today . . . I can't have hit somebody! One of the pieces of paper from his filing system had come to rest in his lap, and as Zoro stared down in shock, he realized he was looking at an old, worn photo of Joey. His little brother's face stared up at him, the grin he'd adopted for the school photograph filling Zoro with reproach and self-loathing. The fire, the screams, the guilt. *Joey . . . Isaac . . . my fault. And now, I've done it again . . .*

With the dread of that tiny thump freezing in his chest, Zoro realized that Carmela was right—she had always been right . . . "You will never be successful . . . Your family suffers because of you . . . We're lucky you haven't killed the rest of us . . ."

Another victim, another little boy, he thought. For a moment he was frozen in the limo, afraid to get out and check. He hadn't set out to find trouble; yet once again, the world had slapped him with a sack full of crap. With the morning sun shining in his eyes, Zoro fumbled for the door handle. He pushed the door open and stepped through the gathering crowd. Across the road, the woman still stood, watching him—*now seeing me for the killer I am*, Zoro thought.

He pushed through the crowd to the other side of the limo, still searching for the boy. But there was no boy. The small blue figure had vanished.

"Where is he? Oh my God, where's the kid I hit?"

A guy in the crowd turned toward him. "It was the kid's lucky day, buddy. Or yours, maybe. Your tires stopped just inches from the kid. He bounced against your front grill a little bit and then took off somewhere. We'll never find him in this crowd."

Zoro should have been relieved, empowered—he should have felt as if he'd been reborn. But instead he felt defeated all over again. He had the absurd thought: *It figures. I can't even run somebody over the right way.* Even knowing he hadn't hurt the kid became just another piece of the never-ending ache that was Zoro's life.

The crowd, realizing the show was over, had started to disperse. Zoro went back around to the driver's side, thinking, *Why me? Why is this life happening to me?*

He climbed back into the limo. He tugged the car into drive, but now he didn't feel secure or in control; he felt cold and heavy, and he swallowed hard. He drove to the end of the block, until a stoplight halted him. Something was always halting Zoro.

A grubby-looking bum shuffled toward him, acting like he wanted to ask a question, and against his better judgment, Zoro rolled the window down. Immediately, the bum's smell assaulted Zoro's nostrils. Even on a cool day like this, the bum smelled of sweat and alcohol.

"Whoa, kid! You got magic brakes?" the bum asked, bracing himself against the window.

"Go away," Zoro said.

"You look like you're about to give up, kid." The bum started chuckling.

"What the hell are you laughing at?" Zoro hit the button to roll up the window, but the old man shoved his arm inside and wiggled a dirty finger in Zoro's face.

"There's only two ways people live, kid," he wheezed. "You either get good, or give up. And you don't look like the type to get good. You're going to end up just like me."

"Get the hell out of here," Zoro yelled, shoving the bum's filthy arm out the window.

The old man backed up a couple of steps. Zoro wanted to get away, but the damned light was still red.

The bum gave Zoro a crazy-ass smile—or maybe it was just mean and spiteful. "I'll be seeing you, kid," the old man called in a voice Zoro could hear, even through the closed window. "See you soon kid . . . See you soon."

"Screw you, you crazy son of a bitch!" Zoro shouted.

At last, the light changed and he could move. Slowly, as he drove, Zoro began to calm down. Steering with one hand, he tidied the limo as best he could with the other, gathering his scattered matchbooks and other pieces of paper and piling them beside him on the seat. At the next red light, he shoved them back under the visor.

Of all the strange and crummy things that had ever happened to Zoro, that moment, that tiny thud and the panic and guilt he'd felt, had been a low point of sorts.

That bum was right, he thought. Then, almost instantly he told himself, *No! There's gotta be something better than this!*

Slowly, his mind moving uncertainly through unfamiliar territory, Zoro decided a change was due—though he had no clue what to do about it. Still clutching the wrinkled photo of Joey, Zoro knew that he would have to start moving. Find a way to get good . . . get rich, make her proud . . . that would prove her wrong—prove them all wrong. *That would change everything*, he thought. *Besides, maybe today is the day everything starts to change. Who knows?* With a little luck, maybe he could even believe it.

The light switched from red to green, and Zoro drove on.

CHAPTER 4

Zoro had finally left the city behind, crossing over into New Jersey. He glanced again at the address on the card Carmela had given him. The suburb he was driving into sure didn't look like a normal neighborhood of brownstones and brick tenements; it felt like he was driving into a freaking postcard—one a rich friend sends you from a vacation you couldn't afford in a million years. Zoro had a habit of attaching feelings to places, and he realized he hated the opulence surrounding him. Still, he straightened his tie.

But looking respectable did little to ease his worry. He'd been driving for nearly thirty minutes since leaving the city, and his mind was still chasing itself in circles. He hadn't expected to feel this way. Today should have been a good day, a fresh start. But then Gina had kicked him out, and he'd nearly killed a little kid, and then the thoughts of Joey . . .

And at that moment, right in the middle of his confusion, he started hearing Isaac's voice in his mind. Zoro thought, *Oh, God! Not today, please!*

Hearing his father's voice echoing inside his head hadn't been anywhere on his list of things to do, but still Isaac's voice was there. *It must have been seeing the mansions that triggered it,* Zoro figured. He had heard that voice many times since his father's death thirty-one years before. Tiny whispers of his father's ideology about success gurgled and sputtered about in his head. He'd heard the whispers before, too many times. When Zoro was younger, Isaac would eagerly challenge him with an endless barrage of stories and mental exercises. Zoro wasn't particularly interested, and forgot them almost as quickly as he heard them. But he learned to appreciate the one-on-one time with his father.

"I promise you, someday this will be important, Zoro," Isaac had said. "I promise one day, if you remember what I'm teaching, I'll give you everything."

"A treasure, Dad?" Zoro's young eyes had widened in wonderment. Isaac would only raise his eyebrows and smile. He never answered. But Zoro always wondered.

And now Zoro could hear his father's voice whispering to him all over again. Not that it mattered; he couldn't remember even one of those damn stories. Zoro might have tried to remember, might even have longed for those father-and-son days if Isaac hadn't kept his promise. But Isaac had kept his word and had given Zoro everything he had—which was nothing.

Before anyone in the family could comprehend the tragedy of Joey's death, Isaac had succumbed to grief. The day of Joey's funeral, something snapped inside Isaac, transforming his crippling sorrow into blinding rage—so much so that he stormed out of his own son's funeral. Apparently, he had moved from rage to despair because, that same night, Isaac jumped from the Tappan Zee Bridge into the Hudson River. On that cold October evening so long ago, Isaac had betrayed Zoro, managing not only to drown himself, but also to pull Zoro into the waters of despair, drowning his hopes and dreams of a happy life.

To hell with you, Dad, Zoro thought with a grimace. He jabbed at the FM radio, then cranked the volume up almost as loud as it would go, trying to banish his dead father's voice from his head. As long as Zoro had breath in him, Isaac would never be more than a distant stain in the boneyard of his mind.

The signal just ahead turned yellow, and Zoro pushed the accelerator to the floor. *Some people would probably be crying right now*, he thought. But Zoro didn't have many tears left. They had evaporated, just like his father's empty promises.

CHAPTER 5

Four and a half minutes later Zoro coasted to a stop in front of a set of imposing, wrought iron gates that looked to be ten feet tall. The armor-plated limo, the gates, and the high, bleached stone wall told Zoro clearly that his new boss was a man who valued his own privacy and had the means to ensure it.

Zoro straightened his tie again, even as he felt himself sink deeper into his seat.

He rolled down his window to speak into the security intercom, but at that moment the iron gate began to slowly swing open. Zoro looked around, trying to locate the surveillance camera, but it must have been very well hidden. The gate opened, reminding Zoro of those scenes in scary movies where a foreboding door would creak open by itself, and you knew the people in the movie were about to walk into an ambush of zombies or something—but you knew they were going to go through the door anyhow. Taking a deep breath, Zoro nudged the limo forward, down the driveway.

Holy shit, is this a driveway or a road into the next county? The driveway was so long in fact, that Zoro had to crane his neck to see to the end. It reminded him of the time he had taken Joey to Yankee Stadium; Joey had to sit on his lap so that he could see over the heads of the people seated in front. *God, enough! Please get Joey out of my head!*

Looking up the drive, Zoro felt the tension creeping in, joining his sadness in a gloomy medley of emotions. He had no idea what he might expect at the end of the driveway. He felt as if he were crashing some reclusive world of scrutiny and private servants—of which he was one.

Despite his misgivings, Zoro realized that his thoughts were gradually becoming less turbulent. Where the sun met the tops of the skyscraping oak trees that flanked the driveway, an almost ethereal luster gleamed through the wind-tossed leaves. The Cisary estate was more than a private compound, Zoro realized; it was a place of breathtaking loveliness. The last autumn flowers, in beds along the driveway, painted brilliant splashes of yellow, purple, and the purest white against the rich green of the grass. Zoro allowed the soothing beauty to caress his mind.

As he made the final turn and arrived in front of the house, his eyes opened in wonder. The Cisary mansion looked like some kind of resort hotel, or maybe a castle that had strayed from Europe and wound up in New Jersey. Soaring towers rose into the sky; graceful archways and intricate stonework made the place look like something from another time. In the middle of the circular drive in front of the house was a splashing fountain filled with figures that looked like they belonged in the Vatican.

As he opened the car door, Zoro noticed a security guard holding the leash of a Rottweiler that was definitely not taking any shit. Keeping one eye on the dog, Zoro stepped cautiously from the limo and moved toward the immense portico that sheltered the massive oak front door.

It seemed to take forever for the front door to open. But when it did, Zoro had to suppress a grin. Standing in the open doorway was a small, wrinkled man with a bald head and prominent ears, wearing a dark suit and tie that looked like it might swallow him. He looked like Yoda on prom night. Zoro took a deep breath, trying to collect himself.

"I'm the new driver for Mr. Cisary." He wiped a sweaty hand on his pants leg and held it out toward the butler.

The butler's eyes slapped his hand away. "You're late. Unacceptable." He waited a second and then motioned for Zoro to follow.

Stepping into the foyer, Zoro heard the quiet click of a motion sensor, followed by the faint buzz of a remote-control camera.

"Please wait for Mr. Cisary at the east tower staircase. And don't cross any red ropes. I assure you, we have quite a sophisticated security system."

What, they think I'm some kind of burglar?

"Fucking Yoda," Zoro muttered under his breath.

"Excuse me?"

"Nothing. Which way to the east tower staircase?"

Yoda raised a hand and pointed a wrinkled, crooked finger.

Zoro was starting to get agitated, and the voices in his head began whispering and chattering. He was grinding his teeth in frustration. But when he stepped into the grand hall, the voices instantly went silent.

He wasn't prepared for that room. Its ceiling was maybe forty feet high; the room appeared to be the size of a basketball court. Great stone arches framed the passageways to long, dark halls that led onward into obscurity. And, at each corner, opulent staircases of marble and brass spiraled up into the four towers he had seen from outside.

The floor of the hall was fashioned from gleaming marble mosaics of brown and tan, interspersed with red berries of quartz. At center court, dozens of sculptures lined a large central staircase that led to the second-floor balcony. Frescoes covered the ceiling, far above. Ancient-looking paintings lined the walls, and to Zoro it seemed that the paintings were trying to tell him something . . . but he couldn't tell what. He felt frustrated, mystified, and—almost against his will—curious.

Zoro stared around for maybe a full minute. "For Christ's sake," he muttered, "this is a bit much."

He closed his eyes. Somewhere in this gleaming marble shrine he could hear a fly buzzing. His senses seemed heightened, and he opened his eyes, only to find that Yoda had vanished. He suppressed the urge to go racing up the central staircase, and slide down the marble banister, screaming, "Screw you, you rich bastard!"

The house seemed empty. Zoro made his way in the direction the butler had pointed. On his way to the east tower staircase, he passed another guard, a muscular man with a short-muzzle Glock holstered at his hip. The guard moved silently through a doorway, clicking the door latch closed behind him. Zoro strode past the guard's door, and with a cool flick of his eyes he stopped at the staircase. Each step was broad, with a small riser that ended in a polished, bull-nose front. A red velvet rope, its ends capped with ornate brass clips, was draped across the first step. "Red rope, bitch," he muttered.

Zoro's eyes climbed the stairs. A picture hung at every ninth step beneath the sheltering shadows of carved marble alcoves. The first was a red chalk-artist's sketch. To the right was an image of an outstretched godly figure. The body was partly translucent, which left portions of the brainstem visible, as if seen through X-ray glasses. To the left of the outstretched figure, another commanding, godly figure pointed to the sun. Below these two figures was a man on his knees with a fist raised high while his other hand pressed a small child mercilessly to the ground. The child looked so frail and helpless, and the man's hand appeared to be pulling the child's skin tight across his face. Zoro was disgusted. "Son of a bitch," he muttered. "Who collects pictures of child abusers?"

Despite his reaction, he was curious about the other sketches. He threw a sidelong glance across his shoulder as he stepped over the red rope. The next alcove contained a drawing of a godlike bearded figure wrapped in a brain-shaped red cloak enclosed by a square outline that framed the figure in the center of the page. Beams of light shot out from the outline, while desperate-looking men within the outline gripped the figure's legs tightly, pulling it back into the drawing. The whole thing looked like some religious zealot's worst nightmare.

Nine steps further up, the next sketch showed two men, one floating on a drape shaped like the higher human brain, while both men's hands reached to meet in the middle of the sketch. And around the outside of the sketch, among a flurry of images, angels danced. *Sick*, Zoro thought. *What kind of person would display this kind of crap and protect it with a velvet rope besides?*

Just as Zoro started for the fourth alcove, a voice came out of nowhere. "You seem to have a good heart."

Surprised by the sudden sound, Zoro felt his heart racing. He heard the quiet sound of approaching footsteps. He was startled, but he did his best to mask it.

"A good heart! Am I the only one who thinks these sketches are wrong?"

"Don't worry about it," the shadowy figure replied, coming down the stairs. "My name is Maximilian Cisary, but you may call me Max. You must be Zorro."

Zoro could hear his new boss rolling the *r* sound in the Spanish style. It happened all the time; everybody thought he was named for the swordsman in the black cape.

Fueled by curiosity, Zoro spun around to head up the stairs toward his new boss.

"Wait!" Max called, holding up a hand. "Look at the sketch beside you. It's Michelangelo's *Adam*."

Zoro felt an overwhelming sense of uncertainty. He looked at the sketch, and it seemed familiar. But there was something else there, a presence . . . something he could almost remember . . .

Then he had it. "Sistine Chapel," Zoro said. "Is that it?"

In the shadows on the stairs, Zoro thought he could make out a smile on Max's face. "Close your eyes," Max whispered. "Think of the sketch as you just saw it, with all the precision of your mind; excavate the images you see. Go beneath the surface of the sketch. Look behind the red chalk marks, as if you were looking at a photographic negative."

Zoro found himself pulled deeper, melding with the artwork. In the sketch, Adam sat on the Earth, reaching, desiring the touch of God. And God, bathed in a river of celestial life, stretched his finger toward Adam.

"Now open your eyes. Do you see it?"

Zoro kept his eyes ahead. *What the hell is this, some kind of weird mind game?* he thought.

"Zorro, God is instilling divine power into humanity. When their fingers touch, a spark of energy will bring Adam life. Do you see it?"

Zoro saw nothing.

"Think of it: Adam means 'Earth,' the source of creation and life."

Zoro felt a hesitant thought pushing into his mind, and then a glimmer of inspiration. He looked up at Max.

"Aha, you do see it!" Max said. "Look there: Michelangelo has sketched God on a red drape that is anatomically shaped like a human brain. Do you see it, Zorro? There, in chalk and paper, God himself, the soul of our souls, is coming to us. Do you see it?"

Zoro nodded.

Max smiled. "No one knows for certain how it's done, but we can all agree that God manifests, and I think Michelangelo knew how."

Zoro held his moment of revelation for a few seconds, but then he remembered the image in the first sketch. He wondered what a man with a sketch of a child abuser really understood about religion and faith and pain. Was Max just a teacher, passing along inscrutable words, or was there more buried beneath the surface?

For some reason, thinking about the first sketch was really getting to Zoro. He struggled to remain calm, but he felt a surge of déjà vu: a sense of helplessness he'd not felt since failing Joey.

With his lips barely moving, he said, "Yeah, whatever. And by the way, I'm Zoro, with one *r*. And your sketches suck! Especially that first one. It celebrates abuse like it was some kind of religion." Zoro threw the words at Max like stones of accusation.

Max paused several seconds before answering. "You may not realize it, Zoro with one *r*, but I am no stranger to religion or pain." Another moment of silence passed, and then he smiled again. "I'm a Bronx boy, too, did you know that? I was a dedicated altar boy. I grew up in a time of soapbox cars and stickball in the streets.

"My mother loved me, Zoro. She loved me . . . and the church. She gave up on marriage though; one day she ended the stench of loveless hoping, divorcing my abusive father. And with that single act she broke her vow to the church."

Max fell silent again, and in the quiet, Zoro had the foreboding feeling that his new boss knew a lot more about him than he realized. *But, hey,* he thought, *at least his mother loved him. More than I can say for mine.*

"Perhaps that's why she insisted on buying me new shoes for church every year," Max said, finally, looking at Zoro again, "as guilty compensation."

"To tell you the truth, I never got a lot out of church, myself," Zoro said, wondering why he was prolonging a conversation he really didn't care about.

Max nodded. "I reached that point too, one day. I found that the priest spoke with an assured and unwavering tone, but in his words there was little wisdom. So I left the church unsatisfied. But you know what, Zoro? To me the Bible is still one of the most beautiful songs ever heard. I read it every chance I get. I used to sit on trains or buses reading incessantly, and its melody was soothing."

Max leaned against the banister. His eyes studied the sketch hanging in the alcove beside Zoro. "Years later I found that same melody in art, after I met Father Ryan. He changed my view of the church. You see, Zoro, Father Ryan wasn't playing at religion. He was studious; he'd labor late into the night, studying the Scriptures."

Max smiled at the memory. "Father Ryan's endless devotion was as inspiring as his kindness. The first time I met him, it was at the Metropolitan Museum. I was standing in front of a painting of Mary Magdalene, and I remember that I almost had to remind myself to breathe."

Max's eyes closed. His voice fell to a near whisper. "She was radiant. I was awestruck; my heart soared with delight . . ." He opened his eyes and looked at Zoro as if he'd forgotten anyone else was there, as if he'd come back from a deep distance.

"Do you know what he told me, Zoro? Father Ryan said that from across the room he could see me looking right through the painting. And that's when he decided to become my art teacher; a teacher of special secrets who never asked anything of me except to receive what he offered and always gave more than he took . . . except maybe for spaghetti." Max gave a quiet chuckle. "If there was spaghetti on the dinner table, Father Ryan could gobble the whole platter."

Descending the rest of the way to the third alcove, Max closed in on Zoro. He gazed into Zoro's face, and Zoro realized he was willing the moment to move more slowly.

For a long time Max didn't say anything. Then he smiled and said in a soft voice, "You look just like your father."

CHAPTER 6

Zoro froze for an instant, unable to believe what he'd just heard, and then his body shivered. He strained as the words scraped against his mind. Zoro had never thought of himself as anything like Isaac, and he lifted a skeptical brow. *Why is he saying that?* And suddenly his insides burned, and the anger was gushing up from deep in his gut. He couldn't stop it. It was as if he was being lost to something deep inside him, something that consumed him.

"Like my father? What the hell gives you the right to say that? You think because you got all this fucking money—"

"No!" Max quickly interrupted, "I have money because I think."

Zoro turned and stomped away, down the stairs, his mind churning like a raging hellhound. He mustered all of his contempt and fury and sent it into his feet, pounding down the steps and hopping back over the red rope, past that hateful sketch of the child abuser. The sketch, the atmosphere in this freakishly huge mansion, Max's words . . . It all had shoved Zoro into a corner of his mind; the sense of helplessness was crushing. It was like reliving the worst days of his life, all at once. *Go to hell, you rich bastard*, he thought.

Zoro had a hard time admitting it, but he was pissed at himself, too, for letting Max get to him. The fact was, Max had a lazy charm about him, and an uncanny way of threading it under your skin.

Max still stood by the third alcove, watching Zoro's retreating back. "I get it; you're angry," he said. "Maybe you need a hug."

Zoro spun around and faced him. "I don't fucking believe this! Now you're mocking me?" The words coiled from his throat, and it was all he could do to keep himself from rushing up the stairs and smashing Max in the face.

"I don't think I'm mocking you; of course, I could be wrong," Max said. Coming down the stairs, Max unfastened the red rope with a purposeful flick.

Zoro had a feeling things were about to turn ugly. He and his mouth had just pushed away his new boss. Zoro was very good at pushing away everything in his life.

But Max appeared completely calm as he looked up at the sketch in the first alcove. "Tell me, Zoro with one *r*, what do you think you see in this first sketch? Be honest. By the way, it's very valuable, you know."

Does he take me for an idiot? Zoro thought. He stared angrily at Max, not wanting to care about his stupid sketch. Rage churned in his gut, his cheeks flushed, and he gritted his teeth. "You wanna know what I think? Okay, here it is: What kind of idiot would pay for something like that?"

"You've got a serious problem," Max grinned. "Actually I'm guessing you've got more than one."

Zoro's fists clenched.

Max held up a hand. "Sorry, that sounded less insensitive in my head," he said.

Despite his anger, it began to dawn on Zoro that in a matter of seconds he'd moved from insulting his new boss's artwork to insulting his boss. His anger drained away and resignation slumped his shoulders. "Where should I turn in the keys to the limo?" *Might as well get it over with.*

"What are you talking about, Zoro?"

Zoro gave Max a doubtful, uncomprehending look. "I . . . you're gonna fire me, right?"

"No," Max said, grinning, "Everyone has the right to be a jerk."

Zoro stared at Max for a couple of seconds, then glanced at his watch, as if he had an appointment somewhere. He turned and walked away down the east corridor. The hall had been backlit on his way to the staircase, but now, with the staircase at his back, the corridor was darkened, almost black. The only lights were tiny yellow portrait lamps that cast intermittent wedges of light across the darkened corridor.

"I think I like you," Max said, his voice carrying down the hallway.

You're as full of shit as a politician, Zoro thought. Still, he searched deep inside for the reason, any reason, Max might be saying that.

Max moved past Zoro, crabbing his left leg as he walked but still moving with surprising agility for a guy who looked so old. *This old man moves like an Apache scout . . . silent . . . He sneaks up on you when you're not looking . . .*

Zoro followed Max, noticing the scent trail of Max's aftershave. He tried to ignore his feeling that this relationship would become a weeping wound in his mind. On the other hand, he couldn't believe his luck; he'd called his boss an idiot. *And yet he likes me*, Zoro thought, although part of him wasn't convinced he was completely off the hook. He went over how he might apologize to Max and started practicing it in his mind, imagining how Max might react.

But it seemed Max had more ways to annoy Zoro than he had imagined. "Your father was a good man," he said, striding along through the small patches of light from the portrait lamps, staying just ahead of Zoro. "I thought you'd like to know that. I hope you can believe the truth about Isaac. It is the truth, you know."

This guy really, really bugs me, Zoro thought. His eyes squinted, his gait stiffened. *I don't give a damn what he thinks about Isaac. I don't give a damn what anybody thinks about him.*

Zoro knew that Carmela was always measuring him against his father, and that he always came up short. Isaac had always kept himself well groomed; he had a slender, upright posture. By contrast, Zoro was stocky, usually unshaven, and most of the time he smelled like cigar smoke and city streets. Zoro kept his hair slicked back and his broad hands were always his first resort in solving any problem. Of all the things in his life he couldn't master, his appearance and behavior were at the top of the list. Zoro could always blame his appearance on his job or use some other excuse . . . so he did.

What the hell does he know about my father, anyway? Zoro thought, staring angrily at Max. *I'll tell this rich son of a bitch what I think of his opinion.* "Isaac . . . he doesn't exist."

"You don't trust what I'm saying?" Max said, stepping through the archway into the grand hall without ever looking back.

Stepping up his gait to close the distance between him and Max, Zoro shouted, "I got no reason to!"

As they retraced Zoro's earlier path across the sparkling grand hall, through the entry foyer, and onto the front driveway where the limo sat shimmering in the sun, Zoro couldn't help but notice Max's hands. They moved rhythmically, reflecting the sunlight off a large silver ring that encircled the third finger of his right hand like the guardian of a sanctuary. Zoro tried to look away as Max moved down the stairs, but he wasn't able to; his head bobbled, following the path of the shiny ring like a kitten following a flashlight on a wall. Zoro instinctively distrusted the ring.

"What the—"

Zoro had been so fixated on Max's silver ring that he missed one of the front steps, lost his balance, and fell toward the mosaic-tiled driveway. Luckily for him, Max had turned at that moment, and he caught Zoro's shoulders as he toppled, stopping his fall.

Max looked at Zoro, smiling. "Well I'll be damned."

*   *   *

As Max climbed into the limo, he thought about when he had first met Isaac. Isaac had always felt exposed by his weaknesses, Max remembered. And he'd had the exact same look on his face as Zoro, just now, when he had tripped down those same stairs—thirty-one years ago! *It seems neither Isaac nor his son were suited to be tightrope walkers*, he thought, smiling. Max watched Zoro as he strode toward the still-open door of the limo, looking angry and embarrassed. It was uncanny how alike the two of them were—though Zoro couldn't see it yet, of course. Having never known his father past his own boyhood, Zoro nonetheless seemed to Max to harbor his father's every thought and mannerism. Max felt a bit like he'd fallen into a powerful, parallel universe, or perhaps that he'd gone backward in time.

*   *   *

Still perturbed, Zoro marched around the front of the limo muttering obscenities, trying to cover his embarrassment. Sliding behind the wheel, Zoro locked eyes with Max in the rearview mirror. He stared at him a heartbeat longer than necessary. "It's difficult to make out what that sketch means, I'll give you that," Max said. "But it's something very special." Max spoke looking directly into the rearview mirror, his eyes seeking Zoro's.

"Great," Zoro muttered. He started the car and pulled slowly around the sun-dappled driveway, circling the fountain to go back the way he'd come in. *At least we're not talking about Isaac anymore.* "So? Aren't you going to tell me what it means? That sketch?"

"Nope."

Zoro shrugged. He guessed there wasn't much sense in arguing with a man who owned a bulletproof car.

And then Max said, "But I was wondering: did you hurt him . . . the child you hit today?"

CHAPTER 7

Zoro's heart began to pound. Had he heard Max right? He felt panic starting to throb in his chest, as though he were trapped in a searchlight. It was the feeling of having lost all control. It took all his concentration to keep the car from running off the driveway into one of the flowerbeds.

How could Max know? A boy he had almost run over . . . a boy so much like Joey . . . He looked in the rearview mirror at Max. "I'll admit I'm a pretty freaking simple guy, just a poor limo driver. But let's cut the voodoo bullshit. Tell me what's going on. How did you know about that?" Zoro was trying to deal with his panic and his confusion at the same time; the effort was fuzzing his mind.

"It's not voodoo," Max said. "I just know things." Framed in the rearview mirror, Max was staring into Zoro's eyes.

Zoro was about to dismiss Max's comment, but then the older man spoke again, and his words jangled the wild horses stampeding through Zoro's brain.

"There seems to be something more that's bothering you, Zoro. I can see the despair. It isn't hard to see because there's no sight as pure as despair."

Zoro summoned what little bravado he had left, pressing his chest out like a Brooklyn-bred mobster. "What are you, some sort of mind reader?"

"Nope. But you need to accept that it's possible that I could know far more about you than you could imagine, even the fact that you almost hit a child earlier today."

Zoro eyed Max, stunned by how Max could know anything about him. *I've gotta figure this guy out.* "So what do you think you know about me?"

"I've seen things in my life, Zoro, things that allow me to understand." In a soft voice that held no malice or accusation, Max began to recount Zoro's life, as if he were reading it from the pages of a book. "Your brother died," Max began, "your mother blames you, and you believe her. And now"—Max hesitated—"you're ready to change, but you don't know how. You just don't know how to save yourself."

As Max spoke, his words carried Zoro back to every painful moment. Grief filled his heart; the ache was unbearable. And it didn't help matters that Max was dead right about every detail.

"And that photo on my dashboard, the one of the young boy . . . I think there's more to say," Max continued. "I think you might like to say it. I think you might even need to say it."

Zoro didn't protest, didn't try to make excuses. In a dead voice, he narrated for Max the story of Joey's death. Like a jailhouse snitch, he fingered himself, all the while thinking that after this, Max might not want to know him. Hell, Zoro didn't even want to know himself.

"There was no moon that night, and all I could think about was Rachel," Zoro began. "She was a year older than me and curvy. Sneaking out to see her for a few minutes at the park around the corner seemed a lot more important than babysitting my little brother. There were so many things that could have gone wrong, and they all did. I smelled smoke, heard the sirens, and somehow I knew it was already too late.

"I ran up to the house, screaming through the scalding gusts of heavy smoke, yelling until my lungs hurt. But I couldn't save Joey." Tears began streaming down Zoro's face. "He was so little. I can't even imagine how much pain he endured. Those flames blistering his body . . . the darkness, the crackling . . . Joey had curled up on the floor, gasping for breath in that pit of hell. I swear I heard him call my name! *Zoro . . . help me, Zoro . . .*" Joey's voice was stuck in Zoro's mind like an echo that refused to die.

By now, Zoro was sobbing. Without him realizing it, the car had coasted to a stop in the long driveway. Max sat very still in the backseat, his eyes still fastened on Zoro's face, reflected in the rearview mirror.

"I would have run to Joey and burned up with him if that cop hadn't caught me and dragged me out of the fire. I wish he hadn't. My dad missed Joey so bad, he jumped off a bridge and killed himself.

"It was all because of me," Zoro said between sobs. "Joey and Dad are dead and Ma hates me. You see, Mr. Max, my soul's been to places even God wouldn't go."

Zoro clenched his teeth, holding his face in his hands. "Mr. Max, I've done everything I can to forget, but I just can't."

"Maybe you should just remember, son. Find your own truth in it." Max's voice was as quiet as ever. If Zoro had been watching him in the rearview mirror, he would have seen the ashen color on Max's face, the tremor in his lips as he struggled with memories of his own.

"It's not right, you know what I mean?" Zoro said, trying to get his voice under control. "One thing comes along and blows your whole life away."

Max took a deep breath. "I'm sorry you've been doing this your whole life, Zoro."

"Doing what?" Zoro sniffed, trying to conceal the red of his eyes from his billionaire impromptu psychoanalyst.

"Believing the self-delusional nonsense that comes out of your mouth."

"You . . . you think this is easy for me? You think I wanted any of this?"

"Zoro, clearly I'm not trying to upset you; I just want you to understand something."

Zoro was silent, drained. Whatever his new guru was about to share with him, he felt powerless to do anything except listen.

Max had a gentle expression on his face. "Everything we lose is a stone in the road, Zoro. And you need to learn to face the stones, pile them up, and maybe even use them to build a road toward the answers and away from the pain. You can always find reasons to give up, but Zoro, you can also find just as many reasons to go on."

For a moment Zoro sat mulling over the idea, then his mind clanged shut like a graveyard gate. He shoved himself up straight in the driver's seat and pushed the accelerator, guiding the limo down the driveway and through the open gate, making a right turn onto the road.

"Right now, I'm too busy hating me to do any road construction," he said. "By the way, where are we headed?"

Just then, they were jolted by a series of bumps. Zoro swore and braked, trying to see what he'd hit or run over. At that moment, Max leaned forward and said quietly, "If you're not moving forward from the past, Zoro, you're going the wrong way. And we're going to Grand Central Station."

Zoro realized that the limo, which had made him feel safe earlier that morning, was now feeling surprisingly uncomfortable. He felt like a polar explorer, stranded in an abandoned outpost, looking out over a vast expanse of frozen nothing. "It's not my fault, you know, the way I am," Zoro said with a sigh.

Max rolled a grin up to the corners of his mouth. "Ah, yes; it's Mommy's fault, is it?" Max started laughing.

Zoro wasn't laughing. His world was closing in on him and he felt like hell. "You don't know shit," Zoro snapped, wishing he could have had Max sign a nondisclosure form before he opened his heart to him.

Max was a distinguished-looking man who appeared tall, even when he was sitting down, Zoro had noticed. No droop in his shoulders, no slump in his posture. Now he leaned forward again. "You're right, Zoro, I don't know enough," he said. "But I do know most people listen to their families all their lives, yet find nothing as comforting as their silence. I'm guessing she's a bit much, your mother; even at your age, always ordering you around . . . eat that, wear this, do that. Does she run your life?"

"Run it? She damn well owns it! She's ruined my life!"

Max leaned farther over the front seat. He put his hand on Zoro's shoulder. Zoro hadn't expected that, and he sure didn't expect to hear what Max said next.

"I'm going to help you, Zoro. I'm going to save you."

CHAPTER 8

If he hadn't considered it before, Zoro was now seriously considering that his new boss might be a nutcase. And yet he was sitting there in the backseat, perfectly calm, volunteering to be Zoro's personal savior. *Christ's sake*, he thought, *this is making me crazy.*

Max must have sensed Zoro's inner reaction. "Please, Zoro," he said, "give me a chance to explain. What if you discovered that your reality was a dream, and all you needed to do was wake up?"

Oh, yeah, now that sounds perfectly logical—NOT!

"Look, Zoro," Max said, "you have something I need, and I have something I can give you."

Zoro was trying to disconnect his ears, to just go on autopilot and let Max's words soak into the upholstery like elevator music. But for some reason, he couldn't keep himself from waiting to hear what Max would say next.

"But, Zoro, for this to work, you need to understand that we need to first break you out of the prison of your own mind."

"I think—"

"What you think is a bunch of crap," Max said, cutting him off. He lifted his head, cocking it to one side. His voice took on an eager tone. "You fidget around in your own head and build illusions of what you think is real. Your knee-jerk responses and bad thoughts are like a virus. You're infected, Zoro, and so is the rest of the world. It's a bloody epidemic!"

Ma! Zoro thought. *I ought to tell Max she's the real virus.* But Zoro was too mentally tired to talk. Although he had the feeling he ought to say something, he just sat there.

"Don't you want to know what I can give you, Zoro?"

"Okay, I'll bite. What?"

"When you know that, you'll already have it." Max grinned.

Zoro sighed and shook his head. More riddles, more bullshit packaged like a proverb. Part of him wanted to believe what Max was saying, and the rest of him was afraid to hear what he would say next.

"Look, you don't wake up one morning with all the answers," Max said. "You either figure life out one mistake at a time, or ..."

"Or what?" asked Zoro.

"Well, you could listen to me," Max said, smiling.

"Why would I listen to you?"

"Because I'm your wake-up call!" Max paused. "Or . . . I don't know, maybe you're right. After all, what could an old billionaire possibly teach you?"

Zoro searched his mind, but he couldn't grasp what Max was talking about. *Wake-up call. Yeah, right.*

They were heading into a steady stream of traffic. Zoro's brow knitted and he frowned as he regretted having confided in Max.

All his life people had laughed at him behind his back. They laughed when he lost the state championship in high school; hell, some sickos probably even laughed when Joey died. And now he wondered if Max was laughing at him. He cringed inside, silently telling himself, *I shouldn't have said anything.*

After all, today wasn't the first time in his life someone had offered to save him. After Joey's death, Carmela had forced him to spend a year at one of Vermont's cheapest centers for troubled youth. After surviving a series of failed interventions followed by attempts to rescue the interventions, Zoro had concluded that staying frozen in his miserable world was the status quo that suited him. It was his easy misery—familiar, like the smell of traffic exhaust.

Looking at Max in the mirror, Zoro's green eyes squinted. "You're wasting your time; after what I did to Joey, I'm not worth saving."

Max sat up even straighter in his seat, if that were possible. To Zoro, it looked as if some wild inner light was glaring harshly from his eyes. "You have nothing to reproach yourself for, Zoro," Max said sternly, "absolutely nothing. Any reproach would be preposterous. You do, however, have the right to dream, to be wealthy, and to have the life you truly deserve. Incidentally, Zoro, your greatest liability—your mind— has gotten the question wrong. The question is not, 'Am I worth it?'; the question is, 'Is it worth my life?'"

"But Mr. Max—" Zoro had fully expected some tough assertions, but suddenly everything he'd assumed was backward and wrong. It was as if someone had thrown a switch in his brain and opened a tiny circuit, and his ordinary thinking would no longer be enough.

"Ask yourself, Zoro, loud and clear, 'Is what you've got now worth your life?' Say it with me, Zoro, 'Is what I've got now worth my life?' Go on . . . say it."

Max was plainspoken and strong-willed. Zoro repeated the words, sounding and feeling like a doofus.

But Max spoke again, his voice kinder. "Everything that's broken, even the worst of it, can be fixed, Zoro."

"But . . . what if I can't be fixed? What happens then?"

"This time will be different, Zoro."

Zoro took a deep breath and shook his head. "All's I know is my little brother died because of me, and then life just went black." *Why am I telling him this?* Zoro thought. And suddenly the tiny, open circuit in his brain slammed shut.

The old man's eyes bored in on Zoro. "I understand, Zoro, really, I do. Life doesn't knock before it mugs you, I get that. But God will find you again; he isn't quite done with you, Zoro."

"Tell me you didn't just say that," Zoro mumbled, "'cause I've had just about all the help I can take from God."

"Zoro, I look at you: It's as if you're saying, 'Help me; I've lost hope and I'm trapped in my mind.'"

Zoro shrugged and glanced at Max, then away. "You know, in high school everything was easy. I could've saved the world then. And now, I can't even hold down a job." *Geez, look at me, all forthcoming, suddenly.*

"You were fearless, weren't you, Zoro?"

"Yeah, I was. What happened to that?"

"Life."

Zoro nodded slowly, letting that thought sink in. "I wish I had known me better, back when I was something. You know how it is, Mr. Max."

"How what is?" Max replied, "Feeling sorry for yourself? Sorry, I don't."

Zoro began to feel like a coward. He started wishing and praying for this ride to end, before he said anything more he would regret—or had to listen to any more painful truth from Max's lips.

He had spent years trying to shake loose his sorrow, but it clung to him like a leech. He'd spent hours numbering the hurtful thoughts in his head, trying to subtract them out. And now Max was shaking and rattling those same thoughts, rumbling over them like the thumping of tires on the expansion joints of the Tappan Zee Bridge.

"Zoro, your mind has created an illusion of who you are and what you're capable of. If you can wake from that, I can help you."

Zoro got the feeling that Max's help would come at a stiff price.

"For now," Max said, "begin by talking to Joey. And before you tell me that's impossible, remember that there are a lot of mysteries we don't understand."

"You sound like a fortune cookie." Zoro chuckled nervously.

Having left Jersey behind, he edged the limo through the clogged streets pulsing with the metal blood of Manhattan. He sat hunched over the steering wheel, his left knee resting against the driver's door, sensing the vibration of the engine. Except for that faint hum, the limo was mostly quiet. Zoro preferred the quiet. This time of day even the homeless guys, the ones who smeared your windshield with spit and wiped it with their coatsleeves, were silent and hidden.

Max was still staring at him in the mirror, clearly expecting him to say something. Zoro blinked. He was tired of thinking about the pain, tired of Max's confusing pronouncements, tired of bleeding tears. He simply wanted to tune Max out.

"I've tried, I really have, Mr. Max. But no matter which way I turn, I just can't face Joey's memory." The jagged thoughts tumbled about in Zoro's head. *Thump . . . thump . . . thump . . .* "So whaddya say we leave Joey and Isaac out of this, and cut to the chase? If you're thinking of helping me, what is it you want from me? Just give me the short version."

* * *

The hair on Max's arm bristled with anticipation; he could feel a decisive moment approaching. Bumping into Carmela after so many years, the urgent call from Domino, his own situation, at first Max had wondered, *What's trying to happen here?* And then, it had all made sense. Max had made the connection and realized the universe had been conspiring to give him a second chance at solving a thirty-year-old mystery, before it was too late.

"I think there's something we need to discuss," he said.

"I don't think I like the sound of that," Zoro replied.

"Good, Zoro," Max laughed. "Then don't think. Park anywhere you can along here. We're at our destination."

CHAPTER 9

Forty-second Street was oddly quiet, and so was Max. And though he wasn't speaking, a loud debate raged in his mind. But in truth, Max had little choice. He needed to tell Zoro everything because, in his estimation, Zoro was the one. Normally cautious, Max couldn't afford to be today.

Zoro came around and opened his door, and Max stepped out of the limo and onto the sidewalk. Max led them into Grand Central Station. Standing on the balcony, they watched streams of humanity coming in from the commuter trains, swirling around the central information kiosk, moving beneath the mural of golden constellations painted on the turquoise-blue ceiling.

"You could say this is the universe," Max said, peering upward. Then he gave Zoro an intent look. "I haven't a lot of time to consider the consequences, Zoro, so I'll get right to the point. I need to give you something."

* * *

Zoro kept his eyes roving over the people milling about in the station, willing himself not to look at Max. He didn't want to appear to be his usual self and blow his chance. He'd hoped all his life things would finally go his way, and here it was—an opportunity. What would it be? Maybe an offer from this rich guy. The endless possibilities sang out in his mind; an explosion of hope and anticipation detonated in his chest.

"So what's this all about?" Zoro said with a little smile, trying to conceal his excitement. He stood quietly, one eye on the crowd, hoping, and still he waited.

"A fortune," Max whispered.

Zoro inhaled sharply. "Like a million?"

Max grinned. "Try bigger."

"How much bigger?" Zoro's eyes were riveted on Max's face now. His stomach was knotted with agonizing, hopeful tension. Could it be all his dreams were about to come true? Zoro's face flushed with anxious impatience.

"Okay, here it is," Max said with a grin. "What was the first thing that went through your mind when you stepped into my house?"

Zoro's eyes widened, as the answer popped into his head. "Indiana Jones. Your place looks like some ancient temple filled with paintings and crap. It was all kind of mysterious."

Max took a deep breath. He laid his hand flat on Zoro's shoulder. "If it felt mysterious," Max whispered, "it's because there's a secret in my house that holds the answer to the greatest and most powerful mystery of all time."

Zoro turned again to look at the bustling crowd below, a thousand questions tumbling through his mind. "Mystery," Zoro muttered, "what mystery?"

"I must admit," Max said, "this is more difficult than I imagined."

Zoro could see in his peripheral vision that Max was watching him intently, as if waiting for some kind of signal or cue. Zoro just stared ahead blankly, not sure what Max was expecting from him.

"So what do you think?" Max asked. "Do you want to know the secret? Because once I tell you, Zoro, there's no turning back."

"I'm not crazy about secrets," Zoro said, swallowing hard. "But I'm not crazy, either."

Max was still watching.

"Okay," Zoro said. "I'm listening."

Max exhaled sharply, his breath whooshing from his throat. "The problem is," he said, spreading his hands urgently, "I don't know how much time we have."

"What does that mean?" Zoro asked.

"Forget what I said; it's not important." Max's tone was dangerously mysterious. "What's important, though, is to tell you that what's at stake here is so powerful that, should it fall into the wrong hands, it could plunge the world into darkness."

Zoro looked hard at Max. Was anything he was saying true, or was he leading him through the shadows of an unstable mind? His eyes squinted with skepticism. "Spooky!" Zoro puckered his lips mockingly.

"Zoro, let me be clear—"

"No, let me be clear," Zoro said. "You're talking out of the side of your mouth. There're no straight answers here."

"All right, fine. You want to hear the simple truth?"

"Yes, damn it, what is it?" Zoro turned away from Max again, shaking his head. *Damn mumbo-jumbo. Why can't he just say stuff straight out?*

"A name . . ." Max said the words slowly, just above a whisper. Yet, somehow, Zoro could still hear him, even above the noise of the hurrying crowds.

"A name?" Zoro gave Max a twisted, sardonic smile.

Max leaned into Zoro's shoulder and looked out over the crowd.

Zoro puffed a hard breath from his nostrils. His eyes probed Max's face for answers. "Means nothing to me," he said gazing again at the crowd.

"Let me finish," Max said. "The Name, should you choose to find it, could make you the most powerful person on earth."

What does this Howard Hughes nut job want from me? Looking back at Max, he shrugged.

* * *

Max was proposing an urgent quest to Zoro, and he was afraid. The minute he explained the story behind the Name, he was certain Zoro would make the only play he was comfortable with. He knew that people never perceive the truth in a way that puts what they already believe into question. So few people in history, with the exception of geniuses like Einstein, Edison, and Michelangelo, were ever able to override the sanctity of their established beliefs. Even powerful, privileged people had failed to understand.

Max stared at the people thronging through the vast hall below them. Not a single person passing through Grand Central Station understood. And yet here he was, about to initiate Zoro into something so far beyond his imagination that it would make his head hurt. But whether Zoro knew it or not, only he possessed the information that Max needed. And with time running out, what was once a pressing need was quickly growing into a matter of desperation.

* * *

Trying one more time to sift through the strangeness, Zoro pressed again, "You're talking about some secret name? So can I assume you're going to tell me what it is?"

Max cleared his throat. He seemed to be thinking about what he was going to say. Zoro scoped the crowd. Everyone was rushing from one place to the next; he and Max were alone on an island of stillness, adrift in an ocean of hustle and bustle. If Max would relinquish the secret, this would be as good a place as any. He could unzip the secret safely here, dead-bolted in the frenzied anonymity of Grand Central Station.

"Zoro . . ." Max's eyes were so focused they looked like they could burn through the station walls, and his voice was as hard as the marble floor. "Thousands of years ago God was believed to have given a divine secret to the high priests in the Holy of Holies of Solomon's temple."

Zoro's heart was suddenly pounding. His attention was stretched as tight as a piano wire. He stood silently, not moving his eyes from Max's face. Despite not understanding, Zoro was now certain he should listen. This had the makings of an adventure, and he'd try anything once, and had had six broken bones to prove it. Though this . . . this wasn't making sense yet. Of this he was sure.

"Look, I'm not dumb, but can you dumb it down for me?"

Max swallowed; his face showed traces of apprehension. In a tone of awe, as if speaking about royalty, he said, "Speaking the Name, Zoro, unleashes the power of heaven."

"But, Mr. Max . . . There's no basis for believing that."

Max began to vibrate with an inner excitement, like a buttered kernel of popcorn in a hot pan. "No one knows for sure how it happens, but something about correctly sounding out that Name can make you powerful beyond your imagination." Max paused again, and to Zoro, the noise in the crowded station suddenly seemed muffled, as if Max's words were the only sound.

How is that even possible? Zoro thought. "So, Mr. Max . . . You're telling me this name is actually real?"

"As real as you and me, Zoro. The secret of the Name has moved through a web of nameless guardians, all hidden away, all stitched together in secrecy for thousands of years." Max leaned a bit closer. "The Name I'm talking about, Zoro, is the true name of God, a divine secret used by those ancient priests to conjure up miracles, feats of biblical proportion."

Zoro felt his head spin like a compass needle. Whether because of emotional fatigue or Max's suggestive voice, he felt powerless. Max's eyes were fixed intently on Zoro, his pupils dilated and dark as the pits of eternity. "Zoro, Zoro," Max squeezed his shoulder tightly. Suddenly Max's face looked different to Zoro. The heavy weight of memories seemed to press on his shoulders. Max leaned on the railing of the station balcony, and it seemed like it was all he could do to remain on his feet.

"With the Name, Zoro . . . the world's hard rain could be stopped . . . Don't you understand?" Zoro was astonished to see a tear on Max's cheek that he quickly wiped away.

Zoro could find no words. He rubbed his face with his hands, pulled in a deep breath, and let it out. Something about Max's sincerity, the passion with which he told the story, made Zoro want to believe what he was saying. A few minutes ago, Zoro wasn't even aware such a secret name existed. And now, the depth of his own ignorance frightened him.

CHAPTER 10

Max blinked, his eyes sharpened, and his face took on a look of purpose. His whole body straightened and he started to wave his hands in the air like a Baptist minister. "Look up at the ceiling," he told Zoro. "The constellations of the universe, rendered in gold.

"Consider, Zoro: the universe is a neat, functioning system."

Zoro shrugged. "Okay, but . . ."

"And the Name, Zoro," Max continued, his voice dipping low, "the most sought-after treasure in the history of humankind—it's the device that allows you to unlock the secrets of the universe. I don't know exactly what would happen to someone who spoke the word, but legend has it that correctly uttering the Name channels the power of God through the speaker."

"Wait here," Max said, glancing over Zoro's shoulder toward the stairs.

* * *

A man ran his hand along the marble banister as he climbed the station stairs. He wasn't the kind of man to set his own world on fire, but what he'd done was necessary. At least he thought it was.

"Over here," Max flagged him from the balcony, meeting him at the top step. The man slid a plain, brown, letter-sized envelope from beneath his coat. Pulling an 8x10 photograph from the envelope, he handed it to Max.

"You're on your own now, Max."

Max looked dubious. "Are you sure?"

"I'm going to melt away." He forced himself to look into Max's eyes. "One can't be too careful. The Holy See has eyes and ears everywhere, others too."

Before Max could respond, Zoro moved toward them. On glimpsing Zoro, the man draped his arm across his face and spun around.

"I can't be seen with him," the man said as he bowed his head, bothered by Zoro.

"Wait," Max grabbed at his coat sleeve just as he turned to walk away. "I need to know if you found out anything else."

"I haven't come up with anything beyond what I've just given you."

"Well that wasn't much," Max said.

As Zoro neared, the man crammed the empty envelope into his pocket and hurried down the stairs, shielding his face.

*   *   *

The veins across Zoro's temples were engorged and throbbing. He found himself wondering about that strange man, as Max slipped the photograph into his briefcase.

Max grinned at him. "I can see the wheels spinning in your head." He reached forward and tousled Zoro's hair.

"Hey, what the hell?" Zoro pulled away.

Max raised his palms toward Zoro, smiling an apology. Zoro went silent for a moment. He tugged at the wrinkled cuffs poking from the sleeves of his trademark black suit.

"Zoro, as I told you, there's something you have that I need, and something I have that you want."

"So what do you need from me?"

"Your mind."

"That's crazy."

"Let me show you something your father knew. Then you decide if I'm a nut job or if we can help each other."

"Okay, but what does my mind have to do with you helping me, or that crazy story?"

"Interesting question—a key question, in fact. If you can give me your mind, I'll tell you the rest of a story that could change your life forever."

"How the hell can I do that? I can't just separate myself from my mind."

"Ah, but let's not rule anything out. Consider this, Zoro. Science has changed how we look at the world. We no longer see just the surface of the earth, we see the parts underneath, that make up our world. We don't think of gravity and electricity as magic; we understand there are real forces and streams of electrons. In the same way, you, your mind, and your reality are not just one big inseparable clump; underneath the surface we can dissect them into parts, like a bunch of worlds all working together in a system."

Looking at Max, Zoro suddenly remembered his grandfather on the day he died. He remembered the sudden strength in the sick old man's voice when he'd said, "We all die, Zoro. I'm off to another world."

Zoro had asked him, "Why are you leaving me, Grandpa?"

The look in his grandfather's eyes had softened. "I'm not leaving, only changing." His grandfather had smiled.

After sitting beside his grandfather's bed for another hour, Zoro had fallen asleep. When he woke to the sound of sobbing all around him and looked down into his grandfather's peaceful, still face, he knew it was all over. He'd never known what Grandpa had meant. And now, listening to Max, he burned with many of the same questions that it seemed Max was about to answer.

Max paused briefly, as an announcement echoed throughout the cavernous hall of the station, and then continued. "According to our greatest thinkers, Zoro, we can dissect our world into three worlds."

Okay, that sounds like total bullshit to me . . . Zoro grabbed the thought that popped up and forced it back to the corner of his mind. *Listen, Zoro. For once in your life, listen to somebody who's trying to help you.* "Three worlds, Mr. Max?"

Max spoke in an animated way, sounding out every syllable. He explained that the first world was the easiest to understand; it was the outside world, the world of physical form. "It's the world where things happen to you, Zoro. When you get the flu, it happens in your physical world."

Max explained the second world, the inner world of mind, thoughts, emotions, and mental images.

Zoro looked at Max, with his cut, angular features, his uncompromising elegance. "You're a lot like my grandfather, though your lifestyle hasn't caught up with you like his did," Zoro said, chuckling.

Max smiled. "What do you mean?"

"Grandpa loved the ponies. His nickname was Derby Dan."

"I'm not much on racing," Max said. "The races are just horses and numbers to me. Maybe I should continue?"

"Sorry, go on."

"The third world is more difficult to explain, Max said. "It is less tangible, for it is the place that transcends the physical and mental world.

"There is a stream of consciousness in the world that is vibrant and alive. And the third world, Zoro, is made up of that essence, that very energy of life. We've come to understand it as an infinite place where our souls go. It is the boundless space between everything tangible."

"Okay," Zoro said, nodding. He had a momentary question about whether he really bought what Max was saying, or if he was just saying what he was supposed to say. One thing was for sure: he'd never thought of things this way. There was no proof of it of course, no way to confirm it. But by its nature the thought of three worlds seemed no less plausible to Zoro than any other one-sided account of the universe he'd ever heard.

Zoro leaned on the banister and looked at Max. "So what does this all mean?"

"Not what does it mean," Max replied, "but rather, what has it caused?"

Zoro's forehead wrinkled in puzzlement.

"Zoro, most people believe they live in only one world, the outer world. They've become consumed by their physical nature, and that's all they understand. And with that shallow view, the world quickly becomes a cold and harsh place where we allow ourselves to be bullied by the outer world.

"But when we recognize the three worlds and understand that they are all interconnected and directly affect one another, a wonderful discovery blossoms. If you have the power to affect one world, you also unknowingly affect the other worlds; after all, they're connected. And the one world that you have direct and immediate control over, the one you can use to affect the other worlds, is your inner world—the world within your mind."

Zoro listened attentively, but he still felt pretty mystified. There was something about Max, though, that made Zoro want to listen to him. Why should a guy like Max care about somebody like him? And yet, he was trying to explain things, trying to get something across to Zoro that seemed really important to him. Not that many people had ever given Zoro that sort of attention. After a few seconds, he shook his head and said, "Go on."

"Zoro, right now we're only interested in one world, your world of the mind: the one we can use to save you. Do you understand?"

"Yes . . . I think so."

"Good, then let's leave it at that."

"What about the rest of that story you promised me?"

"Ah. That's something we need to look at. Follow me."

CHAPTER 11

As they made their way to the nearest exit, Zoro felt as if he had a million question marks buzzing in his head. Zoro held the door open for Max, who, as he stepped outside, was gilded by a slant of autumn sunlight. Tumbled along by a breeze blowing down Forty-second Street, leaves clattered down the sidewalk and swirled around Zoro's feet, startling a flock of preening starlings into flight.

Zoro blinked. For an instant, the whole picture looked unreal. It was perfectly fitting, he thought: this strange image of Max bathed in light with a hundred carbon-copy starlings dotting the skyline behind him. In a curious way, the scene matched everything Max had described so far, things that mostly sounded bogus and hard to sort out. It seemed as if someone had pulled a lever and the world had stopped for a moment, allowing Zoro to ponder this surrealistic image and figure out what world Max was part of.

Nearby, a deep, threatening voice roared like a rumbling steamroller. "Get off my street, you goddamned insect!"

Some guy in an expensive-looking suit was standing over a homeless panhandler. It looked like he had shoved the bum down and now he was brandishing a brass-tipped cane while the panhandler cowered.

"Conrad," Max hissed.

"You know that guy?" Zoro asked.

"Only too well."

People like Conrad usually didn't bother Zoro; he could take care of himself in a scrape when he had to. But he was surprised that a person like Max would ever have had anything to do with someone so cruel. *It's not right for him to do that, not even to a homeless guy*, Zoro thought. At that moment it didn't matter to Zoro how expensive Conrad's full-stretch Mercedes was, or that he appeared to be someone who knew how to get his own way; Zoro needed to stop him.

Moving toward the scuffle, Zoro initially felt a surge of adrenaline. He wanted with all his heart to sock this Conrad character in the mouth for what he'd done. But the closer Zoro got to Conrad, the more ridiculous he appeared. From behind, his blocky stature made him look like a mountain troll. Zoro might even have laughed, if he hadn't been on a mission.

He came up behind Conrad and quickly moved between him and his victim. With his back to Conrad, Zoro helped the homeless man to his feet. "You all right?" He asked.

The bum nodded. Zoro looked into his face, and the homeless man's million-miles-away stare told Zoro this latest insult was just the most recent in a history of similar abuse. Zoro caught his reflection in the man's blood-shot eyes and remembered what the other bum had said this morning, after the accident: "*See you soon, kid.*"

Suddenly the stuff Max had said didn't seem so hard to believe. Maybe Max's offer really was Zoro's way out, a path of escape from a life that was going nowhere.

"This isn't any of your business," growled Conrad. Zoro turned to face him, and felt a jolt of surprise at realizing that this Conrad guy looked familiar. Where had Zoro seen him before?

But if Zoro was surprised at this, he was even more astonished by Conrad's reaction. He stared at Zoro, looking like someone who had just seen a ghost. His lips trembled, and a single, hoarsely whispered word fell from his mouth: "Isaac?"

He peered about frantically, and then spied Max, standing by the door of his limo. His expression quickly changed from one of fear and confusion to purpling rage.

"You two . . . together again!" Conrad shouted. He spun back toward Zoro, menacing him with his cane. His jaw jutted like a boxer's, coming in for the haymaker. "You have something that belongs to me!" he bellowed.

Zoro stared at Conrad's contorted face, then over at Max. He had no idea what Conrad was talking about. He shook his head in confusion.

"Good day, Conrad," Max called. "I hope you don't mind that Carmela acquainted me with her son . . . Isaac's son."

Conrad's forehead knit in concentration. He looked from Zoro to Max, putting the pieces together in his mind.

"And now, if you'll excuse us," Max said, "We need to be going. Zoro?"

"Wait a minute, Mr. Max!" Zoro stood nose to nose with Conrad. "Who are you? How do you know Isaac; how do you know me?"

"I'll explain it to you, Zoro," Max said. "But we really should go— now!"

Zoro stepped around Conrad, giving the broad man a wide berth. He was almost to the limo when he heard quick, heavy footsteps behind him.

"Just a minute," Conrad puffed as he hurried toward Zoro.

"Mason, Conrad Mason is my name."

Zoro recognized the name; Conrad Mason was a wealthy industrialist, part of New York's elite. But something about the man bothered Zoro. He couldn't put his finger on it, until he saw him smile; he looked like he owned the world.

"Your father was my friend," Conrad said.

"Nonsense," Max replied. "You can't afford to wait, Zoro, please now." Max knew that Conrad would now be following their every move. Acting in secret was no longer an option. They had to move quickly, or miss their opportunity forever. Time was not on their side.

They got into the limo, and Zoro turned the key in the ignition. He looked at Max in the rearview mirror. "What the hell was that all about, Mr. Max? How'd you get mixed up with a goon like that Conrad guy? And how does he know Isaac?"

Max looked at Zoro for a long moment, as if trying to decide how much to tell him.

"He's just a crazy, old eccentric, Zoro. Everyone knows to ignore him."

As they drove away, Max prayed to God that his plan would work.

CHAPTER 12

Still staring after the receding limo, Conrad yanked his cell phone out of his pocket. He stabbed at the keys, wishing he were shoving his finger into Max's eye.

In another part of town, a man seated behind the wheel of an expensive brown sedan felt his cell phone vibrate. He pulled it out, glancing at the screen. "Yeah, Conrad."

"Max and Isaac's kid are together!" Conrad bellowed. "I saw them, just now, Alton. In Manhattan, outside Grand Central."

Alton sat in disbelieving silence for several seconds. "Zoro? What are you talking about? That can't be. How could he have contacted Max without my knowing?"

"Damned good question," Conrad growled. "Apparently the old hag arranged to put them together."

"Goddamn it, what could she know after all these years?" Alton had already yanked the car into drive and pressed the accelerator to the floor. His muscles tensed and his eyes worked the road as he sped around the interchange.

"I don't know," Conrad said. In the last few seconds, since encountering Max and Zoro, he had been frantically retracing thirty-year-old footsteps, trying to remember something, anything he'd missed. He visualized everything about Carmela's house, inside and out. He pictured every nook and cranny.

"Any ideas?" Alton said.

"Ideas? You idiot! You make it sound like I could have missed something. I never make mistakes!" Conrad tried to remember every nuance in Carmela's face, the last time he'd seen her. It ate him up that she might have pulled a fast one on him. But why, if she'd kept anything from him, would she have waited this long?

"It doesn't add up," Alton said, swerving quickly to pass a slow-moving taxi. "Maybe it's a coincidence."

"I don't believe in coincidence. They've got something. Get to Carmela's as fast as you can."

"Already on my way. In this traffic I'll be there in five minutes."

"All right. Then handle it," Conrad ordered. "Find what you need to find and get out." Alton clicked his phone shut. He was about twenty blocks from her neighborhood.

When he arrived a few minutes later, he watched the house as the minutes leaked by. When he was sure the house was empty, he stepped from the sedan, and no one seemed to notice him slip into the backyard.

CHAPTER 13

As Zoro drove, the city streets began swimming in front of him. His mind started taking a trip of its own—a strange name, a strange man, a story of three worlds; it was all a confusing mess. Pressing his palm flat against his forehead, he was certain he would need more details from Max.

Lost in his thoughts, he wasn't sure how far they had gone when Max told him to stop. They were in front of the New York Public Library. Zoro shook his head to clear it and looked at the two lion sculptures guarding the entrance. On the north side was the one dubbed "Fortitude" by Mayor LaGuardia, and the lion on the south was "Patience." They'd been commissioned during the Depression years as a symbol of hope for the people. Still, Zoro found it hard to believe that the world was any safer with them there.

Max tugged his sleeve up to look at his wristwatch.

Hesitantly, Zoro spoke. "What's going on, Mr. Max? If you have something to explain, now would be a good time."

"Conrad is an old rival of your father's and mine. And I think the story I promised you will shed some light on that."

"I'm getting sick and tired of being in the dark here. In fact I'm sick and tired of being sick and tired, and I'd like some answers now."

"Then I suggest you follow me into the library," Max said.

Max led the way into the building and upstairs to a room with a sign on the door that said "Special Collections; Authorized Personnel Only." Max pulled a key from his pocket and unlocked the door, propping it open with its drop-down brass door holder. They went inside and Max motioned for Zoro to sit.

Zoro stood for a moment, staring about at the rich surroundings. Just ahead of him was a long, polished wooden table; a runner of maroon tapestry, embroidered with intricate designs, ran down the center of the table. Flanked by several high-backed chairs upholstered in immaculate red velvet, to Zoro the chairs looked almost like thrones. Matching red velvet curtains framed the large windows. Between the windows and elsewhere in the spacious room, bookcases rose almost to the ceiling.

Zoro sat in one of the red velvet chairs. He didn't allow himself to speculate about what would happen next. In fact, the plan he'd made with himself was simple. He'd come to realize it was easier to follow Max than to worry about what came next.

"This room holds one of the world's leading collections of rare books and reproductions of ancient writings, Zoro," Max said. "In here there are some 25,000 books, along with letters and ancient manuscripts."

Max had a thick volume in his hands, and he walked toward Zoro and laid it on the table in front of him.

"But this is the book you should be reading," he said. "Go ahead, Zoro. Open it."

Zoro opened the book and stared at the words. They were written in a language he couldn't understand—even the letters were foreign to him.

"It's Hebrew," Max explained. "It tells the history of the last temple of Jerusalem." Zoro skimmed through the pages, then stopped at an image depicting a man who appeared to be guarding a doorway. The guard stood before a building of immense stone blocks. Zoro stared at the picture for several seconds, then shut his eyes, trying to fix its details in his mind. He could almost taste and smell the dust stirred up by the Roman army as it crested a hill behind the temple. The guard stood firm, his arms crossed in a V in front of his armor of leather and iron. There was a strange design on the guard's breastplate that almost mirrored the shape of his crossed arms: a V with the ends pointed—like the tips of swords . . . and cradled in the center, the embossed outline of two lions following the contour of the V.

"Zoro, Zoro," Max had to shake Zoro from his reverie. He placed three more volumes on the desk beside Zoro.

"Mr. Max, I can't even read the first book you gave me, and now you're giving me three more."

"Don't worry, Zoro. I'm going to give you the abridged version—at least, enough of it to get you started. But I wanted you to see these now. One day, you may want to come back here to learn more for yourself."

"I doubt it. So . . . how about that abridged version you mentioned?"

Max sat down in the chair across the table from Zoro. He took a deep breath.

"I'm glad you chose to hear my story," Max smiled.

Zoro knew all about choice; people loved to talk about it. But deep down inside, Zoro felt that people like him didn't have choices—not really.

As if sensing Zoro's mood souring, Max said in a quiet, insistent voice, "Close your eyes, Zoro; picture my words in your mind."

Zoro decided to follow his new plan: *Just follow Max's lead . . . Don't try to figure it out . . .*

"It's a complicated legend," Max began. "You've probably heard of the Vatican Library, the Bibliotheca Vaticana, the most valuable archive in the world. Most of its treasures were acquired by less than gentle means during the Crusades. It contains thousands of manuscripts and incunabula—even Christopher Columbus's personal notes—all of it stored in a vault the size of a football field.

"But beneath Vatican City lies a secret archive. In a network of tunnels, on miles of shelves, lie treasures from great libraries such as those of Babylon and Athens. Some of the world's most treasured pieces lie there, never cataloged . . . never again touched by human hands."

Max looked at Zoro. "You've probably heard of it?"

Zoro opened his eyes and gave Max a blank look. "Never."

Max smiled, continuing, "Well, as the story goes . . ."

As Max spoke, the sounds of the outside world dimmed in Zoro's ears. The words began to summon images in his mind.

"In the Vatican Library there are ancient writings that speak of a hidden light created by God, a light filled with the secrets of the cosmos. With that light, a mortal person could defeat great armies, could acquire great power and wealth.

"Centuries ago, the high priests of the temple in Jerusalem, the Kohanim, received the secret to accessing that light: a thirty-two letter word for the Name of God, which, when spoken with the proper tone and emphasis, literally beamed the architecture of the universe into their minds. It was the very word used by Moses to part the Red Sea."

"That sounds utterly ridiculous," Zoro said. "I don't remember hearing anything like that in confirmation classes."

Max thought for a second and nodded. "I have to admit, it does. But this next bit should pique your interest, Zoro.

"Because the light was so powerful, any ordinary man who had spoken the Name succumbed to a tormenting madness."

"What about the priests?"

"Excellent question, Zoro. Some certainly did, which is why the priests seized on a plan. They entrusted a single priest, the most powerful among them, to conceal the Name, saving it for the direst of times. The secret of the Name was so important that it was never even committed to writing. It was entrusted only to the mind of a single Kohan, its memory preserved only in the traditions passed in succession from one high priest to the next."

"What happened to the guy who knew the Name?"

"The legend is complicated, but several sources indicate that the last of the high priests was killed when the temple was razed by Titus and his band of conquering Romans in A.D. 70. And with him, the Name was lost forever."

Zoro opened his eyes. "So why are you wasting my time? It's all over, right?"

Max smiled. "Another damn good question. I'll tell you.

"In the early 1500s, a monk named Leonardo di Pistoia was sent out by the Vatican to scour monasteries for ancient writings. While crawling through a narrow catacomb in the ancient port city of Caesarea, he reported being seized by a sudden, inexplicable terror. At that moment, an earth tremor shook the catacombs, and his way out was blocked by wreckage. When he was finally pulled from the ruins three days later, he was clutching a jeweled, golden breastplate. On it were thirty-two symbols."

Zoro grinned lopsidedly. "So this breastplate, it's valuable?"

"Priceless."

"Yeah, see, now we're getting somewhere." Zoro turned toward Max.

"When word of Leonardo's discovery reached the Vatican, Pope Pius III's successor, Julius II, immediately dispatched an army to retrieve the breastplate. It turns out the last high priest had written the Name down after all. Upon its arrival at the Vatican, it was entombed in that secret Vatican archive to be studied. You see, the problem was that the thirty-two markings appeared as neither words nor letters of any known language. They were more like the scribblings of a madman.

"And that's where the story becomes very unusual."

"Funny, I thought we were already there," Zoro said. Max gave a quiet chuckle and continued.

"Around 1508, Pope Julius II called his childhood friend Michelangelo from Florence to paint the Sistine Chapel. Throughout his preparation, Michelangelo was given carte blanche to create an inspiring revelation on the ceiling of the chapel. He was also given access to the Vatican archives to seek inspiration.

"After befriending the prefect of the archives, Michelangelo was secretly led into the locked archive housing the golden breastplate. It is said that after kneeling before the breastplate, Michelangelo suddenly leapt to his feet, jumping wildly through the room as if he were dancing the king's waltz."

"So wait a minute," Zoro said. "You're saying Michelangelo figured it out? What the breastplate said—the Name?"

"I think Michelangelo kneeled in front of those symbols and something clicked in his mind. I think with the mathematical skill of an artistic savant, he deciphered immediately what the symbols meant, translating them with the language he knew best: art."

"What happened next?"

"That very same day somebody set a fire in the archive, completely destroying the golden breastplate. Or so it is said."

"But who, and why?" Zoro asked.

"That leads us directly to the next series of events," Max said. "Shortly after the fire, Michelangelo began to paint the first panel of *Creation* on the Sistine Chapel ceiling, when his theological advisor, Marco Vigerio della Rovere, noticed something very odd: Michelangelo was painting with a brilliant and never-before-seen style, as if he'd been inspired by heaven itself. At first della Rovere was baffled. But when he pieced together events and realized Michelangelo had seen the breastplate, he nearly burst at the seams.

"Under cover of darkness, the Holy Father was rushed to the Sistine Chapel to confront Michelangelo, who had dropped to his knees. Imagine it, Zoro! A thousand candles around him sucked the oxygen from the air. The smoke-darkened stone walls of the chapel blazed under the flickering light as Michelangelo encountered the wrath of the Pope's thundering voice. And under the weight of his presence, Michelangelo confessed he knew the Name."

Zoro leaned forward eagerly, asking, "What happened next?"

"Well, the best I have been able to learn," Max continued, "is that when he was asked what happened when he spoke the Name, Michelangelo kept saying, 'I danced with angels and I'm going to paint their message on the ceiling.' The Pope demanded he tell him the Name, but no amount of pressure could induce Michelangelo to pronounce it in his presence.

"So, a frustrated Pope threatened to excommunicate Michelangelo if he ever painted the thirty-two symbols. And the Holy Father sent him to walk among the people with the burden of his secret locked inside him, burning like the plague."

Zoro realized he had been holding his breath. He released it now, feeling his chest deflating with disappointment. "Then it's done."

"Maybe not Zoro, maybe not. You see, the Pope and his successors allowed Michelangelo to keep painting the Sistine Chapel; in fact, the artist was kept as close to the Vatican as possible for years, in the event that Michelangolo would defy the Pope and let some sign of the thirty-two symbols slip out in his work. That never happened, though Michelangelo took every advantage to paint mockeries of the popes in the Sistine Chapel.

"It is easy to imagine how Michelangelo might've broken under the weight of the Holy Father's authority, although apparently quite the opposite seems to be true. Sometime later, shortly after Michelangelo's death, four drawings surfaced, bearing the title 'Study by Andrea Canossa.'"

"And?"

"Michelangelo always claimed he was a Count of Canossa. Do you see, Zoro?" Max's voice creaked with excitement.

Before Zoro could answer, Max leaned forward in his seat. "In 1563, near the end of his life, Michelangelo fired all of his assistants. And he wrote of himself, 'In spite of my old age, I believe I have been designated by God to do what I will do next.'"

"Most of what we know about Michelangelo comes from his apprentice Ascanio Condivi. He claims that Michelangelo's most prized and most guarded possessions were four drawings upon which he wrote the words 'Study by Andrea Canossa.'"

Max's face tightened and he snapped open his briefcase. "Take a look at this." He pulled the 8x10 digitized photograph from his briefcase and handed it to Zoro. Zoro's face went slack. "My God, there on the stone wall, something's written there."

Max grinned again. "It's called the Vatican riddle. Almost no one has ever heard of it, let alone seen it. But thanks to the bright lights needed for the scanners used to preserve a record of crumbling texts in the archive, it was noticed. And after much probing, I received an unofficial explanation. It seems, Zoro, that these words were discovered scratched into the stone header over the soot-covered entrance to the secret archives."

Zoro swallowed hard. "What does it mean?"

Still grinning, Max said, "Roughly translated from Latin, the inscription reads, 'When you understand the meaning of three, you will discover the fourth.'"

It wasn't unusual for Zoro to miss things, but he really, really wanted to understand what Max was telling him. Despite his best efforts, though, he stared at Max, confused.

"Come on!" Max insisted. "Don't you get it yet?"

Zoro slowly shook his head.

Throwing his hands in the air with frustration, Max barked, "Zoro, the thirty-two-symbol Name is in Andrea Canossa's drawing! . . . Don't you see it?"

Max sighed into the silence that followed. "The Name," Max said tiredly, "is a crossover into God's domain. And if we don't find it now, I'm afraid the chance will be lost forever."

What the hell am I doing? Actually starting to believe this crap? He shot an anxious glance at Max.

Max saw the doubt in Zoro's face and shook his head, looking steadily at Zoro. "Zoro, evolution isn't some biological accident waiting to happen. Evolutionary leaps are awakenings. And with the secrets of the Name, you could do in an instant what evolution has taken millions of years to do—"

"Oh my God!" Zoro suddenly yelled. "This is ridiculous . . . The sketches on the spiral staircase! You're shitting me! They're the ones you're talking about!"

"Yes, Zoro," Max smiled. "Now close your mouth; you're attracting flies."

Zoro shook his head. "Michelangelo's original sketches for the Sistine . . . your sketches?"

Max nodded.

Zoro closed his eyes as the sketches from Max's home surfaced from his memory. The first sketch depicted a godly figure with the outlines of a primitive brain worked into the figure's head while it hovered above the merciless child abuser. A godly figure and beams of mystical light leaped from the second sketch as the figure tried to work its way out of the square outline in the center of the page. And in the third sketch, Adam, as Zoro now realized the figure to be, reached toward God who appeared floating on a drape shaped like the higher human brain. And around the outside of the sketch, among a flurry of images, angels danced . . .

Looking straight ahead at Max, Zoro could clearly see in his mind's eye the tan marble staircase with its series of alcoves. A blurred image entered his thoughts: a subconscious recording his conscious mind had not even been aware he had made. The fourth alcove, the one he'd never reached—three feet high and two feet wide—was crested with an intricately embossed marble carving unlike any he'd ever seen. Perched almost invisibly atop the spiral, below the shadows of the carving, the last alcove was empty.

Max grinned smugly, sensing Zoro's astonishment. "Yes, Zoro, after a lifetime of searching, I've only found three of the sketches."

Zoro cleared his throat. "It's not in the first three sketches, is it?"

"No. But the fourth alcove, the empty alcove, Zoro, is waiting for the fourth sketch, the one your father found."

Zoro's eyes twinkled strangely as the realization dawned. "My father? He found the fourth sketch, the final clue?"

"Divinity itself, Zoro. The key to the mind of God . . . Isaac found it."

CHAPTER 14

Suddenly Zoro could feel eyes on him—but not Max's. He spun around and his mouth fell open.

Conrad stood in the doorway. He was clapping, his stubby hands beating a steady, staccato rhythm as a mocking grin creased his face. He stepped into the room. His eyes were small and dark.

"What the hell is he doing here?" Zoro shot a helpless glance at Max.

"That's quite the story Max is trying to sell you," Conrad sneered.

Max stared at him. In a very even, controlled voice, he said, "Conrad, you need to leave, now."

"Why now? Things are just getting interesting."

Zoro stood slowly, the gears turning in his mind. His mind was grappling with this encounter as if it was a puzzle, and its fragments had him baffled. Who was this man? How long had he been standing there? And why did he follow them here?

"Zoro, lad," Conrad said, "you can't seriously be considering playing along with this insanity."

Zoro stared from Max to Conrad. "Don't worry, Conrad; I'm not suffering from insanity."

He strode quickly across the room and grabbed Conrad by the lapels, nearly lifting him off the floor.

"I'm enjoying every minute of it. And don't call me 'lad'! Now what the hell do you want with us?"

Instead of backing down, Conrad smiled calmly into Zoro's angry face.

"Well, let's see if I've got this right. First," Conrad said, ticking each item off on his fingers, "Max has offered you some crazy story about your father and some magic beans. No, that isn't it. A magic sketch was it? Then he's backed it up with what? These books?" And then he laughed in Zoro's face.

Max darted forward, prying Zoro's hands off Conrad and pushing the two men apart. "That's enough, Conrad."

"I doubt our esteemed colleague here has given you the whole truth, Zoro," Conrad said, straightening his lapels. The sketch your father had, it belongs to me!"

"What's he saying, Max?" Zoro said.

"This doesn't concern you, Zoro. Conrad I'm warning you, keep away from this boy."

"Ooohhh, I'm trembling," Conrad said in a mocking voice.

"Perhaps you should be." Max squared off, clenching his fists. *Damn,* Zoro thought, *Max may be a gentleman, but he sure isn't a monk.*

"You and your damn stupid ideas," Conrad shouted, stabbing a finger in the air at Max.

"Get out!" Max yelled.

Conrad smiled. "Now that I have your attention, lad," Conrad said, his voice dropping in volume, "I'll make it plain and simple. What has Max actually offered you, Zoro? He's trying to convince you of something that isn't true. You want the truth? Come work for me. Help me find the sketch; at least I pay with cash and not pipe dreams!" Conrad stuffed a rigid, anodized aluminum business card in Zoro's pocket.

Zoro loved the sound of cash. But he was having a hard time connecting anything good with this throwback ogre. He thought about what to say next, and before his mouth could hatch a word, Conrad's tree-trunk legs had carried him with surprising quickness around the corner to the exit.

"I'm sorry, Zoro." Max's voice was immediately calmer. "Conrad is . . . just an old competitor. He's a little wacky. I wouldn't listen to a word he's saying. He's a nut job, and no friend of your father's."

Zoro shrugged. "Just some rich idiot. I get it . . . New York's full of 'em."

Zoro tried to sound dismissive, but he had to admit to himself that Conrad's words had planted a seed of doubt in his mind.

Max must have sensed it. He was giving Zoro a worried look.

CHAPTER 15

Once they were back outside, Zoro began to mentally stack up the pros and cons of Max's revelations; the cons started to look insurmountable.

"I'm so confused, Mr. Max. How am I supposed to know what's right and what's wrong?"

"Be patient, Zoro, there's a lot you don't know. But you're going to understand it all soon; you have to believe that."

"I'll believe it if it makes me richer than the Pope!" Zoro grinned.

Without a word, Max reached for the door handle of the limo, opened the door, and got in. He had a strange, troubling feeling about Zoro sometimes, and yet he couldn't explain the rush of warmth Zoro's childish humor brought out in him.

"Relax, I'm kidding," Zoro said as he got into the driver's seat. "You angry?"

"Annoyed," Max replied.

"How annoyed?"

"Annoyed." Max repeated, suppressing a thin smile.

Zoro was still grinning smugly. It was as if something inside him was trying to dismantle all the progress he'd made today. He realized it, too.

"Did you notice how I managed to do that, Mr. Max?"

"What? Annoy me? Really Zoro, I would think today's revelation about your father would have you thinking seriously about the ramifications of finding the Name. I'd just like you to understand why you think the way you do."

Zoro eyed Max. "The inside of my head's a scary place, Mr. Max. You sure you want to go there?"

Max leaned over the seat toward Zoro, his voice quiet. "Maybe I've already been there."

Zoro glanced nervously at Max. "You can't read my mind. People can't do that . . . can they?"

Max just gazed silently at Zoro.

"Look, Mr. Max, I'm already freaked out enough with everything you've told me today. So let's stop talking, because I'm starting to lose my mind."

"Actually," Max grinned, "you're just now finding it."

The electronic tweet of Zoro's cell phone shattered the silence of the moment. He fished it from his pocket and looked at the screen. "I gotta take this, Mr. Max. It's Ma."

He put the phone to his ear. "Yeah, Ma? . . . What? When? Oh, my God! Yeah, yeah, sure, I'll be right there." Zoro's voice started to quiver. "Calm down, Ma, I'm coming, okay?"

He turned back toward Max, his eyes wide with alarm. "I gotta go, Mr. Max. Something's happened to Ma."

"Of course. Take the limo."

"How will you get home?"

"I've a condo nearby, at the south end of Manhattan—not far. Drop me there, Zoro. Take care of your mother, and I will see you tomorrow morning."

CHAPTER 16

A part of Zoro's mind realized he had always been a silent partner in Carmela's delusions. He had been a firsthand observer, and though he saw himself as detached from Carmela's reality, he also often found himself submerged into a world of her own creation, a world where he wandered all alone. Zoro had witnessed a lifetime of uncertainty, of emotional ups and downs—many of them orchestrated by Carmela—to the point that sometimes he lacked the strength to eat. And though his weakness could be glossed over by the occasional drink, Zoro was too vain to admit that, especially lately, he'd been losing control.

As Zoro rolled up to the house, he saw an unmarked police car, the kind with a red cherry flashing on the dashboard, parked in the driveway.

The door closed behind him as he walked through the living room. Carmela was seated at Isaac's old desk, swallowing a Valium.

"Ma! Are you all right?"

Her house was a shambles; upside-down furniture and shattered lamps littered the room.

Standing next to Carmela was a stocky cop who looked like a detective. "Looks like someone's broken into your mother's place."

"No shit, Sherlock!" Zoro said, his anxiety and frustration boiling over.

"Zoro! Mind your manners!" Carmela snapped. "It's all right." Carmela said, touching the detective's hand. "Zoro's here now, I'll be fine."

"When I heard the address on the squawk box I came straightaway," the cop said.

"Thank you, Detective Gideon," Carmela said.

Zoro kept an eye on the cop. He looked old, but there was a crisp edge to his eyes.

"Now, if you're sure there's nothing else I can do, I'll be on my way."

"You might start by looking for the bastard who broke in here," Zoro said, still seething.

"Zoro," Carmela interrupted, "I'm sure Detective Gideon will do his best."

As the detective stepped from the room, his eyes trailed Zoro, like one of those movie dissolves, when a character moves by in silent slow motion, and fades so quickly that you can't remember his face.

"Who was that, Ma?"

"What does that matter, Zoro? Look at this place. Oh, this is the end." Carmela's voice had an edge to it. The brave front she had put on for the detective faded as soon as he walked out the door. It should've signaled the oncoming storm. But as Zoro stood beside her and watched her once-beautiful eyes tear up, he missed the tension in the corners of her mouth.

"Oh, Zoro," she cried, "why, Zoro, why?"

In her hand she grasped a small silver frame that had held a picture of the family. It was the only one she kept out, a special memory. Now the picture, torn ragged from its frame, left nothing but grief for Carmela.

"I loved him once, you know," Carmela said, running her thumb across Isaac's face on the tattered photograph.

Zoro didn't say anything for a moment. "I know, Ma."

"It was the nicest thing he'd ever done for me. He gave up eating lunch all week just to buy me this little frame. And now look at it.

"Few things fall a poor man's way, Zoro. I had the memory of your father's kindness, but now . . ." She looked up at Zoro, desperation in her eyes. "It's like being violated, Zoro. Some vicious stranger just came in here without anybody knowing, and he defiled all my memories . . . my precious memories . . ." Carmela began sobbing quietly.

Zoro began to lift an overturned box from the floor.

"Don't touch it!" Carmela shrieked. "Don't touch it!" Screaming came easily to Carmela—it always had. She moved to the sofa and sobbed hysterically. Zoro sat down and put his arms around his mother for a moment and tried to calm her, but nothing he did could calm her.

He looked around him, thinking that Carmela's house was an island, a walled sanctuary. She tried so hard to prevent the pains of the world from penetrating her refuge. Carmela had imprisoned her past in her home, as if it were a thatched hut built on sticks in a river. And she had made herself just as inaccessible.

It was so hard for Zoro to reach her, a woman who had refused to see what was going on around her. As he scanned the tangled mess left behind by the burglar, he was struck with the thought of how helpless she was. Except for her keepsakes, her home was empty. Though the house was filled with hundreds of trinkets, small ceramic dolls and wooden boxes from oriental shops, none of them could testify against the intruder who had ruined them all so casually. That parade of silent witnesses to the past could do nothing to help her right now.

Looking around, Zoro thought, *You'd sacrifice me in a minute for this, all your trinkets and keepsakes. If you could have chosen between having your house broken into and having me beat to hell, I'd be in the hospital right this second.* He felt like he was sitting next to some dictator who one minute would hold your hand, and the next throw you to the wolves in the name of some perceived, warped belief.

And what made it worse was that Zoro knew she hated half the trinkets. Some were gifts from Isaac and some were gifts from her father. Her father's gifts had been difficult. Unlike Isaac's father, whose passing had left a gaping hole in Zoro's heart, Carmela's father was a manic-depressive man whose love was feared, whose understanding was a disaster. She had wept for much of her childhood and learned that shame could help her through difficult periods. Eventually, Zoro surmised, she came to believe that there was no greater compensation in her life than acceptance by the world around her. And so she had created a perfect façade, with everything in its place. The loss of human dignity was far less important to Carmela than appearances. Now the symbols of her perfect life, the victory on earth she was looking for, lay disheveled and violated. *God, where to start?* Zoro thought, *with the stuff, or with Carmela?*

Zoro tried to smile, "Cheer up, Ma. At least you're okay, right?"

"Zoro, what's going on?" she asked, her anger toned with a tinge of fear. Zoro had the feeling she wasn't just talking about what had happened to her house.

"I don't know, Ma. Since I met Max, things have been happening . . ."

"Max? What kinds of things?" Carmela's voice hardened.

"Nothing, just . . . He's very strange. And the people he knows are, also . . . like this Conrad guy . . ."

Carmela's face went pale. "Where did you meet Conrad?"

"With Max. I don't think they're exactly buddies."

"What did he say to you? How did you . . ."

"Does he worry you, Ma?"

"No. I'm not worried . . . about Conrad. Listen, Zoro, we should talk."

"Ma?"

Zoro stared at Carmela, fearing what he might be about to hear, but unable to turn away.

"Zoro, after Joey died, while you were away . . ."

"Away!" he scoffed. "You sent me to the funny farm for a year because you couldn't stand to look at me!"

"Everything I did was for your own good!" Her voice cracked a bit. "When your dad died, I needed to do what was best for the family. I needed help. I was lonely, Zoro, and he was there, so I let . . . certain people . . . help."

"No, Ma!"

"Yes . . . Conrad."

Zoro looked away from her. The revelation sucked the air from his chest: the suggestion that some bad-tempered troll had somehow played a part in his life left Zoro wanting to punch somebody. It was as if Carmela had spit on Isaac's grave.

Without warning, Carmela slapped Zoro so hard the red outline of her palm burned into his cheek. "How dare you think that?"

"Are you crazy, Ma? Think what?"

"I know what you're thinking about Conrad and me, you filthy-minded little punk! Don't you dare insinuate anything like that; I never want to hear it."

Zoro glared at his mother, angry and uncomprehending.

"He helped me as a friend, Zoro. He even helped Nathan get into the seminary."

"You don't know what I was thinking, Ma," Zoro said, defensively. He got up and walked into the kitchen. "And I don't know what the hell's going on," he said over his shoulder. "All I know is something weird's happening and I don't know what it is!"

Little by little, Zoro could see Carmela's composure returning. Her hands were still shaking, but the deformity of her heart was well concealed now. Like a bird with a broken wing, a cold, stoic look crept over her.

Zoro brought some tea from the kitchen. A fragrant wisp of steam curled into the air from the cups, and as Carmela sipped, Zoro saw some of the tension leave her face.

Soon the varnish on Carmela's personality began to shine once more, and she sat with Zoro on the sofa, reminiscing. Zoro pulled an over-turned cardboard box onto the sofa; it was Isaac's box, containing the few remnants of his world, the handful of legends still left for Zoro to cling to.

Zoro had always thought of his father as a dreamer. But because Isaac spent his life on dreams, he abandoned any traces of Carmela's love. Now, all that was left were his crippled memories in a small box.

They sat together looking through the withered remains of a once-robust man. Zoro turned slowly toward Carmela and slumped against the sofa back. "You did love him, Ma, right?" he asked.

Carmela nodded sincerely. "With all my heart. It was the most wonderful time of my life."

"What happened?"

Zoro's question caught Carmela off guard. "I don't know, Zoro. I don't know what to say. Somehow I lost him." She tightened her face, forcing the wrinkles at the corner of her eyes into a symmetric spiderweb. "I guess he just stopped seeing things the way I did."

For a moment Zoro and Carmela were transported into a young man's past, a young man's dreams. Flanked by memories, Carmela talked of Isaac's early days. He was a Midwestern boy whose childhood reeked of poverty, though that had never cut him in half, never crippled him from struggling against the silent stares of Harvard graduates and Yale boys: boys who'd never detached themselves from the vernacular of wealth or who so loathed Isaac's early success in the face of poverty that they rained down their own inadequacies upon him.

But Isaac persisted; he was determined to work his way to the top of the Pantheon Corporation. He began as a simple clerk, working in Conrad Mason's office. And with her at his side, Carmela figured, success was so close it was palpable.

"You know what they say, Zoro: 'Behind every good man is a good woman, rolling her eyes.'" Under Carmela's scrutiny, the climb would have been exhilarating. She could taste the certainty of social success and prestige.

But soon it became clear that Isaac had come to enjoy his work at the Pantheon Corporation about as much as a spinal tap. He'd go to work every day kicking and screaming and fighting for his freedom. And Carmela soon began to feel betrayed.

"What is this, Ma?" Zoro said, wanting to change the subject. He really didn't want to hear about anything that had to do with Conrad, and his mother didn't need any more pain right now. Zoro had reached into the box and picked up a piece of cardboard with some tattered pictures glued to it, pictures that appeared to be clipped from old magazines.

"It's your father's dream board." Carmela struggled to keep her voice hard. Despite her efforts, though, her face softened as she looked at the pasted pictures. Her cheeks pinked with the pleasure of another sweet memory.

"What's it for, Ma?"

"Your father would rush home every day, bringing old magazines—discarded ones, the ones that were dog-eared—that were no longer suitable to have in the Pantheon waiting room. We'd dream about all the things we wanted to do and have, and your father would cut out pictures of the dreams and paste them to the board." She looked at him. "And you would help, Zoro."

"Me?"

"Yes, you'd sit on his lap. Your little hands were so busy, cutting out the pictures. And your father was always so gentle, despite you cutting up half his pictures. He never got angry; he'd just smile and bring home more magazines."

"Ma—"

"Don't say it, Zoro, don't say it!" Carmela held her hand over his mouth. "It's too hard . . . I . . . I can't go there."

With sadness, Zoro realized he knew what she meant, what she couldn't say: Hearing anything good about Isaac would strike a fatal blow. It was somehow easier to remember him as the source of all her grief than to face the truth that she had lost something good.

One small, ransacked box of personal effects, pulled from Isaac's desk and flung onto the floor by an intruder, had suddenly become the heartbeat of Zoro's world. The real world was full of its own importance, some of it struggling to survive and some which had long died. But here and now, there was nothing more important than that placid field of memories.

Digging deeper in the cardboard box, Zoro found a small decorative wooden box. It was covered with splashes of colored lacquer; it had probably come from one of those shops in Chinatown. Zoro wondered what painstaking memories of its creation it carried, shanghaied from across the sea. Sold by a clerk, far from home, sitting in an open doorway in Chinatown, surrounded by cases of vegetables and the fading echoes of an ancient culture. And as Zoro struggled to open it, he wondered what great meaning it might hold.

He couldn't budge the lid. "Ma," he laughed, "I can't get it open." His observation made them both laugh.

"Oh, give me that, you stupid boy. It's a Japanese puzzle box."

"What's that?"

"It's a box with a secret; your father gave me all different kinds of them."

The Himitsu-Bako puzzle box was a small wooden box decorated with a kaleidoscope of hand-painted designs and covered with a shiny veneer of lacquer. The town of Hakone, in the distant shadow of Mount Fuji, where it was made, was quite renowned for puzzle boxes, Carmela told him. This particular kind of box required a series of intricate moves to open the lid.

"Give me that!" Carmela said. "This one's easy; it only takes four moves to unlock it."

As Zoro studied Carmela's moves, he was startled as the box popped open. He reached inside and pulled out two small photographs.

"Let's have it," Carmela said.

She looked at the first photograph. "I have no idea what this is." He looked at it. It was a black-and-white picture of an observatory next to a building with an old Gothic archway. He flipped it over; he saw the word "Princeton" scrawled in pencil.

"What about the other one, Zoro?"

The other photograph was a small, faded picture of Carmela and Isaac, arm in arm. Isaac was a striking contrast to Carmela: he was happy. She appeared older than her years and without vigor. Isaac was smiling and didn't seem in the least bothered by the collar of his overstarched shirt. Around his neck was a small medallion. He seemed to be wearing it proudly. Yes, Zoro thought: pride, that look was there in Isaac, in that photo. Zoro wanted to ask about the medallion, but Carmela had begun to weep bitterly.

Zoro turned toward Carmela; the plastic-covered sofa squeaked. His foot snagged momentarily on her threadbare carpet, and he felt sad.

"But, Ma, you said you were happy." Zoro motioned to the photo.

"I thought we were happy, Zoro." Carmela paused. Then, twisting her lips into an angry knot, her voice went flat and hard. "My whole life I've been looking forward to being happy, and that day's never come."

Zoro sank deeper into the sofa; he was determined not to speak a word of reproach. *She's hurting . . . let her have that, at least . . .*

"Leave his things alone, Zoro. Put the box down."

"But Ma, it's Dad's . . . he left this . . ."

"Can't you see I'm in pain, Zoro? That's what your father left me: pain that I feel to this day!" Her eyes narrowed. "And you!" She shouted, turning pale. "My own son . . . you've sealed me in this fate."

As was his habit, Zoro tried to justify her anger toward him, no matter how badly it tore him up inside. "I lost my way; but, Ma, I love you."

Her house, her refuge was caging him in as her demeanor darkened. "Don't you dare talk about love to me! You haven't earned my love."

"Earned," Zoro sighed. "A son isn't supposed to have to earn his mother's love."

Zoro hoped the crisis would subside. But Carmela had built walls, and within them she was filled with even greater fear and scorn. Instantly, Zoro was on the outside again, where he had always been. Carmela's cruelty could be relentless, and in that moment Zoro wanted to hide in the remotest corner of the world.

"This is entirely your fault," she said.

"Ma . . ."

Carmela ran to the bathroom, crying.

Zoro crammed the two photographs into his pocket and wandered through the house. Alone in the downstairs hallway, Zoro stared at the door to Joey's room. After enduring an afternoon with Carmela, he wasn't sure if he could stand any more torture, but something pulled him toward the door. Opening it should've been easy; after all, it wasn't really Joey's room. Carmela had built the shrine shortly after they'd moved into Grandma's house. Zoro had never been allowed to see the inside. But the idea of it was a continual reminder.

Suddenly dripping with sweat, his heart pounding, he turned the knob, slowly pressing open the door. The room was a perfect recreation of Joey's old room. It was a crusade into Carmela's denial, a pathetic attempt at keeping Joey alive. A small bed was perfectly made up with a cowboy cover. On the night table was a matching cowboy lamp, and a generous fantasy of toys decorated the room. Zoro's heart ached, and he was on the verge of tears.

He heard the floor creak behind him. He turned to see Carmela, her face a mask of rage.

"No!" she shouted as she stepped across the tiny hallway. "You bastard! You don't have the right to touch anything in here," she yelled hysterically. "Not you, not ever."

Zoro turned and made for the front door. He was tired, his wounds were raw, and he wondered if anything could ever end Carmela's marathon of persecution.

CHAPTER 17

Zoro drove to Johnny's place. Two flights of worn, creaky wooden steps later, Zoro stopped to catch his breath. The hallway was short and narrow, and its time-darkened paneling smelled like an ashtray. He rapped his meaty hand against the apartment door.

"Come in," a voice spoke sternly.

There he is, Zoro thought, stepping onto a scarred wooden floor. Johnny's big silhouette was outlined against a window. From outside, Zoro guessed, he cast an image that must have resembled some desperate monster, locked away behind bars in some desolate forgotten asylum. It wasn't a fitting image for a guy who was as well known on the streets as Johnny. Nor was this a fitting place to live. But there in the stuffy second-floor apartment, sandwiched between a squeaking air-conditioner crudely wedged into the window and the crumbling plaster wall beside him was Zoro's new bedroom. He glanced at the old sofa and cringed silently.

"Thanks for this, Johnny," Zoro smiled.

"You should patch things up with Gina," Johnny said. "Get her something nice. I can help you out."

Zoro didn't argue.

With Johnny's counseling session over, Zoro made his way to the kitchen table and slumped into the comfortable hollow of an old chair.

"You'll never guess what happened to me, Johnny."

Johnny snubbed out his cigar in the ashtray, poured them each two fingers of bourbon, then downed his glass in one shot.

"So, what you got for me?" Johnny smiled.

Zoro mentioned Max's sketches, and Johnny began to grin. Zoro recognized the face.

"Careful, Johnny."

"Look, just as a friend, I'm interested. If there's any way I can help you . . ."

"You wanna help, Johnny, find me some damn aspirin."

Johnny pushed another two fingers of bourbon Zoro's way.

"I don't even know what to start believing." Zoro fixed his gaze on Johnny. By now he knew the look in his eyes. "Put a little cash in my pocket, you know, to take care of Gina, and I think I can cut you in if there's a payoff. But only *if* . . . cool?"

"So what's this sketch worth?"

"Last I heard it's not the sketch, but what's on it," Zoro said. Johnny stared at Zoro, clearly waiting for more.

"Look, it seems there may be more than one person interested in me finding that sketch." He thought about his crazy encounter with Conrad. "If I find it, I'll cut you in for anything I make, to cover the interest on the loan. But, Johnny, it's hands off the sketch; this goes down my way."

Johnny gave him an oily smile. "I promise to do my best."

Zoro studied Johnny and wondered what he was doing trusting him.

It had been a long and very eventful day. Zoro suddenly felt like he might not be able to make it across the floor to the couch. But he did, and a few minutes later he was falling asleep to the sound of the traffic on the street below Johnny's place.

CHAPTER 18

Thursday Morning, Manhattan

Zoro gave the ignition key a twist and the Bentley's engine roared smoothly to life. He had just picked up Max at the condo on the south end of Manhattan. It didn't seem like just his second day at work; it seemed like the world had changed completely since he had first visited the mansion in New Jersey yesterday morning.

They drove down Canal Street, a gauntlet of Rolex pushers and knockoff Gucci bags. Zoro's mind ran back and forth over all that had happened since he'd found himself stuck in Max's story. Zoro could pretend the sketch didn't exist, retreat from Max's story; it would be the easiest thing in the world to do . . . except he was hooked. "So what the hell happened to the sketch?" Zoro finally asked, picking up where they had left off yesterday, before Conrad's interruption.

"Unfortunately," Max said, then hesitated. "When Isaac died . . . that secret died with him."

Disbelief coiled sourly in Zoro's stomach, as he realized what he'd just heard. He cursed Isaac over and over again in his mind. Then he had an idea. "I could look through his things . . . at Carmela's house," he said.

"That's exactly my offer, Zoro," Max calmly replied.

Zoro's eyes narrowed. "Offer, what do you mean offer?"

"It all makes sense, Zoro," Max said. "You want to be rich . . ."

"Damn straight."

"Good . . . You saw the digitized photo of the archive. In light of that new information it's clear the fourth sketch is the key; it's the last piece of the puzzle. And that's where you come in.

Zoro's eyes narrowed. "How?"

"Look, Zoro, the first three sketches aren't without value; they have amazing secrets of their own. Let me teach you everything I know about the first three sketches. In exchange, you help me find the fourth. What I teach you will at the very least make you a millionaire."

He grinned at Zoro. "Bored yet?"

"Hell, no," Zoro hesitated for a moment. "So how do I help? And what's the catch?"

"Too easy, Zoro, too quick . . . the catch is I need your answer to one question."

Zoro guided the limo through the anonymous stream of traffic winding its way through the gray cityscape. Zoro's mind was full of things he couldn't say. But what he did say was, "Sure, what's the question?"

"Zoro," Max grabbed his shoulder from behind. "Where's the fourth sketch?"

Zoro swiveled his head around. "How the hell should I know?"

"Your father did."

"My father and me are nothing alike! I would never abandon my family!" Zoro shouted, liking Max less and less.

Cool down, Zoro, cool down, he kept repeating to himself. He couldn't afford the rage at this moment. Traffic came to a halt, which was probably a good thing because it gave him a chance to suck in his breath, try to tamp down the reactive rage that was clawing its way up his spine. He gave a hopeless shrug.

"Zoro, I'm sorry . . ." Max began.

"Sorry, my ass." The traffic moved and Zoro floored the accelerator, holding up his hand to fend off the words.

"All I can tell you is that many years ago, I taught your father what I'm offering to teach you now."

"You must be a crappy teacher; my family's still poor."

"I'm sorry, Zoro, but your father, my dear friend, passed away before he really had a chance. But, Zoro . . . a father never hides the truth far from his son."

"So why not ask my brother Nathan? Hell, he's a damn priest; he's already tight with God—probably on a first-name basis."

"Because he doesn't have the capacity to believe me, Zoro. You do."

Despite his frustration, Zoro wanted to believe Max. He wanted it so badly to be true that he ached inside. But it was just too unbelievable, and thinking of Isaac was just too painful. "I don't buy this six degrees of separation shit," Zoro growled. "Whatever my father knew, I don't know it."

The nondescript hum of traffic pulled at Zoro like the low drone of a Gregorian chant; his mind felt numb from trying to believe the unbelievable. Max's assertions seemed plainly impossible. And, true or not, to Zoro, they didn't add up. He needed to question Max, to sort things out. *Yeah, I'm done listening for a while; let him listen to me, answer my questions!*

"I'm not sure I can believe you, either," Zoro said, glancing at Max in the rearview mirror.

Max's eyes darted at him. "Can't . . . or won't?"

"What's the difference?"

Max shook his head. "Zoro, you must go through the same process Isaac did, and get into his head. I'm sure Isaac left clues to the fourth sketch's location."

"What makes you think he'd do that?"

"As desperate as things may have been for him," Max replied, "Isaac was always someone I knew and could trust."

Zoro felt himself squirming inwardly as an increasing sense of discomfort took hold of him. He stared at Max, wondering how the hell he was ever supposed to think like Isaac. "How?" Zoro asked, finally. "How am I going to do this?"

Zoro gave Max an empty stare. Max sighed. "Zoro, I can't give you false hope or make you empty promises. But you must trust me; this is the only way. I'll teach you what I taught Isaac about the human mind and those sketches, and with that I promise you'll see the clues.

"I don't know exactly how, Zoro," Max said. "You may not even consciously see the clues. But your mind will. One day you'll turn left when you want to turn right, stay home when you should've gone out . . . just like Isaac may have done. The clues will always bring you to where you need to be. You just have to believe."

Zoro handled the wheel deftly, seamlessly negotiating the clogged streets. Without his consciously willing it, he seemed always to find an opening at just the right moment; the traffic seemed to open before him like Moses parting the sea. *Could it be?* He thought. *Could my whole life ever be this way—effortless?* If he deciphered the sketches one by one, would he see things the same way Isaac had? Could he grow so deeply into Isaac's mind that he could see through Isaac's eyes?

"So what now, Mr. Max?"

"I believe you can tell me, Zoro."

Zoro shook his head. "You're walking around in my mind again. I tell you I've got nothing, no clues, nothing."

"I believe you're wrong, Zoro."

"So why Isaac?" Zoro asked. "Why did he find the sketch and why—"

"I don't know." Max couldn't explain the tragedy beyond words, beyond a thousand excuses that spread unchecked in Zoro's mind.

Zoro's thoughts were all over the map. He found himself thinking about Isaac, his gentle manner, his eyes. It was hard to remember the details of his face. Maybe he'd blocked him out for too long. Or maybe that's how the mind works, he wondered. Then it hit him.

"I can't connect this to anything, but I found these at Carmela's." Zoro pulled the old black-and-white photographs out of his pocket. He flipped over the one of the observatory, where the word "Princeton" was clearly visible.

"What was your father doing at Princeton?"

"I have no idea, Mr. Max."

"This is good, Zoro. It shows that Isaac was clearly on the trail of something. For whatever reason, we need to go to Princeton," Max said.

"We have no proof this means anything. Where would we even start?" Zoro shook his head. *Crazy old man!*

"Have you got anything better at this point, Zoro?"

Zoro took the initiative and headed toward Princeton.

CHAPTER 19

Slouched in the driver's seat, Zoro said nothing. His palms were sweaty and the red light seemed to last forever. It turned green, but the opposing traffic was still in the intersection; he couldn't move. The light went yellow, then red. It was total gridlock.

Zoro's mind felt the same way. With the featureless sound of the traffic walling him in isolation, Zoro watched the light change, blinking a multicolored Morse code message: Green . . . yellow . . . red. Green . . . yellow . . . red. A police motorcycle weaved across the intersection, blasting out splashes of red and blue light that tore through the green-yellow-red.

And then, quietly, from beneath the surrealistic kaleidoscope of sound and color, Zoro heard a whisper, a voice. He glanced around. A couple of dozen cars rolled by, all with windows shut. Behind him, Max had his head buried in his briefcase; he hadn't said anything.

"Wake up, sleepyhead; what's wrong with you?" the voice whispered. A kid's voice. Joey's voice.

Joey? Why am I hearing you? I must really be losing it. First there was Max's crazy story, and now he was hearing Joey, clear as day. As much as he wanted Joey beside him, to hear his voice, to see his smiling face so full of hope, the last thing he wanted was Joey in his head again.

Get out of my head, Joey!

"Maybe I'm in your head. Wait . . . nope, I'm everywhere."

Zoro tried to focus again on his driving, but they were still gridlocked. All he could do was sit there and wait for the voice to come back.

"Don't give up, Zee," the voice said. Joey was the only one who ever called Zoro that. Zoro squeezed the steering wheel until his knuckles whitened, trying to shake free of the cruel game his imagination was playing. For most of his life he had carried his guilt for Joey's blood, and he was tired beyond words. *I gave up everything for you, Joey.*

"What for, Zoro? Look at me, I'm dead!"

Don't say that! Zoro screamed in his mind.

Suddenly Zoro heard a thin, childlike voice singing, "Twinkle, Twinkle Little Star." Joey's voice rolled in after it: "Dead—dead—dead—dead . . . little star . . ."

Stop it, Joey! Zoro shook his head from side to side. But the voice whispered relentlessly.

"You make wishes because you need help. Max is your wish, a second chance I never got . . . the only wrong choice, Zee, is no choice. Tag, you're it!"

This isn't happening, Zoro thought. *No more imagining Joey's voice, no more daydreaming. This isn't real!*

But the tune played on. "Dead—dead—dead—dead . . . little star . . ."

"Stop it, Joey!" Zoro whispered forcefully, out loud now. Zoro felt his sanity hanging by the thinnest of threads, frayed and worn by the battle going on in his head.

"Zoro?" Max said. "Did you say something?"

Zoro massaged his temples, and that ghastly tune began to fade. *Okay, get back on track, Zoro.* "My head feels like a speedball, Mr. Max."

"The light's green, Zoro. Traffic's moving now," Max said.

Zoro felt completely spent. Thoughts of Isaac and Joey had ground him down to a stub of himself. He felt embarrassed. He must seem so transparent to Max, whispering to his dead brother.

"Zoro, you need to decide what you want, because when it happens, you'll have to move fast. So. . . you in, or not?"

When what happens? Zoro thought. Zoro had faced some strange days, but these last couple were by far the strangest. There was no ritual of small talk between him and Max, just some old man's muddied story. It was like watching runway lights at LaGuardia through a rain-drenched windshield: the colored lights would flicker in and out of focus, now clear, now blurring into a psychedelic illusion.

And Zoro was definitely out of focus. He couldn't make up his mind about Max. On one hand, Zoro could just play along, humor him, and get paid for doing it. On the other hand, Max had opened some pretty deep wounds and seemed likely to keep cutting.

Zoro shook his head, and his lips pulled tensely across his face. Most of the thoughts running through his mind began with the words *crazy, crazy old man.* What an unbelievable story. His fingers drummed against the wheel. He yearned for answers—but to what? All he could do was simply move ahead, crawling in traffic.

He needed to decide something fast; the drive was nearly over. Zoro was unsure, and yet he was drawn to Max's insane story. Why did it matter so much to Max after thirty years, why the urgency? And why was he driven to consider Max's offer? Sure, there was the potential for making money, but the craziness of it didn't sit right with him.

The choice was twisting in Zoro's gut, and he had a feeling he was running out of time to make it. *Do I step out of everything I believe and start believing Max? That would sure be a change in the schedule of events,* he thought.

In the last few minutes of that limo ride, they had passed countless lush trees thick with autumn leaves. Max leaned forward with an urgent expression on his face.

"Zoro," Max said gently, "anger burns until it burns you out. You need to stop using Joey as an excuse. He'd want you to have a second chance."

Second chance!

The cards were all on the table now. Here in the limo, a man who until yesterday had been a perfect stranger had an incomprehensible understanding of Zoro's stark reality. And as clear as the choice should have been, Zoro couldn't shake loose from the persistent hopelessness in which he was caught. "We're supposed to get tomorrow, and Joey never did. That's just wrong," Zoro muttered thinly.

"You didn't let him down," Max smiled.

Zoro opened his mouth to say something, and then stopped. "So what do you want me to do?"

"I can answer that without ever saying a word," Max replied quite plainly.

And it seemed Max could. He'd already laid it all out for Zoro, a clear path to a second chance. And all Zoro needed was a little courage, a little faith, and the guts to make a choice.

"Pull in near Nassau Hall, just ahead," Max said.

CHAPTER 20

They walked the cobblestone toward the historic Nassau Hall, the oldest building at Princeton University.

"We'll start here, Zoro. It's an administrative office now, but it used to house an archive. Maybe we can get a lead on this photo."

Zoro looked at the striking pair of lions flanking the front entrance, liking what he saw. "Hey, Mr. Max, these would fit nicely in your place."

Max looked at Zoro who, at that moment, had a carefree grin plastered across his face. That grin wasn't always there. After Joey died he'd worked hard to find it, but he only managed to on the rare occasion. He worked hard at everything, although he pretty much didn't succeed at anything. His relationship with Carmela didn't help either. Life was too damn serious.

"So where do we start?"

Max started to say at the administrative offices, as he pushed through the heavy doors. But he changed his mind at the last second. Max swung left toward the end of the corridor. "Always follow your gut, Zoro. Your instinct will never disappoint you."

Zoro nodded in agreement.

A caretaker, as old-looking as the mop he was pushing, shuffled around the corner. "Now I'll show you something unexpected," Zoro said. "Hand me that photograph."

Zoro pulled a cigar from his pocket and held it out like a large carrot. The old caretaker looked up and bit down on his lower lip.

"Pops," Zoro said, sliding the cigar into the old man's shirt pocket. "Any idea what this is?" He held out the photograph.

"Well, damn," the caretaker said, running his hand over the cigar, "that's the old Halsted Observatory."

"How do we get there?" Zoro asked.

The old man leaned his mop against the wall. He took a moment, as if to remember. "The whole place was flattened about seventy years ago, to make room for Joline Hall. You can see it, there, from this window."

"Have you been working here for a while?" Max asked.

"My whole life," the caretaker laughed. "Never missed a day. I gotta sparkling clean record."

"Have you ever heard anything unusual about that building or its contents?" Max asked.

The old caretaker was a "mind-my-own-business" kind of guy. But Zoro's offering hadn't been a mistake.

"Let me show you something," the caretaker said as he turned and headed down the basement steps.

Overhead in the dark basement corridor ran a hundred feet of heavy pipes draped in old plaster canvas insulation. Leaking water droplets, fat with asbestos, bombed their heads as they followed him deeper toward the boiler room.

"Don't get many visitors down here," the old man said, laughing. "I seem to recall it's here somewhere."

In the room adjacent to the boiler was a string of green metal lockers. In the middle of the room a small metal table and chair made up the caretaker's dining area. Max and Zoro were wondering what secrets the old man would uncover as he dug through the lockers one by one.

"Bill," squawked loudly over the caretaker's two-way radio. "There's a light out on two. Can you see to it?"

"Damn," he said. "Before they bite my head off, you boys might want to see this." The caretaker pulled a large architectural drawing from one locker.

At first Zoro's mind thought of the sketch. Then he laughed at the absurd thought, as the caretaker unrolled the drawing on his table.

"Here, yeah, see here." He pointed to a line between what was once the Halsted Observatory and Nassau Hall. "The story that I've heard is that this building was used as a hospital, even a secret meeting place for Congress during the Civil War. But this here tunnel," he paused to collect his thoughts, "hell, when they started construction on Joline Hall, apparently they tore it open like a can of tuna. Damn tunnel was full of all sorts of Civil War junk." He scratched his head. "It's all backfilled with dirt now though."

Neither Max nor Zoro hesitated. "What happened to all the things from the tunnel?"

The old man dropped into his chair, fiercely rubbing his hands over his balding scalp. "I don't rightly remember, son."

"Try and think harder, Pops."

"Far as I can recall it all went to the Metropolitan Museum of Art in New York, years ago."

"Pops, you deserve another." Zoro popped a second cigar into the caretaker's pocket.

As Zoro turned to leave, the old man jammed the rolled up drawing into Zoro's hand. "Maybe you can use it, son," the old man smiled.

CHAPTER 21

They headed toward the highway that led to Manhattan. The road was relatively empty. Just minutes from the highway on-ramp a dark SUV pulled in close behind them. Zoro wasn't comfortable so he hugged the right shoulder and motioned for the car to pass. But the SUV didn't budge. Instead the driver came down hard on the horn. Zoro signaled again for the SUV to pass, but the driver drove aggressively close, signalling for Zoro to pull over. Zoro pushed down the accelerator and the front wheels caught a little air over a small hill. "Son of a bitch is after us."

"I know . . . he wouldn't pass us," said Max.

Just ahead was the on-ramp, but it was backed up with traffic. Zoro swerved to the right and the SUV trailed closely, its driver still leaning on the horn. Thirty yards further on, Zoro saw a driveway leading to an expensive home.

"Up there," Max said, thinking the home would be the safest place to stop.

"I see it," Zoro said.

Zoro pulled into the driveway, and the SUV followed, turning sharply, nosing diagonally across the driveway leaving them no way out. Two blocky men in dark suits stepped from the SUV. Zoro pulled open the door and stepped out. "What the hell do you want?"

Since no one had come out of the house, Zoro figured they were on their own. The first man approached. He pulled Max's door open and Max stepped from the vehicle, saying, "Who are you?"

"Princeton security, sir."

"Do you have some identification?" Zoro asked.

The second man held up his hand toward Zoro. He was wearing perforated black leather driving gloves. "I'll ask the questions," he said.

"We haven't done anything wrong."

"Sir, you were seen stealing university property."

"We've done no such thing," Max replied.

The first man reached into the Bentley and pulled the rolled-up architectural drawing from the backseat.

"Now wait just one minute . . ."

"It's all right, Zoro, let them have it."

The first man retreated to the SUV, where he unrolled the drawing. Dropping it onto the backseat, he snapped open his phone. Zoro could see him shake his head "no" as he spoke to someone on the other end.

"I'm calling the real cops," Zoro yelled.

The second man beat a hasty retreat to the SUV. Max looked at Zoro. "We don't need to get the police involved."

"Mr. Max, can't you at least call the University and complain?"

"It's a healthy bet, Zoro, that it wouldn't make a difference. Let's go home."

CHAPTER 22

The ride back to Max's house had been quiet, mostly. Zoro's hands were still shaking, though it wasn't out of fear; he was angry. He'd wanted to dress down those goons, mostly with his fists, but Max had held him back.

As the setting sun faintly splashed the windshield, Max's signet ring cast a small reflection on the side of the front passenger seat headrest closest to Zoro. He couldn't make out the ring itself, but it suddenly seemed to him it was a sign of a privileged Ivy League life. If only Max knew what he was thinking about him . . . and Princeton; he still resented the people he considered privileged. Even outside on the streets they were passing, the stores and cafés were crowded with people who looked like they had everything. The air smelled of freshly brewed coffee and everyone seemed to have it all . . . except Zoro. He hoped that something good would come of the trek he was taking with Max. *Anything ought to be better than what I have,* he thought. Still, Zoro was conflicted, because as hard as Max's story was to believe, facing Zoro's coldest demons would be even harder.

With the fading sun barely shining in his eyes, Zoro's face felt hot, as if he'd been battered. He struggled to organize his thoughts. Could he really free himself from his mistakes, or had the ripples of his past already overtaken him and spread to the rest of his life? Did it all come down to an ill-fated October evening when he was fourteen, or was there more to life? Perhaps the curse was bigger than he'd imagined. Perhaps every moment of his life, every thought, every word, was already laid out like an undertow, ready to pull him into deeper water.

The wounds Max had opened cut so deeply, Zoro couldn't bear to look at them. Reliving Isaac's life, retracing Isaac's footsteps with only Max's crazy map as a guide . . . how could he do it? And what if, after facing miles of Isaac's life, only deeper questions remained. Zoro sat back and wondered if, like his father's, the last leg of his journey would find him at the silty bottom of the Hudson River. He pulled a strained breath; the air in the limo felt like cement.

Zoro wished he were somewhere else. But what choice was there? He was trapped in the limo. All his life he had been trapped, inching forward in traffic.

"I feel a bit like a psychology experiment, letting you morph me into Isaac." *Geez*, he thought, *how'd I ever get myself into this mess?*

Max squinted harshly at him. "Is your attitude a by-product of stupidity? Doesn't it seem at all odd to you that I'm offering you the chance of a lifetime, and you're not jumping on it?

Zoro got that, but still he felt this whole journey might mess him up even more than he was. And every time he spoke up Max would chop him off at the knees with some one-line cliché. *When you let go of the things that make you not good enough, that's when you can beat this . . . bullshit voodoo!*

Zoro turned and stared out the window, wondering what he had to lose. To a certain extent all this made sense; they had found a real clue at Princeton, except he kept wondering why. Why was his mind somehow now inclined to go along with Max's thinking. *I better play this close to the vest; if Ma or Gina finds out what I'm doing . . . shit!*

"I'm just thinking, Mr. Max, suppose I told my family about this, they'd say I'm out of my mind."

"Out of your mind would be a good place to start, Zoro."

"There you go again! How do you expect me to believe or understand anything you say?" Zoro swerved hard, cutting into the next lane.

"My advice is, don't believe a word people tell you," Max said. "Anyone who tells you what's what doesn't want you to find out the truth for yourself."

Zoro just shook his head. Max might as well have been speaking Chinese, or any other language; no matter how Max pitched it, Zoro could only hear the words and never the meaning.

CHAPTER 23

"He's dead!" A slender priest said as he stumbled into the mess hall. The others could make out the look of panic on his face. It took ten minutes to calm him down, before he led them to the second-floor bathroom.

Saint Joseph's Seminary, located at 201 Seminary Avenue in Yonkers, sat on a forty-acre wooded swatch on Valentine Hill. Capped with a brick red roof, its gray granite walls were laid in an appropriate Renaissance style. Earlier that evening, Domino Montagino had settled into a bath, in preparation for his return trip to the Vatican. In the guest room reserved for him, he had packed a small carry-on bag, and a classic black suit lay draped over a single bed. It was fitting for a modest representative to the Holy See. Having completed his administrative duties, he was to board a commercial flight bound for Rome at 10 p.m. He had wanted to comb through the souvenir shops at LaGuardia before leaving. Instead, Detective Gideon was combing through his things.

Gideon carried himself with an angry, stoic look. Standing in the bathroom doorway he eyed Domino's body in the tub. All the typical signs of an electrocution were visible, including a 1500-watt hairdryer floating at his knees. But there were distinct signs of a struggle, and the heavy bruising around his neck was hard to miss.

"Who was the last one with him?" Gideon asked.

"He left the mess hall earlier, alone," the rector replied, sounding as if he was upset that Gideon would question the integrity of anyone at Saint Joseph's.

"Did he come to New York to meet anyone in particular?" Gideon asked.

"Actually no. His were regular administrative duties carried out twice a year at the archdiocese. We supplied him with a place to stay and a hot meal, nothing more," said the rector.

Gideon jotted a few notes in his notebook and walked back to the bedside, where a forensic technician had laid out the contents of Domino's coat pockets: a passport and wallet, an appointment book, and an empty, plain brown, letter-sized envelope. Thumbing through Domino's appointment book, Gideon raised an eyebrow.

* * *

Pulling through the condo gates, Zoro caught sight of Gideon leaning against an unmarked police cruiser. His mind raced, trying to come to terms with why the police were here. Max didn't give him a chance to speak. "Wait in the car, Zoro," Max said. Opening the car door, he joined Gideon far enough away from the limo that Zoro couldn't hear what they were saying. It drove Zoro nuts.

Gideon held out his gold shield toward Max.

"Am I about to make the eleven o'clock news, officer?" Max smiled.

"I'm Detective Gideon," he announced, rumbling to assert his authority. "Do you know a Domino Montagino?"

"Why yes I do," Max said.

"He was murdered earlier today."

Max managed to look properly horrified at Gideon's news. "I'm afraid I can't help you in that regard," he said.

"How well did you know Domino Montagino?" the detective asked.

"He was a casual acquaintance, someone with a unique philosophical perspective and a good ear to bend."

"And when was the last time you saw him?"

"Yesterday, in fact," Max replied. "We met for lunch at Grand Central Station. He was fine when I left him."

Gideon asked more questions and jotted more notes. He seemed to be getting less friendly with every question. "In the interest of clarification," he asked, "did he have many enemies?"

Max found the question strange; it supposed Domino had enemies to begin with. "I don't know. I'm sorry but I need to be going."

"Maybe your driver can be of some help." Gideon glanced over at Zoro. Zoro felt his stomach cramp up. *Why the hell are they looking at me?*

"I'm afraid you'd be wasting your time," Max said. "He never left the car, never met the man."

"I see."

Max sensed he didn't see at all. Gideon jotted a few more suspicious notes on his pad.

"Perhaps," Gideon said, "I should speak to him myself."

Max nodded. "That would be our pleasure detective. If you'd like to schedule an appointment with my secretary, we would be happy to join you at the precinct."

Gideon was silent.

"Right now I'm afraid my driver needs to run an errand of great importance. You'll have to excuse me."

Zoro had almost turned himself inside out with curiosity, his head out the open window hoping to overhear the conversation. Coming up to the limo, Max kept his voice down. "I won't be needing you anymore today, Zoro," Max whispered. "Get some rest. Tomorrow we follow that lead to the museum."

"What did the cops want Mr. Max?"

"Nothing to concern yourself with. Go home, Zoro, I insist. We will have our work cut out for us tomorrow at the museum."

CHAPTER 24

By the time he got close to his neighborhood, the limo's gas gauge was near empty. Zoro headed to the nearest gas station, filled the tank, and pulled into a parking spot close to the coin-operated vacuum cleaners.

Standing inside the store as he waited in line to pay, Zoro saw a passing reflection in the glass storefront. The hairs lifted on his arms as he spun around. He could have sworn he'd seen Detective Gideon. But there was no one there.

Suddenly he sensed a tremor in the air that felt like pure bad vibes. An old woman walked toward him, a heavy corrective shoe on one foot that clip-clopped like a horse on pavement. The old gypsy's eyes scanned Zoro.

"You sensed something; I felt that," she said.

"I thought I saw someone. I guess I imagined it."

"I doubt it," she said and grinned, her lips peeling back to reveal a heavy golden tooth.

He tried to subtly distance himself from her without losing his place in line.

"Wait," she said. "Help out an old lady. I can read your fortune." She held out her dirty palm.

With eight people waiting in line ahead of him to buy cigarettes, lottery tickets, and gas, Zoro figured why not. He dropped a dollar bill in her hand and smiled.

She rolled the bill across her palm, twisting it lightly between her fingers like a hand-rolled Cubana. Fifteen seconds later indistinct sounds came from her mouth; her eyes rolled white, like the eyes of a tipped porcelain doll. Grabbing Zoro's arm, she clenched down with a grip like a vise, as the bill torpedoed toward the ground.

"You carry many ghosts in your head that aren't your own," she said.

She was truly strange, Zoro couldn't argue with that. "You're not just good," he laughed, "you're *good* good."

"I'm not imagining this," she whispered. "Someone is looking for those ghosts . . . behind you now."

Gideon! he thought. Zoro spun around, searching out beyond the gas pumps. When he turned back, the shadowy figure of the gypsy woman was gone, though the smell of cigarette ashes lingered.

With her words droning in his head, his mind took a turn down a long dark tunnel. After what seemed like an hour, he got to the cashier and paid for his gas. Walking back toward the limo, he surveyed the parking lot carefully, looking for any trace of Detective Gideon.

*   *   *

Detective Gideon had parked near the synagogue, right across the street from the gas station. After sipping a cup of leftover coffee, he watched the station and mulled over things. Ever suspicious, he needed to know if there was any connection between Zoro and the earlier homicide. Reaching for the door handle, he stopped himself. Something made him ease off; he wondered if this was the right time to confront Zoro. He casually stuck his hand inside his pocket and thumbed his badge. He was only months away from retirement and had no hobbies outside his detective work, no family either. Somehow he felt he just needed to solve this case before retirement left him wondering what he'd do with the rest of his life. Out of habit, he scanned the street. Something made him turn around. It might've been a passing reflection, a face . . . something made his senses tingle. After looking around for a few seconds, he shrugged and started his car, returning to the precinct.

He arrived at his desk, prompt as usual. He spent more time there than he ever did at home. Sergeant Clements had warned him years ago what to expect if he took work home with him, but Gideon hadn't listened.

Thinking about the strange tingling feeling he'd had earlier, he found himself flipping through the pages of a particular file folder again and again. He was having serious doubts about that one case. He was drawn to it like a serial killer was drawn to one type of victim: the same hair color or the smell of a certain perfume. Gideon was obsessing, and he knew it.

The chief called him into his office and looked him squarely in the face.

"You've been out all day, Gideon. And you haven't solved a single case."

"Look, Chief, it hasn't always been this way."

"I know. So what's going on, Gideon?"

"It's just this one case. I need to close it."

"Why? You're a couple months from retirement. Finish your other cases, then buy a fishing rod."

Suddenly Gideon's eyes were ablaze; the chief had no business telling him what to do. "This is bigger than me, or you, or even this department. I can feel it in my gut."

"I get stuck with all the whack-job cops," the chief muttered to himself. "Okay, fine. You making progress?"

"I wouldn't call it progress."

"Then move on. Believe me," the chief said, "you can't solve them all. That problem comes with the territory."

"Chief, I can't let it go. Some people think they have the right to do the wrong thing for the right reasons."

"Maybe," the chief said. "But the universe can't tell the difference between right and wrong, Gideon. It's only concerned with balance. Now, balance the fifteen files on your desk, and get the hell out of my office."

"Chief," Gideon said, holding up his hand, "here's the thing: I can tell the difference, and I can't let that go."

CHAPTER 25

Friday Morning, Manhattan

The next morning, traffic began to thicken, slowly at first, and then cars flowed in larger numbers. Zoro knew they were headed toward Central Park, to the Metropolitan Museum of Art. Coasting steadily through the Manhattan traffic, the limo was more than a carriage; it had become Max's lecture hall, Zoro's classroom.

Zoro had to admit, though, that he liked it when Max was teaching; it kept his mind off other things. Each lesson made him feel better about himself, stronger. Zoro liked that he was gaining control.

"Mr. Max, yesterday at the gas station, there was an old fortune-teller. I let her read my fortune."

"Oh, Lord," Max said, smiling. "That's kind of wacky for you, Zoro."

"Okay, sure, I like everything to be based on reality. I only did it because I felt sorry for her; she looked like she really needed the coin, you know? But she said something . . ."

"Oh?"

"She said there are many ghosts in my head that aren't mine."

"Unusual."

"What do you think she meant by that?"

The limo was cruising along steadily, narrowing the distance between them and Central Park.

"She couldn't tell about Joey, could she, Mr. Max?"

"Ah . . . here's the thing: I don't think that's what she meant."

Max studied Zoro in the mirror for a few seconds. Then, to Zoro's astonishment, he climbed over the seat back and plopped into the passenger seat. He came over with a big grin on his face.

"What the—"

"Do you mind?"

Zoro shrugged. "It's your car, Mr. Max."

"What she was talking about, Zoro, are the subconscious beliefs in your head: the ones that are so out of control that a perfect stranger can sense them."

Zoro just nodded, waiting for whatever Max was going to say next.

"You believe if your crappy life is against you, it has nothing to do with your beliefs; it's because life is just against you. Isn't that so?"

"I guess so," Zoro said.

"Wrong!" Max said explosively, and the force of his voice went vibrating through Zoro's mind. "You can doubt everything around you, doubt everything I say, but you never challenge *your own* beliefs. Why is that? Who told you your beliefs are right and not wrong? Who has proven life's against you? Who the hell has checked your beliefs and made sure you didn't get a defective set? You, Zoro? Your mommy?"

Why does time seem to crawl when he's poking around inside my brain? "I was hoping you could tell me," Zoro said, pulling a foolish face.

"I contend, Zoro, straight up, that your deep-seated beliefs are faulty."

"That old gypsy woman could see all that just by talking to me?"

"A five-year-old could see that just by knowing where to look. Not only that, but since you've inadvertently used that litany of limited beliefs against yourself over and over again, your life is a walking picture of your flawed beliefs. Your subconscious mind has absorbed negativity, failure, and scarcity, and accepted them as truth. And with that it's been working tirelessly, day in and day out, to bring about circumstances and situations that match that truth. If it's hard to make money, it's not your fault, Zoro, isn't that right? It's because it's hard, because the deck is stacked against you. And your subconscious will back you up on that, won't it?"

"I'm afraid that I don't really accept all your contentions," Zoro replied.

"Nor can I accept yours."

And then Max dropped the bombshell. "Because if you're right, Zoro, you killed Joey. That's true, isn't it? Why else would you believe it?"

Zoro's eyes widened, filling with dread and fear. "Fuck you, you son of a bitch! Since Joey died I have nothing, and you're accusing me? I'm never going to forgive you for that, never. You just crossed the line."

"You're a jackass, Zoro! Wake up!"

As Zoro reached the next intersection, he floored the accelerator, shooting across the intersection and barely missing an oncoming truck.

"Kill us if you want, but you can't avoid the question." Max's voice was hard. "Did . . . you . . . kill . . . Joey? Did you? *Did you?* DID YOU?"

"No!" Zoro slammed on the brake pedal, spinning the big limo sideways and the rear tires over the curb. "No," he cried, his face crumpling in grief and confusion. "No . . . no . . . no!"

"Then why?" Max asked, his voice suddenly tender. "Why do you believe it?"

As Zoro looked at himself in the rearview mirror, an unsteady bead of sweat trickled down his forehead.

"I want you to listen to me, Zoro. I've suffered just like you; I've lived in hell. But there's only one way to stop the grief and hatred from rotting your soul. You have to learn to pay attention to your own mind, to be conscious of your subconscious."

Even in his fog of grief and anxiety, Zoro was trying to listen to Max. But the truth was playing Houdini in his head. Bottled away with his hardest pain and insulated with half-truths, Zoro had hidden the real truth deep inside.

Zoro gave Max a stricken look. "Maybe I didn't exactly kill Joey, but everything I touch dies," he said.

"Don't give me that, Zoro." Max's voice was still kind—pleading, even. "I understand your pain, but what you just said is a crock. I look at you now, and I see you teetering on the edge of the most important truth you can discover. Listen, Zoro: it's not your destiny to remain trapped."

Max took a deep breath and leaned away from Zoro, against the passenger door panel. He rubbed the top of his head, giving Zoro a doubtful look. "Zoro," Max finally said, "we see what we look for, and we look for what we know."

Zoro gave Max a sidelong glance. "If this is important, do you think you could quit talking like a Tibetan monk?"

Max looked questioningly at Zoro.

"I can't understand you."

"Fair enough," Max conceded. "Okay . . . Do you remember the movie *Jurassic Park*?"

"Loved that movie," Zoro said, allowing his eyes to connect with Max's. And there it was again: the rush of warmth and understanding that for some reason kept finding its way into Zoro. He felt something when he was with Max that reminded him of the good times . . . before everything started going wrong.

"Zoro, do you remember how the *T. rex* couldn't see anything that wasn't moving?"

"Yeah."

Max nodded. "Its eyes saw what was there all right, but unless the object was moving, it didn't register in the *T. rex's* mind, right?"

Zoro checked the mirrors for oncoming traffic, then carefully eased the rear wheels over the curb and back into the street.

"Think, Zoro . . . the *T. rex* . . . it's there, but he doesn't see it . . ."

Zoro's mind shuffled off in search of answers. He focused. Maybe it was because he'd already come this far, or maybe it was because Max's explanations had signaled a deeper truth. But he refused to go back. *Come on, I need to get this . . . I need to get this . . .*

"I got it!" he yelled. "There are things I could be seeing that my mind doesn't see!"

"Exactly," Max said, smiling. "And what else?"

"And what I do see," Zoro continued, "depends on what the beliefs in my mind are whispering to me."

It's over, thank God, he thought. The waiting was finally over. And though he was sitting down, Zoro felt his legs buckling with relief.

Then Max again asked, "And . . . ?"

Zoro looked over at Max, his forehead wrinkling. *What more could there be?* he thought. Then suddenly it dawned on him. "I'm not programmed to discover my bad subconscious beliefs—what the old lady called ghosts."

"Bingo!" Max smiled broadly.

Zoro's words had brought him all the way back to the issue at hand. In a way, it was like he'd been sleeping. And now he was being asked to awaken and listen to the quiet breathing inside him, to find the corruption hidden in soft murmurs: the corruption that had him bleeding tears for Joey.

His thoughts drifted to Gina, and how she was before they got married. She'd been so carefree. When he'd first met her at the beach and asked her to have a drink with him, he had no idea they'd spend a whole day under an umbrella talking. She was emotional and spontaneous and it seemed like they had so little in common. It wasn't long before he discovered that she put just as much emotion and fire behind her kisses, and that feeling sealed the deal for him. Eventually he asked her to marry him and she threw her arms around him, embraced him, all of him, the good and the bad. Maybe now he could take a lesson from her, embrace all of who he was, but still have a good long look underneath his clunky exterior.

"Zoro," Max said, "if you shut off the sludge pump of corrupt beliefs, guess what happens?"

"I get rich?" Zoro grinned. But his grin belied the look of confusion in his eyes.

Max gave him a direct look. "If you find a heartbeat in money, marry it. But I'm offering you something bigger: your life. You have the power, Zoro, to burn any idea, any thought, any belief into your subconscious.

And those thoughts never sleep; they are always vibrating inside you, always at work, whispering the truth—or lies."

They were at a traffic light, and when it turned green, the limo stalled. Zoro quickly shifted into neutral and cranked the ignition, but before he could move forward, Max scooted over beside him and grabbed the steering wheel.

"Close your eyes, Zoro."

"Huh?"

"Just do it."

He did. He felt Max's foot move onto the accelerator, nudging his aside. The limo began to move.

"Men look at the sky and the earth," Max said, "and try to explain things, but you need to look deeper."

"I've tried to do what you say, Max, but I've never seen anything."

Zoro resisted the urge to look, to take control of the car. Instead, he kept his eyes pressed firmly closed, completely trusting Max to steer. They were in the middle of Manhattan, and traffic covered the roadway. Still, eyes shut, sensing the surge of traffic all around him, Zoro tried to picture what Max was describing.

Max asked Zoro to picture himself looking down on his body, and then picture himself looking down on his home, his street, his city, state, and country. "See the satellite image of your continent, until finally you see the whole, blue planet," Max said. "You'll see the trillions of things happening on the planet from your vantage point in outer space."

And suddenly from nowhere, passing before the kaleidoscope of colors flowing across his closed eyelids, Zoro saw other places, other countries, some suffering war and famine. He saw places filled with happiness, technological advances, and tender stories of the heart. He saw the complexity of the entire ecosystem.

"Now quickly look at yourself," Max said. "See that tiny little negative thought, way down there on the planet? That tiny thought surrounded by an infinite mechanism of thoughts and realities?

"Open your eyes now, Zoro," Max said. "Take over the driving."

Zoro took the wheel and eased his foot back onto the gas pedal. Max scooted back over to the passenger side of the front seat. For a couple of blocks, they rode along in silence. Zoro couldn't get the image out of his mind: the image of the blue planet, hanging in space—and of himself, a tiny part of everything that was going on there.

"Park here," Max said. "We've reached our destination."

CHAPTER 26

Zoro stared at the clerk's eyes. His gut told him something was wrong. He hadn't expected what the clerk said next, but it hit him like a freight train. It was probably the same way Isaac felt receiving the news under the domed arches of the Metropolitan Museum thirty years ago.

"What do you mean no record?" Zoro was livid. "You need to check again."

The administrative clerk punched a few more keys on her keyboard. "I'm not sure what to tell you gentlemen. We simply have no record of ever receiving a donation from Princeton."

Zoro was confused. "Why would Pop have sent us here?"

Max shook his head. "He wasn't lying, Zoro. I'm certain Isaac came here on the trail of that sketch." Before Max could say anything else the administrative clerk interrupted. She had thought of something that could explain this morning's troubling developments.

"The Cloisters," she said.

"Yes, yes, that could explain it," Max said.

"Wait," Zoro's voice was loud, "what are cloisters?"

"Not cloisters, Zoro," Max responded, "*The* Cloisters."

"It's a branch of the museum," the administrative clerk chimed in, explaining that several medieval European abbeys were disassembled stone by stone and shipped to New York, then reassembled in Fort Tryon Park. "They include some magnificent medieval gardens and a wonderful collection of medieval art."

"Can you access the acquisition records for the Cloisters?" Max asked.

"Not from here," the clerk replied. "I can make a call."

Max nodded.

Dropping the receiver back into the phone cradle after her call, the clerk informed them that the Cloisters would get back to her in about an hour. Max thanked her for her effort. Turning to Zoro he suggested a walk through Central Park, to cut the anxiety of the wait.

They walked into Central Park, behind the museum, opposite Cleopatra's needle.

"What do you think explains this, Mr. Max?"

Max blinked. It only took him a second to understand what Zoro was getting at. He had that kind of mind, sharp. It was what Isaac had liked best about him. "It's funny, Zoro; I've been thinking the exact same thing. I can't make a connection between Princeton's Civil War relics and a reassembled medieval abbey."

Zoro had wondered that as well, and had no answer, so he waited for whatever Max was going to say next, but then he abruptly interrupted Max before he began.

"Wait! What if the sketch was hidden inside an original stone block or a statue shipped over for the abbey's reconstruction, but the clue to that information was somehow hidden at Princeton?"

"I think that could be one guess, Zoro. However, I don't think that's relevant. I have no reason to think that the sketch's history will change the circumstances of where we are now. The best thing we've got going for us is to keep reliving Isaac's days, and get into his head, if we are actually going to find where the sketch is today."

Zoro blinked. "This whole thing's a kettle of fish that I'd like to avoid. But if it's the only way, Mr. Max, how quick can we get this over with? We got an hour to kill?"

Max knew that was ridiculous; an hour to unravel the mind. Max raised his hands. His palms were paler than the rest of him, much paler. It was odd, Zoro thought: so much of Max was shrouded in mystery, darkness. Even his voice could sound that way—dark, like rich chocolate. But his palms were lily white.

"Thank you for being interested, Zoro," Max began ever so gingerly. They walked a few paces in the brisk autumn air. "So what do you think changed, Zoro, when a primitive hominid, what you might loosely call a caveman, went from grubbing in the dirt for roots and slugs to using a tool, then using fire, and then imagining language and mathematics and civilizations?"

"I don't know. Something, I guess."

Max slowed his pace, breathing the cool air of the park. "Yes, something changed. There's a profound truth in those words, Zoro. You see, practically overnight—at least, in evolutionary terms—some flash of ingenuity sparked up in the caveman's consciousness. Their brains didn't change overnight, but something awakened that pushed the boundaries of their intellectual evolution."

Max turned to smile at Zoro. "If you want to know what that brilliant spark was that catapulted their brains to new heights, we're going to have to dissect your mind."

"Excuse me? You mean, like, figuratively, right?"

"No, Zoro, I have a scalpel in my pocket," Max said drily.

"Okay, okay," Zoro said. He wasn't going to overthink things, this time, he decided. "I'm all ears, Mr. Max."

"We've seen, Zoro, from an abstract point of view, that we can divide our experiences into the three worlds. So you can probably guess what I'm going to say about your inner world of mind."

"Three minds, right?"

"Exactly! All tangled together in this thing we call the brain, there are three parts to our mind. Although in actual fact, there is a fourth part to the mind outside of our heads. But we can deal with that later. Now, Zoro, the first part, or quadrant, is buried deep within this complex mess of neurons and electrical impulses that is your brain, and it's called the subconscious mind, or the First Q."

"We talked about subconscious beliefs already, or more correctly, you tortured me about Joey," Zoro said.

"And you survived it, right? Even realized some important truths as a result, as I recall?"

"That's true, now tell me more."

"Good." Max knew immediately he'd busted through some of Zoro's barriers. "Now get this, your subconscious mind has a capacity millions of times greater than that of any other part of the mind. It can process millions of bits of information per second as it receives them from your senses, and even has a sixth sense, which you'll understand when you start to grasp how the Third Q works. By contrast, your conscious mind—your Second Q—can only process maybe eighty bits per second of the information it receives from your eyes or ears."

"That's cool."

"It is, Zoro, because it means that sitting inside your head is a remarkable mechanism for recording and cataloging every single thing you've ever experienced. Do you think that's an advantage a successful person could leverage?"

"Yeah!" Another nod from Zoro.

"Our ability to unconsciously record and react to staggering amounts of information frees us from worrying about fleeing danger, remembering to eat, and all sorts of things that we take for granted. And with all the information and subconscious processing looping around in our heads, we also dream and travel in space and time, and invent solutions to problems deep inside our minds, all without ever interrupting the flow of conscious activity of everyday life."

"Whoa, hold on a minute. You make the subconscious sound so great. Yet you just got done bitching about all my messed-up subconscious beliefs."

Max dropped his chin and looked at Zoro askance. "Bitching?"

Zoro recognized the ominous silence that followed. "Bitching, criticizing: tomato, tomahto."

Max smiled. "You're right, and that's something we need to solve first if any of this is going to work for you. May I go on?"

Zoro shrugged and nodded.

"As humans we are very slow to develop, Zoro, and as a consequence we are dramatically linked to the information we receive from a small number of people closest to us during our formative years. As we grow, our brains absorb the world we live in. Nearly everything we learn as children and young adults—language, fears, beliefs, and prejudices—is literally sucked up from the people around us. And those notions bond with each of us as permanent ideas burned into our subconscious minds: our beliefs."

"So that's where my messed-up beliefs come from."

"Everyone's do."

Zoro unexpectedly thought about his prom night. Virginia May Gillian offered up a dazzling smile when she asked him to the prom. He thought she was the prettiest girl in high school—hell, maybe even the world. After the events with Joey and Isaac, he didn't have much of a social life, though he wasn't unpopular. But Carmela had wondered why on earth he felt he deserved to go to the prom, especially with Virginia May. She hemmed and hawed and simply didn't understand why being adored by Virginia May might have been exactly what he needed. Maybe he was expecting too much from Carmela. And Virginia May was expecting a little too much from him. Though Gina later changed Zoro, at the time he wasn't some romantic guy who would buy Virginia May flowers for no reason at all. Maybe she had unrealistic expectations, but he wasn't the kind of guy who wanted to feel passion. And he guessed she didn't feel it either when he kissed her on prom night, because she never kissed him again. Poor Virginia May. He couldn't help but wonder why he'd let Carmela's influence keep him from sharing the passion that girl deserved. That really wasn't fair to her, or him, as a matter of fact.

"Why are you looking at me like that, Mr. Max?"

Max held Zoro with his gaze. "Think about this, Zoro: Your mind can't tell the difference between a good and bad thought. It just records them all and fixes them in your mind as a permanent belief—the very beliefs that have been keeping you from being successful . . . and in these last few days, your beliefs about Isaac have kept you from really opening your mind."

And kissing Virginia May passionately, Zoro thought, grimacing.

"What you truly feel you are capable of—good or bad—what measure of success you can or can't achieve is predetermined and automated by the recorded belief patterns in your mind."

"And I really wouldn't know if that was happening to me?"

"We can only see in ourselves the beliefs we look for, and we can unfortunately only look for the beliefs we know of. The rest are filtered out by our minds and thus invisible . . . unless we undertake to actively explore the beliefs hidden inside our minds."

"*Jurassic Park!*" Zoro yelled. "If I can't see my beliefs, how can I change? Unless I examine them."

"Seems like you've answered your own question, Zoro. Nicely done."

"Don't look so smug, Obi-Wan." Zoro playfully bumped his hip into Max, but he almost knocked the older man down. Zoro grabbed his arm to steady him.

"Sorry, Mr. Max. But I'm beginning to get the picture of why Isaac's trail keeps coming up cold, or maybe even why I never succeeded at anything. Until I understood what you just said, I didn't even know there were thoughts in my mind deceiving me, making me see things from someone else's viewpoint and not mine."

Max nodded. "None of this is mumbo-jumbo, Zoro. You don't need to buy into a brain-sucking cult and dance around in a sheet. Just realize there are tricks you can use to clean up the sludge pump of a brain that you have. It's really all quite logical."

Something struck Zoro on the shoulder. He flinched and spun around; it was a Frisbee, being closely pursued by a golden retriever with a very long, pink tongue.

"Sorry!" a man called, standing about thirty feet away.

"No problem," Zoro said, picking up the Frisbee and tossing it back toward the man. The golden retriever dashed off, its eyes fixed on the flying Frisbee.

Zoro watched the dog and the Frisbee for a couple of seconds, and then he noticed a lone figure, about ten yards on the other side of the man with the dog. The figure seemed to be staring in Zoro's direction, but then quickly turned and ducked behind a tree trunk. Zoro blinked and looked again. Had he imagined it?

He shrugged and turned back toward Max.

"Sludge pump, thanks a lot." Zoro grinned and cut his eyes sideways at Max, but Max was staring ahead, focused on his next thoughts. He could be very intense.

Zoro thought about what he had learned so far. He pondered the idea that his mind had been closed to seeing itself; that a closed mind accepts its belief patterns as absolute truth; that it would then never move ahead to try to repair those beliefs. Suddenly Max spoke, almost as if talking to himself. "Perhaps Jasper can help."

CHAPTER 27

Zoro flicked a few stray raindrops from his jacket. "Who's Jasper?"

Max smiled at Zoro. "Jasper's is one of the most amazing stories you'll ever hear.

"Jasper lived with Delilah, his wife of forty years, in Bridge City, Texas. Jasper and Delilah were both dedicated long-distance runners, and they both had always dreamt of going to Australia and breaking the tape in the Colac Six-Day Marathon. But sadly, the dream ended when Delilah was struck by a fierce and debilitating palsy. Overwhelmed by her illness, Jasper gave up running. He spent his life caring for Delilah. And though she begged him to run without her, he couldn't do it; to him, it felt like betrayal.

"But shortly after Delilah's death, Jasper showed up at the starting line of the Colac Six-Day. He had barely trained at all in twenty years and he was overweight and out of shape. Still, he found a courage that had always been in him; he'd just forgotten about it. Standing in a line of elite, trained athletes, Jasper had a sudden epiphany. Instantly Jasper realized that to understand any successes or failures that are happening to you, you need to first look within yourself.

"Jasper understood that his subconscious mind didn't see things the way his conscious mind did. The subconscious mind would never argue with any of the thoughts he was thinking or picturing in his conscious mind, if those thoughts were in alignment with his deeper subconscious beliefs.

"As the starter pistol cracked, Jasper watched the field of competitors disappear in a burst of speed. And he just smiled, leaned forward, and shuffled off. So, you might think he lost."

Zoro looked away, thinking this might be a trick question. Max grinned at Zoro.

"You won't believe this, but Jasper ran the six-day contest nonstop without sleeping and demolished the field."

They were walking the Bank Rock Bridge; the wooden decking creaked with each step they took. Max roared with laughter. "Born the son of a simple mail carrier, chubby Jasper won the race, all because of the image he held in his mind."

Zoro tried to make the connection. "He won because he was thinking about crossing the finish line?"

Max just stared at him as they walked. Finally Zoro could stand it no longer. "What? What is it?" he yelled.

"Good try, Zoro, really. But not exactly," he said, lacing his fingers. "Actually, Jasper never once thought of the finish. He just imagined Delilah running beside him. And for all the years he carried her in her illness, she now carried him."

Zoro went quiet and studied Max, trying to digest what he had just heard.

"Zoro, what's more important than what Jasper was thinking is what he *wasn't* thinking. You see, it never entered his mind that he wasn't qualified to run the race. It never entered his mind to stop running while the other competitors slept." Max smiled. "When Jasper's conscious mind said, 'Let's run the race,' his subconscious mind opened the file called 'race.' And the only thing in the file were the words, 'Congratulations, you've already won.' You see, Jasper had implanted that thought into his subconscious by repeating it and believing in his conscious mind. No one else's beliefs were there in his mind."

"There you go again, Mr. Max, saying something unexplainable."

"Don't be ridiculous, of course it's explainable. And why don't you drop the Mr. and just call me Max?"

"Okay . . . Max. You think everything is possible, as long as your mind believes it?"

"Isn't it?"

"Is it?"

By now Zoro's mind was all frothed up and begging for mercy. But Max didn't let up. "The thing is, Zoro, Jasper understood that to change anything outside of yourself, you first need to change inside yourself. Your subconscious mind is like a fluid, and it takes the shape of whatever image you hold in your mind.

"Understand, Zoro, that when Jasper crossed the finish line he was holding Delilah's hand. Being first or being last never mattered, because at that moment he'd already won. And that, Zoro, is the belief he consciously fired into his subconscious mind over and over again, until his subconscious mind replied, 'Yup, you've already won.'" Max pitched a sidelong glance through the thinning trees at the open field at Cedar Hill.

They were walking down a broad path that wound beneath overarching boughs laden with autumn-gilded leaves. To Zoro, it seemed as if they were walking through a tunnel of gold—one with no beginning, no end.

Suddenly, Zoro thought he might be getting his fingernails under the edge of what Max was trying to show him. It all seemed so perfect to Zoro. The logic was seamless, the reason unflawed. Zoro was wordless. He'd spent his whole life looking for a finish line that wasn't there. But at this moment, none of that—not even the quest for the Name— seemed as important as walking down this golden pathway, walking along side by side with Max.

"Wait here, Zoro, I have an idea," Max said.

Zoro stared as Max disappeared behind the trees. Glancing behind him, Zoro saw a woman jogging toward him. For a moment he thought she was approaching him to ask him something. She was very pretty, and he found himself grinning foolishly. He half expected her to stop. Instead of stopping, she just kept running.

"Zoro," Max shouted. A quick glance over his shoulder, through a thicket of trees, and he saw Max standing in a clearing by the hill waving a football frantically in the air.

He found out later that Max had paid handsomely for it, purchasing the football from some kids in the park. Right now, though, he shuddered at what he imagined would come next. He pushed his way past the thicket of trees, through an old cobweb he calmly parted with his hands. By the time he made it to the clearing, Max was dragging an empty trashcan up onto a picnic table. Zoro walked over to him. "Are you nuts, Max?"

"I know what happened at the state championship game years ago when you choked, Zoro."

Zoro's eyebrows shot up. He wondered how Max could know so much about him, though he supposed Carmela would have been all too happy to share his failures with anyone who would have listened. He couldn't muster any words.

That foggy day years ago came into his mind, and it sent a chill down his spine. On fourth and goal with seconds on the clock, the ball had come out of the center's hands and bounced off Zoro's chest, while he stood upright and frozen. In his mind, even at that very moment, he swore he'd heard the play whistled dead. But the bone-crushing tackle from an amped-up safety had thought otherwise, and apparently so had the referees, as the clock ran out. His mind ran wildly and he shuddered as he felt his bid for state dissolve all over again in his mind. Then he had drifted over to the bleachers to a seat left empty by a disappointed Carmela.

Zoro came out of his think mode. "I get what you're doing, Max. You want to prove that even now I'm affected by some sort of spell my mind cast on me years ago."

"Think Jasper, Zoro," Max smiled devilishly.

"All right, Max, I'll face this ghost. But it will cost you—a hundred bucks for every ball I make into that trash can."

Max nodded. They looked at each other as if to make a silent oath.

Zoro sucked in a breath and let the first ball fly; it bounced off the picnic bench. "Not to worry, I got this." Another ball sailed two yards above the can. Six more balls and he still hadn't sunk a single one. A hard lump formed in his throat, thinking about that day. He'd been so close to winning state, and he had blown it.

Max turned toward Zoro. Whatever Zoro thought he was going to say wasn't what he said.

"You're missing the mark because your subconscious works both ways. Bad thoughts are equally powerful."

"Both ways?"

"Yes, thinking and wishing you're going to sink the ball isn't enough to counteract your negative beliefs." Max lobbed a ball dead center into the trashcan, granted he'd stepped up halfway closer than Zoro was.

Zoro sighed, watching as Max did it twice more. "I think I hate you now, Max." Zoro smiled.

"When you first met me, Zoro, you did hate me—even before you knew me—just because I was rich. You even muttered obscenities when you walked around my limo. Anyone else would've fired your sorry ass on the spot, and made the thoughts you held in your mind a reality. I mean seriously, Zoro, if you resent the rich, how could your mind ever let you become what you resent?"

"I didn't mean to not like you, Max."

Max cuffed Zoro lightly on the head.

"Ow! What was that for?"

"No one means to, Zoro, but programming is a bad habit. And you've given in to yours."

A silent alarm had gone off in Zoro's head. "I'm the freakin' *T. rex*!"

"It's true, Zoro. And you also throw like a girl."

"Nice, Max, real encouraging."

Max's cell phone rang, and Zoro felt excited. *It must be the museum*, he thought. It was.

"Of course," Max said, "cost is no issue." He clicked his cell phone shut.

"Well?"

"I'm afraid the Cloisters will have to search the archive records manually. That may take until Monday." As they continued their walk, Max gave the football back to the kids from whom he had bought it.

"Here we are." They had made a circle through the park, and now stood next to the limo. "You hungry, Zoro? Good, then take us to the Bowery."

Zoro instinctively took a last nervous look over his shoulder. But there was nobody there.

CHAPTER 28

Max strolled into the soup kitchen as if walking into a friend's house. Three people behind the steam table wearing hairnets instantly recognized him and waved. The homeless people, sucking down free turkey and mash at the collapsible tables, never looked up. The smell was less than pleasant, and Zoro wished he could run outside and gulp down a rush of fresh air.

"Here, Max? You seriously want to eat here?"

"Isaac volunteered here, Zoro. This is where he would have been that Friday at lunchtime."

As Max moved into the room, two people seated at the middle of a long table put down their forks and looked closely at Max. When they stood and hugged Max, Zoro looked surprised.

One of the men started toward Zoro. His open hands came sailing through the air, grabbing hold of Zoro's hand and arm and shaking firmly. Zoro pulled back, a look of disgust forming on his face. A few paces behind him the other man approached, and Zoro realized they weren't bums.

"Zoro," Max smiled, "meet my friends. Vincent and Hershel are executives in my organization; they volunteer here weekly."

Zoro suddenly felt shamed by his thoughts. "Sorry, I thought you guys were just bums."

The man who had shaken his hand, dressed in a T-shirt, jeans, and scuffed shoes, certainly didn't stand out from the other patrons of the soup kitchen.

"You guys finish your lunch break," Max said. "Zoro, come over here for a minute." Max moved to a quiet corner where a single table was set with a red-and-white checkered tablecloth. "Pull up a chair."

Zoro sat down on a chair, facing Max across the table. He felt confused and uncomfortable and was sure it showed on his face.

"I expected you'd be fooled by the crowd here, Zoro."

There was a ketchup bottle on the table between them; Zoro took it and turned it around and around on its base. "Why are we here, Max?"

"Besides retracing Isaac's trail, to prove a point."

Zoro looked at him. "I got this one. You're hell-bent on proving to me that I'm a misfit and that I'm easy to fool. Right?"

Max was about to answer when a man in a hairnet dropped two plates of turkey and mash in front of them. Zoro heaved an annoyed sigh. "I'm not a bum. I can afford my own food."

"Of course you can, Zoro. But I pay for all this. You might as well enjoy it." Max smiled and picked up his fork.

Zoro reluctantly started eating.

"Here's the point I wanted to make, Zoro: a successful person can never presume or assume anything."

Zoro slugged back some turkey. "This is relevant to finding Isaac's sketch?" he asked around a mouthful of food.

"You want to become his mind or not?" Max asked.

Zoro half nodded. "Only if absolutely necessary."

Max stepped up the conversation with gusto. "We've seen how your subconscious mind has affected you and your throwing arm apparently," Max chuckled. "But we are also affected by our conscious mind, which is the Second Q. You made certain assumptions when you saw my colleagues and acted accordingly. Do you understand why?"

"No, but would it help if I said it's not my fault?"

"What's your gut feeling?"

"Just tell me why I acted like that. That will work for me, Max."

"All right, let's confront why you behaved the way you did. The actions your conscious mind takes are based on what you see, hear, and learn from your physical senses. But here's the crux: What we see in our minds is not determined by our eyes, ears, or senses. It's merely a brain-generated re-creation of what our eyes and senses see. Your mind generated a picture labeled 'bums,' so bums were all you perceived."

"Why?"

"Because your brain's re-creation is not a faithful reproduction of the world. Every image you consciously see moves through a series of filters and relays in the brain, all of which affect the final picture. If I asked the Rolling Stones and the New York Philharmonic to play the same song, it would sound completely different. Would you agree?"

"Yeah."

"In the same way, your brain is not a perfect artist. Your brain makes certain guesses about what it sees and summarizes them into a snapshot of the real world. So what you see in your head is actually a fuzzed-up inference and not an exact re-creation of what your eyes or senses see."

Zoro drew back and looked at Max, understanding dawning in his face. "So my actions here today were based on an imperfect interpretation of what I saw?"

"Yup, a filtered view."

Zoro felt the information buzzing in his head. He paused. "So having me look at every place Isaac went up until now was an absolute waste of time. In a sense I could only see things my way, never his way?"

"You say tomato, he says tomahto," Max smiled. "But here's the thing, everywhere we've been is now recorded in your subconscious mind."

Zoro stared down at his plate for a moment, thoughtfully stirring the mashed potatoes, then slowly lifted a forkful to his mouth.

"So what do I do, to see things differently, to get rid of the filtered view?"

"You don't."

"Huh?"

"The reason our conscious images are filtered, Zoro, is because there's just too much going on around us. If you tried to hold on to an accurate, unfiltered image of everything going on around you, you'd simply go nuts."

Zoro scanned the room; seconds passed. He tried to hold an image of every person's face, his or her hair and clothing, the clang of dishes and forks, the babble of words, the colors and sounds . . . The effort quickly staggered his mind.

"Astonishing," he said.

Max reached for his arm. "And so it seems, Zoro, that during the course of our evolution we've come up with this wonderful mechanism to absorb all the information around us subconsciously, so as not to be bogged down in our conscious life. And then our conscious mind projects a simple, incomplete, yet easy-to-handle image in front of our mind's eye and calls it reality—our conscious state of mind."

"My God," Zoro finally said. "If we consider that every action I take is based on what I see in the world around me, all my decisions are actually based on a guess, a semi-accurate re-creation of what's actually there."

Max sat back and gave Zoro a proud look. "What ever happened to poor, misfit Zoro?"

"I believe," Zoro said, "he understands now that all his perceptions are crammed into a little conscious box and all blurred up by filters in his mind."

"Bingo." Max smiled wider.

"Well, hell," Zoro said. "I guess it's time I stopped believing my eyes.

"Everyplace we've been, Max, it's all up here in my coconut, and all's I gotta do to make heads or tails of Isaac's trail is move things around, re-create a better image of what's going on around me, and use that to my advantage."

"How?"

"I . . . I got nothing."

Max groaned. "Get out of your tiny box!"

"So my problem is that I'm small-minded?"

"It is and it isn't. Don't get me wrong; you are small-minded."

Zoro scoffed. "That's right up there with 'you throw like a girl.'" Max was looking at him expectantly.

"Oh, crap. Now you are going to ask me how to fix my mind . . . This is the longest goddamned day I've ever lived through."

Max relented. "I'll give you a hint, Zoro. You need to shift your mind into a higher gear. Remember what I told you about a shift happening in cavemen, something that sparked up their brains to the next level?"

"Yeah."

"Don't you want to know what that was, or more importantly, why the next level of shift isn't happening to you?"

"I do, but it's just . . . I'm so tired. I mean, you go ahead, and if I don't fall asleep, I'll try to listen."

"Okay, Zoro, we'll quit for today. But before we do I want to leave you with a final thought. For your purposes, don't answer it, just mull it over."

Zoro nodded.

"If the conscious and subconscious are two parts of your mind," Max said, "things that need a little fixing, who's the handyman?"

"If you want to stand back and change how those minds work together, doesn't there need to be another part of the mind that does that? Don't we need a different set of biological brain circuits to tackle that job?"

Zoro started to speak, but Max stopped him. "Don't answer, Zoro; just leave it for now."

They walked outside into a flurry of rain and ringing church bells, which soon had Zoro thinking about Gina again.

An August honeymoon in the Caribbean could get wet. Throughout their whole holiday, it had rained. St. Lucia floods when it rains. But snuggling in the fresh bedsheets had been a perfect honeymoon, a perfect memory. The crazy rain noisily battering the hotel windows had sounded an awful lot like the noise in Zoro's head. He'd always had the steady guilty whispers droning inside of him. "I know it's crazy, Gina," he'd said, "but when I'm next to you, it's quiet."

"Zoro, it's time you took me home. And until we hear from the Cloisters on Monday, I won't need your services."

That night, Zoro went to bed early, but sleep didn't come easily.

CHAPTER 29

Saturday Morning, The Bronx

The next morning, thoughts of that mysterious fourth sketch still looped in his head. It was Saturday and the idle time multiplied his second thoughts about the strange opportunity that had come his way. And those second thoughts brought him straight to Father Nathan's doorstep.

Nathan was the gem of the family, just as his church, Mount Carmel, was the gem of the Bronx. It had stood as a symbol of immigrant pride for over a hundred years, though these days, the immigrants were mostly Central Americans, Albanians, and students. Zoro strolled up the front steps, past the emerald-colored marble columns flanking the doors. Inside, a gentle light dribbled through the stained glass, giving the inside of the church a welcoming glow. That warm glow made Zoro wonder how such beauty could have abandoned him so coldly during the days when he had needed it most.

Outside, the rain that had earlier been threatening to fall had peeled back into sunshine, but the wind was still blowing. Inside the drafty church, that wind set the chandeliers in motion, and their shadows flickered as they lengthened and shortened along the terrazzo floor. As

Zoro stood at the back of the church under the swinging lights and the shifting shadows, suddenly a door at the front of the church flew open and the silence was pierced by a loud voice. "Well, I'll be!" It was Nathan.

Zoro's view of Nathan was idyllic: the perfect son, the perfect man. Zoro knew he had done many foolish things in his life, but he never considered himself a fool. Still, he always came up short in comparison to Nathan—and it didn't seem to matter who was doing the comparing. The soft light from the stained glass played on his face as Nathan approached his younger brother, but Nathan's voice and expression were plain and direct.

"What are you doing here, Zoro?"

Zoro gave Nathan what he hoped was a convincing grin. "Can't I visit my brother the priest without all this suspicion?"

"How long has it been, Zoro? I've been a priest here, what, ten years? Aside from Gina dragging you here for Christmas and Easter, you haven't set foot in this church for at least that long."

"Well, don't worry, Nate, I can't stay long."

Nathan pulled his brows tight. "Out of the blue you show up here, and then say you can't stay. Is that the best you got?" Nathan turned to walk away.

"No," Zoro pleaded. "No, wait, I need—"

"What's going on, Zoro? Are you in some sort of trouble?"

"No, why would you say that?"

"When else have you ever come to me?"

"Oh, for Pete's sake, Nate, I only need an answer."

Nathan swung around. His jowled cheeks were red, probably from too much sacramental wine. He gave Zoro a big grin. "Answer, huh? Well, I guess I'm your best shot. With your sins, the seminary wouldn't give you the time of day."

"Very funny, Nate," Zoro smiled, hoping his smile wasn't as thin as it felt. "Listen, you're the one I can always trust, no questions asked—"

"Is it about your new job?" Nathan interrupted. "Ma already told me about it."

"Son of a bitch, does this family tell everything it knows?" Zoro flopped into the first pew, exasperated by his mother's meddling. He slipped his fingers between his shirt buttons and stared at Nathan. He felt a bone-numbing headache start at the top of his head. "It's about Max," Zoro said, rubbing his temples. "He's my new boss."

"I know who Max is."

"He says he's found a secret that could change my life—the world, even. I'm afraid I can't tell you more than that, Nate. But I need your opinion."

Nathan grew silent. After staring at Zoro for what seemed like forever, he held out his heavy hand. "Zoro, I've heard a lot of promises, a lot of rumors, but in the end," Nathan hesitated, "I think you know what I'm going to say."

"No way to substantiate a rumor?" Zoro asked, smiling childishly.

Nathan shrugged.

"Far-fetched, right?" Zoro asked.

"Yup," Nathan replied. "Look, Zoro, I know you and I haven't often seen eye to eye. But I'd really like to help you. I know things are tough for you right now."

He told Zoro he ought to come back to church, get his life in order. After a while, Zoro stopped paying attention; it was clear Nathan wasn't going to give him any answers, and his headache was getting worse.

"Come on back to my place, Zoro, rest for a while. Let me help you," Nathan finished.

"No thanks, Nathan," Zoro finally said. Nathan wasn't going to be any help, and knowing that was clarifying for Zoro, in a way—a strange sort of relief.

Nathan reached out to lay a hand on his brother's shoulder.

Zoro took a deep breath filled with the thick smell of paraffin wax and incense. "So," Zoro looked straight past Nathan, "Andrea Canossa's sketches . . . fairy tales, right?"

Nathan yanked his hand off Zoro's shoulder like it was hot. He stared at Zoro, wide-eyed. "Outside! Quickly, Zoro."

"What's going on, Nate?"

"Shh! Not another word in here." Nathan quickly looked around. He hurried Zoro into the courtyard and crowded him onto a bench in the far corner, staring suspiciously over his shoulder. "Tell me exactly what Max said about this, Zoro, every single word. You know you can trust me."

"I'm not sure I want to get you involved."

Nathan's burly hand grabbed Zoro by the wrist. "If you're on a road straight to damnation, I need to know. Start from the beginning," he said.

Zoro peeled Nathan's hand off his arm and put some space between them on the bench. He held his breath for a second, wondering where to start. "Max says the fourth sketch leads to something called the True Name of God. Did you know there's a secret name, Nathan?"

"Just go on, Zoro, quickly." Again Nathan gripped his wrist so hard he thought it might break.

"Shit, Nathan!" Zoro pulled his wrist free and winced, flexing his wrist. "Give me a chance. Max says he's found three of the sketches, and get this: Dad found the fourth."

Nathan leaned against the courtyard wall, a stricken expression on his face. "Zoro," Nathan whispered, "you mustn't breathe a word of this to anyone."

"What's all this got to do with Dad, Nathan?"

"Forget Dad. Forget the sketches. You understand me? Not a word to anyone, Zoro!"

"Nathan, you're scaring me. I wasn't even sure these sketches were real."

"Oh, they're real enough, Zoro, but you can't do this! You don't know what you're getting into."

"Stop with the scary talk!" Zoro shouted. "Get to the point."

"Keep your voice down." Nathan looked worried.

"What are they, Nathan?"

"I can't tell you . . . the sketches are nothing . . . I mean . . . if they found out . . ." Nathan glanced over his shoulder again.

"Nothing! What kind of answer is that? And who are 'they'?"

Nathan shook his head as he looked at Zoro. "You don't understand, Zoro. You don't realize what would happen if this got out." Nathan was taking shallow, panicked breaths.

Geez, what's going on here? "Let's try and stay calm, already!"

"I told you to keep your voice down!" Nathan's eyes glazed with fear.

Zoro stared into his older brother's frightened face, and then took a few seconds to think. "Nathan, do you realize what it feels like to always lose? Let me tell you: it feels like crap. If this is real, Nathan—what Max is talking about—this could be my chance."

"No, let it go, Zoro! This isn't anything you should be involved in. And besides, there's no real power in the Name, other than what people want to believe."

"So what's the problem?" Zoro asked, pivoting toward Nathan. "If it's no big deal, why do you care so much?"

"The problem is," Nathan looked at Zoro with a stare that shot right through him, "people *do* believe. And they're the kind of people you don't want to be mixed up with."

"But it could be real. You said so yourself."

"Zoro, please. This could get ugly real fast. I have an obligation to inform the Holy See and the Church." Nathan paused, looked away, and continued, more to himself than to Zoro. "And once the Church knows, there's no guarantee that the others won't find out . . ." He turned back to Zoro. "Please, Zoro. You don't know what you're getting into. I can't sit on this for you, but I'll give you some time . . . a day. Zoro, please don't get involved in this."

Zoro stared at his brother a few seconds, and then shrugged. "It won't do any good, Nathan. My mind's pretty much made up. You can't make me change it. And don't go running to Ma, either. You know the way she is." Zoro got up to leave.

Nathan moved to block his path. "This isn't confession, Zoro. I can tell everything you've said."

"I swear, Nathan, if you tell Ma, I'll kill you." Zoro pushed past Nathan to cross the courtyard and headed for the iron gate.

"Zoro, stay clear of this, I'm warning you!" Nathan yelled after him.

"Life's too short to live the same day twice," Zoro said over his shoulder as he disappeared out the gate.

* * *

Nathan groaned. He walked quietly to the rectory and picked up a phone. He clutched the phone to his chest for a minute, then swallowed hard and dialed.

"Hello? Yes, it's Father Nathan from Mount Carmel for Conrad Mason. Please tell him it's a matter of great urgency."

A hard voice crackled over the receiver. Nathan took a deep breath and finally spoke. "I'm sorry to disturb you, Mr. Mason, but it's about Zoro . . . Yes, well . . . I only called because you'd asked to know if Max ever came around . . . I see . . . I wasn't aware you knew already . . .

"I was hoping you could talk him out of this foolishness . . . Well, I agree he's troubled, but not that troubled . . .

"I wish I knew what to say . . . Yes I agree a little religion would do him good . . . So you'll look into it? Thank you, Mr. Mason, I appreciate it. You've always been good to us."

CHAPTER 30

After leaving Nathan, Zoro felt drawn to his apartment. Zoro turned off the street and into a dark, dim, alleyway. The gray sky barely had room to spill between the dirty brick tenements. The smell of garbage was overpowering, and the crisscross of rusty fire escapes made Zoro think of prison bars. The alleyway was a dead end; a narrow crevasse between the last two buildings was the only exit to Arthur Avenue. Zoro could just squeeze through.

Stepping out onto Arthur Avenue, Zoro stared up at the windows of his apartment, and without warning a figure flashed past his living room window. He knew Gina wasn't home at this time on a Saturday. *What the hell?* He dashed across the street and flung open the stairway door.

A fist crashed into his face. The blow staggered Zoro, hurling him back onto the sidewalk. Through the red haze of pain, he was vaguely aware of his attacker leaping over his crumpled form and dashing away to a waiting car.

Instinctively Zoro rose to his feet, but faltered, stunned by the savage blow. Still, he stared after the attacker, and as the man reached for the handle of the vehicle, Zoro saw a V-shaped tattoo on his right hand.

"Goddamn it," he yelled as the car sped away. Zoro had never been sucker-punched before. "Jesus," he said. "This is too goddamned much."

He got to his feet, flung open the front door of the apartment building, and bolted up the stairs two by two. He made a sharp turn at the first landing and raced up the narrow corridor to his apartment.

The front door was partially open. Zoro yanked it open and then froze, staring down the hallway into the living room.

The entire apartment was a mess. Everything was tossed out of place: drawers dumped on the floor; clothes torn from the closet. *This is sad*, he thought. *For a guy who's got so little to get robbed . . . it's just sad.*

Since the intruder had driven off, Zoro was pretty sure there was no one else here now. He walked into the living room and looked around him, and on a side table near the bedroom door—one of the few pieces of furniture in its rightful place—he saw the latest issue of Gina's favorite magazine. It had a pink marble mansion on the cover. She'd circled the mansion twice, in pink highlighter, and it made him smile.

He thought about Gina, miles away at work, unaware of this calamity. That's how the whole world seemed to be: unaware. Zoro walked into the small kitchen, and stared at the open refrigerator, the food tossed onto the floor, the canned goods, dishes, and silverware that now littered the countertops.

As he looked around the dingy apartment, the scene appeared lifeless and frozen in time, like a preview of the extinction of his life. Zoro remembered how at night, the streetlights outside barely leaked through the windows. Even though it was still morning, as he stood in the wrecked apartment, Zoro felt swallowed by gloom.

Suddenly, he heard the clink of glass, coming from his front hallway. His heart raced and he searched frantically for a weapon; all he could find was an umbrella.

He tiptoed across the floor, moving silently toward the hallway. He pressed against the living room wall, trying to make himself invisible. As he listened, he again heard the quiet clink of glass.

Zoro gripped the umbrella. Taking a deep breath, he rushed around the corner and lunged at the figure huddled over a small table in his hallway.

Zoro threw the man against the wall, smashing the front of his head.

The man dropped to one knee and cried out. Zoro drew back the umbrella to strike, and that was when he recognized him.

"Gideon?" Zoro said. "What the hell! Are you crazy?" The detective flopped sideways, holding his head.

"I could've killed you," Zoro said sternly.

Gideon peered up at Zoro, still holding his head, and a grin creased his face. "How? Poke me to death with an umbrella?"

Zoro tossed the umbrella aside and reached down to help Gideon stand.

"I'm okay," Gideon said. "No need to ask."

"Why are you here, Gideon? How did you even get here so quickly?"

"Residents reported a break-in. Imagine my surprise when I heard your name over the radio." He scanned Zoro's face. "It seems like you might have gotten a look at our burglar. Looks like you took a pretty good shot, yourself. Your lip's busted, and your nose is bleeding."

"I'm okay."

"Can you describe your attacker?"

"I didn't see him very well," Zoro said.

"Let's go take a look around." Gideon and Zoro walked back into the living room.

"Anything missing?" Gideon asked.

"How the hell should I know? The place is a mess."

"Come on, you're a bright guy. Trust your instincts."

"Well, come to think of it, there was one thing that struck me as out of place."

"Yeah, what is it?"

"You're here," Zoro said in a deadpan voice. "Is that what you're looking for?"

Gideon shot a hard look at Zoro. "Okay, smart ass. Obviously you know more than you're saying. Sorry I tried to help. Thank you for your time. But I'm telling you, Zoro, you haven't seen the last of me." Gideon looked a final time around the wrecked apartment, then left.

Zoro steadied the shock of his reaction and disbelief and starting cleaning up the apartment. It would save Gina from worrying, he thought.

But the deeper into the task he got, the more he began to worry. As far as he could tell, nothing was taken . . . so what was the motive for the break-in?

Maybe I got here soon enough to keep that bastard from stealing anything, he thought. The idea gave him a twinge of enjoyment, and he smiled, gloating over his victory. "Come on . . . is that all you got?" he yelled at the sky.

Then it struck him: Nathan had been worried for him, and now he was wondering if he ought to worry, too. Was this more than a simple robbery attempt? Visions of Carmela's trashed apartment rose in his mind.

All this started after I met Max, he thought, slumping onto the sofa. Things really were strange, and he wondered if he ought to listen to Nathan and get as far from Max as he could.

And then he thought, *When you hit rock bottom, you've got nowhere to go but up. I've taken every piece of crap life has thrown at me, and I'm still here.*

"Yeah! I'm still here!" Zoro shouted. Then he sat quietly, listening to a small clock on the wall tapping out the seconds. In the street, a blasting truck horn pierced the stillness. Zoro was startled and suddenly felt confined. He got up from the couch, walked pensively down the hallway to the narrow corridor, closing the apartment door behind him. He exited the building onto the street.

He crossed the street, squeezed through the crevasse between the buildings, and entered the dark alleyway. On the other end of the alley he stopped and peered into the street; there was no break in the faceless traffic. He started down the sidewalk, headed toward Fordham Road. From there it would be just a short D train ride to Hank's Auto Body Shop. His face ached where the burglar had punched him, adding to the discomfort of the headache that had started when he was in the church talking to Nathan.

The limo ought to be detailed by now, he thought, and he hoped that the scuff mark Gina had put on the trunk had been fixed as easily as Hank had assured him it would. He was just lucky Max hadn't noticed it . . . at least, he hadn't said anything.

Zoro took stock of his life as he walked. He was forty-five, a simple limo driver whose life was floundering in the wake of his stagnation. He wasn't a bad man. In fact, dogs liked him. And he had physical courage; hell, he had the scars to prove it. But the boy for whom a bright future was once foretold now had to content himself with false bravado and self-deception.

Zoro had to admit that he had become a skeptic, a man who carefully avoided inflicting any feelings on himself. At home—when he was still living there—he took care not to get in Gina's way and watched her change over the years, though she had never seen a change in him. Now he was wondering what excuse could explain a loser like him?

As Zoro walked he noticed again how his neighborhood had changed. The once-busy stores now held little more than abandoned dreams; there were vacant lots where parks once stood. Zoro kept wondering as he looked why things were looking so different to him these days.

He stepped into the alley outside Hank's Auto Body Shop when he noticed a thin man slip into the shadows behind the garage. He continued walking toward the door to Hank's place. And then, from inside the shop, he heard the crunch of glass.

He tore open the door just in time to see someone disappearing out of Hank's broken back door . . . and then he spotted the limo. Immediately, his heart sank. The driver's-side window of the limo had a spider-webbed hole punched in it. It looked like it had taken several blows from a pickaxe to penetrate the reinforced glass.

"Son of a bitch!" Zoro yelled, spinning back toward the alley, but the man was gone.

Then he spotted Hank, knocked out cold on the floor.

CHAPTER 31

Sunday Afternoon, The Bronx

Zoro groaned and rolled over on the couch. He groggily eyed the littered coffee table for any sign of some pain-relieving substance other than the bottle of cheap bourbon that was now half empty. A late-afternoon sunbeam slanted through one of Johnny's dingy windows and lanced him in the eye, ratcheting his headache up a couple of notches and summoning another groan. Zoro decided he was going to have to get up off the couch in order to find any Advil. *Wonder where the hell Johnny keeps his medicine? Ah, the hell with it. I'll just lie here and die.*

The smashed window on the limo yesterday had been the tipping point. Zoro had come back to Johnny's place, and the only thought on his mind was to stop thinking—at least for a while. The bourbon had done the trick for a few hours, but now he was taking stock of the aftermath.

His pants and underwear were twisted together along with his socks, trailing across the living room floor tracing the path by which he'd crawled out of them. A sweet grain-alcohol smell, the kind you only get with a cheap distillation, filled the room. An empty bottle of unlabeled bourbon, the kind of back-alley contraband Johnny kept around, lay in the open, just like Zoro's dignity. He shifted his balance and rolled himself back onto the sofa. A minute later he passed out.

* * *

Zoro found himself suddenly inhaling but not breathing out. *For Christ's sake,* he thought, *exhale.* He knew what came next.

Zoro hadn't set foot in his nightmare for a few days, but it hadn't changed much, though each time it felt brand new and just as frightening. It began, as it always had, with the morning of Joey's funeral. Zoro's memory was washed out and vague, but here, inside the nightmare, everything was crystal-clear—razor-sharp . . .

The turnout had been disappointingly small. Zoro stood on one side of his mother and Isaac on the other. Nathan was in the background. Father Hartley, who had baptized the boys, spoke tenderly of Joey at his funeral.

There was little comfort in the words, and Zoro stared at the casket, his heart aching so much he couldn't cry. He wanted to reach in and pull Joey back, hold him close in his arms, and never let him go. He thought of the many times he'd seen someone weep, overwhelmed by loss, by unrelenting emptiness. But nothing could prepare Zoro for what he felt. Choking on his tearless despair, Zoro felt his legs become limp. He reached for Carmela's hand to steady himself, and she pulled away, as if his hand were hot, or covered with filth.

Suddenly, Zoro was encased in flames, surrounded by the searing crackles of burning wood. He could see the priest talking, but not a sound passed from his mouth. Slowly every grieving loved one and every despairing friend began to fade. Zoro stood alone in the consuming flames and watched helplessly as the casket broke free and dived into the ground. The skies began to curdle and darken, as the raging walls closed in on Zoro.

Then it was night. Zoro turned around to find himself at home, the house and garden of his youth. The flames were still coming, so he ran toward the house, trying to outrun the fire. But the faster he ran, the farther away the house seemed. When he finally reached the porch, he saw the steps had melted and swallowed his shoes.

The house began to groan loudly and shift. Its wooden walls glowed against the darkness as flames licked their way up the siding. The flames twisted like serpentine devil tongues, around every opening, every window. Inside, a voice, barely a whisper, called out, "Zoro . . . help me."

"Joey!" Zoro cried, as he threw himself through the front window without a second's hesitation. And as he clawed his way blindly through the oven of darkness, smoke clogged his lungs. Panicked, he called again, "Joey!" His foot broke through the burned-out floor, and Zoro stumbled and fell to his knees. He crawled forward, sobbing, but there was no rescue, no relief, only blackness and killing heat.

Suddenly blinded by tears, he felt himself scooped up and dropped in the middle of a circle of silhouettes. Carmela's and Nathan's faces danced violently about him. And there was no bubble-gum flavored, lemon-scented compassion anywhere to be seen.

"You killed Joey!" The voices screeched.

But as sadness consumed him, the pace of his nightmare began to shift. He found himself in the Vatican archive. And there was Michelangelo, laughing as a circle of symbols danced through the air to the beat of music with a bohemian flair. Zoro opened his mouth, as Carmela's and Nathan's faces reappeared, but he couldn't speak. He held out his hand and suddenly found himself drawn from the circle of despair and blame. He closed his eyes as he spun wildly. He heard a voice and opened his eyes. There was Isaac who leaned forward and laid a hand on him. The hand was warm, caressing . . . and Zoro woke, drenched in sweat.

Zoro wrapped a sheet around himself and stood up. He staggered to the bathroom, steadying himself against the wall. He turned on the shower and stepped inside, letting the cool water wash away the clammy sweat. As his drunkenness spiraled down the drain, Zoro suddenly became aware that an arm had poked through the shower curtain, offering up a cup of hot joe.

"Don't be late for work," Johnny said on his way out of the bathroom.

Damn, Zoro thought, gingerly sipping the hot coffee, *is it already Monday morning?*

CHAPTER 32

Monday Morning, Manhattan

A pumpkin-orange sun shone past the spires of Manhattan as Zoro punched in the security code for Max's condo. The gate swung open, admitting him to the circular drive in front of the building. Max stood outside the front door, waiting with his briefcase under his arm. Zoro saw him check his watch, and he resented the gesture. It was 11:13 a.m. *Thirteen—how unlucky*, he thought. Considering Zoro had gotten up at 6 a.m. with a hangover to take the limo to Ballistic Securities, a specialty glass shop, he figured Max ought to at least show some appreciation.

With the limo barely at rest, Max slipped into the back.

"Found my sketch yet?" He smiled.

"Very funny."

Zoro waited for Max to say something about the broken window, though Zoro had called to explain it. "An attempted burglary," he said. "My house was robbed, too . . . Bad neighborhood, I guess." Still, he expected Max might have mentioned how nicely the car had been repaired.

Instead, Max snapped open his briefcase and punched up some

high-pitched Indian music on the limo's MP3 player. It made Zoro's nerves scream. He was seriously hung over, emotionally wrung out, and with all the strangeness creeping back in, he brushed his hair from his forehead and frowned. It was all he could do not to lose it.

Without so much as looking at Zoro, Max pulled a small black journal from his briefcase. What the hell was Max doing? Finally Zoro decided to say something. "So . . . is this silent treatment because the window was broken?"

Max glanced at him in the mirror. "Of course not. I've just decided to record what I'm going to teach you, just in case."

Gripping his steering wheel tighter he worked up a little more courage. "Just in case what—I fail?" Zoro watched Max's every move in the rearview, waiting for a sign of anger, impatience. "If I wanted to, I could do this, you know. I'm not a joke."

Max smiled. "Look, Zoro, I'm an old man, so I write things down, in case. But if you're worried about losing your spot with me, don't be. You have to get over the idea that I'm not committed to you."

Max sat quietly, his eyes never leaving Zoro's face. He finally closed his briefcase. "I don't care how many windows you break, Zoro, I made a binding promise. It's you who's all grumpy this morning. What do you want, Zoro?"

"A normal life, I guess."

"That's a bit disturbing, coming from you," Max teased.

Zoro's nerves were worn down to little nubs, and his emotional fatigue won out. But at least Max's sense of humor made him feel a little less like he was being put out to pasture. "A contract! Yeah, that would make me feel better, Max. How about it? Health benefits, four weeks paid vacation at your summer home, I could go for that."

"Hold on a second, Zoro," Max snapped open his cell phone. "That's good news. Just a moment. Zoro, I've got the Cloister's clerk on the line.

"Go ahead; we've got you on speaker phone."

"Well," the clerk began, "I searched for hours, until I came across the original archive records for the donation from Princeton. It seems like you were right, Mr. Cisary, the original donation did pass through the Met first."

"Did you find anything unusual, as we discussed?" Max asked.

The clerk took the initiative. "By process of elimination I cross-referenced the items, such as the Civil War sabers and muskets delivered originally, against the current list of items in our inventory. One thing did strike me as unusual; one small part of the collection seems to have been donated to a private benefactor. It's described in the inventory as a small, black, leather-bound journal, and was donated to the Mason Foundation for the Arts over thirty years ago. Is that helpful?"

"Yes, yes it is, thank you." Max's eyebrows rose as he clicked off his phone. "Conrad, that slippery son of a gun."

"You think that journal led Conrad to the sketch, Max?"

Max didn't answer as Zoro turned onto Sixth Avenue. He liked to drive fast, and especially now, with his nerves all over the place, his foot got heavy, despite the Monday morning traffic.

"I'm not fond of the hospital," Max finally said.

Zoro shrugged, backing off the accelerator. "Look, I'm sorry. I was out of line, before," he finally said. "But does the journal help us or not?"

"No, Zoro. It might have led to the sketch thirty years ago, but Isaac's long since hidden it somewhere else." Max was quiet, contemplating. "This is wrong, Zoro," Max said.

"Speaking strictly for myself," Zoro said, "everything you've laid on me these past couple of days has been wrong. You've asked me to disown my life and step into some kind of dream—or nightmare, maybe, for all I know."

"You're right, Zoro, I made a huge mistake."

"Wha . . . what?"

"I owe you an apology."

"Just wait a damn minute, you're apologizing to me? I'm the one joking around about contracts and shit."

"You see, Zoro, I have a perspective on my life that allows me to see when I'm wrong. I asked you to become Isaac's mind, lead us through his life, and find clues to the sketch. It can't be done that way."

"Whoa, it's not like all bets are off. I can do this."

"Oh, I'm sure you can, but I can't make you Isaac's mind. The right thing to do is to show you how to reach the potential of yours."

"I gotta tell you; right now I'm questioning everything you say. Become Isaac, don't become Isaac. I don't know what to say to this."

Max sipped on a tonic water. He had this look on his face like he wasn't wrong, but damn it, he just had been. It was like being sixteen and living with Carmela. She'd make you turn left, and then say you should have turned right. Zoro didn't have to feign outrage; it was clear in his expression.

"There's only one way this is going to go down. This is about your mind, no one else's. We don't have time to screw around and make you Isaac; I need to tell you about the Third Q now, Zoro."

"You're going to have to prove something to me, Max, right now. I've played along with all your secrets; prove to me why I should believe you now, with this turn of events."

Max leaned forward, a look of desperation in his eyes. "Reach in your pocket, Zoro," he whispered.

"My pocket?" Zoro started hesitantly.

"Yes, do it now! But be careful."

The air in the limo suddenly seemed to be thinning. Zoro nodded and reached into his pocket. He fumbled past a few pennies, carefully running his fingers along the pocket's seam. "There's nothing here," he said.

"Then try again," Max said, "but be very careful."

Zoro's eyes wandered to the rearview mirror, coming to rest on Max. Max's eyes flickered nervously, and he nodded. Zoro felt around again, cautiously. Nothing.

Max sprang forward toward Zoro and screamed, "Boo!"

Zoro's arms flinched upward in a protective reflex, his hands leaving the steering wheel. The limo swerved and Zoro grabbed the wheel again, fighting the limo back into a straight line.

Max was laughing hysterically. "You can file comedy harassment charges later!"

Zoro was furious. "Don't ever do that again! You realize you were one second away from killing us both? What the hell were you thinking?"

Max struggled to stop laughing. "Ever heard of the suspension of disbelief?" he asked.

"No," Zoro grumbled.

"Point is," Max nodded, "for a few seconds, you believed there was something in your pocket. And even though you'll buy that with no proof whatsoever, you still question what I'm trying to tell you."

Zoro drove, chewing on a mixture of his irritation and Max's words. He hated to admit it, but the more he thought about it, the more sense it made. "Okay, fair enough," he replied. He leaned his head against the driver's side window, letting its cool surface take away some of the heat he felt beneath his scalp. He checked the side mirror.

"Then again," Max said, "what if you're right? What if my story is just a fairy tale? What will you do then? What's your plan?"

"I don't know . . . I'd like to own my own limo." He paused a moment, reflecting. "Melvyn Courtland once offered me his limo, but I couldn't manage the $5,000 deposit."

"So why not just give him the deposit?"

"I just said I don't have five big ones."

"Aha, and therein lies the rub."

"Yeah, so what? Maybe I'll just pull the money out of thin air." Zoro checked his side mirror again. Something kept drawing his eyes to the mirror . . .

"Now at least you're being spontaneous," Max replied.

Maybe there was an answer in what Max was saying, but Zoro couldn't make sense of it. He was losing patience again. "Can't you understand plain English? I . . . don't . . . have . . . the . . . money!"

"Hey, it's your dream," Max said. "Why not just find the money?"

Zoro was silent for a moment. "And how am I supposed to do that?"

Max began to laugh again; Zoro, already frustrated, turned even redder. "I'm serious!" Zoro shouted.

"That makes it even funnier," Max replied. "You need to start having a better attitude, Zoro."

"You don't understand. I can't get $5,000."

"But I do understand, Zoro. Let's try a different route, okay? You obviously love Gina. What if she were dying, had only one week to live, and you needed $5,000 to save her life. Could you raise the money then? Could you do anything to get it?"

"Who the hell would make up such a story?" Zoro couldn't figure out how he felt about what Max was saying. Part of him wanted to scream, "Why would you say that?" But he knew why; it was about him, about his way of thinking. But what was it Max was getting at?

"I'm surprised at you, Zoro."

"Surprised at me?"

"You're supposed to be a tough guy." Max grinned. "Everyone thinks so. Isn't that right?"

"Why are you treating me like this?" Zoro muttered. "Nothing but riddles . . ."

"Listen," Max replied, "if you're too scared to raise the money—"

"Who says I'm scared?"

"Okay, then I've got it," Max said. "You're too cheap. Are you too cheap to save your own wife, Zoro?"

"You can be such a jackass!" Zoro said. "Why are you saying this crap? I'm no slouch when it comes to protecting my family!"

Max held up his hand in mock surrender. "For the record, Zoro, I'm not serious," Max laughed. "For crying out loud, I'm trying to make a point. My question is simple: if you needed to save your wife, could you raise the money—yes or no?"

"Yeah . . . of course."

"Are you sure?"

"I'm sure," Zoro said. "I don't treat that sort of thing lightly."

"So why treat your dreams lightly?" Max asked.

Zoro was still fuming. "For the record," he said, "Gina is a hell of a lot more important than any dream."

"You'd think that, wouldn't you," Max replied. "And I agree. So if she needed a $100,000 operation, you could pay?"

"Hell no! Geez, Max, this is crazy!"

Max turned down the volume of his music. *Thank God,* Zoro thought. *He's talking all this smack; at least I don't have to listen to that screechy crap at the same time.*

"Zoro, all these years you've been tortured by your dreams of being rich. And now you realize that maybe being rich is important, in ways you haven't considered, right? In your dreams you claim what's rightfully yours, don't you? But you also carry the people who depend on you."

"If you say so, I'm sure it's true."

"The difference between you and me, Zoro, is that you thrive on being in pain, and I thrive on everything else. Hey, are you hungry?"

Zoro leaned back; his eyes drifted toward Max, reflected in the mirror. Maybe it was time to lighten the atmosphere. "You trying to bribe me into a better mood with lunch? 'Cause it just so happens, that's only going to work a couple hundred times."

Max chuckled.

Zoro studied him in the mirror. "So I gotta tell you, Max, after everything that's been happening . . . sometimes it still seems a little unreal, all this. You know, meeting you, hearing about the sketches, the Name, all that stuff." A few seconds later, Zoro added, "Like, I'm still trying to figure out why you're here, right now, with me."

Max leaned forward. "You want to know the real reason?"

"I'm not sure. Is this another trick question?" It was hard not to take Max's smile as condescending.

"It's no trick," Max said. "I'm here, Zoro, because you created me. And whoever I am, whoever we will be together, it's up to you. You learn the Third Q, find the sketch, and I make you rich, all that, it's your creation."

Max closed the glass limo divider as he snapped open his cell phone. The last thing Zoro heard before the glass muffled Max's voice was "What do the tests show?"

The phone call reminded Zoro to check his messages. He'd left a bunch for Gina, with no reply. Her number on the screen glared at him, and he slid his thumb over to speed dial.

"Gina?"

"What the hell do you want?" Her voice was hard. She clearly wasn't over the argument.

"I just wanted to make sure you're okay, after the break-in."

"I'm fine! And stop stalking the apartment, Zoro! You hear me?"

"Sorry," he heard the receiver drop into the phone cradle.

"Shit!" Zoro's foot flew to the brake pedal. "Damn taxi!" A yellow cab had darted out from a side street. The last thing Zoro needed was a wreck and another run-in with the cops. He braked the limo, his cheeks flushed with the sudden rush of adrenaline.

That's when he saw the brown sedan, starting off big in his side mirror, then quickly shrinking as it braked hastily. Zoro realized the car had been tailing them almost since they left Max's condo. His sudden braking for the taxi had caught the other driver off guard.

Zoro pulled onto a side street a few seconds later and rolled to a stop at a curbside corner store. He got out of the limo and went inside, carefully watching to see if the brown sedan passed or if anyone approached the limo. When he had satisfied himself that they'd lost the tail, he returned to the limo.

"I guess they realized we made them," he told Max. "I didn't see anything." Max nodded.

As they drove on, Zoro continued to study Max in the mirror.

For some reason, Zoro remembered the time Carmela had hauled him down to the church, intent on having him become an altar boy. He was ten years old, he was wearing Nathan's hand-me-down black suit, and his hair was as slick as the icing on a cake. He remembered standing in front of the priest, with Carmela avidly negotiating on his behalf to get him on a crowded roster of altar boys. Twisting his arm painfully, she pushed him toward the priest. "You'd make a fine altar boy, Zoro," she said in a soft, low voice.

"Yes, Mama," he said in a flat, apathetic voice, wishing he were any-where else.

"So," Father Panettone said, "you want to be our newest altar boy?"

"No, sir," Zoro answered. You weren't supposed to lie to a priest, right?

Carmela spun toward him and hissed in his ear. "What would Mama do?"

But the damage had been done. "Surely you understand, Mrs. Mon-tana," Father Panettone said. "If the boy's heart isn't in it . . . maybe in another year or two?"

As she dragged him from Mount Carmel, Mama's lukewarm, false gentility was gone, replaced by icy rage. "You humiliated your mother, Zoro, in front of Father Panettone. I hope you're satisfied." Not another word was uttered. But the sick sin of embarrassing Carmela wasn't soon forgotten.

And now, the same burning guilt and insecurity that Carmela had wrapped him in echoed in his mind. *What would Mama do?* he thought, knowing nothing short of a blood commitment to Max's new plan would do.

Zoro realized that Max was watching him, as if he knew, somehow.

"Zoro, we're going to find your new life," Max said. "I can't under-stand how you can even think about not changing your life, when your life is such a bloody mess."

"I want to believe, Max, but . . . I just feel like you're browbeating me into something I don't understand instead of just giving me what I really need."

"What do you really need?" Max leaned to one side, forcing Zoro's eyes to follow him in the rearview mirror.

"Money," Zoro replied.

"Ah money, Zoro. Makes your life bigger, you know. You sure that's all you want? Because I would never want just that."

"Maybe you wouldn't," Zoro said. "But you got it all, Max! If it's no big deal to you, why not just give me some, and we'll call it even?"

Max shook his head, smiling. "I can't just give you money, Zoro; it would go against the spirit of what I'm teaching. And besides, I've always found wisdom and happiness are as important as money . . . unless of course you want to buy a sandwich. In which case you really need the cash."

"I don't like being laughed at, Max. And it's hard for me to tell when you're joking around and when you're serious."

Max shrugged. "Okay, Zoro. It's like this: money alone is not the answer—trust me on this. And that, incidentally, is why Conrad will never find the sketch."

Zoro knitted his face together in concentration, but he couldn't figure out exactly what Max was trying to say.

"All I ask, Zoro, is that for now, when the silence sets in—and it always does—that the voice you hear in your head should be mine and no one else's."

Zoro heaved a sigh and shook his head. *My brain feels numb—as usual, when I've been around this guy for a while.* "So . . . we gonna have lunch, or spend the whole day yapping?"

"Sure thing," Max said. "Let's get something to eat."

A second later Max's phone rang. Checking the caller ID, Max said, "Zoro, I've got to go a few rounds with this guy. You pick whatever place you want; I'm buying."

"I know just the place," Zoro said.

Holly's . . .

CHAPTER 33

"Zoro!"

Arms went around his waist. Zoro grinned; he didn't need to turn around to know who the arms belonged to.

"Hey, Holly," he said, smiling. He spun around, took one look, and began laughing. "You look ridiculous!"

She was dressed in what appeared to be white hospital scrubs. Zoro gave the outfit an all-over look. "What, Armani? Calvin Klein?"

Holly frowned at him, standing with one hand on her hip. Then she stuck her tongue out. He laughed.

They strolled toward the hot dog stand, a boxy stainless steel cart with two steam compartments and a grill on one end. The surface was scratched, long since oxidized from gleaming silver to dull gray. The flat countertop was littered with crumbs, dabs of mustard, and coffee stains.

"Looks like you already had a pretty good lunch run," Zoro said.

"It just got better when you and your rich boss showed up," Holly said, nodding toward the limo. "And the Mr. Clean outfit was the manager's idea, not mine."

"I figured," Zoro said, starting around toward Holly.

"Customers stay on the other side," Holly barked, pulling a miniature pitchfork from a stack of wieners and whirling it in Zoro's face.

Zoro grinned lopsidedly and held up his hands in surrender.

"Okay, okay. Your new uniform looks pretty." He snickered, "A little Moby Dick, but pretty. Gimme the usual times two."

Holly reached for a Kaiser roll and speared a wiener with her trident. "So, what's up? Tell me about your new boss."

Zoro looked at the limo's dark-tinted windows. Max was still inside, wrangling with whomever had called him while they were driving. "Yeah, my new boss. He's one hilarious guy, all right."

Holly gave him a careful look as she smeared mustard on the sausage. "What's going on, Zoro? Is he okay? I mean, from the looks of that ride . . . You're not mixed up in anything, are you, Zoro?"

The wind swirled under the cart's red-and-white striped canopy, scattering dry leaves along the sidewalk. Zoro watched the leaves for a few seconds, then leaned a little closer and said, "I can trust you, right, Holly?"

Her eyes widened. She got very still.

"Maybe I shouldn't be telling you this," Zoro whispered, "but he's got a crazy secret that can make me rich."

Holly kept staring at Zoro.

"What?" he asked, finally.

"Zoro, are you sure? I mean, you don't know anything about him. And he's talking crazy secrets. Maybe he's just crazy?"

Zoro sighed and looked away.

"Maybe, Zoro," she paused to wipe down the cart top, smearing the dribbles of condiments into a Rorschach blotch, "it's not the best idea that you're telling me this."

"Come on, Holly! We're friends; I trust you."

"I like you, too, but you need to be more careful." She wrapped Zoro's sausage and roll in a napkin and handed it to him.

Zoro gave her a twenty and took a bite out of the sausage. "Not everything's a conspiracy, Holly," he said, chewing noisily.

"I'm not so sure," Holly muttered, filling a styrofoam cup with coffee and sliding it across the counter to Zoro. "So what're you gonna do?"

Zoro shrugged. "Don't know yet."

"What does Gina say?"

Zoro's eyes shifted. Holly broke into a fluorescent smile. "Oh, my God . . . she doesn't know?"

Zoro wouldn't look at Holly. "Hell, she kicked me out," he said. "Why should I tell her anything?" And yet, Zoro knew that at some point he'd have to square things with his wife, whether they were living in the same space at the moment or not.

The thing was, Gina was the kind of girl you saw once and wrote a song about. A couple of rounds with Gina could have a guy wondering if he was still alive—and when her temper kicked in, he might not be. He knew she'd kick his ass if she knew even half of what he was holding out on her.

"Look, Gina's not feeling well, so I'd appreciate it if you didn't say anything, Holly."

Holly laughed as she wrapped another hot dog in a napkin. "Yeah, right. And if somebody does tell her, you'll be the one who's not feeling so well, right, Zoro? I'm surprised she hasn't had a nervous breakdown, living with you."

Zoro rolled his eyes and gave a grudging grin, though deep down he knew Holly wasn't kidding. He could only imagine the confrontation with Gina. *Hey, Honey, I'm heading out to hunt for a secret name—don't wait up.* And then, kaboom! Nuclear Gina!

Zoro finished his food and drained the last of the coffee from the cup. He crumpled the mustard-stained napkin inside the cup and tossed both into the garbage can standing beside Holly's cart. "I'll see you around, Holly. Thanks, it was good."

"Hey, Zoro. Aren't you forgetting something?"

He turned around. She was holding out a sack. "Your boss's food?"

Holly smiled at Zoro. Her eyes made him stop. *Damn, Holly. If I was a couple years younger and a whole lot less married to Gina . . .* And then he shook it off. "Take it easy," he said, taking the bag and turning to go.

"Think about what I told you, Zoro," she called after him. "You need to be more careful." She whirled her finger through the air making the crazy sign and crossing her eyes.

"Thanks, I can take care of myself," he laughed over his shoulder.

Zoro had mixed emotions as he got behind the wheel. Were all the voices buzzing in his head—with Holly's now added to the mix—just trying to warn him, keep him safe?

He reached over the seat to hand Max his hot dog. "You won't regret it, Max. Holly makes the best hot dogs in New York," he said.

"Have you been friends with Holly a long time?" Max asked.

"About a year, I guess. She's all right." Zoro started the car.

"She said I'm crazy, didn't she?"

Max was staring at him in the mirror with an expression that hinted he already knew the answer. Zoro looked away guiltily. "Max, she didn't mean . . . I'm sorry."

"Save it, Zoro; what's said is said. Apologies don't change outcomes."

CHAPTER 34

Holly watched Zoro drive away. Then she moved around to the front of her cart to start scrubbing it down, since the noon rush seemed to be tapering off. She'd been working for a few minutes when a car rolled to a stop behind her. She was waiting for the driver to roll down his window and tell her what he wanted, but instead a horn blasted in her ear.

Asshole! she thought, and flipped the driver off without turning around.

The next instant, the driver's door flew open and banged into her, knocking her to the pavement. A heavy arm circled her waist and began dragging her backward, toward the car. Her attacker shoved her through the door; she struck her head hard against the door frame. She slumped across the passenger seat and onto the floorboard, dazed by the blow, and heard the sound of squealing tires. She tried to shake the fog out of her pounding head, to grab the door handle and dive out of the car before it got up to speed. And then she smelled it: the odor of a blood culture in agar.

"What the hell do you want?" she asked.

*   *   *

Zoro drove north, heading for the Rockefeller Preserve according to Max's instructions, given around a mouthful of hot dog. It was early afternoon, so Max had suggested the slow route, straight through Manhattan. Zoro soon found the limo squeezed in between two delivery vans, blindly weaving across the lanes. Being lighter, the limo had more pickup. And when it came to driving skills, Zoro knew those sweat-soiled truck jockeys couldn't compare to him.

He saw an opening and shot from between the vans, the limo's engine roaring. In a few seconds, the limo was cruising along easily, relatively free of surrounding traffic. He checked the mirror to see if his sudden move had startled Max, but the older man was sitting as if he were at home in an easy chair.

Zoro watched Max, who was gazing about at the passing cityscape like someone who'd never seen it before. That was something Zoro had started to notice about Max: it seemed that no matter what was going on, Max was always tuned in, always totally aware. Zoro guessed that made sense, given all Max's talk about the importance of the mind—or minds . . . whatever. In fact, Max was one of the most focused people Zoro had ever been around.

Actually, it seemed no matter what Zoro thought or did, Max's resolve was luminously clear. "You know, Max, I don't get you," he said, finally.

"How so, Zoro?"

"Holly insults you, and you just . . . let it go. You forgive."

"Not to worry, Zoro, everything is fine. And I know I keep asking, but are you ready to try this a different way?"

* * *

The first time Holly ever saw Alton, he seemed pretty ordinary. But the more you looked at him, the more it wasn't right. His boxy face barely moved when he spoke. It was as if he was built of little bits of faded newspaper.

He looked across at Holly now as he drove, and a weasel grin smeared across his lips. His grin was narrow; it couldn't get past the stiff lines on his brittle face.

"We need to talk," he said, thumbing the electric door locks.

"I was going to call you."

"Really? I had to find out from Conrad that Zoro has made contact with Max. Is that really what I've been paying you for, Holly?"

"Look, I only just found out."

"Let's assume you're telling the truth—"

"I'm not lying! Stop and let me out." Holly leaned forward, scrambling for the door handle. Alton leaned across and aimed a backhanded blow that connected with her jaw and bounced her head off the passenger-side window. Dark flashes exploded in front of her eyes. She felt his hand gripping her windpipe.

"Just give me a chance to explain," she gasped.

His grip relaxed slightly—very slightly. "I'm listening," he said, gunning the brown sedan down the road and driving with one hand while he kept her in a chokehold with the other.

"You can do anything you want to me," she said, "but I just don't think Zoro's someone you have to worry about. Why don't you stay away from him?"

He let go of her throat, but only to cuff her across the face with the back of his hand. Then he started choking her again. She ran her hand under the seat edge, trying to find something, anything she could hit him with.

They were weaving through midtown traffic, but the glass was tinted and Holly was sure no one could see or hear her. She struggled to breathe.

"There's nothing I can do, Alton," she gasped.

His voice turned angrier, "Don't be too hasty, Holly. There's always something you can do."

*   *   *

"For the record I don't think you're crazy, Max, but I'm still not really sure what I'm getting myself into," Zoro said.

"I think you don't need to worry about it so much," Max said. "I'd say if you're willing to go along with me, do whatever needs doing, I think that's where you need to begin."

"I have no idea where to begin," Zoro replied. "I just think maybe there's an easier way for me. I mean, first you try and cram me into Isaac's head, and now that I'm part way in you pull me out."

"True." Max realized that wasn't fair. So he'd specifically arranged a demonstration at the institute. The way he figured it, Zoro needed to get a handle on his mind as quick as possible.

Zoro clamped his fists on the steering wheel, his middle fingernails digging into the flesh of his palms. He was afraid to say what he was thinking, but he knew it wouldn't get any easier. "What, if I gave you $5,000 instead of using it to buy a limo?" he asked, thinking of Johnny's Savings and Loan. "Maybe you could just, like, show me how to get rich without all the nonsense. You know, without the hunt for your lost Picasso and all that spooky shit."

"Michelangelo."

"Whatever. But $5,000, from the sound of it, that's a pretty good deal right?"

"Hmmm . . . Not exactly," Max replied.

"What do you mean, not exactly?"

"Take it easy, Zoro, don't get excited."

"I really wish you'd stop telling me what to do." Zoro stared in the rearview mirror. "God, I think I need a drink." Right about now he wished he was back at Tommy's throwing back a cold hangover cure. He tore open a lemon-scented wet napkin from Foo's Chinatown Café and wiped down his face.

"Look, Zoro, $5,000 is a decent offer for you to make; it shows you're serious. But you have to understand: the only way to succeed is to undergo a shift in personal consciousness. That's the no-holds-barred truth, and you need to believe that. And if it were you trying to convince me, I'd already believe you."

Zoro moaned.

"Look around you, Zoro. What do you see?"

Zoro shuffled his eyes from window to window. "Nothing."

Max smiled. "I see your second chance."

*   *   *

Alton loosened his grip on her throat, and Holly struggled to steady her breathing as waves of pain knifed through her head and face. "What kind of game are you playing?" she asked.

"One where I make the rules."

"If it's about the money, just take it back and leave me alone!"

"Oh, there are things at stake here that are much more important than money, dear girl. And may I remind you that you have an obligation to me, a pledge sealed in blood. Much more important, wouldn't you say, than your misplaced infatuation with Zoro? Blood, Holly . . . blood is so much more important than money, wouldn't you say? Oh, and one more thing, don't make the careless mistake of betraying me again."

"I told you, I was going to—"

Before Holly could finish, he twisted his hand tighter, completely shutting off her air. Her limbs twitched violently; her face purpled. Her world faded to black . . .

*   *   *

"So, what do you say, Zoro? Will you—"

"What the hell!" Zoro shouted, staring at his side mirrors.

A car had moved up close behind them: closer than someone who was just trying to move ahead in traffic. Zoro immediately recognized the brown sedan that had been following them earlier.

"What is it? Someone behind us?" Max said, swiveling around in his seat.

"Yeah. And I think they want to play hardball," Zoro said. "Hang on, Max."

Zoro swerved suddenly onto a side street, and the brown sedan followed him. He slammed on the brakes, jammed the limo into park, and threw the door open, ready to yank open the door of the brown sedan as it stopped to avoid colliding with the limo.

But the other driver was too quick for him. The brown sedan swerved around the limo with a scream of tortured rubber, and then blew by at getaway speed.

For the fraction of a second the driver was in view, Zoro's eyes scanned his face, his hands, anything he could see. He had a chiseled, blocky look about him, and his eyes were coal black. Nothing about him was familiar—until Zoro saw the V-shaped tattoo on the back of his hand. *The son of a bitch that broke into my place!*

Zoro turned his face to catch Max's half profile in the window.

"Anyone we know?" Max asked.

"I'm not sure," Zoro replied, crossing over to the limo.

"Zoro, we've got better things to do than chase after phantom cars."

Zoro slid behind the wheel, slamming the visor down. His face was pulled, wrinkling the skin ever so gently, like fine fissures over thin ice. "I think that's the guy who busted up my apartment this weekend."

"Really? Why?"

"He had the same tattoo on his hand."

Max's face suddenly had a stricken look. "A V shape?"

Zoro swiveled around to look at Max. "Yeah! How'd you know?"

Max didn't answer, but his expression told Zoro this was not a good development. "So, I'm guessing this guy is with our buddy Conrad?"

Max glanced at Zoro, then away. "I'm afraid Alton is much worse than Conrad, Zoro. Much worse."

They sat in the limo for a few seconds as the engine idled quietly. Max leaned forward in the seat and gripped Zoro's shoulder. "Zoro, I fear that we're running out of time. Unfortunately, now that . . . certain other people are involved, you may not have the option of walking away from all this."

"What do you mean?"

"Even if you never see me again, Zoro, I'm not sure you'll be able to convince Alton, Conrad, and the others that you don't have what they're looking for."

"The sketch?"

"Among other things."

"Damn it! What kind of crap have you got me into, Max?"

"Listen, Zoro. In one way, nothing has changed. You still want a better life, right?"

"Yeah . . . I guess so. Of course, I'd prefer not to have to live it while looking over my shoulder."

"And you won't, if we're successful, Zoro. That I can absolutely promise you. You must believe me, Zoro, and you must agree to help me! You'll be helping yourself at the same time. More than you can possibly imagine."

Max stared at Zoro's reflection in the rearview mirror and Zoro stared back. He could feel his heart pounding; he knew that this was a knife-edge moment. No matter what he did right now, nothing else in his life would ever be the same.

"Sure," Zoro said, finally. "We'll do it your way . . . Exactly what is your way?"

Max took a deep breath and appeared to relax slightly. "Pull over, turn off the engine, close your eyes, and listen. This is where the rubber hits the road."

Zoro rolled the limo to the curb. He killed the engine and leaned back in the seat, closing his eyes. "All right, we're in the Zoro cone of silence," he said, chuckling.

"Okay, Zoro. To find the fourth sketch, in fact to succeed in any way, you need to accept that the world around us is controlled entirely by our minds. And now I need to give you a crash course on the third part of your mind."

"Give me a moment to, like, get my head around this."

The cadence of Max's voice began to slow, his tone deepened. "You believe you are your thoughts and have come to identify with your mind. Even though you've learned that your conscious mind is made up of poor re-creations, you still assume they are absolute. You forget that your perception is broken."

Zoro rubbed his eyes, but kept them closed. "I am not my mind?"

Then he had a thought, "So . . . wait a minute. My mind is somehow broken . . . Yet, Isaac's the one who jumped off a bridge . . . and his mind was okay? Is that what you're saying?"

Max sighed. "Let's not make this any harder than it needs to be."

"But you still make it sound like my mind is worse than Isaac's ever was. It's not . . . is it?"

"It is."

Zoro sighed. "You're supposed to say everything is going to be okay, Max."

"Everything's going to be okay," Max whispered.

"Too late," Zoro said, giving a sad little chuckle.

"Why are you here, Zoro?" Max asked softly.

"I don't know."

"You're still with me, Zoro; there must be something you want."

Zoro didn't answer.

"I think I know," Max said.

Zoro felt Max probing, seeing his every thought, right down to his soul.

"Okay, I'm listening . . . eyes closed, everything."

"I think," Max said, "that you stopped being angry a long time ago. Now you're just afraid. That's why you need me. You believe you deserve what you got, and you're afraid of letting that go. Because if you stop punishing yourself for just a minute, you might wake up and realize everything you believe, everything you stand for, is based on lies and your mind's faulty re-creations."

"I don't think that's me."

"People don't usually think beyond their thoughts."

"Not me!"

"Okay then. There's nothing wrong with your life and how you think. Everything is hunky-dory. My work is done. See you."

"Wait." Zoro's arm went up.

"Wait, you say? You feel the hair bristling on the back of your neck, Zoro? You disagree with me, but by instinct you can't get around the truth? Is that it?"

Damn. He's got me nailed down. No matter how much Zoro tried to disagree, he felt himself melting into Max's words.

"No amount of pretending will change the truth. Your mind is just a river of thoughts, always changing, always moving. But you've dammed it up and created a stagnant pond. Sure, the water's calm there, but it's also a filthy stink hole, a cesspool."

"Lovely image," Zoro said. "I hope you're going somewhere with this."

"Come on, Zoro, keep up with me," Max whispered intensely. "When I say your mind is worse than Isaac's, you don't need to get defensive. Because your mind is not real. Your brain is, your consciousness is, but your mind is only an abstraction of thought, thoughts that you can control and change.

"Look, Max, I've heard this sort of mind improvement crap a million times before."

"Oh, I assumed that. But you've never heard the real truth of it. Not all words are true, Zoro; only the best ones are."

"Max, I'm sure people have analyzed me in this way before. Convince me why your analysis is the uncompromising truth."

"This doesn't have to be difficult."

"Always the optimist, right, Max?" Zoro smiled. He was beginning to think Max should open a small office, hang a sign . . . Billionaire Psychoanalyst.

"Look, Zoro, the reason you're not succeeding is simple. Your mind has become mean, vindictive, and out to get you. It will do anything to keep you trapped in your life, circling the drain. Want to know why?"

Zoro nodded yes.

"Your mind exploits your fears and weaknesses and grinds you down until you're nothing. As long as it's in control, you will never question its beliefs. But when you try to change your beliefs, when you try to move out of the comfort of your boundaries, you threaten to rewrite the very program of your mind. Your mind perceives the danger and reacts; it's in a fight for its life. And make no mistake about it, your mind is clever."

Zoro heard voices. He looked in his side mirrors and saw two young boys on the sidewalk, coming toward the limo.

"Dude," one of them said, "check out this car. Looks like it belongs to Jay-Z or Dr. Dre, or something."

"You better get away, Jamal," the other boy said. "You don't know, might be some badasses in there. Come on, man, don't be messing with that limo, dude."

The boys continued down the sidewalk, one of them casting backward glances at the limo and the other hurrying away without looking back. Zoro watched them go, reflecting on their lives, what they were thinking right now. Each of them carried an image of the car and its occupants—one based on excitement and admiration, the other on fear and avoidance.

Which kid was he? Zoro wondered. If Max was right, his mind was telling him how to react to situations, based on all the scripts written into his life from the day he was born. He closed his eyes again as Max resumed speaking.

"Your mind knows your every fear, every intimate detail of your life," Max went on. "It's tricked you into believing your life is unchangeable and whispers in your head, *You're not good enough . . . you can't do that . . . what the hell is Max talking about, he's a quack . . . don't you dare change!* That voice is your mind deceiving you, Zoro. Those abstract thoughts are your mind controlling you, lying to you. Isn't life hard enough without believing the deceiver that's buried in your head?

"And yet you believe you *are* your mind. 'If I believe it, it must be so,' you say. 'If I hear it in my head, it must be true. Those thoughts, that mind, that's me, that's who I am. How can I betray myself?'

"Rubbish!" Max shouted, suddenly. Zoro jumped, startled by the sudden noise.

"Geez, Max! You scared the crap out of me!"

"Good! That's exactly what I'm trying to do."

"Very funny."

"No, it's not funny at all, Zoro. Your head is filled with bad recreations of the world around you, with worn-out old stories and unhelpful guidelines about how to react to life.

"You're loaded down with unfulfilled expectations. And the bigger the gap gets between those expectations and your life, the more miserable you become. You see the world go by from inside your tiny box, wishing and praying for a way out."

Zoro realized he'd been holding his breath. He let it out, his chest deflating like a leaky air cushion. He had nothing to say.

"Open your eyes, Zoro."

Zoro blinked. He could hear the sounds of the city murmuring around them as they sat in the limo. The daylight seemed slightly brighter . . . or maybe his eyes had just been closed too long.

"The good news is that there is a way out," Max said, "and I'm going to help you find it. Do you believe me?"

Zoro nodded.

"Good. That's enough for now. Start the car, and let's get to the Preserve."

CHAPTER 35

Feeling the buzz in his pocket, Zoro struggled to pull his phone free of his trousers.

"Nate, I can't talk now," Zoro murmured.

"You're with him, right now, aren't you?" Nathan asked.

"With who, Nathan?"

"With Max, of course. Look, Zoro, don't say anything, but you need to know there's something fishy about him."

"What are you talking about?"

"Oh, for crying out loud, Zoro. He's got a cunning mind."

"Oh, yeah? How's that work?"

"Think about it, Zoro. He tracks you down after thirty years. He reads you up and down and feeds you exactly the story you're desperate for. And you turn around and punch his dance card."

Zoro glanced in the mirror at Max; he seemed absorbed with something in his briefcase.

"I think you're being paranoid," Zoro said.

"I've done some checking, Zoro. Every time something happens, that guy's around. He comes into our lives and Joey and Dad die. He shows up again, and Gina tells me you got robbed."

"Coincidence, Nate, that's all."

"And Ma's place? Coincidence too?"

"I don't know, Nate."

"Zoro, there are people who would kill to keep that sketch from surfacing again. And I just don't know where Max fits in. Has he told you anything?"

A sudden fury rose in Zoro, like a hot flash filling his veins. He had finally started trusting Max, and now Nate was trying to jerk him around, drag him back to square one. "I don't know where you're getting this crap, Nate. I've haven't seen anything worrisome. He's taught me about my subconscious beliefs and conscious thoughts. Come on, is that so scary?"

Zoro pulled up to a stoplight. Nathan could always make him seriously angry. But this last part, that was the worst of it. He was finally getting one leg up on his life, how his mind worked, and the first thing Nathan wanted to do was pull the rug out from under his good leg.

"Zoro, whatever Max is saying, he's screwing with you because he knows you're not strong enough to say no. If you need me to, I'll do it for you."

Zoro hated how smug Nathan was. His eyes shifted and he fidgeted in the seat, as the light turned green. He raised his voice, momentarily forgetting that Max was in the backseat.

"Shut up, Nate! Just shut up, okay? I gotta go."

Max looked up in surprise. "Zoro?"

"Zoro, wait!" Nate said. "There's something you need to know. I've spoken to—"

"Good-bye, Nate."

CHAPTER 36

Zoro snapped his phone shut, but as hard as he tried, he couldn't get his older brother's warning out of his head. There was plenty he disagreed with Nate about, but one thing they lined up on was that there was stuff going on with Max that Zoro didn't understand. Zoro glanced in the mirror. Max was watching him, plainly curious about his outburst on the phone.

"That was my older brother, Nathan. Says he's worried about me."

"I see."

"So . . . what's really going on, can you explain it? Seems like it's the least you can do, considering you got me involved in this mess I can't walk away from, like you said."

"What did Nathan say?"

"Let's see . . . he said the sketch is dangerous and there's people who don't want it found. Is that true?"

"Yes. But I wouldn't worry about it."

"Max, I can maybe see why you wouldn't worry, but I gotta tell you, I'm a little nervous, especially now that I know I've got some tough guy tailing me."

"You know what, Zoro? I had a special treat planned for you, but I think that can wait until we settle this. There's a nice café at the museum just up ahead; pull over, and we can walk from here."

"Sounds good. I was getting kind of thirsty, anyway."

The outside of the American Museum of Natural History clearly signaled it was a building with a serious purpose: huge doors, massive columns, heavy stone blocks. The Rose Center's glass cube structure stood in sharp contrast, as if a futuristic spacecraft had landed amid the Greek Revival surroundings.

Zoro and Max went in the main entrance and walked beneath the Barosaurus exhibit, the immense, upright skeleton looming over them like a weird, gothic street lamp.

Threading the corridors past the café, Max guided Zoro to the Rose Center. Max disappeared along the four-hundred-foot walkway that cut through the "scale of the universe" exhibit. After a few twists and turns, Zoro caught up. Through the crystalline glass they could see the entire exhibit, which showcased the infinite vastness of the observable universe.

Max stretched dangerously over the rail, like a bent periscope, and scanned the room. "I just want you to see what we'll be talking about after I straighten you out," he said. Then he ducked through a side doorway at the end of the exhibit.

Zoro followed as they hurried through a seemingly locked door, taking a shortcut only Max knew, apparently. Guiding Zoro through a back lobby behind the IMAX Theater, they finally emerged at the Starlight Café.

Max picked up a tray and bought two iced teas. He looked around and spotted a table in the corner; they made straight for it. He wiped his glass with his napkin, again and again; Zoro figured he probably had the cleanest glass in Manhattan. Then he drank his whole iced tea in one long draught.

"Well?" Zoro said after Max put his drained glass down. "I've indulged you, now you indulge me."

"The Temple Guard . . ."

Zoro tilted his head as he tried to remember.

"You remember the book at the library? The picture?"

Zoro nodded.

Max looked at him for several seconds, as if he were trying to decide what to say next. "I'm fairly certain the bloodline of that very ancient brotherhood still exists today. And I suspect your brother Nathan is certain also."

Zoro leaned across the table. "How do you know this?"

"It's a rumor that's been around for centuries."

"Oh, good," Zoro breathed out, "I thought you were going to tell me you were one of them."

Max's voice was a faint murmur now. "The original Temple Guards were noble, guarding a divine treasure. But over the centuries the few remaining descendants were lost to a perverse obsession with the Name. Their identities are kept secret; no one knows who they are. And more importantly, their reverence for the Name will permit them to stop at nothing to keep it from what they regard as unworthy hands."

Zoro's eyes widened. "Stop at nothing, you say?"

Max nodded.

"But it's just a rumor, right?"

"Yes, Zoro. No one's documented an encounter with the Temple Guard in almost two thousand years."

Zoro remembered how Max had reacted to his description of the tattoo on the back of the hand of the brown sedan's driver. "What about the V-shaped tattoo?"

"Think about the picture again. Remember the design on the Guard's armor?"

"Yeah . . . same shape. So this Alton guy's one of these Temple Guards?"

"I guess you could say that's another unsubstantiated rumor."

Zoro stared at his tea for a few seconds, then turned the glass up and drained it, much as Max had his own, earlier. "Well, I guess there's no way to substantiate a rumor. Let's go."

"Seriously? Just like that? Something's made you more confident, Zoro."

"Anything wrong with that?"

"No! By all means, let's go."

CHAPTER 37

Once they were back in the limo and cruising north on Central Park West, Zoro said, "Okay, Max, let's see . . . before my brother called, you were explaining to me that my mind is full of crap and that it's pushing me around and ruining my life. Oh— and I'm not my mind, right?"

Max gave him a wide smile. "That's my boy. As I promised earlier, I'm going to tell you how to fix that using the third part of your mind, the Third Q, and then I'll share a surprise with you."

"What's the surprise?"

"It wouldn't be a surprise if I told you. Later, okay?

"Okay, so what's the Third Q?"

"There's a hidden part to the mind, Zoro, at least it's partly hidden in your case. And it's got a couple of important jobs, not the least of which is creating your reality."

Zoro didn't have to second-guess himself. "Your question at the Bowery, about what controls the subconscious and conscious minds, the Third Q, right?"

"That's right. There are hidden circuits in your brain that observe the mind, tap the subconscious, and are responsible for some abstract and pretty cool things the human mind can do. And without even knowing it, you're doing some of them right now."

"Like what?"

"For example, Zoro . . . humans are profoundly cooperative and connected. We are linked through cities and moving relationships, and abstractions like the Internet, keeping track of hundreds of acquaintances and their mental makeup, and so on.

"In fact, our mind searches for connections and meaning everywhere it looks. It even tries to project itself into the heads of others to try and see what they're thinking. We're the only species that tries to figure what makes the rest of us tick!"

"You're bigger than life and also harder to understand, Max. I can't see how anything you've said is possible."

"You really think so? Bigger than life?" Max was grinning. "So anyway, these strange things our minds do are possible it appears, because our human brain has evolved special circuits that bring us these uniquely human abstract abilities.

"I hate to be the one to tell you this, Zoro, but evolution has left you with a brain that's about seven times larger than it has to be, from a strictly biological perspective."

"My brain, too?"

"Even yours, Zoro."

"Cool."

"And that human brain of yours is wired like the wiring of a house."

To a certain extent it all made sense to Zoro. "I got this next part, Max. The question now becomes, if my brain is wired to give me cool abstract abilities anyway, can I rewire those special circuits now and fix my—what did you call it?—sludge-pump brain?"

"Aha! I'm getting more proud of you every minute, Zoro."

Zoro's smile widened.

"Scientists doing functional magnetic resonance imaging on groups of special and successful people discovered that those people lit up their brains in a special and different way," Max said. "It seems areas of the brain, responsible for abstract and sophisticated thinking, had become rewired. And that gave them the advantage of refereeing their subconscious and conscious minds, in this quagmire we call a brain."

The more Zoro thought about it, the more excited he got. "I like it! All I have to do is rewire and build Third-Q circuits that control the other parts of my mind."

"Now that's a useful deduction, Zoro."

"And here's the best part. The ability to rewire your brain in that way is neatly woven into our brains by virtue of us simply being human. Every brain cell at the genetic level can build Third-Q circuits."

"Sounds a little like *Ripley's Believe It or Not*," Zoro smiled.

"It's all true. There is a real biological explanation for success." Max hardly paused. "But at the same time, those same circuits are also responsible for some pretty powerful abstract things we do."

Zoro half expected there'd be more to the Third Q than its effect on the conscious and subconscious minds. On impulse he eased off the accelerator and the heavy limo slowed quickly. He coasted to the curb and dropped the gear into neutral. The whole time he sat there, a mosaic of rust buckets and expensive cars filed past the limo.

"It turns out, Zoro, that those same special circuits light up like crazy when we think abstract thoughts and relate to people in a way that evidently has us jumping into another person's head to see their motivation, intentions, the thoughts they're thinking. And those circuits are also active when we're making a deeper connection with the universe and are trying to manifest.

"Apparently we have a tool in our heads that links us to similarly thinking people and the universe, to help manifest our thoughts. Isn't that amazing?"

"I'm sorry, this is nonsense. I'm supposed to think thoughts in my head, and things will just manifest in my world. I don't buy it," Zoro said flatly.

"The truth is, Zoro, that kind of manifestation only works if you're first wired correctly. Otherwise, it's like trying to run Windows on a Commodore 64 . . . the hardware and software don't match."

Zoro pulled away from the curb, mulling over information that was harder to grasp than a greased pig. To say his mind was getting tired was putting it mildly.

"Of course," Max added, "there's one other time when those special circuits are up and firing like crazy. That happens when you're being still and present."

Zoro imagined his mind, filled with tiny electrical pulses firing through his brain.

CHAPTER 38

Zoro's phone rang. He was a little perturbed. *If this is Nate bugging me again . . .*

"Holly? Whoa, whoa, slow down! Are you crying? No, no, it's okay . . . Sure, I can meet you there in ten minutes." He clicked his phone shut.

"Max, something's wrong with Holly. She wouldn't say what, just said if I wanted to hear what she had to say, I needed to meet her in a public place. I promised to meet her at Bryant Park."

"Then I can't imagine not keeping that promise." Max whirled his hand through the air, motioning for Zoro to hurry up.

* * *

They walked past the huge, pink granite fountain that dominated the Sixth Avenue entrance to the park. The central building of the New York Public Library sat opposite the park.

"I can't see her cart anywhere," Zoro said, scanning the area. "This is where she usually is, this time of the day." He was getting worried; Holly had sounded pretty shaken up.

"Walk with me, Zoro. She'll show."

Zoro tried to think of the last time he felt this worried. Other than the night of the fire, he couldn't pin down a date. Walking through the park, Zoro was nervous enough to chew iron nails.

"I can calm you down if you like," Max said.

"I'm not even sure why I'm so nervous, Max."

"Just as an exercise, Zoro, forget the memories that absorb the present moment and also the thoughts that travel into a worrisome future for Holly. What your mind is thinking, when seemingly you're not thinking anything, is where you need to be."

"Sounds like we're entering the Twilight Zone."

"I prefer to think of it as the Light-of-Day Zone," Max said.

"Umm . . . okay." Zoro's eyes were still flicking back and forth, searching for Holly. He could feel his pulse ticking fast with worry. He tried to stay focused on what Max was saying, but it was hard.

"Zoro, I want you to calm down and be as still and present as you can. Because that, my boy, is the only other time when those special circuits in your brain can fire like crazy."

Zoro saw a flash of white clothing and a lock of long, dark brown hair. "Hang on a second, Max, I think that's . . . No, never mind. Not Holly. Sorry, you were saying?"

"The concept of being present, Zoro, is very confusing."

"Yeah, I think I'm already confused . . ." Zoro's words trailed off as his attention drifted toward a group of people gathered around a female figure. He suddenly strode off quickly toward them, forgetting all about Max. And then, a pebble hit him in the back of the neck.

He whirled around to face Max, who was just straightening up from the ground, readying a pebble in his hand, apparently for another throw.

"Damn it, Max! What the hell?"

"You can't help Holly by going off chasing everything you see," Max said. He strode up to Zoro. "Close your eyes, Zoro."

"What are you . . ."

"Just do it!"

Zoro, taken aback, closed his eyes.

"Now hold your breath."

"Max, this is—"

"Shut up and hold your breath."

After a few seconds, Zoro let out a gasp. "I can't hold it any longer."

"Okay, good. Now you're present. Now, listen to me; stay with me, Zoro. When we think of being present, it immediately brings an image to mind of some Tibetan monk squatting on a mat chanting, while his brain is turned off doing nothing, thinking nothing, right?"

Zoro nodded.

"Well, that's all wrong! The idea of being truly present is to stop your voluntary, consciously forced, useless worries and memories from overwhelming the resources of your mind, your computing power."

Zoro nodded.

"When you do this, a very surprising thing happens. By virtue of those special circuits we've talked about, your brain is uniquely adapted to unconsciously use that time to think about and plan your future. We are predesigned to run thousands of scenarios in the background of our minds: daydreaming, silently planning out every coming moment. In that quasi-conscious–subconscious state of Q thinking, human beings are incredibly skilled at jumping out of their heads and thinking about the future, scanning the tons of recorded information in the subconscious mind and predicting what might happen next. Even what next steps you take to help Holly.

"When you remove the filters and thoughts and belief patterns and create the circumstances in your mind that allow the natural machinery in your head to function, that's when you gain insight and foresight."

"Hmmm . . . Is that why I get my best ideas right before I wake up, or when I'm singing in the shower?"

"Exactly! In those special moments, in the crack between the conscious and subconscious mind, when our minds are seemingly daydreaming, doing nothing, that's exactly when our most successful ideas and answers are created. That's when Third-Q circuits come to life.

"For example, when Albert Einstein drifted off to his world of imagination, he saw himself sliding down a rainbow of light, and awoke to discover the Theory of Relativity. Like him, our incredible ability to channel the resources of our minds into those special analytical brain circuits allows us to grow the circuits and experience things we never thought, things that don't yet exist. In your mind, Zoro, you can travel in space and time and build a bridge to the moon. You're unlimited!"

Just as Zoro opened his mouth to reply, he heard someone calling his name. He turned around; it was Holly—and she looked like she'd been through a meat grinder.

"My God, Holly! What the hell happened to you?"

She ran to him and he wrapped his arms around her. She was sobbing incoherently into his chest.

"Here, Miss," Max said, pulling the white silk handkerchief from his breast pocket. "Let me clean your face."

"Zoro, you gotta be careful," she managed to say, finally. She looked at Max, then Zoro. "Some people, they're not happy."

"What are you talking about, Holly? Who did this to you? We can take her to a doctor, right, Max? Come on, Holly, the limo's right over here—"

"No!" she said, backing away. "I can't go, not with him." She was staring at Max.

"Young lady, I assure you, I'm perfectly sane—" Max began.

"No, I can't!" she said. "I need to be as far away from you as I can. And don't try and follow me, Zoro." And then she turned and ran into the crowd surrounding the fountain.

"Holly! Holly, come back!" Zoro shouted. "Max, we gotta go get her. She needs help!"

Max was staring at the place where Holly had been. "I wonder, Zoro . . . did you consider that seeing Holly at this particular moment might not be a coincidence?"

"I don't get it."

"Remember what I said about the Temple Guard? What they're capable of?"

"Wait . . . you don't think Holly's mixed up with this somehow? The sketches?"

"Maybe not directly, Zoro. But maybe she's being used. To watch you . . . or distract you."

Zoro stared at Max, and doubt once again started digging a hole in his mind. "But . . . she's my friend."

"Which would make her a perfect tool . . . in the wrong hands."

Zoro's shoulders slumped. "So what do I do, Max? How can I help her?"

Max put his hand on Zoro's shoulder. "By helping yourself, Zoro. The sooner we reach our goal, the sooner all this is over. Then no one will have any reason to hurt you or anyone you care about."

Zoro shook his head, neither denying nor accepting. "I don't know, Max . . ."

"Stop right there," Max said, "I do know!"

"I . . . I guess so, Max. If you're really sure this is the best way."

"The best way, Zoro, is to keep you pointed in the right direction, toward our goal. Because if you don't know where you're going, you'll probably end up somewhere else."

The truth won't change, Zoro; it will always wait for you to catch up . . . only problem is, I don't know how much time I've got, Max thought.

Zoro stared across the park filled with people from all walks of life. As the sounds and textures began to dance in Zoro's head, tangling with his worry for Holly and himself, he felt a migraine taxiing onto the tarmac inside his skull. For what seemed like an eternity but probably wasn't much more than a minute, Zoro stood, wondering.

A toddler walking along behind his mother caught Zoro's eye. The tyke was dressed in a bee costume, probably for an upcoming play at school, or something like that.

Zoro wondered what life would be like as a bee. If he were a bee, there would be no colossal leaps of understanding. In fact, life as a bee was simple: a bee was just a soldier in a colony—no need to think. *And as a bee,* Zoro thought, *if I screwed up, what's the worst that could happen? The sergeant bee would pull off my stripes.* He began to laugh, picturing himself as a stripeless bee.

"Interesting creature, the bumblebee," Max said, once again seemingly inside Zoro's thoughts. "Engineers will tell you that bumblebees shouldn't be able to fly. It's a question of physics: their wings are simply too small to lift their large bodies. And yet they manage to do it. Why do you think that is?"

"I guess no one's told the bee," replied Zoro.

Max stared at Zoro for a moment, silent and expressionless. "So close to the answer, Zoro, and yet . . ." He looked away, then turned back toward Zoro. "There's no sign of Holly—she's gone and there's probably nothing you can do, for now at least. We have to get to the limo. Our next destination is my facility near the Rockefeller Park Preserve."

Zoro took a long, last look around the crowded park. He sighed. "Okay, Max. But have you got any Advil? My head is really starting to pound."

CHAPTER 39

The brown sedan snaked through Harlem and pulled into a warehouse garage. Yanking the chain pulley, the metal doors roared shut and soon the dimly lit garage fell completely dark. In a deep dirty sink near the back wall, he washed a trickle of Holly's blood from his bruised knuckles. From outside he heard the sound of children playing, and Alton gripped the edges of the sink.

Even though the room was dark, Alton doubted anything could match the darkness now engulfing his mind. Memories came flooding into his head in bits and pieces. They were memories of childhood beatings and desperate screaming moments. He counted his breaths and realized the voice in his head would never leave him alone. So lost in dissociation, it was as if he was sharing the inside of his head with someone else. He could feel his alter ego coming to life and yet was powerless to do anything about it.

Games are not for you, his mind spoke with his father's deep voice.

Alton spun around in the darkness. He wondered, if he had suddenly been given a pardon and was able to go back to a time when he could go outside and play, would he?

Alton stared through the darkness, thinking about his existence. His father had given him life, and then beaten it out of him again and again.

"You were born for one purpose," his father had told him. "You must protect the Name." That was made perfectly clear with every lashing, every closed-fist punch he'd received.

Over time he learned to protect himself by taking on a second personality, his father's. And in moments like these, under the stress of fear and disappointment, his father's voice whispered to him, as the second man inside of his mind came to life.

"I'm not asking to go play," Alton said. "I understand my calling."

He made his way in the dark toward the fridge, but there was no food or water, and the fridge light hurt his eyes.

Things have changed so quickly, you shouldn't have let her go, the deep voice spoke again in his mind.

"I won't let you down," Alton replied. "I won't let them find the Name. With my blood, my life, I promise you this." Alton returned to the sink. Cupping his hands under the spigot, he drank; he was thirsty.

If you can't find it, you know what you must do, the voice spoke.

"I understand, things could be leading to the Name, or could just be another dead end. Either way, anyone who is a threat is expendable," Alton replied.

He removed his holstered gun and bloodstained shirt, replacing it with an identical beige shirt. It was sad in a way, a noble beginning ending in a perversion of truth and purity. Alton wasn't even aware he'd become two personalities, one with no remorse, like a black widow. His whole life he'd been fooling people, covering his tracks, being careful never to let his alter ego surface. Though now, so close to finding the Name, his alter ego was growing and suffocating him.

The laughter from outside broke the silence. He thought again about the children playing. Back then, during his childhood, there were no games, no laughter.

Why are you thinking about the children again? The voice was hard.

Alton sucked in a breath. "I'm not, father."

I will not accept weakness from you. You cannot accept it from yourself.

Alton gripped the edges of the sink. "I'm sorry, father." Reaching for a short strand of frayed string, Alton clicked on the lightbulb hanging above the sink. He was completely alone. In the half-broken mirror in front of him, he could no longer recognize his own reflection. In that moment, everything around him seemed bent, and he felt as if he were no longer looking out through his own eyes.

Who are you, Alton? His own voice was deeper now.

"I am a soldier, father."

Who are you? Again Alton spoke with his father's voice.

"I am the Guard," Alton said as he thrust his arms across his chest.

Completely lost to his dissociation, Alton believed he was his father. He reached for the doors' chain pulley, and soon the brown sedan swung from the alleyway and rocketed across Manhattan.

CHAPTER 40

When Zoro got to Max's building, he led the way up a modestly large staircase fronting a gray granite building across the street from the Preserve. It didn't look like it belonged among the trees. Above the staircase, framed on the stone façade, was a tablet engraved with the words "Academy of Intellectual Freedom."

"I never heard of this place, Max."

"The Academy was founded in the nineteenth century, Zoro. Its purpose is to encourage independent thinking, social justice, and as the name says, intellectual freedom. But come along; there's more important information to cover."

Entering through a double-paneled oak door complete with a heavy brass kickplate, Zoro heard the gleaming voices of preschoolers. After passing through a framework of bone-white marble arches, they entered a series of classrooms. The rooms were an odd mixture of the classic and modern: dark oak walls and ornate, floor-to-ceiling bookshelves enclosed rooms full of sleek laboratory tables and cupboards filled with all manner of Pyrex beakers, test tubes, and specimen jars. The young students seemed more like a fraternity of Oxford lab rats from the 1960s.

"This way, Zoro," Max called.

Jogging to catch up, Zoro flew round the next corner, only to slam into a Plexiglas wall. His face flattened as his cheeks were forced up against the clear plastic cage. Zoro's eyes popped closed in his head, when Max suddenly grabbed his arm and pulled him off the wall.

"I don't think you've ever seen anything like this, Zoro."

Behind the plastic wall was a group of adults boxed into dimly lit Plexiglas cubicles. They were seated at wooden tables, some with their legs crossed at the knees, and half the group held cards against their foreheads. At the far end was an electric scoreboard that silently flashed out the red numbers 50:50.

Max released Zoro's arm. "They're guessing the cards," Max said evenly. Then he flung open the Plexiglas door. *Only Max would enter a room without knocking*, Zoro thought.

"I do apologize for the intrusion, Malcolm," Max smiled, speaking to a man in a white lab coat.

"Maximilian, come in." The scientist smiled, shaking Max's outstretched hand.

"Zoro, please meet Malcolm Greer, one of my most trusted research associates." Zoro stepped into the Plexiglas room, which smelled sweaty and stale. Malcolm Greer, though, was fresh and good-looking. Zoro instantly hated how good-looking Malcolm was. It made him feel better to imagine Malcolm living in a dirty flat in the projects.

"Seems like an awful lot of trouble just to guess some cards," Zoro said. "Why are we here?"

Suddenly, Max grabbed hold of Zoro's wrist and swept him with his leg, karate style, into an empty chair.

"That's not funny," Zoro said. "What the hell did I ever do to you?" *And how can an old guy put a move like that on me?*

Max faced Zoro. "Sit still, Zoro, and work with me." Max opposed his hands at the wrists, making a V. Pressing his palms into Zoro's neck, he pushed his fingers into the base of Zoro's skull along the mastoid bony prominences. Instantly thoughts began to fly through Zoro's mind. Then the room went dark.

"I don't know where I am," Zoro said feebly.

"Don't be afraid," Max answered.

"What's going on, Max? I can't see."

As his eyes came back into focus, Zoro suddenly felt as if a zero-degree wind had blown through him.

"Are you okay, Zoro Montana?" It was the first time Max had called him by his full name.

"I don't know what happened," Zoro said. "What did you do to me?" He was starting to get angry.

"Don't get caught in the drama, Zoro," Max smiled. "I just gave you a little Vulcan mind probe."

"A mind probe . . . yeah, right." *You damn near choked me to death*, Zoro thought. He gazed doubtfully at Max. "What do you want from me?"

Max leaned on the wooden table beside Zoro. "Zoro, as you faded out you saw Joey, then your mind flashed forward to your father jumping off a bridge. Before everything went black you pictured Isaac hiding the sketch, though the details of where were foggy and incomplete. And now you're struggling to bring that image into focus."

Zoro's eyes flew wide and he slammed his heels to the ground, firing the wooden chair out behind him as he jumped to his feet. "How the hell did you know that?"

Max held a finger to his lips; with his other hand he motioned for Zoro to follow him out of the Plexiglas room. "Your mind is very susceptible to suggestion in a semiconscious state, Zoro. Those who know the right questions to ask can learn a lot about you when you're in that situation."

"I would have liked some warning, Max."

"I understand, Zoro. But please just trust me a little longer, okay?"

At the end of the corridor was an old, gray steel door. Its double-level bar latch was counterweighted with a cable attached to a thirty-pound steel weight.

Great, we're headed into the boiler room, Zoro thought.

"I don't want you to talk to anyone about this," Max said. "Now where's that key?" He fumbled in his pockets. "By the way, in the worst case," Max said, "there is a second entrance buried behind the service grid out back."

"You've got to be kidding," Zoro muttered, stroking his unshaven face.

Max's expression turned to a smile. "Ah, here's the key. What do you think the odds are that this is the right one?"

Turning the key in the latch, Max pulled the heavy door open as the counterweight clinked along the wall. "There are miles of corridors down here, Zoro, and no maps," Max warned. "Easy to get lost; you'd better stay close."

"This place looks centuries old," Zoro said. "Are we allowed to be in here? I mean, you probably are . . . but can I come with you?"

"Yes," Max said, lighting the way with his iPhone, "but you may never be the same."

CHAPTER 41

s they made their way into the restricted research area, the
floor had a slight downward tilt. As they moved deeper, the air
turned to a heavy must.

Moments later, at the end of the long steel corridor, a figure appeared.
The man flicked on a set of overhead lights, guiding them to where he
stood. Each yellow light was covered with a wired grill that cast a check-
erboard across the gray steel walls. Thirty twelve-foot sections of steel
wall were connected by a series of large, hand-hammered rivets. The
corridor resembled the inside of a battleship and smelled like the inside
of a sneaker.

"Hello, Charlie," Max said as they entered the door the man opened
for them.

The integrated PET/MRI lab they entered was cramped, and Zoro
felt claustrophobic. From where he sat, through the glass, he had a clear
view of the scanner, and it reminded him of a giant doughnut. A concrete pillar half concealed him from the door, and Zoro felt trapped and
a little uneasy.

Charlie stumbled through the door, turned toward Zoro, and stretched
out his crooked fingers. "God to metz youz, Zoro." The words swarmed

from his mouth like someone trying to speak with a mouth full of bees. "Look at thizz," Charlie buzzed, tossing a model of a sectioned human skull and brain at Zoro. Zoro fumbled the open skull, causing the plastic brain to flop onto the floor. Charlie scurried over and scooped up the pieces of plastic brain, yanked the empty skull from Zoro's hands, then charged from the room, muttering to himself.

"Charlie doesn't know what the Third Q is, Zoro," Max whispered. "Charlie's a scientist. Poor slob's all wrapped up in having demonstrated a new part of the brain, but hasn't a clue what it does."

Max ushered Zoro to the specially modified machine, which was both a combined MRI and PET scanner. They stood beside the big metal doughnut as Charlie hustled back to the room behind them and pecked on a control board. When the scanner fired up, the room was filled with a piercing metallic clunking noise. As the doughnut began to whirl and clunk, it pounded on Zoro's Monday-evening nerves. They quickly retreated to the control room.

Zoro watched Charlie adjust the scanner with precision. "Charlie is an excellent technician," Max said. "After years of studying invisible things, he is uniquely qualified to study the Third Q. And although Charlie isn't sure what the Q is, it nonetheless doesn't stop him from proving it's there—like love, a feeling you can't see or touch, but you know it's there. He's found a way to measure the invisible."

Max stepped up beside Zoro. He appeared excited, ready to share. "Years ago I discovered that certain nuns and monks had something extraordinary going on in their heads."

Zoro stared at Max, intrigued.

"At first, I couldn't say anything, until I had proof," Max said. "But the emerging technology of integrated PET/MRI scanning allowed us to measure energy activity in different parts of the brain. See here, Zoro."

Max twisted around to the monitor and pointed at a scan outlining a human brain in yellow, green, red, and blue colors.

"We of course needed to authenticate our findings," Max said. "But now we know they're quite reliable."

Charlie was hunched over a control console, madly punching an orchestrated sequence of lit buttons, flailing about like the Phantom of the Opera.

In the room beside Zoro, the MRI clunked and hummed. The giant apparatus housed a magnet capable of generating 10,000 times the force of Earth's gravity: so powerful that it was able to realign a person's atomic particles at the level of every cell, then measure how quickly those particles returned to their normal state. And it could just as easily drive a metal cufflink through a concrete wall. But as formidable as this technology was, the specialized integration of a PET scanner into the MRI would be even more formidable.

"I need some quiet," Zoro said, making for the hallway between the labs.

"Sister Clarice is in the hallway, Zoro," Max said, nodding toward the door. "Please give her my greetings."

Sure enough, a small woman in a nun's garb sat in the hallway on a folding chair. In fact, she was tiny, perhaps no more than four feet eight inches tall. Still, there was something about her even Zoro noticed; she had an aura far larger than her tiny frame could contain.

In her hand she held a sandwich wrapped with neatly folded wax paper. She broke her meager sandwich, of homemade sourdough and cheese, into two equal pieces. Holding one half out toward Zoro, she said, "Why so bitter, young man? God wants you to be happy."

Zoro wanted to ignore her and keep walking, but he couldn't move; he couldn't even look away.

"Everything happens for a reason, young man," she said. "And the reason is always inside you."

"Zoro, come in here. I think you'll find this interesting." Max stood behind him, gesturing to the lab.

Inside, Charlie was setting out a step stool in front of the scanner table for Clarice. As Max and Zoro took up positions behind the control console, she climbed onto the table, and Charlie strapped her firmly in place between supporting blocks of foam. He gently inserted a Teflon catheter into her arm as the injection pump gurgled faintly. The isotope tracer flowed slowly into her veins.

Charlie rejoined Max and Zoro at the console. There, he pushed a small white joystick and the scanner table slid silently forward. As Clarice disappeared into the giant doughnut, Zoro saw her glance over at him.

Zoro waited a full five minutes. He sat next to Charlie at the console, trying to hide his anxiety. Only the occasional clunk of the magnet disturbed the silence.

"Care to tell me what's happening?" Zoro asked.

Max gently laid a hand on Zoro's arm. "A normal brain scan shows low activity here, in this region, Zoro." Max pointed to the first monitor. "But watch what happens when Clarice prays."

"Okay, Clarizz," Charlie announced over the speaker. "Anytime youz ready."

Suddenly the scan of Clarice's brain began to glow brilliantly. Beyond the view of the human eye, in the depths of the brain, lay a centuries-old secret. There, in Clarice's brain, the imager mapped out a hot zone, more brilliant and active than any other part of the human brain. But the more Zoro reflected on it, the smaller was his comprehension.

"This doesn't prove anything," Zoro said.

"What iz youz talking about?" Charlie said. "Right therez." He pointed to the second monitor.

"I don't see anything," Zoro said, mostly to irk Charlie.

"Iz youz going to start lying? Do youz ever tellz the truth?" Charlie snapped.

"Listen, I'm not a liar. I can see the part of the brain that lights up, I'll give you that."

"Zo youz do zee it!"

"Yes, but that doesn't astonish me," Zoro said.

Charlie smiled in a quirky sort of way. "It'z a good thing I'z been zaving the bezt for lazt. Watch the monitorz, Zoro."

"Clarizz," Charlie said, pressing the intercom button. "I'z going to pull youz out now. Keep praying, pleaze."

Charlie pulled back on the joystick that controlled the movable table. Sister Clarice was slowly drawn from inside the magnet. And as she emerged from the scanner, the energy glow on the monitor should have stopped. But instead, the glowing energy she was emitting streamed backward from her head into the scanner in a vibrant, twisting rainbow of colors, long after she had been pulled from the scanner.

And then, suddenly and silently, Zoro was shaken by a charge of adrenaline that felt like the shiver of cold water going down his back in the morning shower. Only this shiver began at Zoro's waist, his center, and traveled upward through his entire body. Then suddenly the feeling was gone, and Zoro tingled in its wake.

He went weak in the knees. Were those special circuits Max had just spoken of linked to the universe in a real way? Was he actually standing face-to-face with concrete proof that a connection to something greater was possible? That some invisible energy was not invisible at all, that it existed? He had seen it streaming from Clarice's head into the world.

Zoro stood motionless, wrangling with the reality, no longer able to deny the power of the mind to connect to the universe and perhaps even a God that he'd so long abandoned.

He felt dizzy, then nauseous, and flinging open the lab door, he ran into the hallway. Emerging from the dark lab, the hallway's fluorescent lights flashed in his eyes.

God, Joey! Would things have been different that night if he'd known then what he knew now? *Could it be that God didn't ignore me?* he thought. *Maybe God couldn't hear me because . . . I was mute.*

No, he couldn't bring himself to accept it. So, Zoro did what he had always done: he read a pre-programmed file in his mind, reacted to the belief it dictated, and discredited everything he had just seen and felt. His subconscious mind could not accept the notion of a greater world that had been waiting for him, all along, without his knowledge.

Then suddenly, as Zoro stood wavering in the hallway, thoughts roaring through his head, his every sense became heightened. The lights in the hallway glowed with blinding brilliance, and he felt a thousand pinpricks in his eyes. Sounds thundered in his ears as suddenly he went crashing backward to the ground. Zoro passed out. And as he fainted into a world free from the harsh slings of his new reality, a singular cold tear ran down his shivering face.

CHAPTER 42

Zoro was back in his apartment, standing in front of his bathroom mirror. He lingered in front of the mirror, staring straight into his own eyes.

He saw duplicity there, and it sent a chill through him. His face went slack, and with his reflection held in the death grip of his eyes, suddenly it came to life. His reflection lurched from the mirror, and with its forehead pressed against his own, it grabbed at Zoro's neck.

* * *

Zoro awoke, thrashing and gasping for air. He realized he was face-to-face with the floor of the hallway outside the scanner room. He had a hollow feeling that usually signaled the need for a good liquor soaking.

Zoro grabbed two handfuls of floor and pushed himself to his feet. He turned and saw Max standing behind him. He gave Max a cold, weighted stare.

"It wasn't me that did this to you," Max said. "And for the record, I wasn't expecting you to pass out."

Zoro's head was buzzing; he shook from side to side like a wet dog.

"We should stop for today," Max said. "It's getting late."

"No, I'm good."

"You sure you're all right?"

"Well, it's a definite possibility that all of your talking has short-circuited my brain." Zoro smiled. He spotted a chair in the adjacent room and headed straight for it. "That was intense. What the hell just happened to me?"

"With you, I don't know," Max said. "But Clarice just proved that the universe is a living breathing thing, affected by the same forces that hold our atoms together, or move the tide, or breathe life into a newborn baby."

"Damn intense," Zoro rubbed his sore head.

Max looked hard at Zoro. "Here in this very building, Zoro, it's been proven that there is a bridge between the inside world and the outside world. There is a bridge between mind and matter. Everything I've told you about Third-Q circuits has been proven."

Zoro leaned back in his chair and looped his hand over the top of his head. "I must be imagining things . . . this can't be real."

"You're wrong about that, Zoro. Anything your mind can imagine can be made real. Not with voodoo or some hyped-up emotional special effect, but with real forces we can't see with our naked eyes, or completely understand—though that doesn't make them any less real."

Zoro wondered if that was how the Name worked . . . like some invisible force of nature.

Max stared thoughtfully at Zoro for a moment. "Zoro, everything in the universe is made up of a dynamic connection of energy and matter. Control the connection, the bridge, and you control everything. And the Third Q is the bridge we use to connect to something deeper. Do you get it?"

"Yes. I think so."

"You still want the secret to being rich?"

Zoro nodded.

"It's all about connecting to something bigger than yourself."

"It's easy for you to talk like that, Max. You're rich."

Max edged in closer to Zoro. "Look, whether you know it or not, you and I are the same, Zoro. We have the same potential, the same power to achieve and become what we choose to be."

"How so?"

Max patted Zoro's shoulder. "If you break a mirror into pieces, you don't see half your face in one piece, and your ears in another, do you? No, you still see yourself completely in each piece of the mirror. Each piece, each cell, contains the whole of your image.

"And in the same way, we're all a piece of the universe, Zoro. Just like the DNA in a single cell or a broken piece of mirror contains an entire image of us, so too do we each contain an entire image of the universe. Every imaginable resource is already contained in us by virtue of the deeper connections we share.

"When you use the Third-Q circuits to look into your subconscious mind, like looking into a piece of a mirror, you begin to see not only what's in your mind, but things that are beyond your mind: things that only your imagination and intuition can pull from the universe and bring to life.

"What I'm trying to say, Zoro," Max continued, "is that you are not just you, but a reflection of the entire universe. Everything is you, Zoro. That means that the knowledge of every Nobel laureate, the energy of every supernova, every quasar, travels through you at the speed of light. And if that energy exists, regardless of how imperceptible it may be to you, you can use it to attract people and ideas and answers. And that's how you sculpt your thoughts into real things in your life."

Zoro looked at Max; he was beginning to see the man behind the words. His fate, the strength and fragility of his life, his success—all were now a constant reminder that Max's methods were his way to a successful life, a life he was trying to make possible for Zoro. In a sense, Max was handing him the keys to the family business. And though Zoro didn't understand completely, he was taken by the thought of all the special secrets he might learn by connecting to something so big it was too small to see.

He thought about that connection, that space between matter and energy. He wondered if that was where some infinite consciousness—God?—resided.

One thing he felt sure of: That connection was where the creative process was born. And that substance that connected everyone and everything was what Zoro needed to embrace. When he learned to touch it in the smallest of ways, magic would happen.

They were just starting to exit the room, walking down the narrow corridor of steel, when Zoro suddenly shouted in a way only Zoro could, "Diana Ross and Marvin Gaye!"

He smiled at Max and asked, "You remember the song 'You Are Everything'?" He looked at Max. "You know . . . the mirror?"

Max grinned at him. "Everything is you," Max said in a raspy voice. "Good, Zoro! A perfect metaphor for the connection. Have I ever told you about the healing power of song?"

"Just sing, Max," Zoro smiled. "Shut up and sing."

Walking side by side, surrounded by proof of the truth, they sang that perfectly fitting song, "You are everything . . ."

CHAPTER 43

Before he had a chance to twist the ignition key, a text message pinged on the screen of Zoro's phone: "Where are you, Zoro?"

"It's Holly," Zoro said. "At least she's talking to us again."

Max nodded. He leaned forward in the seat. "Okay, Zoro, we should see what's going on with your friend."

The way he said it touched Zoro: he really cared. The man obviously was bigger than his money or any mission he happened to be on at the moment. Zoro keyed a quick query to Holly. Her text came back in reply: "Still at park."

"She's at the park," Zoro said. "I really appreciate this, Max."

"Of course. But here's the trade-off, Zoro: I'm going to finish our discussion, give you the quick version though," Max glanced out the rear window.

"That's fair . . . just give me the quick easy," Zoro said, pulling the car into drive.

"Hold on a second," Max said. He slid out of the backseat of the car, rushed around, and got into the front passenger seat. Pulling the door closed, he said, "'You are everything.' Big words. But I'm sure you're wondering, where's the magic in everything I'm saying? How tangibly can our thoughts connect to something bigger and change things?"

"The thought had crossed my mind," Zoro said, feeling the cast-iron question mark in his head shrink in size as he pulled into the street.

"What would you say, Zoro, if I told you that your thoughts, the images of your inner world, are real forces with a real cause and effect?"

"I'd say it sounds a little California-culty and infinitely weird."

Max laughed, "Your honesty can be refreshing, Zoro—sometimes. Only two things are infinite: the universe and human stupidity."

Zoro grinned foolishly. "Sorry, Max. I should keep my mouth shut."

"No, I understand, Zoro. You're struggling to be yourself, and yet stay open to my teaching. This is a struggle every great mind must win, sooner or later. Okay, so consider this idea: thoughts, Zoro, are as real and effective to the inner and infinite world as your hands and feet are to the outer world."

"Frankly I'm having trouble understanding that."

"In what way?"

Zoro shrugged. "I'm not sure. And my head still hurts."

Max gave Zoro one of his easy smiles. "Zoro, imagine a wave spreading across the water. Silently it travels, tipping every boat, slightly rearranging the boats' positions all along its way. Eventually that wave, that vibration, has traveled from one end of an ocean to another, practically another world. Each wave, with the power to affect thousands of boats, thousands of miles away, is followed by thousands more waves. And enough waves make a tsunami."

Zoro's eyes widened, though he held them aimed down the roadway.

"Now imagine, Zoro, that the human brain emits a powerful and measurable energy field: a wave, like what you saw in the lab. Each singular thought that you have is the source of a tiny electrochemical signal that creates a ripple in the waters of your reality. And the most powerful, constant energy is emitted from your subconscious mind. So you can see why controlling it with your Third Q is important."

Zoro furrowed his brow. Preoccupied with the sound of Max's voice and the incessant pounding in his head, he'd forgotten to worry about Holly. Instead he wondered, and not for the first time, how Max had gotten so damn smart. Max meanwhile checked the passenger-side rearview mirror. The road behind them was empty.

Zoro drove the long road and Max went on to explain how five hundred years ago, no one knew what electricity was. Five thousand years ago, magnetism was just voodoo. And fifty million years ago there was no one around to understand gravity. Still, those things existed.

"The point is, Zoro, thoughts are not meaningless nothing. Each single thought you have is a tiny but powerful, measurable force. But in fact you never think about the effect of your thoughts. You never think of the implications of the energy you emit."

"Hold that thought," Zoro said, as he swerved around a delivery truck loaded with crates of canned vegetables that suddenly braked in front of them. "How can such tiny bits of energy be so powerful?" he asked as he moved back into his lane.

"Thirteen kilograms of plutonium." Max said, smiling.

The smile didn't quite reach Zoro. "I'm supposed to understand that, right?"

Max went on to explain that thirteen kilograms of plutonium was needed to make an atomic bomb. But when that plutonium was unrefined, spread out in small piles of radioactive rocks, those bits of plutonium were weak forces and not explosive at all. But according to atomic law, a force existed within the rocks that multiplied exponentially when thirteen kilograms were placed together in a single, concentrated clump. "And when you concentrate it—squish it together—kaboom! Atomic bomb."

"Aha." "Kaboom" made him think of the fight with Gina.

"Like any force, Zoro, the more concentrated thought is, the more powerful it becomes. The thousands of scattered, unproductive thoughts that you have each day do nothing to change your life. But your thoughts are like bits of plutonium, and within them lies unimaginable power. When you control them and reach a critical mass of organized thought . . . boom! . . . your thoughts explode and affect the universe in order to support your dreams and desires."

The words surprised Zoro. It hardly seemed that Max's evidence was conclusive. But to his astonishment, Zoro already knew that thoughts were real forces—only he didn't know it, exactly.

He realized that he felt their power in his lightheadedness when he fell in love with Gina, and again in the pit of his stomach when Carmela was near. And each kind of thought felt different and powerful and real. *No wonder Max was excited*, Zoro thought.

Max was still talking. "I won't bore you with countless explanations, Zoro. I would, however, like to point out that there are only two things that can change your life: your thoughts and your actions. And since you can't have any action without first having a thought, then ultimately those mystical forces called thoughts determine the outcome of your life."

"So my thinking needs to be rethunk."

The limo stalled at a traffic light. Zoro swore softly, pulling the gear into neutral and reaching for the ignition. *For such a damn high-dollar ride, this engine is sure a pain in the ass*, he thought.

"Did you use premium gas when you filled up, Zoro?" Max asked.

"I'm sure I did," Zoro replied, though he really wasn't.

And then, in the instant between touching the key and twisting it to restart the engine, he remembered his imagination . . . Here and now, that very real force had him flying high above the world, ready to make breakthroughs. In his mind he could see himself at the gas pump choosing regular gas. And suddenly he realized everything that was happening to him in his life was the sum total of his choices.

Max's voice came softly from right beside his ear. "Open your eyes, Zoro."

Zoro did, surprised to realize that he had closed his eyes in the first place; the engine was running and the light was green. He pressed down on the accelerator. *My imagination really is powerful; I was traveling above the clouds and sitting at a red light at the same time*, he thought. *I need to work on keeping my eyes open when I'm driving, though . . .*

Max laid his hand beside Zoro's, on the wheel. "You should realize by now that your past failures are irrelevant. Only today's thoughts move your life—"

"Look out!" Zoro yelled, shoving Max's hand off the wheel.

A deer had leaped onto the road and frozen; Zoro reacted instinctively, like a fighter pilot. Steering the limo across the yellow line, he swerved around the deer.

Max was flung across the seat by the sudden maneuver, banging into the passenger door. There hadn't been time to warn him. If Max was hurt, Zoro would never forgive himself.

"You all right? You okay?" Zoro asked.

"Don't worry about me," Max said, rubbing his shoulder as he repositioned himself in the seat. "And good work swerving around the deer."

"Thanks. When I'm behind the wheel I don't even think about it. I had a buddy who flew jets for the air force, and he used to say, 'Up there, if you think, you're dead.'"

Max stared into Zoro's cockpit and smiled. "Have you ever wondered why when a deer steps onto the highway, it freezes?"

"Ummm . . . nope," Zoro said, baffled by Max's calm manner. As if nothing had happened, Max just continued, the recent tense moment becoming fodder for his next lesson. "Could you at least pretend to be shook up, maybe? Just for me?" Zoro said.

Max shook his head. "Listen to me. When the deer sees the car coming, it rushes to its primitive mental filing cabinet, searches for the file that says 'something's moving,' opens the file and reads, 'movement: predator—freeze!'"

"I knew I could count on you to put a picture in my mind," Zoro said. "And for the record, I get it. The deer thinks it's in the woods; I'm right, right?"

"Yes. No matter how much the deer's conscious mind says 'get the hell off the road,' the force of its subconscious mind overrides it, and says 'freeze.' It's like trying not to shake when you're afraid, or cry when you're sad . . . you just can't do it. It doesn't react that way on purpose;

that deer just doesn't have a Third Q to take over its thoughts when the rest of its mind fails. But you do."

"So . . . my preconceived notions are so powerful that they control my life and keep me frozen in the road, unable to tap the power of my thoughts and make the deeper connections I'm capable of."

"Bingo."

Zoro tumbled the thought around in his mind: he had real forces at work inside him that could fix his mind, even reach out beyond it—into the universe. What he had wanted was that fix, a quick fix.

Zoro leaned back against the driver's seat, bracing his left foot against the floorboards. "You know, Max, it's kind of like I stopped thinking and forgot to start again."

"Well, now you're started, Zoro. And that's a good thing."

CHAPTER 44

They circled Byrant Park twice, but there was no sign of Holly's cart. It was still early evening and nice enough outside, so Max suggested they wait in the park. Zoro figured she would return the cart at the end of her shift and ought to be there soon. They found an empty park bench and Zoro leaned back to listen to the excited buzz coming from Max's mouth. He was like the Energizer Bunny, and Zoro was starting to worry that Max could keep going longer than Zoro could listen.

"You once told me the more you think about things, the more difficult things seem to get."

Never good at waiting, Zoro was glad, though, that Max was distracting him from worrying about Holly. "Yeah, you know, I've been knocking myself out all my life, trying to think myself rich, and still I'm a poor slob. Explain that." Zoro kept scanning the park for Holly.

"Your ability to reason, Zoro, is supposed to make things easier."

"You'd think so."

"So where is your way of reason now, Zoro? When your reason, your thoughts, seem to be making things worse, then your reason itself must have some role in your lack of success. Wouldn't you agree?"

"Yeah, I'd say that."

"So it stands to reason," Max smiled, "if your conscious reasoning is at fault, then reason itself needs to be fixed."

Behind Zoro, in the nearby café, he heard the cappuccino machine hiss and sputter a fragrant song.

"Okay, how?" *Holly, where the hell are you?*

"The process of fixing something Zoro, is exactly that," Max replied. "It's a process. To fix things we take them apart, look at them, and clean and replace worn, broken parts. But in your mind, parts like the subconscious and the conscious aren't easy to get to. You can't pull out a bunch of mind and stick in a replacement part."

"So tell me how to rewire my circuits."

"Aha! Yes, that's it! I want you to realize that every obstacle to success, every habit, every shortcoming of your brain can be overcome by one thing, and one thing only: your free will, choice. Because every thought you choose is turned into a biological, flesh-and-blood reality, what we've called circuits in the brain."

"How is that possible?" *Holly . . . Holly . . . God, let her be okay . . .*

"Every cell in your body has the same genes; genes that can be activated to give a cell its unique characteristics. And each type of cell responds to a different activation trigger to ultimately make it what it is meant to be. In our uniquely human brain, it so happens that the neuroenergy of thought, that tiny electric force generated by thinking—something that can actually be seen with the right equipment, as you now know—is the trigger for our brain cells to grow and form new and different synapses and circuits.

"So fundamentally, each type of thought that you carry out in your mind acts to alter gene expression in a brain cell. And different thoughts create different changes."

"You have evidence of this?"

"Absence of evidence is not evidence of absence," Max said confidently.

Zoro winced. He hated Max's one-liners.

"But as a matter of fact, Zoro, it is scientifically proven! You can will your brain to do anything you want by thinking the thoughts that alter the gene expression. In turn, you create new success circuits capable of all the wonderful abilities we have already discussed."

Zoro looked out along the road, back to a crowd of people. But still no Holly.

"Zoro, stay with me here . . . Now that you know this, you have found an entry point, a place at which you can act. Maybe even help Holly, if we ever figure out what she wants."

"So what happens now?"

"What happens now is that I see you finding the present moment and searching deep within for answers, intuition, and guidance from the invisible mechanisms in your brain. I see you firing up gene activity of special neurons in your mind and creating specific links to share experiences with others, and thereby learning to understand someone or something that person may be doing or deciding to do, without ever having done it yourself. I see you perceiving, instantly and automatically, the motivations and intentions of the people around you. I see you developing new and powerful circuits in your mind to instantly see clues—"

"The sketch?"

Max kept going. "Pulled deeper into a sense of connectedness with the boundless energies of the universe, and manifesting a successful future. And I see you conquering your beliefs and boxed-up conscious thoughts and letting imagination, foresight, and creativity sneak into the forefront of your mind, silently guiding you."

I'd like it to guide me back to Gina, he thought. And then it hit him. In all honesty he should have seen it coming that morning. Gina had spent the night before comparing her life to that damn magazine, marble mansions and lives of the rich and famous. And here he was the very next morning driving off right back into their old life. In fact, he didn't realize in driving off, he was one step closer to losing her. When was the last time he'd been spontaneous, passionate, or even let her in? It was Virginia May all over again. Something had to happen; he guessed the fight was better than the alternative. *Mystery solved,* he thought. Now all he needed was the solution to make things right; hopefully one not as crazy as the Name. Max's voice faded in.

"Then I see your breath taken away when you realize that this wonder that is your brain contains unknown and invisible forces working to change the course of your life.

"And finally, I see you making an effort of will and then trying again and again until change brings you the success you dream of."

Pressing back against the bench, Zoro closed his eyes. "Max, people are going to think I'm crazy."

"Who you offend with your thoughts is irrelevant to the truth, Zoro."

Max stood, and Zoro followed.

"No, no I get that," Zoro replied. "It's just . . ."

Out of nowhere, someone slammed into Max, knocking him to the ground and ripping his briefcase from his hand. The thief raced across the sidewalk bordering the park, across the street, and headed for a nearby subway entrance.

"Damn! Max, are you okay?"

Max nodded, pulling himself upright and onto the park bench.

"Wait here. I'll get that son of a bitch."

Zoro sprinted across the street and flung himself down the stairs to the subway. He had a strange, unsettling feeling he couldn't explain: this wasn't just some tackle-and-grab mugging. There was something vital in Max's briefcase, something the attacker had known about. Zoro had to get it back—and get some answers.

Running recklessly, smashing through a thicket of pedestrians, Zoro felt the ground slip under him as he hit the first wet step into the subway. He hurdled the turnstile. Ahead on the platform he caught sight of Max's assailant. Zoro was gaining on him: twenty yards . . . fifteen . . . ten . . .

The train arrived at the platform with a rumbling roar, but Zoro watched the man leap off the platform and race into the darkened tunnel, along the tracks. Zoro followed, into the damp, oily darkness. He could hear the attacker's racing footsteps crunching the gravel just ahead, could see the shadowy form pounding down the tunnel. With a final burst of speed, Zoro reached forward and grabbed the guy's collar, yanking him backward violently and slamming him against the grimy wall of the tunnel. His knuckles connected with the mugger's face, then his solar plexus, then his ribs.

With a groan, the guy dropped the briefcase and tried to shield his face with his arms as Zoro punched him blindly, again and again.

"What does Conrad want with this briefcase, you son of a bitch?" Zoro panted, grabbing the guy by the front of his shirt and shaking him. "Tell me!"

"Who the hell is Conrad?" the man whimpered.

"Aren't you with Conrad?"

"Just take the case, man," the assailant cried, pulling his body into a tucked-up ball. "I'm sorry I robbed the old man . . . just take the case."

Zoro grabbed the man's hands and turned them over in the faint light. They were clean: no tattoos, no scars.

Shit. This poor fool was just a mugger, after all. And even worse, Zoro had no answers. He picked up Max's case and started walking.

CHAPTER 45

B y the time he got back to the platform, Zoro's heart had finally slowed and he could breathe normally again. He also realized that his knuckles were really sore.

Then he looked up and saw Max, slumped cross-legged on the platform, eyes closed.

Goddamn it; something's happened to Max! He leapt up the steps, hurried over, and dropped onto wobbly knees beside Max. "Max, are you all right?"

The train had pulled out, so the platform was mostly empty, and the few people on the platform just ignored them, pretending not to notice, in typical NYC bystander fashion.

"I'm fine, Zoro."

"You don't look fine."

"No dear boy, you don't understand. I was just lingering in my mind, visualizing the outcome of your chase."

"I can't believe this," Zoro said, sinking down to sit beside Max. "I'm chasing some goon down a subway tunnel, and you're sitting here playing mind games?"

"I know," Max replied. "There's so much going on beyond your perception, it would freak you out."

"No. No that's not what I mean," Zoro frowned. "I mean I could've died in that tunnel . . . and you're here screwing around. You're supposed to be my backup. You know . . . bad boys, bad boys . . . "

"Maybe it's just me," Max responded with a little smile, "but 'could've died' isn't nearly as permanent as 'died.' And how do you know I wasn't backing you up?"

Max's sense of humor didn't appease Zoro in the least. "I can't take this anymore," Zoro said. "I thought I could this morning, but this is screwed up."

Zoro tried to deduce what Max was thinking, but things were too flimsy. He tried to ignore the pressure within. He felt as if one false move, one false deduction, and this whole Third Q thing would come apart in his mind. What was Max up to?

Max's teachings flashed through Zoro's mind, as he examined each one. Sending mental probes into his imagination, suddenly Zoro said, "Were you praying for me, Max?"

"Interesting word, 'prayer.'" Max replied.

Zoro suddenly had the feeling that something bigger was about to unfold.

"Zoro, do you think the universe is just a ball of unconnected, chance events? Because I have to tell you, God's more organized than that."

"Is that good news or bad news? I have no idea what that means."

"It means, Zoro, you are infinitely intertwined with the universe."

"So . . . bad news then."

Max conjured up a smile. "The truth is, you don't know the limits of what you're capable of."

Zoro shrugged, but he was still listening.

"The human body is made up of a few dollars' worth of chemicals and a few gallons of water; still we live and think and love and pray and create because a life force exists in all of us."

"I've come to the conclusion," Zoro said, "after spending as much time with you as I have, that it's less of a burden just to agree with you."

Max smiled. "You understand the three worlds, three minds."

"I'm not entirely sure, but I'm trying."

"Then it should be no surprise to you, since so many things come in threes," Max said, "that you are also three people: 'me, myself, and I.' Come on, let's head back outside, and I'll explain."

Max rose to his feet and made for the exit. Zoro followed, eager for Max to explain, but not willing to interrupt the silence. He knew better by now than to interrupt one of Max's dramatic pauses.

But suddenly Zoro felt amazement blooming in his mind. Exhaling slowly, he felt the skin around his raw knuckles tighten and burn; he sensed the air as it slid in and out of his lungs. The electrical energy of a brilliant insight filled the air. "That's it," he whispered, as much to himself as to Max. "'Myself' is my hands and feet, the physical me. You can see it, Max," he said, eyeing one of his scraped knuckles. "*I* hurt *myself*, see?"

Max rolled through the turnstile and Zoro followed behind like a page trailing a knight. He was trying to keep his voice steady and unemotional, though he didn't succeed.

"And here," Zoro said, rushing beside Max, keeping pace now, "'*I* am a loser.' That's what my mind said. 'I' is the label created inside my mind."

"That's a healthy way of looking at it," Max said enthusiastically, turning sharply to face Zoro. Zoro jumped back. His eyes alert, he paused. A few days ago he never would've had an answer. But now it was all so clear.

"And 'me,'" Zoro grinned so widely it must've hurt, "'me' is who I am, my essence, something not even Ma can take away from me."

I remember what you told me, Dad . . . Zoro smiled inwardly *. . . 'I' can be eaten by monsters, but monsters can never eat 'me' . . . now I understand what you meant.*

Max laughed joyously, not trying to push aside the importance of the moment, but reveling in its splendor. "Today for the first time in a long time—maybe ever—you realize that you are more than your thoughts! Zoro," Max said, taking him by the hand, "in the gap between two thoughts—that's the real you."

Zoro smiled and said, "When my mind is blank, I'm in a pure state of mind."

"And that's where I was on the platform, Zoro: inside the stillness firing up those Q circuits." Max thought for a moment, then looked at Zoro again. "The Third-Q connection, Zoro . . . does it mean anything else to you now?"

"Should it?"

"What do you think?"

Joey . . .

In a peaceful voice, Max eased Zoro into the brittleness that had been the norm of his dreams. "Even your beloved Joey and Isaac still live in something deeper, Zoro. Maybe they're the light people claim to see in a near-death experience—who knows? But one thing's for sure: you can get over a lost briefcase, but you never get over Joey—and you don't have to. That's because he still is. And you can never argue with what is, because it already is."

"Max," Zoro's eyes widened, "the Third Q . . . there's more to it than just brain circuits and thoughts and beliefs. I truly feel that. But what, Max? What am I not seeing?"

"For the past few days, Zoro, I've been trying to simplify the most complex thing known to humankind: our brains. And in coming to understand the most difficult thing in the world, we've come to understand the origins of creativity, foresight, and imagination. But no amount of investigation, no amount of scientific exploration on a biological level can ever tell us why we have those thoughts. Why am I creative, why was I created, why am I me? What we cannot do on the physical level is know the origin of consciousness.

"However, we can accept that our brains somehow miraculously bring us, out of nothing more than neurons and electrical circuits, human feelings, love, empathy, the expression of art, religion, invisible creations, and dreams."

"And clearly, you're telling me a biological mechanism alone cannot explain that." *Damn, where did that vocabulary come from? Zoro, old buddy, your mind is definitely changing . . . for the better . . .*

"Yes, Zoro. Again I'm going to ask you to set doubt aside and consider the following. If the things that make us uniquely human—such as our ability to jump into people's heads to see their thoughts, and the ability to jump out of our own heads and travel in space and time to imagine and foresee the unimaginable—if that is fuelled by the neuroenergy traveling along Third-Q circuits in our brain, then perhaps that neuroenergy is special also."

"I'm . . . still in the dark. What is it?"

"Again, setting all doubt aside, could it be that that neuroenergy, that consciousness and source of creativity that is unexplainable in any scientific way, is your soul?"

Without needing a second to think, Zoro realized that Max had just confirmed what he already felt. At first it hardly registered with him, then the fog in his mind cleared and he made the connection.

Zoro swallowed hard, fumbling the words. "My soul . . . it's merely the energy flowing on those pathways in my mind, isn't it?"

In a voice that sounded almost like prayer, Max said, "Genesis, Zoro. The book of Genesis says the Lord breathed life into humankind and we became living souls. A living soul, Zoro! A soul that fills our hearts with tears and joy and dreams and the ability to make choices. When we find the courage to make changes, Zoro, that's when things change. In those moments, when your Third-Q mind is willing change, that's when change is created: real, tangible, biological change in this masterful thing called your brain. In those moments when your mind is nowhere, that's when answers are created and pulled into the here and now. Because that's when you touch your soul!"

"And that's why you said I can connect to something deeper when I connect to the Third Q. I'm reaching my soul, Max. God Almighty . . . my soul . . ." Wonder filled Zoro's mind like a sunrise.

"You now have an opportunity for a great adventure, Zoro: to travel through space, time, and imagination . . . to fly through the inner workings of your biological mind, making new connections, training your mind, and making any dream, any thought a reality. The road to money, love, dreams, and desires lies vividly planned out in your mind, guided by your soul . . . just beyond your reach, but within the reach of your Third Q."

Zoro grinned. "If I use it."

"If you *choose* it," Max whispered.

Stepping onto the sidewalk, for the first time in his life Zoro's vision was clear. He had to find the fourth sketch. And he suddenly knew he had overlooked the most important clue.

"Zoro!" called a woman's voice—behind him.

CHAPTER 46

Zoro saw her, jumping past the crowd and surging forward, a flamingo-colored hoodie partly covering her face. She carried a nylon bag almost the size of a shipping trunk.

"Holly!" Zoro shouted.

She stepped into the street, coming toward him, just as a brown sedan gunned its engine, tires screeching as it leapt forward. The sedan slammed into Holly, tossing her twenty feet in the air; her body smacked into the pavement with a sickening, flat sound. The sedan squealed tires and burned rubber as it accelerated down the street.

"Son of a bitch!" Zoro screamed. He took off after the sedan, his lungs sucking air and his legs pumping. The sedan was boxed in traffic up ahead; Zoro was actually gaining on it. Powered by a surge of adrenaline, he hurled himself across the hood of a halted yellow cab, barely noticing the pain as his shoulder slammed onto the hood of the brown sedan.

"Stop, you bastard!" Zoro screamed, pounding on the hood. He scrambled to the side and yanked on the passenger door handle; the door came open. Zoro leaped in, fear and rage souring his mouth. Zoro wrapped his arm around the assailant's neck. They fought. Zoro could see the V-shaped tattoo on the back of the driver's blocky fist as it came toward his face, slamming into his jaw.

Suddenly, he felt a sharp pain across his cheek, and at the same instant he was blinded by a sudden blaze of light. A snub-nosed revolver was in the driver's hand. Zoro flung himself backward through the open passenger door, crashing onto the pavement. Horns blared and tires screamed as the traffic dodged him. He scrambled to his feet and ran, ducking low as another shot whizzed past his face. The sedan lunged forward, and Zoro somehow managed to get to the sidewalk. Behind him he heard the roar of the sedan's engine as it tore off down the street.

Zoro panted, his hands on his knees. He saw a splash of blood on the sidewalk at his feet and put his hand to his cheek. It was a miracle; the bullet had barely nicked his cheek. He heard a siren in the distance.

Holly! My God, Holly . . .

He jogged back to the scene of the accident, willing his legs to move faster than they could. Max was down on his knees cradling Holly in his lap. The crowd gathered around was as quiet as night.

Max looked up as Zoro pushed his way through the crowd. "The ambulance is coming. Somebody already called 911." Zoro nodded. Max stood and moved aside for Zoro, then backed away, into the crowd.

Zoro knelt beside Holly. Her shirt was bloodstained and her eyes were glazed, uncomprehending. Her face was bruised, swollen, and bloody, her lips split, and her breath rattled in shuddering gasps.

Her lips were moving. He leaned down, his ear next to her mouth.

"I won't lose you . . . be careful," Holly mumbled.

"What are you talking about? You're the one who needs to be more careful."

"Don't trust him!" she said in an agonized whisper.

"Who? Don't trust who?"

Her breath rushed out of her then, and it didn't come back. Her face slackened; the light went out in her eyes. She was gone.

CHAPTER 47

Stepping over the yellow tape, Detective Gideon turned toward Max and Zoro. Zoro looked at him. "You again; you're freaking kidding me. You're like a bad penny, Gideon, turning up anytime something goes wrong."

Gideon looked at Zoro, then Max. "You were a friend of the victim, I understand?" Zoro nodded; Gideon could see the look of horror in Zoro's eyes and scribbled something on his notepad. He didn't feel the same sincerity from Max. There was no obvious repulsion at what had just happened to Holly. "And of course he works for you?" Gideon said looking at Max. Max nodded. More scribbling.

"Can you think of anyone who might have wanted to kill her?"

Zoro shook his head. *No way I'm telling this clown about the Temple Guard. I'm sorry Holly, God I'm sorry.*

"Why were you in the street . . . and why was she following you in particular?"

Zoro shrugged. "I don't know."

"In fact, Detective," Max said, "she was coming to see me."

Zoro stared at Max, who gave a small shake of his head as if to warn Zoro against saying anything.

"I see," Gideon muttered, scribbling.

"So, she was crossing the street to see you—why?"

"I'm afraid I can't say," Max said.

"You say she was coming to talk to you when she got hit, but you don't know why?"

"I didn't say I don't know; I said I can't say," Max said.

"And you, Zoro," Gideon said. "You're the hero, from what witnesses say. You chased the car on foot; quite spectacular, I understand."

One of the cops directing traffic around the crime scene leaned toward Gideon. "Skin a hero and underneath lurks a monster."

"What's that mean, buddy?" Zoro demanded. "You got a theory you wanna share?"

"It means you two guys are as pure as driven charcoal," Gideon said. "There's another side to this story and I know you're hiding something. Did you get a plate number, anything?"

"No, sorry," Zoro said. "I guess I was a little too busy dodging traffic . . . *and bullets.*"

"Nothing at all, Mr. Montana?" Gideon asked with a sneer. "Nothing to help us break this?"

"Help you break this? . . . Holly's broken, Ma's door too, and you haven't done a goddamn thing!" Zoro glared at Gideon, his jaw set tight.

Max began slowly moving closer to Zoro, shifting silently as he kept an eye on Gideon and the other police officers.

"A broken girl, a broken door . . . some coincidence, wouldn't you say?"

"Yeah, you oughta look into that, I guess. And Ma's fine, thanks for asking," Zoro replied. "Though between her door and my face, I got the worst of it."

"You were attacked?" Gideon looked up from his notepad. "The driver, he injured you?"

"Yeah. Tried to shoot me, and he busted my nose a couple of days ago at my house."

"The same man you said you couldn't identify then, do you think you can identify that attacker now?"

Max leaned toward Zoro, grabbing his shoulder. "I'm sorry, Zoro, I've . . . I don't feel well. Do you think you could help me to the limo, to rest?"

Zoro exchanged a glance with Gideon and shrugged. "I need to take care of my boss. If you don't mind, of course."

"Help me understand something first. You just now recognized him as the same man who attacked you in your own home, and yet you can't identify your attacker? " Gideon pressed his line of questioning.

"Yeah. So my place was hit, you already knew that, too. But I never saw the guy clearly," Zoro said. "Shady neighborhood, you know."

"Tragedy just seems to hang around you two." Gideon scowled at them.

"I could say the same about you, you know? We about done here?"

"We know nothing about why she was run down, Detective," Max said. "We watched it happen, just like the other witnesses; you must already know that."

Gideon wasn't satisfied with that answer. He opened his mouth to speak.

"Can I help Mr. Cisary to the car now?" Zoro asked, turning away. He wasn't sure why Max was as intent as he was on telling Gideon as little as possible, but he knew better than to fight it.

"Go ahead—no, hold on a minute. There's one more thing . . . the mark on the victim's hand. I don't suppose you know anything about that?"

"Mark? What mark?" Zoro said.

Gideon took them to the ambulance. He reached beneath the sheet covering Holly's body and pulled out her right hand.

"I don't see anything," Zoro said.

Gideon rubbed the back of her hand, wiping away a layer of skin foundation cream to reveal a V-shaped tattoo.

My God, Holly . . . a Temple Guard?

Before Zoro could say anything, Max spoke up. "Why should we know anything about a tattoo? Can we go, Detective? I'm not feeling very well."

Gideon turned away without answering.

"We're in danger here, Zoro," Max whispered as they walked toward the limo. "Follow my lead."

"No problem. But Gideon—"

"He's not trying to help," Max replied. "Well . . . not us, at least." Max held Zoro in his gaze. "Let's go! I know what I'm talking about; we can't trust Gideon. And there are certain people who will be very upset by Holly's death."

"If we can't trust the cops, Max, who can we trust?" Zoro's voice quivered.

"No one."

Holly's last words echoed in Zoro's mind: *Don't trust him . . . Don't trust him . . .*

Max and Zoro made it to the limo. Zoro helped Max inside, and then went around to the driver's side. He got in, and a moment later he pulled the limo slowly from the curb, feeling the weight of being a hunted man.

CHAPTER 48

Conrad darted from the corridor to his private express elevator. It stopped abruptly at the fortieth floor, which served as a meeting place and the nerve center of Pantheon operations. Conrad trudged by his office, its walls lined with hundreds of books. There were no sagging wooden bookshelves, only rigid metal runs of anodized steel shelving, running up to a fathom of domed ceiling.

Conrad continued down the hall to the "fishbowl": a central control room not unlike the one at the Kennedy Space Center. A central lower deck housed several small workstations and a large bank of digital screens. A half-tier higher, a platform encircled the room, protected by a slatted, angled railing. In banks of conduits in the ceiling and beneath the floor ran a freeway of green, red, and yellow lights, racing along corridors of fiber-optic cables. Great wisps of frosted air from the core computer's cooling system seeped through the perforations in the floor and ceiling. The core computer was the nerve center, the most powerful computer system the twenty-first century could conceive—the heartless pulse of the Pantheon Corporation.

Under Conrad's leadership, the Pantheon Corporation had become one of the largest commercial entities in the world. Its political and financial influences were felt everywhere. Its public persona was one of innovation and environmentally friendly technology; however, unknown to all but a few, its immense wealth was primarily generated by the manipulation of world resources and the induction of political and economic instability, from which it profited greatly.

Conrad walked across the perforated floor, the clanging of his footsteps a counterpoint to the hum of billions of bits of data being processed beneath him. Conrad's life was a counterpoint also, dancing in harmony with a nightmare. But he wasn't looking for a way to wake up. Instead, he was looking for a way to bridle his nightmare, to rein it in for his own purposes. Conrad was perfectly willing to find admirable qualities in a madman. After all, Hitler had once said, "How fortunate for governments that the people they administer don't think." Conrad liked the way that sounded.

He heard footsteps and looked up. It was Alton.

"You. I've been waiting for you," Conrad said.

"This isn't a good time to get sentimental," Alton replied.

Conrad strode across the room. He grabbed Alton's square-boned, papier-mâché face in one hand and wrenched it sadistically, twisting it counterclockwise.

Alton spun out of his grasp. "What's this then? Cross with me?"

"You goddamned snake!" Conrad shouted.

Alton turned his head and cocked it slightly to the left, still smiling, as if to mock Conrad. "Is that the heart you want beating inside you?" Alton asked.

Conrad yanked a pistol from his vest. He pressed the barrel of the .38 against Alton's cheek.

"Imagine my surprise, my dismay, at getting a call from Max, the last person in the world I want to hear from, telling me my man on the ground has gone crazy."

Crazy: the word sickened Alton. He had always seen himself as more of a holy warrior, not some cut-rate, crazed assassin like Conrad. And now, this fool was handing down orders that would stall him in his tracks.

"Just stop, Alton!" Conrad bellowed. "You almost killed him! What would we do then? We're following my plan, not yours."

"You expect me to roam about, doing nothing, risking everything?"

"The only thing you need to concern yourself with is getting my god-damned sketch!" Conrad yelled.

Alton turned abruptly. "Oh for God's sake, stop wasting my time."

Conrad slammed down his revolver and grabbed a handful of papers, flinging them across the room. "Look at me!" Conrad shrieked, as Alton walked away. "Look at this room! I hold the lives of millions in my hand. I could crush whole countries with war or famine . . . do you understand who I am? Do you?" Conrad asked.

Alton turned and shot a look at Conrad.

"I can see that look in your eyes, Alton. It's fear, and you're damn right to fear me."

Alton ran the odds in his mind. He'd made the mistake of putting his own agenda ahead of Conrad's; he knew he'd slipped up.

"Is he dead, Conrad? Did I kill him?"

"No," Conrad admitted, grumbling the word.

"Good, then you have nothing to worry about, do you? Why don't you make some practical use of your omnipotence, Conrad? After all, you said it yourself: you're about as dangerous as they come, a man with such an operation, such a reach. No checks, no balances, no one to be accountable to. So why worry?"

"Understand this," Conrad growled. "I control the money that controls the world. I have the power."

"Ah, but you still don't have the sketch," Alton replied. "Funny, isn't it? A man so powerful, so far-reaching, still unable to fulfill such a simple obsession?"

Enraged by Alton's disrespect, Conrad snatched his revolver from the desk and struck Alton across the face. With whitened spit foaming at the corners of his lips, Conrad yelled, "The wrong time to discover you haven't lived is the moment you're about to die." Then, cocking the hammer all the way back, he yelled, "You think I need you?"

Alton watched as a cold calm came over Conrad. He needed to say something, to change the momentum. *You don't understand, Conrad,* he thought. *You can't possibly understand the difference between us. My kind has been doing our duty for centuries—for reasons an egotistical, money-grubbing tyrant like you could never understand* . . . "Conrad. Listen to me. Everything is still in play. Don't complicate things more than necessary."

Conrad stared at Alton a few seconds longer. The .38's muzzle wavered, then lowered. He snapped his finger out toward Alton. "I want the sketch. That son of a bitch Isaac took it from me. And no way is Max going to get it. Make no mistake," Conrad said. "I will get my sketch." Locking eyes with Alton, Conrad added, "You ruin Max if you have to, but Zoro stays alive. You do whatever it takes, or I will."

Alton nodded.

*   *   *

Max shifted uneasily in his bed. His dream turned cold as his nightmare came to life. These were not the thin, dim visions of a poorly recalled dream, but an overwhelming, clear horror that flickered in his mind with the vivid colors of a kaleidoscope.

The sky filled with starlings; they blocked out the sun, saturating his dream with an unbearable darkness. One by one the birds plummeted steeply from the sky and shrieked as they splintered onto the ground. Beside him a killing field burned, and he choked on the sweet, thick smoke from burning flesh.

The smell of death turned his stomach, as his dream pulled him into a darkened asylum. He stumbled through the hallways, forcing himself to concentrate, but the unholy screams behind every door made it impossible. With a familiar ache in his chest, he felt his legs begin to weaken. Every step forward moved him closer to a black hole that sucked the life from him, and he fell to his knees.

With raw courage he gazed into the first doorway, where a little boy stood beside a woman's corpse, her body now a sick shade of gray. From her head a stream of colored life force flowed into the child, trying to transport him beyond fear.

Max pushed himself to his feet and stumbled forward into a bedroom where a man grinned as he pulled the covers from a sleeping boy. With the smell of incest and sickness about him, Max ran from the room. He climbed stairs that went on without ending, growing tired, until his faintest breath fled from him.

Ringing in the pit of his mind, he heard a black-hearted laughter. Streaks of light and noise began to spill from the doorway beyond him. Dragging his weakened body toward the chaos, he looked into the eyes that laughed maniacally.

Max dared to face the disquieting horror of Conrad. Amid a room stirring with fire and flames stood Conrad, holding the fourth sketch high above his head. A thousand streams of divine energy fused into Conrad from an infinite well of souls.

Max's body shook. His heart and hands trembled, and his life force left his body as he realized he couldn't stop the catastrophe that Conrad would wreak.

Pulling a suffocating breath, Max woke, feeling a concern he'd not known since boyhood. "Zoro," he cried. The sound faded to nothing in the darkness.

CHAPTER 49

Tuesday, The Bronx

The sultry voice of Diana Krall crackled over the speakers of Johnny's cheap stereo, though Zoro wasn't really listening. He sat at the kitchen table, spinning his breakfast Cheerios round and round in a bowl of milk, half lost in thought. He wondered if Johnny, seated across from him, could imagine he was sitting at a table with a man who'd just been shot at, a man whose friend had died in his arms. Johnny sucked down his second Corona. No, he sure as hell didn't suspect anything.

Zoro stared at Johnny, wondering where their lives were headed, where his own life was headed. He knew the story of his own life as well as anyone.

When Zoro quarterbacked at Regionals, he could throw a perfect spiral right on the money to a speeding wide receiver, but now the only thing spinning was his head. He could hardly believe what had happened to Holly yesterday. He knew now, with certainty, that the only way out was to find the sketch . . . with some maniacal killer hot on his heels . . . Well, that was another obstacle. And now Gina had shown up, looking seriously unhappy—which didn't make things any easier.

Gina stood in Johnny's doorway, tapping her foot. Gina was a slender woman, and though she wasn't tall, she carried herself in a way that made her seem taller. "So what harebrained scheme have you gotten yourself into this time, Zoro?" she asked, sounding like Wilma Flintstone scolding her hapless, caveman husband.

Stepping through the door, she gave Johnny an inquisitive glance.

"He's in a bad way," Johnny said. "He showed up late last night, wouldn't say nothing, just went straight to bed. Take it easy on him, Gina."

Zoro massaged his temples. Gina walked over to him. "Hey," she ran her hand across his shoulder. "How's it going?"

Her voice sounded almost tender. Zoro turned and hugged her around the waist. Fear, confusion, desperation . . . that was the answer to her question, though he couldn't put it into words.

"Damn it to hell, Gina" he said, putting his hands on his forehead. This wasn't Gina's problem; it was his mess. But right about now he needed someone to share that mess. But how could he possibly tell her, even begin to make her understand?

"Zoro," Gina began apprehensively, "I'll listen to you, but you've got to level with me."

He looked slowly up at her. He didn't know where to begin. How do you tell your wife a whole story you can barely believe yourself? He shrugged uneasily. "I don't know what to say," he said.

"You're an ass, you know that, Zoro? You never tell me anything!" She stomped over to the sink then whirled to face him. "I've seen you do a lot of stupid things, but I never thought you'd be keeping secrets from me."

"What are you talking about, Gina?"

"Please don't, Zoro. I'm not some dumb bimbo. I can tell something's wrong; I can smell your half-truths."

Zoro heaved a sigh. He looked at Johnny, then at Gina. He started to tell her about Holly. "An accident," he said.

"You're not telling me everything, Zoro."

"Gina, I swear."

Johnny stood up from the table. "Man up, Zoro. Tell her about Max and his pinched sketches."

Gina's dark eyes cranked wide open. She stared at Zoro, accusation plain on her face. Then she spun around and leaned over the sink, muttering, "Damn it," over and over.

Zoro stared pointedly at Johnny, making a cutting motion across his throat, silently signaling for an immediate end to any mention of the sketches.

He looked at Gina. *Maybe he should go to her, say something nice. Maybe she would welcome an old familiar tenderness*, he thought. *She always said how amazed she was that such large rough hands as his could caress her so gently.* Listening to his thoughts, he took two steps forward.

Then she spun around and a plate flew past Zoro's head. He ducked and the plate broke into pieces against the far wall.

"Hey! Those are my plates!" Johnny yelled. "Jesus, Gina, you're crazy!" He got up and left, slamming the apartment door behind him.

"What the hell, Gina?" Zoro said.

"Don't give me that crap," she said, coming toward him and shoving him until he felt the wall against his back. "What sketches, you bum? What are you holding out on me?"

He swallowed hard and motioned for her to sit. He told her most of the story, conveniently forgetting about Conrad and Alton.

"So let me get this straight," she growled when he was finished. "Some rich old dude's gonna dig around in your head . . . you're going to find a stolen sketch . . . and we're gonna be rich, just like that? Why? Why'd he pick you?"

Zoro paused for a moment, weighing his answer. "I don't know. Not really."

"Oh you . . ." her lips twisted into an angry knot.

"You don't believe me?"

"Look, Zoro," Gina said, looking him in the eyes. Suddenly, she looked as tired and confused as Zoro felt. "It's not that . . . it's just . . . our lives have been crap for so long . . . Nothing much has ever changed, despite your best efforts."

"Is that what you think, Gina?"

"I just don't want you wasting our lives, chasing something we can't have. I've given up on pink houses, Zoro. Maybe it's time you did, too."

"Why can't you just believe in me?" Zoro asked quietly. "Maybe Max picked me because he thinks I can be good at something. I'm not just a no-good bum, Gina; I know that now—in my soul. If he sees it in me, why can't you? For Christ's sake, you're my wife."

Gina had seen him without his clothes plenty of times, but she'd never seen him this naked. She was suddenly overwhelmed by a vulnerability she'd never seen in Zoro. She reached for his hand, unaware tears were running down her face.

"Baby, I do believe in you," she said. "I just can't take it anymore. It's always the same thing: some sucker play, some harebrained scheme, and we always lose. Sometimes I wonder if we'll ever make it."

Zoro's voice dropped to a whisper. "But that's what I'm trying to tell you, Gina: this time is different. I know it. I swear."

She could hear a strangeness in his voice, and pulled her hand away, afraid to fall into another one of Zoro's schemes. "You always say it's different, but it never is."

Zoro knew it wasn't Gina's fault that she doubted him. "Gina, I know it's hard to believe me, after all the dumb things I've done . . ."

"No, no," she said quickly. "I wasn't trying to imply anything."

"No, Gina, listen." His voice was firmer now. "I finally realized my best wasn't good enough. You see, baby, I didn't fail because of my harebrained schemes. I failed because of *me*."

"Stop it! Zoro, don't think that way. Look in my eyes," she said, moving closer and holding him tighter.

Zoro welcomed her embrace, he hugged her tenderly. "Max told me if there's something I don't have, it's because I don't know enough, because I'm not thinking in the right way, or doing the right things. That's the beauty here, baby." Zoro sat forward on his chair, suddenly eager to explain. "I don't know enough. As a matter of fact, I know nothing, and don't care if the whole world knows it."

Suddenly Zoro jumped to his feet and shouted, "I don't know any-thing . . . nothing, not anything! And that's great!"

Gina stared at him, starting to look panicked. "Zoro! Sit down, you're scaring me."

Zoro sat down, still grinning.

"So what's in it for him, this Max Know-it-all?" She looked doubtful again. "Is he conning you, Zoro? Don't you dare give him any money."

Money, Zoro thought, remembering the wad of bills Johnny had handed him a few nights ago. *Damn, it's just like Max said; I changed my thinking, and money's already starting to find me . . .*

And then he let it slip, "I don't even need to give him Johnny's money."

Gina got a look on her face like he had just jabbed her with an ice pick. "You took money from Johnny! Oh, shit, Zoro, you idiot! Now we're dead. You know how Johnny is—you don't pay him back, he'll kill us both."

"Gina, that's not going to happen. I still have all his money; I'll just give it back. No worries, see?"

She still looked doubtful.

"Come on, I can handle Johnny. He's not what you think he is. You've got to trust me, Gina, even if you don't believe me. That's something I learned from Max."

Gina's look softened a little. "Okay, so if Johnny doesn't kill you first, can you find the sketch? Do you know where to look?"

"Not a clue!" Zoro said, laughing. The more he talked about it, the more exciting it became.

Even Gina seemed to be getting more interested. She looked at him for a long time, and then said. "I still don't get it, Zoro; knowing noth-ing is good?"

Zoro studied her for a moment. There was an innocent radiance about her. "Gina, do you remember when we were piss-poor?"

"Kinda like now?" She smiled.

"No. I mean when we started out, not even a place of our own. Everyone said, 'You don't know nothing, you won't find out how hard life is until you grow up.' But none of that mattered to us, right? Alls that mattered was that we had each other. We didn't know any better, and every day was a great adventure. Do you see, Gina?"

"No."

"We didn't know shit. And it was the best time of our marriage."

"But you're saying you don't know anything now . . . I'm confused." Gina sighed.

Gina wasn't arguing with him now. She just seemed so vulnerable. He took her face into his hands.

"That's right, baby. I thought I had all the answers, but all I really had was other people's answers. That's why I was unhappy."

"So what now?" she asked, her voice trembling.

When your mind is blank, it's in a pure state . . .

"So we start over with a clean slate, ready to learn the right answers," Zoro smiled. "Not someone else's idea of the answers. Not the answers handed down by our friends or family. We start without the garbage we inherited. I mean, baby, when I met you, you were a smart and feisty broad . . ."

"Oh, so now I'm a dumb slob?"

"That's not what I mean! What Max is trying to teach me is to forget all the garbage in my head."

An uncertain look came over her face. "Does this have anything to do with Joey?"

Zoro slumped. "Yeah, yeah, I told Max about Joey. And it was as if he already knew everything I felt . . . I was a good kid, you know."

"I know." She nodded.

"I was an empty slate. I never broke the rules until one time, on my fourteenth birthday, I crossed the line. And Joey died because of me. And now wherever I go, I can hear him screaming."

His face became so still she was afraid. "It's not your fault, baby." She looked into his eyes. "I love you."

He met her gaze. "I need to change, Gina, because somewhere, somehow, there's a better life for you and me. And when I find it, every-thing is going to be okay."

"You're a bad liar, Zoro. But okay." She started crying. "Okay, baby, I believe in you. I guess I always have."

Zoro wiped a tear from her cheek. Then he softly sang the song: "You Are Everything."

"I adore you, you beautiful idiot," she whispered. She kissed him, then just as quickly pushed his head away and stood up. "But you make sure Mr. Midas Max don't rip you off, you hear me? Don't you give him Johnny's money!"

Zoro didn't know what else to say, but he'd already decided what to do. Grabbing his phone, Zoro speed-dialed Max.

Tolbert answered on the first ring. Zoro turned toward Gina and shrugged apologetically. Seconds later Max's voice roared a big hello. "Max, it's me, Zoro."

"Zoro!" Max said, his smile so big Zoro could feel it through the phone.

"I need to tell you something, Max."

"Okay." Max waited.

Zoro's voice trembled. "I'm going to trust you found me for a reason. But whatever we're going to do, it needs to be now, before . . . before . . ."

The room was starting to spin around Zoro. What was happening?

"Zoro?" Max's voice came over the phone. "Zoro, what's wrong?"

And then Zoro's phone fell from his hand as he slumped uncon-scious to the floor. He heard the faint sound of Gina screaming . . . then nothing . . .

CHAPTER 50

A dark rain drummed softly on Zoro's face. He awoke to the sound of his name. "This way, Zoro, quickly."

Zoro could've sworn it was Isaac's voice. He opened his eyes, terrified. Surrounded by darkened stone blocks, he looked up fifty feet at a circle of sky filled with moon. His first thought was that he'd fallen down a well. He spotted a small opening to one side. He moved toward the shelter of shadows. He found himself wishing for sunlight, and he trembled.

"This way, Zoro." Again the voice. He followed. He entered a maze of darkened stone catacombs, and ran. Stumbling and ducking beneath blackened archways, he suddenly found himself outside under the night sky. He staggered across a dark field, stopping only for a small breath of relief. He was thirsty, cold, and wet. He ran. The sound of his footsteps swished through the damp grass. His chest was tight and he felt like some infamous prisoner on a wild and frantic prison break.

Suddenly the night went silent, followed by a gentle whisper. "My son."

In front of him a figure stepped from the shadows. It was hard to make out. "Dad, is that you?"

The figure moved closer and stretched out a hand. "Come," the figure said.

Looking suddenly upward at a single, brilliant star shooting across the night sky, Zoro fell forward. Grabbing the figure's hand, suddenly Zoro was whirled through the air in a blinding, violet light. His eyes rolled in his head as he found himself flying through the heavens. He passed millions of stars and planets as he crossed a cold and empty space. Circling the fringe of the universe, he soon found himself hovering over a most extraordinary sight: Earth. Against the backdrop of barren planets he'd circled, he suddenly realized the majesty of his beautiful, blue planet. The gift of life, given uniquely to humankind, was laid out before him in all its splendor and pain. And in the shadow of his glowing planet, he could've sworn he felt Joey and Isaac beside him. Zoro fell into a well of peace, and he couldn't find his voice. But his thirst was gone.

*   *   *

"Can he hear us?" Gina blinked a lingering tear from her eyes.

"I can't be sure, but it's possible." The doctor pushed a few buttons on a monitor and the signal changed color.

Zoro blinked. He heard voices, but couldn't tell where they came from. "Did I die?" His voice sounded strange, strained.

Gina flung herself onto the hospital bed, weeping and laughing with relief. "You're not dead, baby," she said. "But if you ever scare me like that again, I'm going to kill you."

Zoro reached for her hand. "What happened to me?"

A doctor flashed a penlight into Zoro's eyes, checking his pupillary light reflexes. "You had a transient ischemic attack, a ministroke. Can you tell me where you are?"

"Umm, the hospital."

"Good. And what's your name?"

"Zoro." A twisted smile stretched across his face. Then suddenly he looked around. "Do I need to worry? Am I brain-dead?"

The doctor laughed. "The human brain is seven times larger than it needs to be; no one knows why." He patted Zoro on the hand. "You'll be just fine, Zoro."

"How are you feeling?" Gina asked him.

"I can't stop thinking about what I saw—while I was out."

Sitting beside him, she studied his face. Something came into his eyes, something she recognized as hope.

"Gina, something happened to me," he said. "My mind is doing things without me even knowing." His cheeks flushed. "I went places in my head."

"What places?" Gina continued to look at him.

"I don't know, Gina. I'm just seeing weird things."

Gina let him know she was there to listen, though she assumed anything he experienced was probably due to being unconscious. He rubbed his hands over his face. "I want you to understand," he said.

"Take your time, Zoro. I'm here, baby."

"When I was a kid," he said, closing his hand over hers, "my dad used to take me on long car rides."

"Where did you go?"

"Nowhere," Zoro said. "We just drove. But those days felt like heaven."

"It's good that you're telling me, Zoro."

"Close your eyes, Gina," he whispered. "Pretend you're eight years old, without a care in the world. That's the moment. That's what it felt like."

Gina smiled.

"I was in Dad's car again, Gina, safe. I've missed that." Zoro took a deep breath. "It was like magic; I was the magic."

Her first inclination was to doubt him, patronize him. He read it in her eyes. "I'm not crazy . . . just out of my mind, and I'll be back in five minutes," he teased. He hoped the humor would take the pressure off, give her a chance to think things through.

There was another voice in the room. "Now wait just one minute, who's out of their mind?" Zoro recognized the voice. Max stepped into the room and approached the bed slowly.

"Been here the whole time, Zoro . . . wouldn't have missed it. I've never heard of anyone denting the floor with his head before." Max smiled.

Zoro's eyes latched on to Max's. "I don't know what to do, Max."

Max marched straight up beside him. "I'll tell you what you're going to do; you're going to relax."

Gina had a relieved smile on her face.

"There's no reason for concern, Zoro," Max said. Then he reached into his pocket as his phone vibrated. "I can't talk right now," he said quietly. "Is it done? . . . No, no he won't be a problem, at least not for a while."

Now Gina was looking at Max with a worried expression.

Max hung up the phone, seating himself on the bedside chair.

"I saw things, strange things," Zoro continued, as Max dropped his phone into his pocket.

"Don't worry about it." Max smiled.

Zoro's head was ringing with thoughts; sensations of emotion would soon overtake him. "Since you reached out to me, Max, I'm not afraid anymore, but I still hurt." The words strained against his breath. "I think . . . I think I saw Joey and Isaac, but I never got a chance to say good-bye. Maybe I should've stayed dead."

Gina's face was now wax-pale.

"Then say good-bye," Max insisted. "They can still hear you."

"How, Max?"

"It doesn't matter how, Zoro. It only matters that they can."

"Yeah, yeah, you're probably right." Zoro looked at Gina. He realized his emotions had come from everywhere at once, and she wasn't used to that. "I could really use some coffee, Gina."

"I'll have to ask the doctor," she said. She began to walk toward the door.

"Max," Zoro whispered, momentarily forgetting Gina. "Why didn't Isaac want me to find the sketch? He could've just given it to me."

"Interesting question, Zoro." He leaned against the bed rail. "But I think he did; I'm willing to bet on it."

Zoro pulled himself up against the rail, close to Max. He didn't see Gina, standing by the doorway, listening.

"I've been thinking this through," Zoro whispered, "wondering if we should continue."

"And what did you decide?"

"When do we start?"

Max grinned eagerly. "So much is about to happen, Zoro."

"Yes," Gina said. "And it's time you came home. Where you belong."

CHAPTER 51

Wednesday, The Bronx

Johnny swung the sedan into a no-parking zone and parked. He lit a cigar and flicked the match through the open window, into the street. Looking up at Zoro's apartment, Johnny hesitated. He had hoped to keep Zoro close—and the sketch closer.

They hadn't always been close as kids, though Johnny had grown up in the same neighborhood as Zoro and Joey. But when Johnny had tried to entice Zoro into running small bags of money for the bookmakers, figuring no one would ever suspect a clean-cut young man carrying a small paper bag, Zoro had been smart enough to push Johnny away.

As luck would have it, years later, fate had brought them together again. Johnny would never forget the day Zoro had come upon some goons, beating the hell out of him over a disagreement about a temporary loan. Without thinking, without hesitation, Zoro had charged in like the cavalry, bowling over two of Johnny's attackers at once and then putting up an impressive, noisy fight until a beat cop showed up and the goons took off.

Zoro had saved Johnny that day. And though Johnny, crude and violent, was older than Zoro, a poor student, their friendship was instantly bonded. No words had been spoken that day; one look was all it took for Johnny to become Zoro's adopted uncle. And Johnny had repaid his debt many times, over the years.

Lately, though, Johnny had grown colder, more dangerous, and the bond lessened. Now Johnny's loyalties had become impure, heavy. He got out of his car and walked to the apartment building. He rapped his knuckles on Zoro's door.

The noise throbbed in Zoro's head like a drum, and he sprang from the sofa. Gina had already opened the door. He stared at Johnny, trying to figure what kind of bad thing was about to go down.

Johnny smiled and waved. "How are you, buddy?" There was no real warmth in his voice.

Gina looked at Zoro; nobody moved.

"Do I have to force myself in?" Johnny asked, already halfway across the living room.

Zoro lifted his hand as a fake smile formed on his face.

"Gina, how you doing?" Johnny smiled, pursing his grayed lips toward her. She lifted her head to face him, pulling a lock of hair behind her ear.

"Sit down, Johnny; gee, what a surprise," her voice creaked. Behind Johnny's back, she made a helpless, scrunched-up face at Zoro.

Heavy-jowled Johnny slumped into a kitchen chair as Gina wiped two glasses with her apron. Zoro spun a chair around backward, and sat facing him.

"What do you want, Johnny?" Zoro asked.

"What kind of a friend would I be if I didn't visit my adopted nephew when he's sick? Let's talk, Zoro." Johnny said. "Not here though," he added, "outside."

"Look here, Johnny," Zoro protested, hoping not to rouse Gina. But it was too late, Johnny had already climbed through the window onto the balcony. Zoro didn't have any choice except to follow.

He pulled the window shut behind him. "Why are you here, Johnny? You shouldn't be here. It's only been a day since I got home. If it's about your money . . ."

"Relax, Zoro. I'm not here to protect my investment. I'm just worried about you. Can't a friend be worried?"

"Yeah, I guess." Zoro looked doubtful.

"Straight as an arrow, that's what I am, Zoro. I'm the nicest guy you'll ever know." Johnny had an unpleasant grin smeared on his face.

"I appreciate that you . . ."

"Don't fucking interrupt me! I've told you before not to interrupt me."

Zoro shook his head and waited.

"Look, Zoro, just cause you're sick doesn't mean you don't owe me."

"I have your money, Johnny, just take it back." Zoro felt a sense of apprehension, knowing he probably shouldn't have taken the money in the first place.

Johnny scoffed, "But that wasn't our deal. The deal was no interest for a cut of what you get for the sketch. If I'm making nothing off the sketch, you owe me 20 percent interest up front."

Zoro couldn't help glancing back at the window. He wished Gina was somewhere else, so he could release his fury on this contemptible asshole. How dare Johnny come to his home, call him out like this, in front of Gina?

"Tomorrow, the next day, the day after tomorrow . . . days come by quickly, Zoro. You don't want to see the day come when you're sitting here asking yourself, 'How could I have been so damn stupid?'"

"Johnny, don't pull this shit with me, I'm not one of your damn loan customers."

"Relax, Zoro," Johnny laughed. "I'm just after what's mine."

Zoro stared back at Johnny, his arms crossed over his chest.

"How's Gina handling all this, Zoro?" Johnny's tone softened. "You know, she deserves better than this neighborhood. Anything could happen to someone on these streets. Beautiful woman like Gina . . ."

"Johnny, don't even go there! Just cut the shit; I know who you really are."

"But do you know who I'm becoming?"

"I was hoping for a better person."

"Me too, Zoro, but there are many ways to be human."

CHAPTER 52

It had taken longer than Zoro had anticipated to get to Arden Finnegan's shop. It was late, almost closing, and inside the shop, Arden was putting away some small jewelry boxes. Zoro had pulled up silently. So silently, in fact, that no one on the street heard him, or perhaps they were so preoccupied with their lives they didn't notice.

Zoro's mind was playing with him, waffling, keeping him from making a decision. He decided to try and apply the lessons he'd learned from Max. *No harm in trying, at least.* So he sat, staring through the windshield and scrunching his face, making loud, straining noises.

Zoro was trying to tap his subconscious, to force a change that might help him to see things differently. But the answer he was looking for didn't come. What came instead was rain: heavy rain. The big, fat drops clanged a melody as they beat on the limo roof and ran in rivers down the windshield and across the hood.

Zoro's mouth was dry. He kept trying and hoping and squeezing his face together even harder as he prayed that some invisible thing might jump out at him, guide him away from the path he had put himself on. But still no answers came. And the harder he tried, the harder it rained.

So Zoro decided to change tactics, outflank his dilemma like a good general. He would manifest the answer he needed; surely the Law of

Attraction ought to work. Max had said so, right? He began to visualize how he would find the answer for his dilemma.

Still nothing. Max had unfolded the convolutions so plainly, explained it all, and still it wasn't working for Zoro. He sat wishing and wondering, hoping that everything—something—would lead him to an answer.

Frustrated, Zoro wondered how Max did it. Surely Max could do it: it was flat-out in the open and plain to see. Max was wealthy; he lived in a mansion, an impressive display of decorative ironwork and cut marble; his home nestled on an estate of scalloped and trimmed gardens. And he owned oil wells, Zoro thought to himself, *oil wells, for crying out loud.* Sure as hell, that Law of Attraction and Third Q stuff was working for Max. And not marginally, like a weak, occasional trickle that you could barely call a stream. No, Max's wealth raged and broke out like the torrent of a river running over its banks.

Yet, the harder Zoro tried to find an answer, the more he failed. So he settled back, analyzed why things were working for Max, and not for him. And then he was hit with a brilliant moment of misconstrued logic: *Maybe Max had no bad files in his subconscious,* Zoro thought. *Maybe that was why he seemingly succeeded effortlessly where Zoro failed.*

But nothing could have been further from the truth . . .

* * *

Miles away, in his darkened bedroom, behind locked doors guarded by loyal professionals and the best electronic security money could buy, Max was facing his own silent enemies, his own inner demons. He tossed and turned, longing for rest—but sleep wouldn't come. Tonight, there were too many memories . . .

Hunters say they remember their first kill most vividly, as if they feel the wound themselves. That horror sticks with them, hooks them. But what they forget to tell you is that the prey they hunt feels the first wound just as intently.

Max lay in the darkness of the night, and it came alive around him— the gouge of that first arrow. He was almost nine when his loving mother died: quickly and with dignity, so everyone had said. But when he thought about it later, he recognized what a load of bullshit that was. No one dies with dignity, Max thought; the best we can hope to do is to live with dignity.

And so a tender Bronx boy was shuffled alone through various foster homes. At first it was little more than monotony, routine. But then he met Keith Shank, his new foster dad. He never thought ahead to what Shank might rain down on him, but Shank was messed up. He had that creepy ability of getting into your head, of becoming you. And once in your mind, he'd grind you down, until there was nothing left of you.

That's when he'd strike. And soon, under his cold stare, a hug became a grab, until Max was smothered with the ruthlessness of abuse. And if Max believed the world was evil, not because he wanted to believe it, but because it was, of course he could have.

With Shank in his head, evil lurked everywhere and was capable of anything. At school he became afraid of his teachers; he would vomit when forced to change for swimming at the pool. It all got so bad that he'd scream every night, until no home would have him. Back then orphan boys didn't believe in God, and Max hadn't found God either. But Max got lucky . . . he found someone else.

Her name was Clarice, one of his foster sisters. She was only fifteen, an orphan herself and not yet a nun, but devout beyond reproach, and her words would help him push past his demons.

For Clarice was a fierce demon hunter. Clarice had taught Max the secret of how to use the mind with laser precision to zap hell-spawned memories, though she didn't know how she did it.

At first it had been difficult for Max to kill demons in his head. In those days he did it without knowing how. It was a quiet, unconscious competence, which had no clear methodology or explanation. He was like the lucky few who strike it rich, never knowing how or why, never being able to repeat the recipe. But as he practiced, he got better, his ability more pronounced—yet still awkward.

Eventually he grew stronger, his strength nurtured by a young girl who had persuaded him to fight back against the darkness of his own mind.

And though his unconscious competence held him safe, the darker side of his mind pulled him, tried to drag him back down. And those constant repeated failures continued until the day he met Conrad's father.

Joshua Mason had good instincts and a good heart. And he took it upon himself to mentor a struggling but gifted young man named Max. Unable to reconcile the differences between himself and his only son, Conrad, Joshua took Max as his unofficial surrogate son.

This, of course, fed steroids to the monster inside Conrad. When Conrad learned that his own father, his own flesh and blood, had for some reason forgotten to share a little nugget of information about a secret sketch, he vowed that Max—and Joshua, his own father—would see evil up close. And though Conrad's vengeance was stopped short by Joshua's death only one year later, he never gave up trying to derail the developing bond between his father and Max, his hated rival. Joshua was only able to thwart Conrad's hateful resolve when, on his deathbed, he gave young Max the box containing the first sketch and sent him down the secret stairway, escaping Conrad's wrath.

In the years following Joshua's death, Max had spent every penny he'd serendipitously earned to find the next two sketches. And along with the journey to find the sketches, came an explosion of truth; he was finally able to put into words, into definable thoughts, what he and Clarice had known but hadn't been able to define.

* * *

Sitting in front of Finnegan's Pawnshop, Zoro, like young Max, didn't know much. He had never ventured near the cavern of pain that Max harbored; he was too busy with his own haunted past. All Zoro ever saw was a quirky old rich guy with a recipe for success. He never understood that Max couldn't manifest what he *wanted*, but only what he *was*. And the same would be true for Zoro.

And so there Zoro sat, in front of Arden's shop, thinking of how easy this decision would've been for Max to make. He twisted his ring onto his finger, and his heart grew heavy, heavier than his regional championship ring. There hadn't been much for Zoro since Joey had died, but for a while, football had been Zoro's demon hunter. Running plays in his mind, imagining the routes on the field, freed him. And the regional championship win, well, that just paved the road to glory . . . until he came up short in his bid for the state championship. Why was it, Zoro wondered, that all the wins that got them to state seemed to evaporate with the sound of the ending whistle when they lost that last game? Why weren't any of those previous victories enough to keep him from feeling like a loser? And why hadn't Carmela been able to find it within herself to comfort her devastated son in his loss?

He looked down at the ring. His grandfather had somehow found the extra money to have a real ruby set in the ring Zoro and his team-mates were awarded for winning Regionals. Grandpa, God bless him, was trying to make him feel better, Zoro guessed, but after losing the state championship game, Zoro had never worn the ring. He didn't feel he deserved it, somehow. He'd also never picked up a football again.

Arden had offered him $500 for the ring. That, plus the money from the jar in the kitchen, combined with Johnny's original "investment," would get him settled with Johnny, interest and all. One problem solved, at least.

He wiped his face with a handkerchief as he thought of the unbearable discomfort of giving up his ring. But that wasn't his true dilemma: willing himself to decide was what was difficult. He knew he needed to pay Johnny back now, before things got worse. Dodging the mysterious tattooed man while things escalated to a higher degree of violence was plenty to think about without a vindictive Johnny making his life miserable, maybe even threatening Gina.

He zoomed in on the ring and tried one last time, scrunching his face. *Come on, Third Q, come on* . . . But there was no miracle. So, like any other schmuck getting bossed around by his own mind, Zoro decided he'd just sell the ring and do what needed to be done. He pulled his collar up, got out of the limo, and dashed through the rain into Finnegan's Pawnshop.

Arden was all right, a hard worker. He'd inherited the old store, and also his sense of fairness, from his grandfather Kyle Finnegan. Old Man Finnegan, originally a jeweler by trade, had often played on the sound of his name and claimed he could restore anything, make it "fine—again." Zoro remembered a lot of childhood outings to Finnegan's; this was where Isaac shopped on every special occasion, every birthday, every Christmas. In those days, Finnegan's was the poor man's Macy's. Only now it wasn't Christmas, and Zoro wasn't with his father. Arden buzzed him through the second security gate, and he walked to the counter, reluctantly.

"You sure, Zoro?" Arden asked.

"Not much choice, Arden." Zoro had made a plan, calmly and decisively, and selling the ring was part of it.

Arden sighed. "Okay, I'll keep it out of the showcase as long as I can. But the wholesalers get a crack at melting it down, nothing I can do about that. It's got a good stone, too."

It was hard for Zoro, and Arden knew it. But business was business.

"Zoro . . ."

"I'm fine, Arden."

"No, you're soaking wet, and not fine."

"It's just my jacket and pants. They'll dry."

Zoro nodded. He took off the ring and placed it on the counter, then crammed the $500 Arden had counted out into his damp pocket. Oddly, having the money seemed much less fulfilling than he'd imagined. Zoro huddled into his coat and shuffled back toward the cage, as Arden buzzed him out.

"Zoro," Arden called. "Catch."

Zoro turned around, and Arden tossed him a silver pen, printed with the store name.

He grabbed for the pen; it was cold consolation. Still, Arden had a heart. Zoro smiled as he caught the pen through the bars.

"Thanks, man."

There was no turning back, and as his face narrowed, Zoro stepped through the door. The rain came down harder now; each drop stung as it spattered on Zoro's face.

He scrambled to the limo, again flicking up the collar of his jacket. He stopped in a puddle as the autumn downpour ran across his shoes, streaming its way to the sewers. He smiled as the water seeped into his shoes. At least he had made a decision: one that maybe even his mother could understand.

CHAPTER 53

Thursday, The Bronx

Nathan didn't know why Carmela had been so insistent this morning; she said she just had to visit the church because it was bingo day. But Nathan knew she missed bingo day whenever it suited her purposes. He suspected it was something about Zoro; she was probably going to try and corner him and try to convince him to do something on behalf of his errant younger brother. Even though Nathan loved Zoro, there was something about him that Nathan's heart could not accept.

Carmela conducted herself as if she owned Nathan's church. And she might as well have, because around her, Nathan was small, insignificant.

He felt stuck between his devotion to Carmela and his pure and gentle love of his lost little brother, though sometimes he still wanted nothing more than to strangle Zoro. But all it took in those moments was to remember there was a time when he held Zoro's hand and walked him to school, a time he remembered when a skinned knee could be magically cured by a big brother's funny face. Around him the church bells chimed the hour, and the ringing filtered through the church, humming at the doors. And suddenly Carmela's tyranny seemed to hem Nathan close.

* * *

That day, despite the cold, the sun had been working overtime to warm the pavement. And as Conrad arrived at Mount Carmel, things were about to heat up even more. A subliming vapor, rising from a basement heating vent, curtained the church's front entrance. Conrad passed through the swirling vapor and tugged on the heavy front door. He walked up the center aisle to where an old man was kneeling, praying.

Looking at the old man as he walked past, Conrad wondered if he ought to ask him if he'd made a true discovery. What would the old man's report have been at the end of a lifetime of faith?

Conrad continued on, toward the back stairs. He descended slowly to the basement, guided by the sound of the bingo ladies' laughter and gossip. He stepped into the basement fellowship hall and called out in a loud rasp, "Carmela!"

Carmela was immediately up and out of her chair, straightening her dress. She was beside him in a matter of seconds. A dried-out smile twisted the edges of Conrad's lips; and under the fluorescent light he had the color of a spoiled hamburger. Conrad grabbed her hand and turned his back on her, and with Carmela in tow, he quickly climbed the twenty steps back up toward the rectory.

"I'm confused about something, Conrad," Carmela said, quickening her pace. "It's been so many years, and you want to see me now, here?"

"You lied to me, Carmela."

"Pardon me?"

"All those years, when Isaac had abandoned you and the kids, my generosity got you through."

"Yes, Conrad, yes it did, but . . ."

"And you lied to me."

"Lied . . ."

"Not here, Carmela, we'll speak in the Rectory."

No one, not even Carmela, knew who Conrad really was. He had just appeared one day: a forceful young man, the son of a wealthy philanthropist and founder of the Pantheon Corporation. Conrad was a silver-tongued man whom Isaac had aspired to imitate, at first.

Isaac had been drawn into the Pantheon Corporation, a fraternity through which he hoped to surpass the wistful hopes of his immigrant father, who had labored to eke out a better life for his children. But soon it became clear that Conrad was polluted. Under his leadership, the Pantheon Corporation was a fraternity of merciless greed, not the answer Isaac had hoped for.

So Isaac had mutinied, defected to a new fraternity: an invisible brotherhood that existed among all people of goodness. It was the same fraternity to which Max, Isaac's future mentor, belonged. It was the sort of invisible alliance that one might recognize during a crisis—a flash flood, in wartime, a disastrous storm—when one human being helps another without questions: the type of crisis where there are no Catholics, no Jews, no black or white, rich or poor . . . only people doing the right thing.

Max had aspired to build such a fraternity, one of enlightened people who would strive to empower themselves and the world: people who lived by the Third Q.

But Conrad despised Max and utterly rejected his invitation into a fraternity of goodness. Conrad had chosen to work in the dark, with the lights out. It better suited his temperament and intentions.

Today, the man who had come from nowhere and had still not found where he was going would, without question, rain down his frustration on Carmela.

Nathan was seated at his desk as Conrad and Carmela arrived. A weakened beam of light played through the heavy leaded glass in the rectory, barely lighting the grainy pages of the paperback he was holding.

"Out!" Conrad commanded.

"Mr. Mason. What an unexpected surprise."

"I apologize, my dear boy," Conrad said, as he caught Nathan by the sleeve. Nathan could feel his robe twist as Conrad hauled him out of his chair.

"Get out of here," Conrad growled.

Carmela, hugging the frame of the door, said, "It's all right, Nathan, we need the room."

Nathan got up reluctantly. He stared at Conrad, whose physical presence drummed him down, like some sort of Roman general. "What do you want with Ma, Conrad?"

"Nathan!" Carmela said. "It's not that I don't appreciate your protective instincts, but wait outside."

"If you harm her . . ." Nathan warned.

"I'll make no trouble for you," Conrad said, smiling sadistically. Nathan went out and Conrad slammed the door behind him.

"Sit, Carmela." She moved toward Nathan's chair, but Conrad blocked her path with his cane.

"Over there," he said, pointing to a plain wooden chair in front of the rectory desk.

"I pegged you for more of a gentleman," Carmela said. "You've changed, Conrad."

He grabbed her arm and shoved her toward the chair.

"Let go of me. What do you want?" She sat, and he stood over her, still holding her arm. He tightened his grip.

"I do want something." Touching her hair, he said, "Carmela, you're still so beautiful."

"Bullshit," she said, tugging her arm free. "All right, Conrad, out with it. What do you want?"

"What would you do, Carmela, if you could have something back: something you thought you'd lost and could never get back again?"

"I'd give anything. What are you getting at?"

"You can understand me, Carmela, you always have. You know what it's like not to have something that's yours, something you want back."

"What?"

"Damn good question. What is it that I want that I don't have?" Conrad's eyes glazed over, dulled like the eyes of a shark: cold, cruel, and lifeless.

"Isaac's suicide," he said finally, "wasn't about Joey, Carmela."

"What are you talking about?" she asked in a horrified whisper.

"You'd think he'd be at peace—Isaac," Conrad said. He leaned forward. "Guilt can be a terrible burden, even for the dearly departed."

"What do you want, Conrad?" she asked feebly. "What are you trying to tell me?"

Conrad reached into his pocket. He pulled out something shiny on a small chain and wound it around his finger.

"Do you know what this is?"

She shook her head.

He opened his hand and a small pewter medallion tumbled out and spun on its chain in midair.

"Isaac's medallion!"

"Wrong!" Conrad said. "It's mine!"

Grabbing her hand, Conrad put the medallion into Carmela's palm.

"See?" he asked, pointing. "It's inscribed with my name, right there."

Carmela sank into the chair, refusing to let go of the medallion. "But Isaac . . ."

"But Isaac, . . ." Conrad said, mocking her. "Isaac would have his name, right here," he said, flicking at the back of the medallion. "I know this," he added, "because we got them at the same time. Only I was strong enough to tear this wretched relic from around my neck. Isaac wasn't strong enough to make that break. But he was strong enough to steal from me."

"That's not possible," she said. "Isaac may have been a lot of things, but he wasn't a thief!"

"Of course," Conrad laughed. "Neither am I."

"Just tell me what the hell you're looking for and I'll find it." Carmela's voice sounded defeated.

"A sketch," he said in hard tones.

Carmela began to laugh mirthlessly. "You're out of luck, then. Every painting we had burned up in the fire."

"But not my sketch."

Carmela's eyes rolled back in her head. "That's why you helped me, to spy on me? Thinking I was hiding something . . . You bastard!" She started to get up, but he savagely jammed her back down in the chair. He leaned into her face.

"Let me make myself clear, Carmela. Your little Zoro and that termite Max Cisary are somehow involved with this whole thing."

"Zoro? That's absurd and you know it!"

"When they find my sketch, Carmela, I want it back!" Conrad shouted, flecks of spittle hitting her in the face.

Then the look on his face softened. Carmela recognized the expression: the face of duplicity, manipulation, it was very familiar to her.

"Surely a good mother could impress upon her son to do the right thing. Before the wrong thing happens."

A cold chill clung to Carmela. Conrad didn't need to embellish, rattle, or scream. His blank shark eyes had said it all as he laid the clear and present danger squarely into her lap.

"Are you a good mother, Carmela?"

"Yes . . ."

"Are you sure? Because time is running out. Ticktock, ticktock, soon it may be too late."

CHAPTER 54

Thursday was a big market day in Little Italy and the streets were crowded. Zoro walked slowly, his arms swinging idly at his side. The doctors had told him to take it easy after his ischemic attack. But all the prescriptions in the world couldn't stop Zoro from shopping for sausages. The aroma of grilling sausage was his cocaine. And after sampling his way through islands of roast beef and mountains of sausage, Zoro headed home.

"What the hell is wrong with you?" Gina said as she let him in the door. "What have you gotten mixed up in now?"

Zoro watched in surprise as Gina collapsed, weeping, on the couch.

"Carmela told me everything," Gina yelled. "I've always stuck up for you with her, but this time you've gone too far."

Making for the kitchen to unload his groceries, he saw his mother sitting at the kitchen table. And the way she was looking at him at this moment somehow made Zoro forget the ugliness in her heart. Instead, she seemed frail, scared—vulnerable.

"I came to see you," Carmela said, "to warn you. There's going to be trouble."

The tone of her voice was message enough. He looked at her carefully. "Trouble? What kind of trouble?"

Gina stepped into the kitchen doorway, hugging herself and looking scared. Zoro looked at his wife, then turned again toward Carmela. He noticed how the tracks of her tears grooved deeply through the layers of foundation. He sat down across the table from her.

"Go on, Ma."

Carmela described her run-in with Conrad, her emotions spilling out of her like a waterfall. She laid it all out, and Zoro listened. He leaned back, allowing himself time to think. There were so many questions that touched him. And though he wanted to run out and smash Conrad, instead he explained and apologized.

It was precisely what Carmela had wanted to hear. Not his words; they just droned on and labored under Zoro's exaggerated apology. After a while, Carmela had stopped listening. No, the words didn't matter to her; what mattered to Carmela was that any compromise she'd made with Conrad could now be blamed on Zoro. It was, quite simply, Zoro's fault. She turned her head sharply, and her words weren't well thought-through.

"It's been a long time," Carmela said, interrupting Zoro's explanation.

"Excuse me?" Zoro knew better than to expect Carmela to easily accept anything from him that she didn't dictate, but he still wasn't prepared for what she said next.

"This . . ." she closed her eyes to collect her thoughts. "This thing you're mixed up in—you and I both know what you did wrong."

"Oh, so I did something wrong?" Zoro seethed; only his newly found mind-power kept his anger in check.

"Yes. You did something wrong; you believed in something your father did. You believed there was something worth holding on to in all his nonsense."

Zoro took a deep breath and held it, hoping to hold off her mercenary attack. "Why the hell are you saying this?" He shoved himself up from the table as his anger grew.

"Why am I saying this? Look at what's happened. Gina and I are all alone here while you're off doing God knows what."

"Now hold on a second, Carmela," Gina said, uncertainly.

Carmela rushed ahead. "Whatever your father was mixed up in, forget about it. Everything that's happened to us revolves around that stolen sketch. I don't know if your father took it, but I do know that Max is no god, with answers to all the mysteries. And he's putting us in harm's way."

Zoro had the strongest urge to strangle his mother. In his condition, getting upset was about the worst thing he could do.

"The sketch, Zoro: recognize it for what it is," Carmela said. "It's all about a valuable art treasure—nothing more. The sooner you get that through your head . . ."

"But Ma . . ."

"Don't bother trying to deny it," she said. "Anything else is a charade, Zoro. Conrad, Max, this artwork you're all searching for . . . they're all conning you in their own way, to get at the sketch they think your father took. It's all about money, Zoro, and that's it."

Zoro couldn't believe it. Max couldn't be part of some patiently constructed evil plan that revolved around money. "Not Max," he said defiantly.

"It's a con! Do you honestly think they're after some mystery wisdom? Think about it; you're the one who's been investigating—what did you learn? There's no mystery answers, Zoro, only greedy men."

Despite his indignation at the way Carmela was painting Max, Zoro thought about Holly's dying words. The top of his head started aching; even the skin on his head hurt.

Carmela was pulling him back into his empty existence. He felt the rise of emotion and he couldn't hold it back. There was no denying the logic in what Carmela had said; it all made sense to Zoro . . . more sense than some mystery Name and ancient sketch. He looked at Gina out of the corner of his eye, and she looked a bit dazed, too.

"The robbery," Gina said. "So that was Conrad?"

He went into the living room, his eyes fixed on the box of his father's memorabilia that he'd rescued from Carmela's place. He dug frantically through Isaac's things, again and again. He hoped for anything, any clue . . . Zoro kept digging. There had to be something . . . anything . . .

But there was nothing, just a few trinkets, an empty wooden Yosegi box, and an old dream board. With a bear-like swipe he knocked the box to the ground.

"Zoro," Gina said, "What are we going to do?"

His mother and wife were scared—it was obvious. Zoro knew it, and he needed to do the right thing to allay their fears. What was it Conrad had said that day, back in the room at the library? *At least I pay in cash* . . . Maybe Carmela was right. Maybe it just came down to money—those who had it, and those who didn't. If money was what it took to make all this go away . . . "Don't worry, baby. I'll handle it," he said, finally.

Gina's face was a portrait of fear. "I just . . . I don't want to die!"

Carmela came over to him then, gripping his arm. She had a terrified look in her eyes. "Handle it? What's that supposed to mean?"

Zoro's voice creaked with defeat. "You want me to put your fears ahead of my dreams, Ma, so that's what I'm going to do. Like I said, I'll handle it."

At that very moment it became clear. Instead of moving forward into the future, Zoro had decided to move forward through the past. Just a couple days ago he'd regained consciousness, filled with new hope and direction. And now the punishing nightmare of repeating his past mistakes was about to awaken. Zoro would handle things the way he always had, the comfortable way. But first he had to tamp down his mother's rage and his wife's anxiety.

"Ma, Johnny gets his money, and then I quit." *Yeah, I quit,* he thought, hoping that wouldn't be a death sentence. He reached into his pocket and flung a stiff role of hundreds, wrapped with a thick rubber band, onto the coffee table.

He looked at Gina, knowing she'd realize he'd raided her stash in the cookie jar. He knew he shouldn't have taken the money without asking, without explaining, but even so he didn't feel bad about it. All he had wanted to do was jump-start his life—and then Johnny had turned on him. Gina had to know that, he thought. Why on earth wouldn't she understand?

But it probably wouldn't be so easy. It was no coincidence Gina had always saved a little money, just like her mother. She'd save a little something for those special occasions or the tragic ones. It was no coincidence Zoro had taken it either. Somehow she'd known he would because that's what her daddy had always done—at least, that's what Gina said.

Zoro knew there were times when Gina wondered what made Zoro tick. He had always been so committed to his get-rich-quick schemes. There were still things she needed to know but didn't.

"Zoro, you should have asked," she said.

Carmela put her hand over Gina's mouth. "Zoro, I'm telling you, you're doing the right thing."

CHAPTER 55

Friday, New Jersey

The next morning, Zoro headed straight for Max's. But his mind was somewhere else. Despite his decision to take the obvious path yesterday, something wasn't adding up.

He tried over and over to put the parts together. And though he had tried to get excited about the possibility of Conrad's offer, everything was still based on assumptions. What were Conrad's real motives? Why was Max in his life? And what of Isaac's sketch, Zoro wondered.

And as soon as he asked that question, more questions shot through him. Was Max holding something back? Was he somehow involved with Isaac's death? If Max really wanted to do the right thing, this would be the time to start, he thought.

In the shadowy worlds of Max and Conrad, Zoro guessed, loyalties could shift overnight. And without question, there were times when Zoro doubted Max. His passion for daydreaming about the fourth sketch was worrisome, to say the least. And there were questions about Max's plan, which, Zoro suspected, even Max hadn't sorted out.

The ride seemed short, and soon he found himself turning up the long driveway. The limo had been less of an escape today, and now, with all the windows rolled down, Zoro idled in the driveway, needing a little more time to think. He sat motionless, eyes shut, enjoying the slight, unsteady breeze, not knowing what his next step should be. The offer of immediate cash that Conrad had dangled in front of him in the library's Special Collections room was tempting. And yet, he had learned so much from Max. Could he really just toss all that aside? Zoro took a deep breath. One thing was certain: regardless of whom he ultimately gave the sketch to, he nonetheless had to find it first. And the closely guarded secret of his new plan had him lying to Gina *and* Max.

Startled by a sudden tap on the door, Zoro bumped his head on the sun visor as he turned toward the open window.

"GPS down?" Max said, grinning.

"What?" Zoro replied.

"Forgotten how to find the house?"

"You seem far too amused by this," Zoro said, somewhat annoyed.

"Hardly. Move over Zoro, I'm driving today."

"You forgot to say 'Simon says.'"

Max grinned. "You look very professional today. Are you ready to go?"

"Yeah, but I'd rather drive," Zoro said.

"Good, I respect your decision. Simon says—you drive!"

Zoro caught a whiff of Max's cologne as he settled into the backseat. In the rearview mirror, Zoro saw Max trying to shake the ink from his pen. Zoro smiled as he pulled Arden's silver pen from his pocket and offered it to Max.

To his surprise, Max grabbed the pen and stared at it as if it were the key to a pharaoh's tomb.

"Where did you get this pen, Zoro?"

"That? It's from Finnegan's Pawnshop, in my neighborhood. It's just a pen. You could have it if you like."

"Stop babbling, Zoro! This is much more than that!" Max quickly reached for the door handle and pulled open his door.

"Whoa, hold it!" Zoro said, stepping on the brake.

"Come on, Zoro, let's get to the house. We haven't a minute to waste."

"Okay, okay, but why don't we drive? It'll be quicker."

Zoro didn't realize it at that moment, but his plans for the future were about to take another unexpected turn.

CHAPTER 56

Max led Zoro to the rear of the mansion. A path through an ornate English garden ended at an iron gate. Passing through the gate, Max ran ahead to a small door at the rear of the west tower. Zoro followed, and looked uncertainly at the door. Max flung the door open into near-total darkness.

They went inside and immediately began climbing a circular set of marble steps. Round and round Zoro climbed, stopping only briefly to clutch at his side. There was no railing on one side, and an empty pillar of stale air ran dangerously down the center of the staircase. As he ascended, Zoro leaned closer to the wall on the other side and avoided letting his eyes skim over the edge. Max was somewhere far above, hurrying ahead in the darkness, with apparent disregard for the imminent danger of death by falling.

A weak beam of light crawled across the top step, and Zoro could hear the faint sounds of classical music. He took a moment to catch his breath, hearing Max's rapid footsteps, and saw his shadow bobbing around the corner in the weak light.

As Zoro turned the final corner, he saw a scarred oak desk, washed in the light of an antique brass lamp. Zoro walked forward slowly, raising his eyes to see.

"Max?"

"Back here." Max's voice sounded softly from the corner behind the desk.

The silence of the room seemed to crowd Zoro. He stood for a moment, pouring over the details. The circular room was lined by bookcases twelve feet tall; not a square inch of bare wall was visible. Above them, the room was capped with a museum-quality copper dome. An impressive gallery of antiquities and sculptures sprouted from pedestals, looking like a thousand years of civilization sprung to life.

"Zoro! Get over here!"

Zoro walked into the room and leaned across the desk. "Where? Where the hell are you?"

"Zoro! Up here."

Zoro raised his eyes. A thin smile parted his lips as he saw Max, balanced above him on a wooden ladder. The top of the ladder was fixed to pulleys that ran on a metal track around the circumference of the study, giving access to the highest bookshelves. Zoro crooked his head and leaned back just in time to see Max pull a brown box from a dark recess.

"Catch, Zoro," Max said, dropping the box.

What the hell—Zoro caught it and he shook his head. "Max, you're gonna make me crazy."

"I'm trying to save your life, Zoro."

"My life?"

"Open the box, Zoro. We're going to solve a mystery."

Zoro quickly pulled the lid from the box. It was filled to the brim with stacks of framed photographs. Max quickly joined him in looking through the photos, and his face came to life as he pawed through the frames.

"Aha, this would be it," Max said. He pulled a simple wooden-framed photograph from the box.

Zoro leaned in closer to look at the photo. "Isaac?"

"Yes. This is your father and me."

Max and Isaac stood on the bow of some sort of dilapidated fishing boat, with a huge fish that appeared to be the result of a genetic mutation crammed between them. The picture seemed out of place. In this room, against the backdrop of the dignified neo-Renaissance décor, Zoro wondered what insurgency had made Isaac's world collide with Max's. Zoro looked at Max.

"Ma told me you were friends."

Max smiled. "Actually, we were" he said, running his fingers along the frame of the picture. "Strange."

"What's strange?"

"Ah, there it is," Max said, his voice dropping to a whisper as he pulled a water-stained sliver of paper from the backing behind the picture. Max planted his hands on the desk, and fell into his chair. He picked up the paper, then tipped backward and carefully unfolded the paper along its dried, brown creases.

Zoro stood with his hands in his pockets, waiting.

"When your father passed," Max began, "and Joey, of course, I was in Tibet. When I returned from Tibet, I found this rain-soaked letter stuffed in my mailbox." Max scooted it across the desk toward Zoro. "Look at the letter. It's from your father."

Zoro read.

> *Dear Max,*
> *I found it!*
> *It's somewhere safe now, and soon everything will be fine again.*
> *Isaac*

Feeling like an entry-level schmuck, Zoro just stood there, staring blankly at Max.

"Oh, come on, Zoro," Max said. "For years I wondered why Isaac sent this note . . . 'everything will be fine again.' The damn clue was right here under my nose the whole time!"

Zoro's eyes lit up and a tight smile pinched his lips. "Fine again—Finnegan," Zoro murmured. Dropping the note, his expression was clear, like a lightbulb had just gone off in his brain.

"We need to go to Finnegan's!"

Max nodded, grinning.

After a drive into the city that seemed to take forever but was only about an hour, they pulled up to Finnegan's. This time Zoro didn't feel alone or adrift; Max was right beside him as they ran into the shop. Zoro could hear the clink of the lock as the outside door closed behind them. And quickly, Arden buzzed them into the area behind the security cage.

He was slurping spoonfuls of hot tea through a sugar cube lodged in his back teeth; an antique samovar gurgled on a table behind him.

"Arden," Zoro said nervously, "we gotta talk."

"So? Talk," Arden replied, talking around the sugar cube. "I still have your ring, if you're worried."

"No, no, that's not it. Arden, you probably remember my dad, right? Did he leave something in the shop to be restored? A sketch, maybe?"

Arden was surprised. He shifted sideways and laid his arm across the counter. "Not possible," he replied.

"Think, Arden," Zoro pressed. "Anything, is there anything he could have left?"

"Could it perhaps be in storage somewhere?" Max asked.

"No," Arden said, shaking his head, "there's nothing."

Overwhelmed, Zoro groaned and grabbed at Arden's sleeve. "It can't be. That's not possible. There must be something. Give it to me!"

Arden pulled back sharply and shot Zoro a stern look.

"How old are you, Zoro?" Arden asked.

"What? I'm forty-five, but . . ."

"And how old do I look?" Arden asked.

Geez, I don't have time for twenty questions, Zoro thought. He forced himself from the frazzled state he was in and tried to think. Arden ran his hand back and forth under his chin, like a game show model displaying the prize.

"I'm younger than you, Zoro," he said. "Almost everyone here in the neighborhood is older than me. I never even met your father, may God rest his soul."

And suddenly the truth was pinging bright in Zoro's head. "Older than you!" Zoro shouted. "This is the new store!"

"Yeah," Arden replied. "Before Grandpa died, the old place was condemned. In fact, the whole neighborhood's gonna be rolled over soon, probably. Any worthless crap is still there, in the old place. It's vacant, falling down, practically. Go see for yourself."

"Do you mind?" Max asked.

"Knock yourselves out," Arden said. "But you'd better hurry—the whole neighborhood's slated to be demolished any moment now."

CHAPTER 57

Minutes later they were rolling over the bridge, just shy of Bedford-Stuyvesant. They drove the last few hundred yards in silence, staring about them at the stark tragedy of a whole neighborhood that was decaying into dust.

"Your father was incapable of leaving you, you know," Max said into the silence.

Zoro didn't respond.

"I don't think anything short of death would have kept Isaac from you, Zoro."

Zoro turned his eyes to look in the rearview mirror. "You're joking, right?"

"No, of course I'm not. Zoro, I've no idea what we'll find in the old store. But I do have an idea who Isaac was."

"Why would he abandon us, Max? You tell me why . . ." His voice choked off, halted by the lump suddenly rising into his throat.

"That's what I'm trying to say, Zoro. There's no way. No way Isaac took his own life. I refuse to believe that."

Zoro fell silent. Zoro pulled alongside an old, bulky building and parked in a weed-grown gravel driveway. He realized his hands were shaking; he shoved them into his pockets. They got out and crunched slowly across the gravel.

"What do you think, Zoro? Isaac just happened to send that letter . . . and I just happened to keep it . . . and you just happened to get that pen. Is that what you think, Zoro?"

"Coincidence, I guess."

"That's the most ridiculous thing I've ever heard. I think there's no such thing as coincidence; I think Isaac set this whole thing in motion."

Zoro made a scoffing sound.

"No matter what we do or don't find in there, Zoro, I want you to know your father loved you. You're worthy of knowing that your father loved you; if you don't feel worthy yourself, how will anyone else feel you're worthy?" Max turned to Zoro, grabbing his arm. Zoro stood still. "I still believe in him," Max said. "He's led us here, Zoro."

They had stopped abruptly in front of the old, crumbling store. Max laid a hand on Zoro's shoulder. "Whatever we find in there, we're in this together."

Max loped ahead of Zoro and reached for the door handle dangling between two splintered and graffiti-tagged boards. The wind tugged at his hair; he pushed hard and bounced back off the door.

Zoro laughed, "You gotta be kidding me. Locked?"

"Locked," Max replied, staring at the doors.

"Heads up!" Zoro said. Max spun around to see Zoro careening, shoulder first, toward the boarded-up doors. Like a linebacker, he slammed into the old, weathered wood, which gave way with a loud, splintering *crack*!

Zoro turned toward Max and hummed a triumphant "Ta-da!"

"A bit unorthodox," Max smiled back.

"I'm just following your teaching, Max," Zoro replied. "We were locked out, so I manifested a solution. And presto, we're not locked out anymore; problem solved."

"I don't disapprove of your solution, but I'm not crazy about spending the night in jail."

"Hey, no worries. Arden gave us the okay, remember?"

The old store was half-buried in random piles of rubbish. Zoro got busy, digging among the dust-encrusted refuse. Max just stood silently. There were old boxes, trinkets, a worn-out pair of skates, a helmet with glitter glued all over it . . . but no sketch, nothing else. After a while, Zoro gave a disgusted grunt.

"Don't give up, Zoro."

"I've tried Max, I really have. Well, that's it, then," Zoro said. "You almost had me believing in him."

Max tilted his head and then shook it slowly. He fell backward into an old chair, disappearing into a cloud of dust.

"Are you coming," Zoro said, heading for the door. He rubbed his suddenly-sore shoulder, disappointed he'd let his emotions override his sound judgment and drop him right back into Max's delusion. In the interior gloom, Zoro could barely see Max's face, though he could feel the glare. There was silence.

"Thing is, Zoro," Max whispered, "I hear something."

Zoro stopped, listening, "I don't hear anything."

"You have to listen to where the answers are," Max said. "Because there's always something left behind, there's always a clue. And you never know what day your miracle is coming. If you're not listening for it, you're going to miss it."

"Well, there are no miracles here."

"You've merely stirred around all this old stuff, given it a good shaking. But you're missing something, Zoro."

"That's the best explanation you can come up with?"

"I don't know," Max replied. "But just for a minute, forget what you're thinking, Zoro, really forget it."

"Sorry Max, there's nothing here." Zoro had pawed through everything in the place, twice already.

"That's just it," Max replied. "I wouldn't have heard it, if it wasn't here."

In the grayed light everything had the same gray color. And then a tinge of color glided over everything as a passing cloud shifted the sunlight that was falling in the cold afternoon. It was like some sort of alchemy: as the shifting light traversed the store, glittering colors came to life and then died again in the darkness.

"Zoro, look up," Max said calmly.

Zoro was standing, not leaning, but looking down at his feet. "Max, it's all right. I'll be okay, just give me a minute," Zoro said, reduced to a whisper by his disappointment.

"No, Zoro, I mean literally, look . . . up!"

Zoro gazed at the upper walls of the store until he got to the space behind the old counter. "Hello, baby," he chirped, his spirit renewed.

A row of cubbyholes banked the wall above and behind the old counter. Eight small wooden doors, held closed with blackened brass catches, held out hope.

Zoro hopped onto the counter and began rummaging through the cubbyholes one by one. From the first he pulled a roll of moth-eaten cloth. He allowed himself a self-pitying sigh. He then simply took stock in himself and carried on. Soon he'd gone through the middle doors, and still nothing. By now he held out little hope. Zoro barely grazed Max with a glance, intent on getting to the last door.

Max rose to his feet as Zoro pushed open the last door and flicked his lighter. In a fluid and frantic burst of clatter, about a dozen bats erupted from the cubbyhole. When the echoes of fluttering wings stopped, Zoro was still huddled over, his hands covering his head. He cautiously rose up and looked inside.

"Max!" Zoro said breathlessly, donning a high-voltage smile. Under the flicker of his lighter, dangling by a length of hemp twine, he saw a small tag, labeled "Maximilian Cisary." Zoro, hardly daring to breathe, put his arm into the cubbyhole and gave a little tug.

"Well?" Max asked.

A tingle of excitement caressed Zoro as a small wooden box plunked into his hand. He wobbled down off the counter, his legs shaking. Wide-eyed, he said, "Oh, this is it, Max. This is what you heard."

CHAPTER 58

"Let's get this outside in the daylight so we can see it," Max said.

Zoro was already holding the door open. They went out, and Max set the box gently on the hood of the limo. With his fingers shaking, he reached for the lid. They both leaned forward eagerly as Max raised the cover.

There was nothing inside; the box was empty.

Zoro clamped his teeth against the wail of despair that was suddenly fighting to get out. He turned away in disgust. *To hell with the Third Q, to hell with my subconscious, to hell with Max, to hell with everything! When am I ever going to learn that life just plain sucks, and that's it, and there's nothing I can do about it?*

Zoro turned back, ready to get back in the limo and drive Max back to his place, now that they'd reached the final dead end. To his surprise, Max stood with his eyes closed, holding the box to his chest as if it were a long-sought treasure. After several seconds, he opened his eyes and looked at Zoro.

"You okay?" Zoro said in a sour voice.

"I'm much better than okay."

"What are you doing?"

"Being quiet, and giving praise."

In all honesty Zoro should've seen it coming. Max was a master of surprises. But he was too frustrated, disappointed, and disillusioned to care, right this moment. "Whatever, Max. You ready to go?"

"Zoro, I can see the exhaustion circling your face. You look like a wreck."

"Yeah, well, you have a nice day, too."

"I haven't given up, Zoro," Max said. "Don't you get it? The box is another clue to breaking the mystery."

Carmela accusing me . . . Gina scared, doubtful, just waiting for me to screw up again . . . Johnny's threats . . . Conrad's arrogance and spite . . . Max's riddles and psychobabble bullshit . . . Joey's death . . . Isaac gone forever . . . All my hopes and dreams, pinned to some fairy tale told by an old man with so much money he forgot how the real world worked . . . a letter from the past . . . a stinking wreck of an old store . . . and now, an empty box, empty, just like everything and everybody in my shitty life . . .

It all boiled over inside Zoro then; his rage exploded, burned away all his caution, all his understanding, everything except his blinding anger. He grabbed the box out of Max's hands, flung it to the ground, and then stomped on it. "There, Max! I've broken the goddamned mystery. Happy now?"

Max stared at Zoro's feet, at the wreckage of the box. Then he smiled serenely.

"Now what the hell is it?" Zoro said. "What's with the bullshit smile, you crazy old loon?"

"Down there," Max said calmly.

Zoro half turned, looking down at the shattered box. An onrush of emotion smacked him across the face. From within the splintered box, a tiny glimmer struggled to be seen.

"What the hell?" Zoro gasped.

"Well, take a look!" Max urged.

Zoro dived to the ground, tossing the bits of splintered wood aside. "A tape," Zoro said, his voice now frenzied and high. "A cassette tape!"

Inside a secret compartment in the box, a tiny Dictaphone tape had lain hidden.

"See, Max," Zoro grinned foolishly. "My lower self works just as well as the Q self."

Max knelt down beside Zoro until they were eye to eye.

"It wasn't your lower self, Zoro, that found the tape," Max replied. "It was your intuition, smashing through the last obstacles."

Zoro shrugged his shoulders. "Never mind what it was. We've got a tape to listen to."

They sped back to the mansion. Zoro swung into the circular drive, tires squealing in protest. They ran to the front door and threw it open, rushing past the short, disapproving figure of the butler.

"Hi, Yoda; sorry, can't talk right now," Zoro sang.

Max laughed, cantering through the lobby ahead of Zoro. "His name's Tolbert—but I like Yoda, too. It fits him."

"Sorry, Tolbert," Zoro called over his shoulder as he and Max reached the main staircase, and started straight for the study.

Max sprinted past Zoro, leaping the stairs three at a time.

"Sir?" Tolbert said, staring after them, dumbstruck at the sight of such pedestrian conduct.

By the time Zoro reached the upstairs corridor, the study door was closing in his face.

"How does this old guy always beat me?" Zoro muttered, yanking open the door.

Max was digging through one of his desk drawers as Zoro walked across the study floor. He pulled an old Dictaphone, wrapped in its curly cord, from the drawer, and slammed it firmly on the desk. Zoro began to understand how that oak desk had become so scarred. Max fumbled the cassette into the Dictaphone without uttering a word.

"Careful with that tape," Zoro said.

"I'm glad to hear you think something's sacred."

"I think a lot of things are sacred!"

"Like the truth?"

Yes! Zoro thought. *I finally get it!* Gripping Max's arm, Zoro said, "Whatever we do or don't hear on this tape, whatever happens . . . Yes, it is! It is!"

Max smiled broadly at him, then took a deep breath, his finger poised on the Dictaphone's play button.

"Whatever it is, it is . . . but Zoro, here we are," he said.

Zoro waited for a couple of seconds, until he could stand the suspense no longer. He slammed his hands on the desk. "Damn it, Max! Just press the button, for God's sake!"

Max leaned forward and pushed the play button. From the speaker came a solemn voice. Zoro felt a chill go up his spine. It was Conrad!

"Do you have my sketch? Good. Then if everything goes as planned I'll meet you at the lodge in four hours. When you get there leave it inside . . . Then no one touches it but me. Am I clear?" Then there was the sound of a slamming receiver.

"The sketch," Zoro muttered.

"Ssh!"

The tape was still running. They heard the sound of a door opening in the background.

"Conrad," a woman's voice spoke uneasily.

"What is it?" Conrad snapped.

"They're ready for you in the conference room," she replied.

"That's Sherry's voice," Max said quickly.

"Who?" Zoro asked.

"Ssh."

With an enormous, sprawling voice, Conrad started issuing commands. "If the meeting runs over three hours, find some excuse to get me out of there. And tell Isaac to transcribe the Lincoln file on my desk." With that, the tape ended.

"That's my dad he's talking about," Zoro said anxiously.

"Yes, Zoro."

"So what does it mean?" Zoro asked.

"Why . . . it means precisely what it says." Zoro gave him a hopelessly puzzled look.

"Clearly, Zoro, the Dictaphone was accidentally left on during Conrad's phone call. And your father must have stumbled on to the tape. There's no question in my mind, Zoro, that Isaac beat Conrad to the lodge and snatched the sketch right from under his nose." Max laughed. "Oh, Conrad must have bitten someone's head off when he found out the sketch was missing. What I would've given to have seen his face!"

Zoro stared at Max. "Help me understand something, Max. Isaac, Conrad, and you were racing along the same trail all along? You want to clue me in?"

Max looked at Zoro, appearing to come to a decision. "Zoro, many years ago, Joshua—Conrad's father—became my friend and mentor."

Zoro looked at him uncertainly.

"Joshua was an art historian and a private collector. He discovered the first sketch in the rubble of a burned-out temple in Prague in 1949. Just before he died, in order to protect its secret from Conrad and to keep the truth from ever dying, he gave it to me. And since then, Conrad's been racing me to the finish line."

Zoro looked even more troubled. "You're saying you stole Conrad's sketch, too?"

"No! It was a gift from Joshua, retrieved from the ruins. Only Conrad thought it ought to be his." Max grinned. "Years later, when Conrad realized I'd beaten him to the next two sketches, he made an end run at the fourth sketch. I don't know—maybe he thought he'd be able to leverage the first three sketches from me, or maybe he just figured the fourth sketch was the key."

Zoro looked over. "And Isaac, he was your inside man. You used him."

"We were working together, Zoro."

"Together! Screw you and the horse you rode in on, Max."

"That's not fair; I loved Isaac like a brother. I wish every day he hadn't made a move without me."

At first Zoro's reaction was one of disbelief. It just sounded so crazy. Another conspiracy of secrets and betrayals had been alive and breathing, right beneath his very nose.

Contemplating his dilemma he decided Max did care about Isaac, after all. That part was true enough, he could see it in his eyes. "All right, Max, let's say I believe you, what about the girl?" Zoro asked. "Sherry? How does she figure in all this?" He wondered if maybe she'd been the one who'd given Isaac the tape.

"Sherry was Conrad's personal secretary and lover, the only woman who could ever penetrate his hellish character."

"And the tape," Zoro asked. "Why leave the tape?"

"Don't forget the note, Zoro, and this tape. It seems your father left us a map of clues. Granted they're not the greatest clues."

Zoro stayed focused. "So the only question is, how do we find the sketch?" he added. "Because right now we got nothing."

"The more interesting question, Zoro, is why Isaac hid the sketch in the first place. I can't help wondering why he sent these strange clues, instead of just revealing the sketch."

"So what now?" Zoro asked.

"Now we find Sherry," Max replied.

CHAPTER 59

Zoro ran his finger along the lining of his new suit. It wasn't tailored, but it was snug. He had to admit, Max had good taste; the suit Max had gotten him was stylish enough to be edgy; it framed Zoro with an alluring European flair.

The neighborhood they were driving through was identical to Max's. Up ahead in the darkness, a ribbon of torchlights lined the edges of a long driveway. Kerosene smoke wafted up from the torches and curled through the surrounding groves. An endless snake of luxury cars slithered a half mile up the driveway, like an invading armada. At the end of the torch road stood a perfect re-creation of the Pantheon, lit by a series of flaming cauldrons. "I know what I'm doing, Zoro," Max said, sensing Zoro's nervousness. "This is how we find Sherry. You're going to have to trust me."

"By coming to Conrad's gala." Zoro swallowed hard. "You sure about this, Max?"

"I'm trying not to think about it."

"You and me both."

"You having second thoughts, Zoro?"

"Let's just do this," Zoro replied.

They got out of the limo, and Zoro straightened his lapels and shot his cuffs as they walked toward a house glowing with light and beautiful people.

With no invitation, Max tried to quietly move them past the guards at the front door. But they were ushered to one side, and Max was soon engaged in a heavy argument with one of the guards. From around the corner a broad, stiff man appeared.

"May I see some identification please," he said coldly.

"Absolutely," Max said, and he pulled his wallet from his breast pocket.

The man carefully studied Max's driver's license, as if committing it to memory.

"And you," he said, turning to Zoro.

"I'm Zoro," he replied. "If you want to identify me, why don't you ask Conrad; apparently he knows me. I'm sure he'll vouch for that."

"Wait here," the man replied. He reached for a nearby wall phone, and covered the receiver as he spoke. A moment later he returned and handed Max his driver's license. "Mr. Mason welcomes you," he said stiffly, motioning with his hand for them to enter.

Max smiled and walked ahead. Zoro tailed him, pushing out his chest.

He furrowed his brow at the cold opulence that surrounded them. Forty-foot columns supported the ceiling rotunda of domed concrete, arched vaults to the heavens. Max laughed.

"What's so funny?" Zoro said.

"Oh, I was just thinking to myself that Conrad isn't even aware that the Pantheon is now used as a tomb. The arrogant son of a bitch is living in his own grave."

Zoro was soon seduced by the buffet table. "Nice to see that almost dying hasn't hurt your appetite," Max smiled.

Zoro crammed three more cocktail wieners into his mouth and shrugged haplessly.

"No vegetables were harmed in the making of your dinner, Zoro—"

Before Max could finish, a tall, balding man grazed Max's arm. "Mr. Cisary."

"Hello, Dr. Arcello," Max said. He and Zoro followed him to a quiet corner where no one could overhear, and Max turned his full attention on Dr. Arcello.

"It's been a long time, Maximilian," Arcello said, hunching to make himself seem shorter. He leaned into Max; his breath smelled to Max of martinis and caviar.

"Yes, it has. The last time we were together, young Conrad was still wet behind the ears; he'd barely learned how to read a balance sheet, as I recall."

"Why the hell did you come here?"

"Oh, we just decided to show up," Max grinned.

"I don't think it's a good idea . . . not that I'm not glad to see you, Max . . ."

"Good," Max interrupted, "because I need your help."

Arcello scanned the room, contemplating how many eyes were on him. "I need to go," he said.

"Not yet." Max grabbed his arm, clamping down on his bicep. "I want to ask you a question: Did you ever keep track of Sherry, and was she someone worth your attention?"

Arcello leaned back against the wall, hoping to blend among the many columns. "She doesn't want to be found, Max."

"Do you remember why?"

"No, but I remember something else," Arcello answered. Arcello again searched around him. "She had a second cousin who owned the . . ."

His words were interrupted by the sound of a beating drum and the blast of trumpeters, as Conrad emerged from a doorway at the top of a broad, veined marble staircase. Max's mouth twisted at the absurdity of Conrad's grandiose entrance. His hands outstretched, like a golden effigy, he claimed the room. His fierce eyes hid his dreams and dark desires from everyone, desires that were spawned from a depth that could devour the human soul. He smiled, proud that his true self was not known to anyone. "Friends," he said, raising his hands and pointing to Max. "Welcome, everyone." Thunderous applause. "I am looking forward to a splendid evening. What was, is once again. Even my beaten-down enemy has returned as my friend."

All eyes followed Conrad as he descended the staircase. With an awkward groan he pressed a twisted smile from his tense lips and walked toward Max. His eyes darkened, his voice stiffened as he crushed Max's hand, shaking it violently, an obvious display of gentility for the crowd. "Please, everyone," Conrad broke the frozen silence, "enjoy the buffet while I catch up with my old friend. Maestro, music, please."

"I always say, keep your friends close, and your enemies closer," Conrad said to Max.

"It's no good, Conrad," Max said calmly. "Zoro and I are working together. You have no chance."

Conrad turned to Zoro. "I hope you have more luck with Max than your father. Didn't he kill himself after your younger brother's death?"

Standing behind Conrad, Alton smirked.

Zoro grabbed the front of Conrad's shirt. "I'll kill you, you son of a bitch."

Grasping Zoro from behind, Alton threw him to the ground. Zoro sprang up, spoiling for a fight, but Max bear-hugged Zoro. "That was a stupid thing to do," he whispered urgently, as Zoro struggled to break free. "I get it that you're angry, but we need to back off."

Max slowly released Zoro, who straightened his lapels and appeared to be calming down. Then suddenly, Zoro blasted Alton with an open-palm strike, and then gave him a second helping.

The crowd fell totally silent, appalled. Conrad turned to his guests with a delighted smile. "Ladies and gentlemen, that concludes tonight's entertainment. See yourself out, Max, and take your goon with you," he said, fully transformed into a calm statesman.

Zoro still felt the raging contempt burning inside him as Max pulled him to the door by his sleeve. "What the hell was that, Max? You didn't stand up for me."

"Zoro, you need to think before you act."

"But he pissed me off! You heard what he said." Zoro's heart ached. "I could kill the son of a bitch."

"Oh, he'll be dead soon enough, or wishing he was," Max grinned devilishly. "Trust me, Zoro, without that sketch, Conrad's reason for living will be pulled from existence. When he realizes we beat him, he'll welcome the opportunity to put a bullet in his own head."

Heading slowly toward the doorway, Zoro tried to swallow his anger. At that moment, a waiter pressed up beside him and grabbed Max's arm from behind. "Sir, pardon me. Someone said you dropped this." The waiter pressed a silk handkerchief into Max's hand. Max smiled and without a word he crammed it into his lapel pocket.

"Guess you dropped your hankie," Zoro said.

"No, I didn't," Max smiled.

Safely back in the limo, Zoro spun around as Max unfolded the handkerchief and held it up. Scrawled in fountain pen were the words, "Smokey Oval Diner."

It couldn't be that simple, Zoro thought. Then he smiled; he instantly knew.

"Don't tell me, Max, I know: Sherry," he said, pushing the accelerator to the floor.

CHAPTER 60

*Z*oro lowered his eyes from the rearview mirror. A minute ago he'd been furious with Conrad; now he was assessing Max. His head felt as if it had been hollowed out and filled with a thousand screaming voices. And most disturbing of all was that the mercenary voice in his head wanted to kill everything. It would be so much easier to run away back to his old life.

Fighting for success was harder than Zoro had ever imagined. And he wanted nothing more than to wake up from this dream. His hands gripped the steering wheel, ready to turn around at any moment if Max's answers didn't satisfy him.

"Max, all of a sudden I'm not even sure whether this is my journey or yours."

Max nodded and chuckled lightly. "Don't you get it? I'm part of your journey, and you're part of mine."

Max studied Zoro in the mirror. "I know you've been hurt, Zoro, and I know you're confused. But your scars tell where you've been, not where you need to go. I'm just saying."

In front of them cars jammed the road, honking and spewing exhaust. Ahead in the distance was Smokey Oval Park, a silhouette of trees against the moonlight. Max was staring at Zoro, nodding lightly. "Being present, being a Third-Q thinker has nothing to do with passivity. Trust me, we're not done with that son of a bitch Conrad," Max said.

Before Zoro could say a word, Max continued, "We need to get out ahead of him and hit him with some hard rain, Zoro. But we need to do it on our terms."

A smile was forming on Zoro's face. "So we keep fighting?"

"And we win!" Max said. "Allowing the calling of consciousness to be served by who we really are doesn't mean we don't fight and win. We just stay present and don't get tied down by our hang-ups."

As the streetlights skimmed past the limo, Max's words became clearer to Zoro. He couldn't wash away his life with tears or emotions, treading water to stay afloat. Instead, he needed to fight.

Zoro tried to visualize the future, to make it real. As he built Third-Q pathways in his mind, they'd stream billions of bits of brilliance from his subconscious into his conscious mind. And as his conscious mind filled, like air pushing into a balloon, his conscious box would grow and expand, bringing a flurry of brainstorms into existence. The secrets of the mind and soul would reveal themselves to Zoro in the simplest ways, giving him the tools he needed to win.

Zoro worked the limo around Smokey Oval Park, then stopped under a canopy of maples next to the diner. "Well, here we are."

Zoro had found the diner quite by accident. It was lodged in a gritty neighborhood, though the park beside it, he suspected, looked magnificent in the autumn daylight.

The diner wasn't crowded, and they went inside and sat in the last booth from the door. The scent of curry sweetened the air, and Zoro thought the Asian music blaring from a shortwave radio behind the counter might appeal to Max. Soon, a waitress walked over to their table. She was a short and corpulent woman. She turned and flashed her deep blue eyes at Zoro. But through the blue, he recognized what he saw in those eyes: they were empty and afraid.

"Hello, Sherry," Max said calmly.

Her eyes went wide, and her pen slipped from between her fingers and ricocheted off the worn table. She took a small step backward.

"You must be mistaken," she replied. "My name's Leanne." She motioned to her nametag.

Max smiled and put his hand on her wrist. "My name is Max." He was fairly certain she would remember.

"I remember," she whispered, quickly glancing over her shoulder. "Just wait a minute, and I'll be right back with your menus."

*   *   *

Slipping into the kitchen, Sherry pulled a crumpled business card from inside her apron. Checking the card, she dialed the number. It began to ring. When it finally connected, her voice was uneasy.

*   *   *

"So what's the story with her, Max? She doesn't exactly look like someone who belongs in the same world as someone like Conrad," Zoro said.

"Something happened to her, Zoro. That woman was tough as nails, and then one day she just up and disappeared. No one ever knew what spooked her."

"Here she comes," Zoro said, leaning away from Max as they watched Sherry approach.

Making her way back to the table, she hesitated. "Here, gentlemen," Sherry said returning to their table and handing them menus. "Can I get you something to drink?"

"Sherry," Max said, "we need to talk."

"Sorry, the name is Leanne. And there's someone you need to talk to other than me. Just order something and wait, please."

"Of course," Max replied.

As she scurried away with their order, Zoro shrugged at Max, as if to say "what the hell." Max shook his head, already moving into a deeper contemplation.

"Clearly something or someone has got her spooked."

"How long do we have to wait?"

"Ten minutes," Max said.

"Ten minutes?"

"I don't know, Zoro, however long it takes."

* * *

A man briefly huddled under the tattered awning, trying to shake off the sleety rain that had begun to fall. As he sputtered through the front door, Zoro was the first to spot him.

"Him? Oh, Christ," Zoro said.

Max spun around to see a soggy-looking Gideon.

"What's he doing here?" asked Zoro.

Gideon made his way over to the table, trying to appear less bedraggled than he was. He flashed a mighty smile at Max.

"You don't look surprised, Cisary," Gideon said.

As Gideon spoke, Zoro observed him closely. His face was sharp and unshaven; he had the profile of a meat cleaver with stubble. He acted hard, though he seemed like a man with heavy worries.

Zoro waited, listening to the clanking of plates as the short-order cooks slid them onto the shelf for pick up. Gideon never flinched.

Zoro suddenly found himself staring at Gideon's feet. The detective was wearing Crocs. It just didn't add up; if he was some hardboiled, old-time detective, an expert in human behavior, why the hell was he wearing clogs?

Gideon squeezed into the booth bench beside Max and ordered coffee. "Quite a long mess," he said.

"I know that," Max replied.

"Goddamn it, Max!" Zoro tossed his fork down beside his half-eaten apple pie. "You're the expert. If you've figured this out, you wanna tell me why he's here?"

"Thing is, Zoro," Max said, "Detective Gideon is here for a reason of his own. He was the rookie cop assigned to your father's suicide."

"It's been many years, Zoro," Gideon said.

Zoro suddenly realized why Gideon had looked familiar. "I met you at the time of the fire." Of course. The big arms, the burns. The wide face. Gideon was the one who had responded first to the scene of Joey's death. He had held Zoro back from rushing into the flames. He had tried to face the heat and get Joey out. And then he had tried to comfort Zoro about losing his brother.

Zoro stopped breathing. It shocked him. He hadn't expected that.

A passing waitress brought Gideon his coffee and left a coffee-filled carafe on the table.

"And consider this, Zoro: Gideon's worked out a theory about all the break-ins and problems involving you and your family. Haven't you, Gideon?"

Gideon had polished off a half cup of coffee and still looked sleepy. Without saying a word, he refilled the coffee cup from a container in a brown paper bag he had in his coat pocket. He placed the bag on the table, closest to Zoro.

"Wow, you're a regular genius, Max. You want to let me in on what I'm thinking?"

It was a cop's tactic, leading a witness. In fact, it was Gideon's specialty. He'd simply ask the right question, and in a minute he'd have people saying all kinds of things. The average perp didn't stand a chance.

"You see, Zoro," Max began, "Gideon here has already spoken to Sherry, judging by that crumpled NYPD identification card I saw sticking out of her apron. And you know what that tells us?"

Zoro held up his hands. "I got nothing."

"It tells us, Zoro, that he already knew where Sherry was. Didn't you, Gideon?"

Gideon was amused. "I'm off duty, let's talk off the record." He stared at Max and fell silent.

"All right," Max replied, "me first, I guess."

Max turned toward Gideon. "You've been putting things together, wondering what the connection is. It's been driving you crazy; you can't seem to find the thread that's got us all tied together. But here's the thing. I can't help wondering why a thirty-year-old suicide would be that interesting to a smart guy like you."

"Maybe he's not that smart," Zoro said, reaching for the paper bag. Max pushed his hand away.

Gideon reached inside his trench coat pocket and pulled out a rolled-up stack of stapled papers. "These," he said, "they just don't tell enough. But there's enough here to keep a mind busy for thirty years."

Max slowly turned the curled cover page, and Zoro's breath suddenly emptied from his lungs. Max was holding a copy of Isaac's autopsy report. Zoro stared at the papers, then at Max, and then at Gideon.

"Are you certain you want to hear this?" Gideon asked.

Zoro kept staring at the pages. He nodded his head.

"The official report was massive trauma," Gideon said. He hesitated and looked at Max.

"Just give me the facts, I can handle them," Zoro said.

"All right." Gideon's voice was dry. He took another sip of his ninety-proof coffee. "First of all, jumpers don't usually die on impact. Bones break, hips smash, the skull can fracture. You basically go from doing eighty miles an hour to zero miles an hour in one nanosecond. And because of inertia, even when you stop, your internal organs keep going."

"I already guessed that," Zoro said, "but how is that important?"

"Your internal organs tear away. Your liver weighs the equivalent of five hundred pounds on impact. That causes it, your spleen, and the aorta to rip and shred."

"Lucky for Dad," Zoro winced.

"Look, Zoro," Gideon said, "I'm not a pathologist, but my mind's been working overtime. And what I'm telling you is only my opinion."

Zoro had a sick feeling in his stomach. Gideon knew something about the reports. And for certain Zoro felt he was about to be devastated by it.

"Jumpers go over all the time. A few die almost immediately on impact from massive internal hemorrhage. The rips and shreds. And others splash around painfully, drowning. But there are always signs."

"What are you trying to say? My father's case wasn't like that?"

"No. Look here," Gideon said, pointing to a line on the report. "Notice anything unusual?"

Zoro gazed at the line. "Cause of death: multiple blunt force trauma."

"Now check out the next line," Gideon said.

It only had four words written on it: "Lungs clear; no fractures."

"No chance in hell that was just a coincidence," Gideon said.

From the expression on Gideon's face, Zoro realized things didn't add up. He struggled against the impact of the image, and suddenly it hit him. "So how did my dad jump off a freaking bridge and break nothing?"

"Exactly," Gideon replied. "The only way not to break bones is to be relaxed enough not to tighten up on impact. The only way I know that can happen is if the victim was unconscious," Gideon said.

Suddenly, Zoro's head filled with a combustible memory. Zoro's eyes fixed on Gideon. "Drunk! They said he was drunk when he died."

Gideon filled his cup from the paper bag, grabbing the carafe and adding just a drop of coffee for color. He held up his hand indicating Zoro should wait, and he downed the cup.

"The pathologist did a good job. It was a clean autopsy," Gideon said.

"And?" Zoro probed cautiously.

"Look," Gideon repeated, "the pathologist did a thorough job. He took blood tests, fluid from the eyes for toxicology, the works."

"And in Isaac's case?" Max asked.

"Clean." Gideon nodded.

Zoro looked surprised. "You sure?"

"Yes. The toxicology report was clean. Isaac was sober as the Pope when he went over. Still, I don't believe he was conscious." Gideon looked like the kind of cop who could break your legs just for speeding, and he had been about as delicate as a ballet of drunken elephants, but he was sure about his hunch. And to him that was all that mattered.

"This is bullshit," Zoro said. "How could he kill himself in that state?"

"The inescapable fact is that Isaac was unconscious, not drunk, Zoro," Max said. "And unconscious men rarely jump off bridges."

"Your father didn't commit suicide," Gideon said.

Zoro felt his entire world coming unwound. "No, no, this is bullshit! You're a goddamned fuck-up, cop!"

"Maybe so," Gideon said, turning toward Max. "You're mixed up in this whole mess, and you can be sure I'm gonna find out how."

"Screw you, Gideon! Just leave—get the hell out of here!" Zoro's tone was defiant.

Gideon cranked his stubbled face around, slid from the booth, and headed for the exit without another word.

Max put a hand on Zoro's arm. "Zoro, I know this must be hard for you, after all these years . . ."

"Don't, Max! Just . . . don't." Zoro held his head in his hands, trying to figure out how to feel about the shifting of every assumption he'd ever had.

Sherry was back. "You might want to look again at the menu. There's a special I'm sure you'll enjoy." She laid the menu on the table between them, and the look in her eyes was clear.

Inside the menu was tucked a slip of paper bearing the words "the lodge," followed by a scribbled address.

"Let's go to the lodge," Max said.

"No," Zoro insisted. "This is one journey I have to make on my own. Give me that, Max, at least."

CHAPTER 61

Saturday, Harriman State Park

The lodge had once served as a playhouse for Conrad and his cronies, a secret place for cloaked assignations. Its exact location was hard to pinpoint, but it was somewhere near Harriman State Park. And Zoro found it quite easily from Sherry's directions on the note. In the distance he could make out the crippled outline of the lodge. After so many years of being forsaken, it was slowly being swallowed up by nature.

There were no rolling green meadows, just a moss-covered log cabin that leaned like a crooked tombstone. Civilization hadn't reached that far into the ominous shadows of the mountain. The cabin lay plunged deeply into the blackness beneath tall trees. The only links to civilization were two simple, washed-out gravel trails where the access road once ran. There was coldness to that place, accompanied by the smell of moist earth.

Nearing the cabin, Zoro saw it more clearly and noticed that it was much larger than it had first appeared. Its blackened, creosoted timbers melded almost organically into the treescape. And the only other sign of humanity was a small, two-rail sled hung on a shed behind the cabin that perched dangerously above a ravine. On either side of the cabin, the property slid away down tree-covered hills.

Zoro stepped from the limo into a blistering rain and ran blindly to the front porch. He was easily able to jimmy the cabin door's lock. As the door slowly creaked open, Zoro didn't move. He stared into the room, realizing there was no alternative but to proceed. He caught his toe crossing the threshold and fell forward, his hand snagging across something in the darkness as he landed with a heavy thud.

"Shit!" he said softly, realizing his hand was cut and bleeding and the knees of his pants were soiled with dampened grime. He turned and looked back out the door; a rain-blurred hue of daylight leaked across the floor. He followed the trail of light through the room to an imposing stone fireplace framed in wrought iron. In the middle of the ironwork was forged the word "Pantheon."

The room was empty and still, and Zoro swallowed as he stared through the clouds of dust he'd stirred up by his entry.

There was a table, two matched leather chairs—covered with mold—near the fireplace, a small window, cracked but still holding out the streams of rain, and, in the middle of the floor, a bucket diligently catching drops from a precipitous leak from the roof.

For some time he studied the room. There were no clues dangling from the log rafters by neatly cut pieces of hemp twine. And as his thoughts wheeled in his head, it became clear there was nothing useful in the lodge.

The wind wailed through the trees outside and in through the cabin door. A large, dust-covered chandelier, suspended by chains above the table, swung gently, blown by the draft. There was a flash of steel-blue lightning, followed quickly by a peal of thunder.

Your conscious reality is a re-creation . . . break the box. The thought rocketed through Zoro's head, the words seeming to whisper from every corner of the cabin. *Break the box . . .*

"All right, Max, you win," Zoro said. He squeezed his face tightly, hoping to wring the awareness out of his mind, re-create the room. Still there was nothing.

Without warning Max's voice again flashed in Zoro's head. *Be still Zoro, and let the Third Q connect you*, whispered in his mind, over and over. *Be still, be still . . .*

For a moment there wasn't any sound in the cabin except Zoro's breathing. He heard the rush of air running down his windpipe, and it felt cool and moist.

As he slowly turned toward the table, he levied his trust upon the universe. Suddenly, stillness overwhelmed him. Every thought flew from his mind and there wasn't anything left; he was a perfect, blank slate. In that very instant there was no past, no tomorrow, no Joey or Carmela, no fleeting hopes. There was just a cabin and a chandelier twisting over a table.

Zoro's eyes narrowed as every sound in the room became a sound unto itself, until even the rain on the tin roof fell silent. He was aware of every nuance, of every trail of moisture that trickled down the window in an endless barrage of silent raindrops. He turned his head to the right and saw the outline of the bucket on the floor. He saw the silent splash of water dripping from the ceiling into the bucket, making absolutely no sound. It was as if he were hearing with his eyes.

Moments later, feeling his blood coursing through his veins, Zoro felt an intensely peaceful sensation. Feeling a contradictory sense of peaceful exhilaration, he sensed the room beginning to sublime, like a heated vapor over hot desert sand. One by one, each piece of furniture seemed to melt away. Zoro now stood in what appeared to be a completely empty room.

A clap of thunder broke his concentration. Instantly the room was filled with furniture and he no longer felt sublime. The thoughts rushed back across his mind and quickly released him from the state of profound and peaceful contemplation he had been in just seconds ago.

Drenched in sweat, Zoro stepped quietly to the right and fell to the ground as he tripped over the water bucket. The dusty floor seemed to suck the water from the overturned bucket, draining it of its last drops. As Zoro rolled to his side to hoist himself up, the trail of water funneled past him through a riverbank of dust. Following the trickle of water,

Zoro focused his vision, and in that moment of stillness the room stood once again empty.

As Zoro stared down at the empty floor, he could make out a tiny crack at the far end, near the fireplace. He observed how the trail of water spiraled as it ran into the crack and disappeared. Zoro crawled across the floor like some wounded creature, creeping forward until he saw a beam of light from the window sweep across the crack in the floor.

He stared at the crack, but all he could see was darkness. He tugged at the cracked floorboard, chipping away a splinter of wood as a gleaming silhouette flickered under his fingernail. With all the force he could muster, Zoro jammed his forefinger and thumb into the crack and pulled from it a rusted and stained medallion. As a streak of lightning flared through the room, Zoro saw the medallion's silhouette outlined against his hand. He made out a singular drop of brown dried blood, a starburst in the center of the medallion. Slowly and silently, the medallion swung back and forth in the air before his eyes; Zoro had found Isaac's lost medallion.

Zoro staggered to his feet and collapsed into one of the moldy armchairs. As his awareness expanded, Zoro built a vivid image in his mind . . .

Wild, bohemian music filled the air, and he could imagine the fireplace blazing a yellow light across the floor. Zoro ran his fingers over the arm of the chair. It was stubbled with unusual linear marks, and bits of frayed rope clung in the stubble.

Isaac's bloodied medallion . . . the rope marks etched into the chair . . . it was all suddenly so clear.

Zoro's imagination summoned an image of Isaac, tied to the armchair. Conrad, and a crowd of Gucci-shod gargoyles huddled around him, leering at him.

Conrad pulled at Isaac's restraints until they bit into his skin, and tears began to run down Isaac's cheeks. Isaac's face was bruised and bloody; Conrad grabbed him by the throat, choking Isaac into unconsciousness.

As Conrad squeezed tighter and tighter, Zoro cried frantically, "Please stop!" And the room fell silent and empty once more. There was nothing but a dust-encrusted table under a swinging chandelier; rain was falling outside. Desperately clutching at his own throat, Zoro collapsed in a heap and screamed, "Max . . . Oh my God, I'm sorry."

CHAPTER 62

Zoro tore up the mansion steps and frantically pounded on the front door. The entire ride back from the lodge he'd wished he'd not decided to go there alone. He was chilled by the secret he discovered, and could think only of Max's consoling voice. When Tolbert finally opened the door, he stared at Zoro strangely. As Zoro pressed through the door, he protested, "No!"

"I need to see Max, now!"

"I'm very sorry, Mr. Cisary is in the hospital."

An unnerving feeling came over Zoro. "Hospital? What happened?"

"Conrad . . ."

"What? What about him?" Zoro said, shaking Tolbert by the shoulders.

"Mr. Conrad," Tolbert said, grimly.

"Which hospital?"

"Einstein," he replied.

"You'll have to come with me," he said, pulling Tolbert by the arm toward the limo. "You can tell me about it on the way."

CHAPTER 63

Only a few seats in the emergency room were still occupied when Zoro finally reached the hospital. The search for Max became its own kind of agony. "Max, Max," Zoro began to shout, drawing the attention of the whitecoats.

A doctor hooked Zoro by the arm. Zoro spun on his heels, stopped and stared uncomfortably. It was Dr. Granger, who'd treated him for his ischemic attack.

"Max," Zoro whispered. "Is he—"

"He's alive. Do you remember me, Mr. Montana?" Dr. Granger asked.

"Yes, I do. He's alive then?"

"Yes, but I'm afraid . . . well it's very strange." Dr. Granger's tone was apologetic.

"Damn it!" Zoro shouted, trying to push past the crowd of white-coats. "Just tell me what's going on. Max . . . Max!"

"Zoro, something strange has happened to Max," Dr. Granger said. "Try to calm down, and I'll tell you about it. Come with me."

The crowd of whitecoats began to part as Zoro followed Dr. Granger into the intensive care unit. Pale yellow walls were offset by a blue curtain, draped half around Max's bed. Dr. Granger fiddled with his chart as Zoro caught a glimpse of Max. His eyes were closed; his chest rose and fell steadily. "Is he asleep?" Zoro said.

"No, he's in a coma. And we don't know what's causing it."

Confused, Zoro just stared at the doctor. *He should know these things*, Zoro thought, *he's a doctor*. But the neurologists were stumped, Dr. Granger said. The entire team had never seen anything like it.

Max lay motionless in the stark room overrun with baffled white-coats. A small crucifix draped across his folded hands. Two unmatched chairs sat next to the bed.

Dr. Granger pointed to a bank of monitors. It also seemed, he said, that Max had more going on than just his coma. Having lapsed into deep unconsciousness—apparently following the tumultuous confrontation with Conrad that Tolbert had briefed him on during the drive—Max was exhibiting incredible and unexplained bursts of brain activity, even while comatose. The bank of monitors measured activity hundreds of times more powerful than anything they had ever seen, the doctor said. "No one, especially no one comatose, ought to have such brain activity," Dr. Granger said. "And I'm afraid it's been getting more pronounced. At this rate, I don't know how much more he can take before his brain simply burns out."

"Can he hear me?"

"I'm not sure." The doctor turned and checked the monitors.

In the dim light, Zoro stared at the bank of pulsing monitors. Against the glare of lights from the monitor glass, he saw only the reflection of his own troubled face. He knew there was only one way to help Max: He needed to conquer the darkened quarters of his heart. And he who had never been certain now believed.

Zoro sat at Max's bedside in one chair; Tolbert sat silently in the other. Placing his hands over Max's crucifix, Zoro's eyes gazed upward, and he prayed with a reverence he had never felt before. After a moment the words ceased to pour silently from his mind. He began to make the sign of the cross and paused.

"And one more thing, God," Zoro whispered. "You never asked me if

I wanted to see the truth, but I got it anyway. And now you're messing up the story." Zoro twisted uneasily in his seat. He couldn't understand why he felt so deeply about a man he'd only met a few days ago. But he felt that if he lost Max, he would lose everything all over again.

"Please, God, don't take Max from me. He's all I have in this miserable world. Come see for yourself. And don't send Jesus; my life is no place for a boy. Come see for yourself. I'm not invisible. Come see me—you owe me that."

As he prayed, Zoro felt butterflies doing a West Coast jive in his stomach. Then suddenly, as if pricked by a needle, Zoro shuddered. Looking uncertain, he froze, unsure what to do, and then it came again, a tiny twitch beneath his hand.

"He moved!" Zoro shouted.

*   *   *

About a half-hour later, Max's eyelids flickered, then opened. He moved slightly.

"Max," Zoro whispered.

Max recognized the voice; a tiny smile flickered across his lips. Zoro began to cry as he leaned over the bed.

"Hello, Zoro," Max said feebly.

"Don't you ever scare me like that again, Max."

"My heart rate was up a little, that's all."

"I know you don't mind dying, Max, but could you spare me the fun?" To Zoro's surprise, he was able to smile as he said it. "You can't die, you hear me? Promise you won't."

"Everything's going to be okay," Max said, his strength waning with every word. "I missed you today, Zoro."

Zoro squeezed his hand. "I missed you too. I . . ." He hesitated. "I went to the lodge without you, Max."

Max's brow quivered as he tried to raise his head.

Zoro went on to describe the events at the lodge, and then suddenly, the child within him surfaced as he described the scene of

Isaac's murder. He grabbed at Max's hand as he told the story. Zoro had been so determined to get answers, answers that he now regretted knowing.

"So much sadness," Max said weakly, touching Zoro lightly on the forehead, "in here."

Zoro brought a damp cloth from the bedside table to Max's forehead, and Max grabbed Zoro's hand.

"Have I ever told you about the worst day and the best day of my life?" Max said.

"No," Zoro replied.

The room slowly emptied, a chorus of muffled murmurs fading as Tolbert corralled the interns into the hallway.

"It was the morning of Christmas Eve. I was almost nine years old, a half day shy of my ninth birthday," Max said. "My mother had a heart attack. By the time I got to her, it was too late. But I had to try. That's what you do, Zoro."

There were times Zoro had wished he'd known more about Max, knowing what made him tick. But now he wished he understood better why Max was telling him this.

"So there I was, Zoro, just a boy, who a few moments earlier had been delighting in the Yuletide décor on the mantle. And one second later, I was on my hands and knees, trying to think of some way to save her. I couldn't, of course, but I kept on trying. I never stopped."

Zoro struggled with emotion.

"And, Zoro, if you're wondering why it was the best day of my life, it's because that day my mother went to sleep so I could awaken."

"Why are you telling me this now, Max?"

"The sketch, Zoro . . . it's a glimpse of heaven. But even if you find it, it may not be the answer you're looking for. You see, you've been making the unconscious assumption that success, heaven, is a future event. But it's not. It's here for you now, aligned in the moment with your inner purpose. So I'll tell you one last time: let your personality and your life come to serve your soul, then it can shine through in every moment and you won't ever suffer and bang your head against life again. My mother came through me, hoping I would one day see that. And I'm teaching you the same. You have a choice."

Zoro struggled against the words as Max rested from the exhaustion of speaking.

"Max, I'm afraid I won't ever find it on my own."

"Zoro, every moment of your life is a step, with or without me. There is always only this one step, this one moment. And underneath all your thinking there is goodness, an intention, a consciousness that flows into all things you do." Max paused to catch his breath. "Find that, and you'll be fueled by the light of God. With the Third Q in you, you can do it, Zoro."

"I see that sketch everywhere. Why is that, Max?"

"It's because your life, Zoro, is nothing more than a sketch. And losing Joey punched a big hole in it."

"It punched a hole in me, too."

"I know. But, Zoro, behind life's sketch is a light. It's the light of consciousness that's you, and Joey, and Isaac. And when you accept that hole and stop trying to plug it with pain and suffering, the light can shine through, and the hole will be filled with light instead of pain."

Zoro collapsed against Max's hands.

"Zoro, you know I love you like a son."

"I know, but your words can't save me, Max."

"How many lost dreams have you forgotten, Zoro? You can't lie to yourself anymore, trying to fill the hole in your heart with the things you're chasing."

"But I think I should . . ."

"Zoro, stop thinking! Stop painting your life with your thinking brush."

A heavy, moist wind rattled against the window. "Zoro," Max whispered, "believe you're worth it. Because whether you believe you can succeed or you can't, either way, you're right."

Max's head flopped over, into the yellow glow cast by the bedside lamp. As Zoro reached over to right Max's head, he put his trembling hand across the light of the lamp, and the room suddenly dimmed.

"Zoro, if you were Isaac," Max said through his failing breath, "Where would you hide the sketch?"

"Somewhere safe," Zoro said softly.

"Then that's where you must look: in your safest place."

Zoro was too sad, too devastated to consider the meaning right now; all he could do was watch as the life ebbed from a man who had been the best friend he'd ever had—though he hadn't really understood that until now.

"It's time, Zoro. I'm finished with dividing myself between the worlds."

"No, Max, don't—"

Max raised a trembling finger and pointed at the floodlights on the opposite wall.

"What is it, Max?"

Max's voice was extraordinarily soft and barely audible. "Choose the bright light, Zoro; the dim one's too heavy."

And with absolute helplessness and utter peace in his face, Max released his grip on Zoro's hand and sank into an everlasting sleep.

Zoro stood beside the bed, looking down on Max, now pale and forever mute. An icy stillness tortured his heart as he stood motionless. In that pure moment, the world seemed to stand still. And through the sudden darkness, something seemed to flash swiftly toward Zoro. No one saw what was happening except him. In an instant, it had passed.

A rush of energy filled him, left him trembling against the sensation. And when the feeling was gone, so too was the horrible abyss of nothingness. Instead of Zoro's soul bleeding, wounded, it pulsed with new life. Submerged beneath the wave of energy, beneath that mighty power stronger than steel, Zoro had felt it. Stretching to the unrealizable beyond, Max's soul had passed through Zoro.

In that moment, the catastrophic weight of Max's death was lifted by the ribbon of love that had flooded from the stillness through Zoro's body. And in that moment, Zoro was greater than his mind, or his body, or his soul, or anything that was just one part of him.

But then, with a sudden, steady hail of memories, he saw himself being pushed from behind by Isaac as he climbed into his childhood treehouse. Joey was next to him and they giggled as Isaac patiently constructed the finishing touches of their hideaway.

And then it hit him: his childhood treehouse was the safest place on earth. He turned and ran from the room.

CHAPTER 64

Standing now in front of the place where his former home had been, a quake of emotions spilled out of Zoro. Some developer had torn down the old, burned-out wreck of Zoro's childhood home and built what used to be a clean, efficient rental unit on the lot. But the neighborhood wasn't that great—if it ever had been—and the dwelling had been vacant for a long time. Like the rest of the neighborhood, it would soon succumb to the right-of-way for a new tollway. With his hands in his pockets, Zoro's thoughts returned to his boyhood and that magical feeling his old neighborhood held.

As soon as he walked through the side gate, Zoro could see the old treehouse in the yard. In a field behind what had once been his home street, the clanging of heavy machinery announced the impending burial of most of these memories. The entire neighborhood was being demolished.

While the road construction would breathe new life into an old, abandoned neighborhood, the new pavement would do something else; it would cover over secrets that Zoro and Isaac had been afraid to share. Zoro stepped quickly to the yard, trying to avoid the whispers that began to rattle his brain. It didn't work.

"What a perfect time to build you boys that treehouse," Isaac had said.

"Now, Dad? In the winter?"

"Perfect time! No leaves to clutter your view."

Despite the icy cold, they had had no trouble building the treehouse. They had hung half an old door across the front, on which the boys had carved their initials with Isaac's pocketknife.

It had seemed so high then, the treehouse, though now Zoro could reach the door on his toes. He huddled in his memories and ran his fingers across those initials. As he climbed up and squeezed through the door, he melted into a memory of Joey.

"Dad's coming! Quick, hide the pocketknife," Joey whispered.

"Joey, you know we're not supposed to have it."

"Get the box, quick."

They hid the knife in an old coffee tin, their safe-deposit box for treasures of string and Popsicle sticks. Zoro reached into the gap between the roofline and wall, wondering if the tin was still there. As he pulled the tin from its shadowed lair, he hesitated, then slipped the lid from the tin. The pocketknife was still there. And there was something else beneath it. A yellowed piece of paper, a note. Zoro realized a son's secret lair is never far from his father's reach. His hands shook as he began to read:

Dear Zoro,

I know you don't play in here anymore. But I also know eventually you'll find your way back to this place.

Today as I began to write this letter, I remembered a conversation we had when you were only a little boy. I was pasting some pictures on to an old frame with paint as creased as my hands are now becoming. It was my dream board, my way of releasing my dreams to the universe. You had wanted to know what the universe was, and I told you it's the sunlight that warms your shoulders; it's the whisper on the wind; it's the beating of your heart when I hold you tight. You scrunched your face up, not knowing what the heck I was talking about. It made me laugh. You laughed too, probably not even knowing why. And then out of the blue you asked me if I would live forever. When I told you I would always be with you, you began to cry. Even at that young age you had an incredible power to see what others couldn't. And through your tears you asked me, "What will I do if I'm sad, Daddy?" Then I'll hold you up high, where the sunlight sings on your face, I replied. "But what will I do when I'm scared?" Then I'll wrap my arms around you, and carry you through the ends of the universe. "But what will I do if I get lost?" you asked. Then I'll remind you to dream you are found, I said. Then you grabbed me tightly and asked, "But Daddy, how will you do these things if you're gone?" To which I replied . . . I already have.

Zoro, my dear son, it's not your fault that Joey died, it's mine. Today I'm going to right that wrong. And I want you to know that I love you, and that I will always be beside you. But, should anything happen to me, you must promise me you'll go and see Max. Trust no one else; only he can keep you safe.

Love,
Daddy

The letter stirred a forgotten memory in Zoro. He saw Isaac at Joey's funeral, running breathlessly toward a man in the distance. A man he now knew as Conrad.

"You bastard!" Isaac had yelled, right before he was stiff-armed by a man with a tattoo on his hand—Alton.

The fire . . . Isaac's anger . . . the sketch! Zoro's mind whirled in a tornado of realizations. The arsonist hadn't known anyone was home. Zoro realized that Conrad had started the fire to teach Isaac a lesson. *I could have stopped them if I'd been home,* Zoro's mind boiled with anger.

In that moment of bitter remorse, Zoro slammed his head against the treehouse wall, sending a shock wave down the tree trunk, knocking over an old sled perched against its side. And like a bolt of blue lightning, an image of the old sled he'd seen hung on the shed at the lodge flashed through Zoro's mind.

Everything was clear. The letter to Max, the note in the treehouse, the wooden box at Finnegan's . . . it was all Isaac laying a trail of clues that led inexorably to Conrad.

CHAPTER 65

As Zoro returned to the lodge, bits of his history flashed through his mind. He imagined how Isaac must have felt, trapped inside the lodge as Conrad's henchmen rolled up to the building. He must have known he'd never make it off the property with the sketch. Zoro reckoned he hid it, and made a break for it. At least that way if he did get caught fleeing, he'd have some leverage with Conrad. That's what Zoro would have done, if he'd been in Isaac's head at the time. Thing is, Isaac had gotten away all right, but not without being seen. Figuring he'd be heavily watched by Conrad, Isaac must have done the best he could, leaving the most innocuous clues in the little time he had before the fire. Zoro wondered: if Isaac had known the price he would pay would be Joey's life, would he still have done it? Gripping the steering wheel a little tighter, Zoro supposed that perhaps Isaac's destiny had already been written. But many things written seemed suspiciously tidy. Isaac should've known life wasn't like that; life was messy.

But whatever choices Isaac had made, that was in the past. And now, the best Zoro could hope for was to stop trembling as he rolled up to the lodge.

Behind the lodge stood the shadowy outline of the small storage shed he'd noticed the first time he was here. Hung on its side was the old two-rail sled, almost identical to the one he'd knocked over at the treehouse.

That small shed, tilted over a ravine, was the last place anyone would have thought was safe. Stepping swiftly from the limo, Zoro could feel his heart pounding in his chest. Now inside the shed, still trembling, Zoro reached up into the gap between the wall and roof. He ran his hand around the circumference of roofline, hoping to find a narrow space just like in his treehouse. At the far corner his hand jammed against something, and he dislodged a small cylindrical canister. It fell into his hands, and Zoro clutched it to his chest as he ran outside, where he fell to his knees.

With the case clamped to his chest, Zoro wondered for a moment about all the great designs he had had for his life: designs unattempted. And with a dry swallow, he thought of all his great attempts: attempts unfinished. But all that mattered little now, for he held the secret of heaven close to his heart.

The moldy leather case with rusted metal clasps had been wax-sealed with a coat of arms, half of which had fallen away over time. But it wasn't the azure coat of arms of Caprese Michelangelo, the Tuscan home village of Michelangelo. Instead, it was the lion-crested red seal of the Canossa family coat of arms that had been pressed into the soft red wax by the hand of Michelangelo himself. And beneath the seal were words written in Latin.

The phrase, "Beware all who enter here," rang through Zoro's mind.

As he reached for the clasp with a trembling hand, suddenly a shrill cackle broke Zoro's concentration. Grinning maniacally ear-to-ear as he screamed with laughter, Conrad appeared with Alton at his side. Those jackals had followed him!

"You—No!" Zoro gagged.

Words began to spill from Conrad's snarling face as his tree-trunk legs struggled through the gravel driveway. "Now, if you would step over here to my other side and hand me my sketch, that would be just fine," Conrad said.

Zoro swallowed hard. A scream tried to work its way out of his mouth, but ended up in an awkward, "No. No, Conrad."

Alton trailed behind Conrad, flipping back his coat to reveal a holster. Zoro knew no matter what he chose to do, his quest was about to end. He glanced at Conrad. "You owe me this, Conrad. You killed my little brother." His voice was hard.

Conrad was silent for a short moment. "Considering the circumstances, the best I can do is let you walk away, right after you hand me the sketch."

Never . . . never ever, Zoro whispered in his mind.

"Nice and neat, hand it over." Alton unclasped his holster, pulling out his revolver.

"Fuck you, you miserable son of a bitch," Zoro said, gripping the case to his chest.

"Mind your temper, boy," Conrad said, his voice stiffening. "You have no idea what I'm about to become. Now I'm afraid I must insist."

Gazing triumphantly at Zoro, Conrad looked like someone who could taste his destiny. He snatched the case from Zoro and held it above his head. Even before opening it, he shouted, "Now I am God!"

But as soon as he had spoken, strawberry red foam squeezed from the corner of Conrad's mouth as a blistering *crack!* rang out. Conrad fell to his knees, flinging the case to the ground. Zoro looked up to see the wisp of hot smoke curl from Alton's revolver.

He watched as Conrad crawled desperately toward the case, toward a prophecy. He whimpered as he reached for it, like a poisoned man reaches for the antidote. Zoro was surprised how little sympathy he felt for this man dying at his feet as he took the case from Conrad's twitching hands.

Forgetting momentarily about the shooter, Zoro rushed to clumsily open the case.

"That's not meant for you, either." Alton's voice never quavered.

He raised his gun toward Zoro, his face turned icy cold, but before he could pull the trigger, another deafening *crack!* erupted. Alton wobbled backward, a bright red hole appearing in his belly, quickly followed by a rapidly spreading red stain. As Alton's hand clutched his gut, Zoro saw clearly the V tattoo on his hand. Alton fell lifelessly onto the gravel.

Zoro looked toward the trees and saw a dark figure approaching, stumbling as he moved forward into view.

"Johnny?" Zoro gasped.

Johnny lost his footing and crashed onto his knees. Looking at the smoking gun, he tossed it from his hand and broke down. "Oh my God, I'm going to hell. Zoro, what have I done?"

Johnny's secret, the one Zoro had kept for him all these years, had finally caught up with him. He was a local hood, a leg breaker, but he was no killer.

"I didn't have a choice, Zoro! You saw; he was going to shoot you!"

Recognizing the empty look in Johnny's eyes, Zoro held out his hand. "I can help you, Johnny."

"You get the hell away from me! This is your entire fault! You ruin everyone's life!"

"Johnny, everything's going to be okay."

"Damn straight it is. You've got the one thing that can keep me from spending the next million years in purgatory. I'll take that case, Zoro," Johnny said, fumbling for his gun.

"I don't understand," Zoro said bitterly. "You said you didn't want the sketch. Is that why you followed me? You lied to me, Johnny."

"I lie to everyone."

"Don't give it to him, just don't," Conrad moaned, hanging on to life by a thread.

Zoro held his palms out toward Johnny as if to ward off any potential attack. "What's going on, Johnny? Talk to me."

"I got nothing to say to you. Just give me the damn sketch."

Zoro grabbed Johnny's arm. "I swore to Gina, Johnny, over and over again, that I wouldn't die. Don't make me a liar, Johnny! For God's sake, don't make me a liar."

"I'm not going to kill you, Zoro. I've always trusted you, counted on you. Hell, you saved me, that time. I never forgot that."

"Right now I've got my doubts about that trust," Zoro said, as if try-ing to lead both sides of an argument.

From the ground behind them, Conrad groaned. "Open it, open it, show it to me," he demanded. "Don't be weak like your father."

Zoro whirled around to face Conrad. "My father wasn't weak!"

"He cried more than your little brother did," Conrad snarled.

Screaming wildly, Zoro raised the case above his head, as if to smash it down on Conrad.

"What are you waiting for?" Conrad said. "You can't kill me; you're weak, like Isaac. The best you can do is forgive me."

"Forgive you?"

"Isaac did, with his dying breath. Now you must follow in his foot-steps," Conrad moaned. "Forgive me, and open the case, Zoro. Show it to me now!"

"Don't you dare tell me what to do, after what you've done to my life. I've been going out of my mind." He stared at Conrad coldly. "And now it's your turn to go to hell!"

Conrad whispered, "You will forgive me."

Zoro took a deep breath, so deep it went beneath his fury, beneath his pain. He leaned slowly toward Conrad, and opening the first clasp on the leather case, he whispered, "I forgive you." Then snapping it shut again, he added, "but hell won't!"

"Nooo!" Conrad moaned, as Zoro turned away. "Show it to me, it's my destiny." Conrad groaned, then gurgled . . . then was silent.

Zoro heard the sound of tires crunching on gravel. He looked up to see Johnny's car, rolling along the path in front of the lodge. Johnny walked over to Zoro, the gun awkwardly dangling in his hand.

"Is he dead?" Johnny said, nodding toward Conrad. Zoro nodded.

"You know, you really suck at this," Johnny said, snatching the case from Zoro and running back toward his car.

Zoro ran behind him, as Johnny whirled around, raising his gun.

"You're a bastard, too, Johnny, you hear me?"

Johnny jumped into the seat and slammed the door in Zoro's face. His tires spun noisily against the gravel as he punched the accelerator.

Zoro slammed his hands against the quarter panel of the sedan. "Johnny! Don't do this! My dad bought this with his life, Johnny, you know that!" But Johnny just kept going, driving down the gravel path, back toward the highway.

As Zoro watched the hope of a perfect reality vanish, he wondered what Max might say at that moment.

"Adversity, Zoro, is the true test of courage," he'd say. "And every action has a price, and every price has a purpose—even this, Zoro."

Zoro watched Johnny leave, the fourth sketch becoming just another empty craving. But then, the sedan skittered across the gravel and ground to a halt. Through the open window Johnny's boisterous voice rang out. "Here you go, Zoro!" Johnny laughed wildly, like a crazy person, and flung the case and the sketch from the sedan. Then he sped away.

Zoro sprinted down the gravel driveway to where the sketch lay in the dry, brown grass. He picked it up reverently, his mind grappling to understand the essence of everything good that he would soon discover. One look at the sketch, he thought, and he would hear God speak.

Standing with the sketch in his hand, Zoro realized that the universe had indeed conspired to bring back Zoro's destiny. He carefully unrolled the parchment sketch, almost afraid to look at it.

He allowed his eyes to look, then, puzzled, he looked closer. In a few seconds, he began to chuckle, then laugh, then laugh so hard his knees buckled.

Zoro had always thought that God was mysterious, but he'd never known God was a comedian. By now, he was laughing so hard he could barely breathe.

He held the sketch up above his head with his right hand. There was an ornate signature in the bottom right corner of the parchment, and even without being able to read Italian, Zoro recognized the name, Andrea Canossa. Above the signature, the parchment showed . . . nothing.

The fourth sketch was blank.

CHAPTER 66

Wednesday, a New York Cemetery

A frosty ground fog ebbed beneath the gravestones. Now in the rawest part of the early evening, a little before sunset, Zoro seemed caught between the swelling fog and the sun that floated wearily just above the horizon. On such an evening, engaged in the endless cause of thinking, thoughts tripping on one another, running his mind against the words, Zoro couldn't help but wonder why things had worked out the way they had. It was real, he was experiencing it, and yet it felt like a memory. Not like déjà vu, but rather, like a strange sense of rapture, as if his future was his now, and his present was about to unfold.

Standing alone in the stillness of Max's grave, Zoro had prepared only one question. He felt a knot tighten around his heart.

"Why, Max?" he whispered. "All this pain for nothing. First Joey, then Isaac, and a life of misery, all for nothing."

Deep inside, standing in the iciness he felt, Zoro's whole life seemed like a comedy of errors.

"Now I don't even have you. Everything I've been through, and all I've got is this crummy medallion and a useless, blank sketch."

Without concealing his rigidity of mind, his inflexibility of purpose, Zoro leaned over Max's grave.

"Here, you have them," he said, dropping the medallion in the dirt.

Then he stepped forward to lean the empty sketch against the black granite tombstone. Tipping to one side, it rolled through the dirt, and Zoro's world swung upside down. Like the drum of an old-fashioned printing press, the cylindrical roll of parchment picked up a trace of dust from Max's freshly dug grave.

Zoro gasped, as his decision to throw away the sketch, without deep thought or care, had led to an astonishing discovery. In that moment the sketch revealed an intimate glimpse into its secret. Though he'd seen nothing on the canvas before, now the thin layer of dust that had settled on it outlined a faint script, scratched without ink into the parchment. With the finesse of a diamond cutter, Michelangelo had plied an inkless reed pen against the parchment.

Zoro held the parchment up to the light, trying to make out the scratch marks, but the words were unrecognizable, as if the artist, in a final fit of malice, had reached from beyond the grave to tease Zoro with this last riddle.

Zoro stared at the parchment, tilting it from side to side, rolling the grains of earth into the scratch marks to heighten them. Squinting closely, he could make out six random words, apparently Italian. "What does it mean?" he mumbled.

Opening his mind, Zoro felt himself drifting beneath his conscious mind into the Third Q. He felt Max's mind, his powers of insight, assisting his efforts at tapping into his subconscious.

Little by little the bits of Italian his grandfather had taught him wiggled their way back into his mind, and he could translate the words. They flashed before his eyes as if the words he read were as plain as the Queen's English.

"The Name lives where angels dance," was all it said.

Zoro fell down on his knees. In that solitary moment, with no one to see that he was alone, Zoro watched the withering of the blossoms laid upon Max's grave. Wondering if he could ever understand the meaning of those words, Zoro watched as a solitary bumblebee moved slowly from beneath a mat of dried leaves and began to sluggishly buzz about the wilting blossoms. *It's autumn; what's a bumblebee doing out?* And then, his spine tingling with intuition, Zoro began to listen to the message of the bee.

Without the distraction of other thoughts, Zoro gazed at the bumblebee. And as he vividly called upon his mind to damp out every sight and sound, the picture of that solitary bee bent his eye.

Suddenly, as if pinched hard, his ears blazed with his own words. "I see now," Zoro said, stretching his hand out toward the bee. "You fly, little fellow, because you choose to."

In defiance of physics, of all things flesh and blood, that solitary bee, too big to fly, its wings too small for loft, still flew.

And seeing that bee choose to fly, Zoro began to laugh. There was a word for men like Michelangelo, he thought: brilliant.

Michelangelo was supposed to immortalize the church in stone. It had always been quite simple, chipping and polishing the marble into a face. But forced to trade his chisel and hammer for a brush, he'd been struck powerless. Terrified by the eternal damnation he was promised by the Pope, he never did reveal the Name in paint. But Zoro couldn't help but wonder if perhaps he had risked it all for the light he saw in every living soul. Michelangelo was a sculptor, not a painter. And so surely, Zoro thought, Michelangelo would have immortalized the Name in stone, not paint.

Suddenly Zoro could feel his future rushing up behind him, and something in his mind changed that felt like freedom. He realized that just like him, Michelangelo had always wanted the answers behind the Name. He always wanted wings to fly with the angels. Whether Michelangelo spoke the word that day in the archive and was beamed into heaven, or heaven was beamed into him, one thing was for sure: Michelangelo understood there was a back door to the light. It was a door in our minds, left slightly open for those who choose to find it: for those who chose to fly.

Zoro realized you could call it a primitive superstition or a romantic notion. But the Third Q, the flesh and blood of it, those tiny circuits in his brain lit with a very special energy, they were real. They were the back door. And though that back door might seem like a longer, harder road, it ultimately led to something larger than a Name; it led to freedom and creation he could control.

Michelangelo knew that, that was the message in his blank sketch, his Q message to Zoro. *I guess you could say Michelangelo got his chance to dance with the angels after all,* Zoro thought, *only this time he was doing it through a man named Zoro.*

Zoro's head was an echoing chamber of loud messages, but it didn't matter, because there was always the comfort of Joey's resting silence to compare it to. His road was now illuminated by a light peeking through a tiny crack in an open back door. And he wondered if maybe somewhere in heaven, Max was the one who'd opened it.

He stared at the clue on the blank sketch and again wondered if Michelangelo had actually hidden the Name in a sculpture of angels, or whether all he was trying to say was that all angels have one thing in common: they can only be freed by us.

In that instant, Zoro's mind was no longer a pit of dreadful creatures, of corrupted files; he was free. He would let go, let go of all that was bleeding his mind and soul dry. The pain of Joey and Isaac was instantly gone, replaced by the peace of knowing they still existed, as Max had assured him. And the temptation to sell his soul for a piddling past or future was gone, too. Zoro knew it was all right to hold on to what he could, as long as it didn't hold on to him.

It was all so clear now. The future was unwritten, like that blank sketch—like the purity of a mind transformed into a blank slate—and where it went was up to Zoro. He could dance with angels on the blank canvas of life; he was free to create his own masterwork, without ever again wasting time trying to figure life out at the expense of living it.

And here and now, in a long and graceful perspective, Zoro understood why Michelangelo etched nothing on the fourth sketch; nothing past, nothing future, nothing hard, nothing real.

Zoro knew, with no far echoing voice, but with clear, heart-deep certainty, that he was nothing more than the sum total of his thoughts and choices. And with no half-assured plunge into the sands of uncertainty, Zoro knew no vortex of negative energy could ever drag him down again. In a mind charged with burning purpose, Zoro understood that he was the manifestation of the universe, and his will and God's will were one and the same.

In that striking instant, Zoro realized that sometimes the bigger picture is something really small. Smiling, he realized that small, blank sketch was his life; he alone was the artist. Life wasn't about how he ended up or came through, but how he was, who he was, and that he was, at this and every moment, true. Raising his chin to the sky, he called out, "My life lives for itself!" And he knew instantly there was only one choice: to paint his life with all the color in his soul.

But then, gazing at the faint scratches on the sketch, it called to him, and he realized that his ultimate choice was yet to come.

CHAPTER 67

His phone buzzed; it was Gina.

"You need to get back soon, Zoro. She's fading."

"Okay, baby. I'll be there soon."

Carmela had taken a sudden turn for the worse on that morning a few days ago when Zoro had left after the confrontation over Conrad's threats. Her health, fragile for these many years, had begun its final decline under the strain of the emotions she had unleashed on him that day. Now, Zoro's mother was dying, and he knew that he needed to be getting back.

Arriving at Carmela's house, Zoro stood on the walkway for a moment and watched as hordes of well-wishers flooded inside. He just stood there in front of the house Carmela had grown up in, the one her parents had died in, and no one noticed him. He didn't mind; those people, that house didn't hold any happy childhood memories. It was just an old-fashioned wood frame house, filled with lies coated over with so many coats of paint, like its sticking windows, which he could never pry open.

Zoro was beginning to wonder how he had ever been able to breathe inside that house, with its swollen-shut window frames. Isaac wouldn't have lived there, he thought, walking a few paces forward. Isaac was a romantic, and would've found the house too suffocating, too hermetic.

Then again, Isaac had always balanced what he wanted with what Carmela wanted. He clearly adored her, and Zoro wondered what Isaac had seen in her. Maybe she had been different before—everything. Casting his thoughts aside, he stepped forward.

Soon he made his way past the crowd outside. At the front entry he wiped his feet carefully; he did that every time he came here. He stepped inside, but before climbing the stairs to Carmela's bedroom he looked around. There was nothing out of the ordinary. Still, as he retraced his memories, the place felt somehow wrong. Zoro was uneasy. A minute later, without realizing it, he was standing in front of Carmela's bedroom. He must have tuned out while walking upstairs.

Everyone around was silent. The bedroom smelled of fresh sheets, and Carmela lay on her back. This morning the room had smelled bad, although Carmela had been so rosy and ripe with life. Now, the room had more life in it than she did.

Her skin was pasty white and colorless, and her chest heaved and collapsed into itself with every breath. She looked so close to death, so broken, it pained Zoro's heart. Yet in her, he knew the devil had done his work.

Nathan kneeled at her bedside and prayed. "It's been a long time since we've all been here together," Nathan said, looking up at Zoro. His voice was frail.

"Nothing's changed," Zoro said.

Nathan raised his face to look at Zoro. "Nothing? You call this nothing?"

"She always put her beliefs ahead of everything." Zoro's voice was hard, though he didn't look angry. "Even me, even the truth . . ."

"You bastard!"

"Oh no, no, Nate, please don't fight with me. We can't look at the ocean and argue over where one drop of water begins and the other one ends, not anymore," Zoro said. "So I won't argue with you." He motioned for Nathan to move over.

Zoro's logic outweighed his words, so Nathan nodded in approval, making room for Zoro at Carmela's bedside.

Zoro kneeled beside Carmela and held her hand. "A lifetime of love and turmoil: that's us, Ma. And I spent it trying to make things up to you. I know this is something you'll never understand, but I forgive you for that, and I forgive me, too. You did the best you could with what you knew, Ma, and I'll always love you for it." He brushed a lock of hair out of her closed eyes. She barely moved. "Good-bye, Ma," Zoro whispered, slowly releasing her hand. And with that simple gesture, Zoro kissed her on the forehead and sealed his farewell. He rose to his feet and paused, studying the others for a moment, and then he turned to leave.

Nathan caught him by the arm. "Don't forget your way home," he said and smiled.

*   *   *

Zoro walked in the front door of the apartment, and Gina barreled into him. She grabbed him, wrapping her arms around his neck, her legs around his waist.

"I love you," Gina said. "I'm glad you're alive."

"I know, me too. I'm gonna take a walk. Do you want to come?"

"Yeah. I'm not letting you go, ever again."

They went outside and walked down Arthur Avenue.

"How's she doing?" Gina said, after they'd gone maybe half a block.

"Worse."

"Do you want me to go by again, later?"

"Good Lord, no! She's got an army of followers watching over her. Besides, I need you here with me."

"You want to get something to drink?"

Zoro looked down the street, speckled with shops and cafés. "I love this place. I can see why we wanted to live here."

Gina smiled. "We've got a lot to talk about," she said. "I have so many questions."

They crossed the street to a small café. The tables were decked out with pink linen. Zoro ordered a pot of tea. He poured a cup for each of them. It smelled warm.

She smiled at him. "Tea. That's a little different for you, isn't it?"

Zoro grinned. "I don't see any reason to make things any tougher for my mind than they already are." He got a serious look on his face. "Look Gina . . . I know I haven't said a word to you these past few days . . . and I'm sorry I didn't tell you everything. And maybe I didn't love you enough . . . I know you deserve better."

Gina looked at him for a long time. "You're nervous, Zoro, but you don't have to be. You're trying to work up the nerve to apologize for . . . I don't know, a lifetime of hurt. But you don't have to. Honestly, yesterdays don't matter to me so much, anymore."

She drew a long breath. "You're okay, that's all that matters."

A moment later the waiter brought a blueberry-topped slice of cheesecake they'd ordered. "Two forks," Zoro said. "Thanks."

"This is delicious," Gina said, a little later. "I haven't eaten since you left, earlier."

Zoro's elbows were propped on the table. "Gina, I want you to know that after what I've been through, I'm different now."

"Why are you telling me this?"

"Because I want to share my life with you, my whole life, everything. I thought that's what you wanted?"

"I did . . . I do."

"Then let me talk."

She nodded.

"It was never easy for me to accept the truth. But I've learned that my mind has a living presence in our lives. And I alone am responsible for it." He paused. "Look, I don't want to push anything I believe on you," he said.

Gina's eyes were glistening. "You've learned so much, and you still haven't learned a thing, Zoro. I get you, exactly who you are or who you're becoming; I get you."

Sometimes it was hard for him to believe she was there with him. But he saw it now. Even in the worst of times, she'd been there. And he had to admit, it felt good that she got him.

He pulled her close and kissed her, vowing never to leave her side.

Gina whispered in his ear.

"Really? Zoro grinned foolishly.

"That's my miracle," she smiled. "Now go finish yours. Go, Zoro, go now," she said.

Zoro stopped only for a moment, and surrendered to it. Then he headed straight for the exit, knowing today was no foolish game. And he had one last play he needed to play. He knew he had to go back to the beginning, the very beginning.

CHAPTER 68

Zoro drove along the same route he'd driven the first day he met Max. Though his memories of that day pounded in his head, the uneven pavement beneath him seemed somehow smoother. And with no agony of impatience, no hurry, he drove toward the corner of Third Avenue, the corner that almost shattered the life of an ordinary person.

Zoro's thoughts drifted, and he rubbed his hand over his eyes. That day, like so many others, Zoro had been agitated, unfocused, and he missed the best part of the moment, the drive to Max's. He loved driving, sometimes spending hours on the road for no reason at all. The soft vibration of the steering wheel in his hands, the revolution of a good engine, the freedom of movement, he loved it all. But on that first day, he'd forgotten about all of that. Instead, he was caught up in the noise and chaos, the menacing cabdrivers who'd cut you off just as soon as run you down.

But today Zoro felt different. He had embraced the Third Q, and it was beginning to leave its mark. Zoro was in the zone: he could see not only what he saw, but what he ought to see. Zoro stopped the limo in mid-street near the corner of Third Avenue and smiled at his newfound power of foresight.

He now realized that the mesmerizing woman he had seen that day wasn't flagging a cab; she was trying to warn Zoro about the little child darting into the street from between two parked vehicles. And when Max had guessed about the accident that morning, he had put it together from the water bottles tumbled onto the floor of the limo, Zoro's grief-reddened eyes, the spilled coffee, the crushed picture of Joey on the dashboard. That magical clarity, that skill like prophecy, that Max had had, was nothing more than the Q at work, opening his mind to what was already there, if only one had the ability to see it. And yet it was everything.

*   *   *

It didn't feel right, his backseat being empty, but Zoro kept going up the driveway. Walking up the front steps, he missed Max terribly. As he reached the front door, it swung open and Tolbert stepped out to embrace Zoro. Then Tolbert stepped back through the door, pointing at the spiral staircase, where the red rope had been taken down. Zoro paused as if there was more to say, but then just kept walking. He gazed back, nodded to Tolbert, and walked toward the staircase, clutching the fourth sketch to his chest.

Fixed now on the first sketch, the one of the man pressing the child to the ground, Zoro almost stumbled in mid-step.

"Hello, Max," Zoro said, as he reached the first alcove. "I think I get it, but did you have to make it so hard? As if it wasn't hard enough for me . . . Don't get me wrong, I'm not trying to pick a fight, but come on! How on earth was I supposed to figure it out? I suppose you were right; in the end, your plan has come together."

For a while Zoro stared at the first sketch, before finally releasing his breath. Then reaching forward he touched its frame, and instantly, as if in a dream, a blue light flashed and he saw himself in the lab at Max's facility. At first he didn't understand what was happening, though he was perfectly lucid. He saw himself watching over Sister Clarice, and he thought about how he'd fought with everything in his mind to deny what he'd seen in the lab that day. Sure, he knew he could trust his own eyes; he had seen the lights beaming from Clarice's brain in her scan, and yet belief wasn't in keeping with what he'd been thinking. The simple fact was, people didn't believe in ghosts, and at first neither did he. But now, with fond memories of Max, Zoro understood that the ghost, the voodoo, wasn't the Q, it was his old mind. For a moment he heard Max's voice, and no matter how he phrased it, it was always the truth. "Three people, knucklehead, living in three worlds, connected by the Third Q."

Suddenly, things that hadn't seemed all that important were. And suddenly, what had been such a nasty-sounding word wasn't, and Zoro believed. Without attempting to explain what he was feeling, Zoro embraced the power of his subconscious beliefs and realized, *He's not hurting the child, he's saving him from choking.* Not abuse . . . rescue. It fit.

Making for the second alcove, Zoro gazed triumphantly at the sketch of God in action, escaping the conscious mind's box. Reaching for the sketch, Zoro could guess what would happen next. Touching the frame, his mind was thrown into a blinding, whirling light, and it took an instant for things to come into focus. When they did, Zoro could see himself outside of Finnegan's old store, and he could hear Max say, as he stood beside the limo, "The box is another clue to breaking the mystery, Zoro," just as Zoro smashed the puzzle box on the ground.

Zoro had hated not knowing what was going on, but now he knew. The clear crispness of the slow playback in his mind made it easy for him to see the things he'd missed. And he admired how he'd come to open his mind and see things differently, to find a way to make things work, even at the expense of that little puzzle box. He had found a way to change his perspective of the world. And thinking in that new and broader sense made Zoro conscious of things he'd never noticed before. He was literally thinking outside the box.

It was simple enough. He was smart enough to figure it out on his own, and he felt his feet dancing along an invisible line drawn by his mind. In an instant his feet swiftly carried him to the third alcove.

"Adam," he said, "the Third Q, the road to my soul."

Pushing his hand forward toward the frame, Zoro found himself flying through streams of trailing lights until he came to the gradual realization that he was at the lodge. And there, he saw himself block out all of his senses except the one he needed the most, and all the answers came into focus. When he needed to hear, no noise was a distraction, and when he needed to see, he saw what was really there, not just what he perceived. In defiance of all logic, Zoro had found the way to be in the moment, in the middle. There wasn't anything mystical about it. It was an undeniable truth, he realized, that we are something more than just flesh and blood. And there is a power we can't understand, and it's got a hold on us. Zoro couldn't stop thinking about how amazing that was.

He breathed deeply, and then, crossing his legs one over the other, he walked up the stairs. His skin flushed a little as he reached delicately toward the fourth empty alcove, placing the rolled sketch where it rightly belonged.

"Don't worry about me, Max. I know I had to walk up these stairs to learn, and I have to walk down the stairs to understand." Before the words had completely rolled from his lips, Max spoke in Zoro's mind: *When you bring your soul into your conscious mind, a living, breathing light fills your life.*

With a peaceful glow of dignity charging his soul and the power of revelation streaming through his mind, Zoro felt as if a whole new world had opened up. And no matter how true or untrue the legend of the Name of God might be, Zoro sensed he understood that no legend mired in blood could ever be as powerful as his mind and soul.

Something jumped inside him as he caught sight of the door at the top of the tower. Unable to pull his eyes from the door, Zoro's feet moved him upward. After nine steps, Zoro drew a long breath and paused in front of the door.

He pushed open the tower door and was quickly drenched in a softly colored light. The stone room was encircled by tall, stained-glass windows. Through them beamed narrow spears of twilight, faintly illuminating the shadows that obscured Zoro's view of the tower. He was conscious of no fear, no past, and no future. Zoro was now. He stood by the door in the beaming light for some time. And in that light, all the devouring monsters his mind could conjure up died out forever.

His eyes traced the flagstone floor to the end of the tower, where something moved. He rubbed his eyes. There, peering through the hazed light, he thought he saw a man.

"Max?" Zoro said, taking a step forward. And immediately, as if startled by Zoro's step, the man moved—and grew larger! Bewildered, Zoro stopped, and the man stopped instantly.

Then Zoro chuckled. Against the far wall, in the shadows, was a mirror; he was seeing his reflection. *Don't lose it, Zoro*, he told himself. And then, nearby, he noticed a simple, claw-footed chair. He walked over to it.

On the chair were three articles, spaced neatly, evenly; a black cap, a downturned silver ring, a small black book, and in the fold of the book's pages, a parchment letter.

The cap was a staunch black cap with a shining bill, the pride of any limo driver.

"Nice of you to get me a new cap, Max," Zoro smiled.

And as he started to flick it onto his head, to christen it as his own, he noticed a small, broad marking of indelible ink. He grabbed the back of the chair to steady himself, feeling both faint and humble as he read the word "Max" printed inside the driver's cap.

"Max, my God . . . you were me!" He smiled. And suddenly, with a mind less crowded by doubt, anything seemed possible.

He brought his attention to the ring. He turned it to the right, hoping it might somehow be his championship ring, but it wasn't. It was Max's ring. A ring of solid silver, stamped with a gallant and noble letter: Q.

Recalling how proudly Max had worn the ring made Zoro miss him with a sudden intensity. Feeling a little remiss, he pulled the ring onto his finger and watched it glisten in the light.

Quickly his attention turned to the black book, layered almost imperceptibly in a fine dust. Zoro traced a jagged-edged Q across the book.

He shivered as he stood for a moment in the silence, hearing only the soothing cadence of his breathing. He flipped open the book and read:

"Today I met an extraordinary man named Zoro, with one *r*."

Holding Max's journal in his hand, it was clear to him; life was a never-ending journey. And it all began with one small dream, one small choice, and one small moment.

As Zoro emerged from his contemplation, he leaned against the back of the chair, again looking off toward the light, but found his eyes trailing back to the parchment letter. Holding the journal in his trembling hand, Zoro pulled the letter from between its pages. Unfolding Max's note, the words caressed him with a lingering tenderness and compassion:

Dear Zoro,

I knew I would never find the fourth sketch. Perhaps deep inside I never really needed to, though I knew in my heart that you did.

Remember Zoro: everyone is someone, and everything is something. And if by now you still believe that you are ordinary, if you still believe that your mind has been appointed by decree of the universe, and your life has been shaped by the will of God alone, then remain who you are. Or make a little room in your heart and mind, and choose. Choose to fly, Zoro. For it was once written, if you choose to be a far better thing than you have ever been, then I know that you were sent to me by angels.

Love,

Max

EPILOGUE

Zoro and Gina woke up, cuddled together under the blankets. They just lay there for a while, staring into each other's eyes. He loved looking into her eyes. Sometimes, he found it hard to believe he was really here with her. Gina said she felt the same way, insisting he hold her tightly.

She ran her fingers through her hair. "How'd you sleep?"

"No bad dreams," Zoro replied.

"Still dreaming about Max?" she asked, sitting up.

"Uh huh. Max is the best thing that ever happened to me."

"Except me, of course!"

"Except you, of course." Zoro slid up beside her. "You've always been there for me, Gina. You're the reason I stayed alive and holding on, all those years."

Gina blushed childishly.

"You deserve the truth," he said, clearing the sleep from his throat.

Gina nudged up closer, against him, and kissed him on the cheek. "Joey's up, I gotta get going."

"I can't have you keeping our son waiting." He rolled onto his belly. "Hey," he said as he smiled, "You know what today is?"

"What, Mr. Smart Guy?" Gina asked, turning toward him.

"Another amazing day."

She placed her hand gently on his cheek, and he caressed her hand with his. "Now, I gotta hurry Gina, I'm late."

*   *   *

The limo came to a sudden stop at the end of a long driveway flanked by rows of newly planted trees. Ahead, he saw the marble building, which seemed to fill an entire block. For a moment he felt envious, wondering if he could ever live in such extravagance. Walking to the door, he dropped his head just a little.

The door opened, and his eyes panned across a pair of handmade Santoni shoes. They were dark gray, with just a tinge of blue, and matched perfectly a crisply pleated Armani suit. For the second time that morning, he felt envious.

"I was beginning to worry about the time," his boss said. "You're late, Johnny."

"Sorry, Zoro," Johnny replied. "And I appreciate the job . . . 'cause no job, no parole."

"Three years inside can change a man. You deserve to have someone believe in you."

"I get why *you* were at my parole hearing, but why Gideon?" Johnny asked.

Zoro smiled, "He's a good man, that Gideon Kohen."

"Besides, this job is more than just keeping up with your parole. If you want out of the nightmare, this is where we start saving you."

The great door swung closed behind Zoro, as he stepped lightly toward his limo. He turned and waved to Gina, who was standing in the upstairs window, framed in pink marble. She looked good, he thought, in her pink mansion. She was where she belonged.

They stepped quietly to the limo. That silent moment gave Johnny time to wonder. "Dude, I can't stop thinking about it. Max wills away all his money, leaves you nothing except those sketches you keep promising to show me, and still your life ends up so amazing."

"I get lucky a lot, these days."

"Still, it's got my mind wandering all over the place."

"Johnny, don't let your mind wander. It's too small to be left on its own."

"Nice, dude. Nice," Johnny replied.

Zoro smiled.

Johnny yanked his flask from his pocket and pulled two quick gulps.

"You've gone three years without a drink, Johnny, and you're breaking out the sauce on your first day?" Zoro asked softly.

Johnny caught Zoro's disapproving reflection and realized his gaffe. "Sorry," he said, popping a mint into his mouth to cover his breath. Johnny searched for a snappy comeback, but instead, his voice cracked with emotion. "Zoro, is it stupid to want what you have?"

"Sometimes, Johnny, you need to draw a line in the sand and say, 'My turn now!'"

"I feel a lecture coming on," Johnny snorted. "Is this going to be a regular thing with you?"

"Only until you learn to control the toxic mojo in your mind."

"You never give up." Johnny stared at him.

"Only because I don't want to . . . Hold on a second, Johnny." Zoro bent over and scooped Joey's nerf football from the lawn. A few seconds later it sailed dead center through an old tire hanging from the bough of a tree.

"Let's go, Johnny." They got into the limo.

"So where are we going anyway, Zoro?"

"To dance with angels."

—THE BEGINNING—

ABOUT THE AUTHORS

Arnold Francis has brought his expertise in medical sciences and philosophy together in his first novel *The Third Q*. A successful entrepreneur and inventor, he has built several million-dollar businesses. A championship dog breeder, amateur sculptor, musician, and scuba enthusiast, the pastime he loves best is sharing his success secrets with those in need.

Robert Luxenberg has been a swimming champion, a member of the Canadian national team, and the leader of the Canadian contingent to one of the largest international sports games. After attending university on an NCAA scholarship, Robert worked in commercial real estate and subsequently went on to develop several cutting-edge business ventures. Robert is an accomplished speaker, trainer, writer, and philanthropist whose journey of growth inspired him to explore and share the visionary wisdom of *The Third Q*.

www.TheThirdQ.com